HORSE PLAY

Jo Carnegie

WINDSOR
PARAGON

First published 2012
by Transworld Publishers
This Large Print edition published 2012
by AudioGO Ltd
by arrangement with
Transworld Publishers

Hardcover ISBN: 978 1 445 85020 7
Softcover ISBN: 978 1 445 85021 4

British Library Cataloguing in Publication Data available

Printed and bound in Great Britain by
MPG Books Group Limited

To Rhys Charles Williams

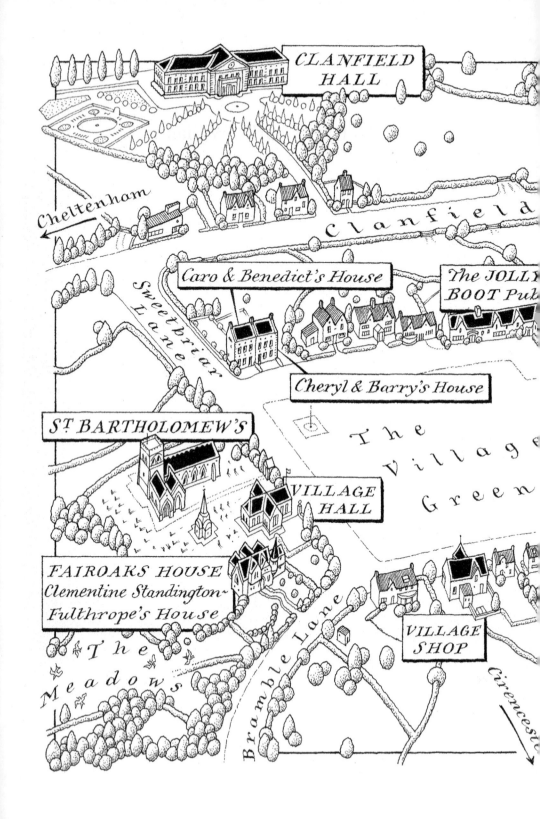

CLANFIELD HALL

Cheltenham

CLANFIELD

Sweetbriar Lane

Caro & Benedict's House

The JOLLY BOOT Pub

Cheryl & Barry's House

St. BARTHOLOMEW'S

VILLAGE HALL

The Village Green

FAIROAKS HOUSE
Clementine Standington-Fulthrope's House

Bramble Lane

The Meadows

VILLAGE SHOP

Cirencest

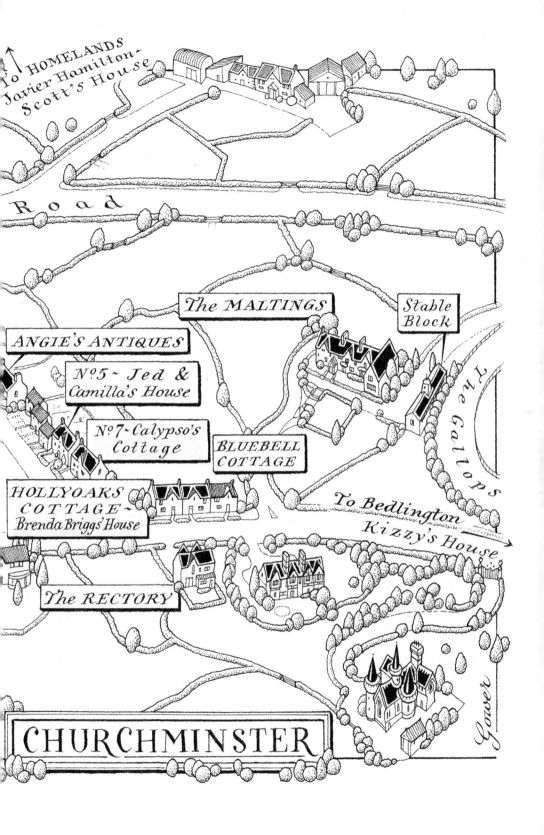

To HOMELANDS
Javier Hamilton-
Scott's House

R o a d

The MALTINGS

Stable
Block

ANGIE'S ANTIQUES

Nº5 ~ Jed &
Camilla's House

Nº7 ~ Calypso's
Cottage

BLUEBELL
COTTAGE

The Gallops

HOLLYOAKS
COTTAGE ~
Brenda Briggs' House

To Bedlington
Kizzy's House

The RECTORY

CHURCHMINSTER

Gower

PART ONE

PART ONE

CHAPTER ONE

Six months earlier

The tinkle of champagne glasses rang out in the peaceful spring evening. As the guests assembled on the outdoor terrace of Clanfield Hall, they were all in agreement that it was hard to find a more beautiful view of the Cotswolds. Before them five hundred acres of deep wooded valleys and rolling hills, all in exuberant bloom.

As stunning as the backdrop was, the conversation soon swung back to the things typically talked about at these parties: politics, sport, money and sex. Young waiting staff passed through the black-tie crowd offering mouth-watering canapés: slivers of rare Hereford beef and smoked wild salmon, asparagus picked that day from the kitchen garden. It was a pleasant start to the evening before the party moved inside for the eight-course dinner in the ballroom.

At the end of the vast lawn, a horse and rider emerged from a thicket of trees, going like a bat out of hell. The official bridleway curved round to the right, away from the stately home, but the rider either didn't know or didn't care, as their mount thundered across the bottom of the field. One by one, the distinguished guests broke off their conversations to watch the horse, a muscly bay thoroughbred, hurtle towards a five-bar gate. Sat on top of the huge beast was a tiny figure bent forward, with a long blonde ponytail flying out behind.

'Christ,' someone said. 'Is that a *girl*?'

Down on the field, 24-year-old Kizzy Milton gave a cry of exhilaration. Oblivious of her audience, she crouched even lower in the saddle. A big building appeared on her left in the blur of green, but Kizzy had no time to take it in. She gave another whoop; this was what it was all about! A perfect spring evening when the fields opened up in front of you, and it felt like you could go on for ever . . .

The five-bar gate was coming up. Kizzy grinned and pressed her heels into Juno's side. Moments later they flew over the fence as though it were nothing, landing perfectly on the other side. But instead of ending up in the field she'd been anticipating, Kizzy found herself cantering across a front lawn the size of a football pitch. Immaculate stripes were mown into the grass, the same stripes Juno was now churning up with his great hooves. As Kizzy's eyes travelled up the garden she was confronted by the most breathtaking house she'd ever seen.

Actually, forget house. Kizzy took in the rows of windows and turrets, the purple wisteria blanketing the golden stone. It was a bloody stately home—and she'd just careered right through the middle of it.

Shit! With Herculean effort Kizzy hauled Juno up in front of an enormous ornate fountain. She could make a quick exit and no one would be any the wiser . . .

'What on earth do you think you're doing?' a cross voice called out. 'This is private property!'

Heart in mouth, Kizzy looked back up the lawn. A terrace full of people in dinner jackets and cocktail dresses stared back at her. An elegant blonde woman, who reminded Kizzy of Joanna

4

Lumley, was standing at the top of some steps leading down into the garden, looking completely horrified.

'Sorry!' Kizzy called, painfully aware of forty-eight pairs of eyes on her. 'I got a bit lost. I had no idea I was on your land!'

The evening sun glittered off the woman's cream jewelled gown. 'Please get off the lawns! We've only just had them re-laid!'

'I am *so* sorry!' Kizzy felt her face burn with embarrassment and exertion.

'The bridle path is that way,' the woman said pointedly. 'If you wouldn't mind . . .'

'Of course! I didn't mean to disrupt your evening . . .' Kizzy looked apologetically at the people on the terrace, registering the smooth, well-fed complexions of the rich and privileged. A lone face, striking and angled, grabbed her attention, and Kizzy caught a quick flash of amused dark eyes. Next moment there was a resounding *clang*, making Juno rear into the air. As Kizzy fought to calm him down she saw a butler open the terrace doors, holding a gong.

'Dinner is served,' he intoned, only showing a glimmer of surprise at the dusty-faced girl on a sweaty horse carving up his employer's grounds.

Oh God! She'd only gatecrashed *Downton* bloody *Abbey*! Kizzy half-expected them to get the shotgun out, but, already bored of the impromptu sideshow, the guests had started to file indoors. Kizzy grabbed the chance to escape. Wheeling the horse round, she took off back towards the wood in a fast trot. *I don't belong somewhere like this.* The sooner she got away, the better.

CHAPTER TWO

The charming village of Churchminster nestled in the very heart of the Cotswolds. Even in a county already awash with chocolate-box cottages and fine Georgian houses, its prettiness and charm stood out. With its honey-gold stone, glorious gardens and community spirit, it had come fourth two years earlier in the prestigious competition: Britain's Best Village.

Gastronomy fans flocked from miles around to eat at the Jolly Boot, the gorgeous low-beamed pub famed for its Michelin-starred chef, and champagne on tap. St Bartholomew's, an ancient church mentioned in the Domesday book, stood on the other side of the green. Still in a slight state of disrepair after a fire a few years back, St Bartholomew's was considered one of the most historic buildings in the district. Like a benevolent grandfather, it kept watch over the village and its colourful inhabitants.

Tonight, however, the tranquillity of the place was about to be shattered. A bright-pink Cadillac screeched on to the green, music blaring out of its open windows. As the car ground to a halt outside the line of thatched cottages, a tangle-haired blonde in the passenger seat leaned across and passionately snogged the sexy, dishevelled-looking man next to her. The couple had one final clinch, hands and mouths all over each other, before the blonde kicked her door open and unfolded her long legs. Carvela strappies in one hand, clutch bag in the other, she climbed out and blew the driver a kiss. The Cadillac revved its engine appreciatively and roared off, a neon spaceship disappearing back into the night.

The taste of aftershave and liquor still in her mouth, Calypso Standington-Fulthrope pushed open the white picket gate of the end cottage and started up the path. Everything about her screamed 'dirty stop-out'—smudged eyeliner, battered man's leather jacket over a short black dress barely covering her fabulously lithe five-foot-nine body. Despite the chilly October evening her legs were tanned and bare, a coating of Chanel Rouge Noir polish on her toes. Wincing as the hangover began to kick in, Calypso opened her bag. An empty cigarette packet fell out on the ground as she started rummaging around for her keys.

It was soon evident that they were nowhere to be seen. *Bollocks.* What had she done with them? Calypso shivered as a gust of wind hit her. As she looked across the green the welcome sight of No. 1 Mill House greeted her; the tall, big-windowed building lit up like a beacon in the gathering gloom. Jamming her heels back on, Calypso set off down the path.

It seemed to take an age negotiating the piles of horseshit and potholes round the green, but she finally reached the pale-green door. Reaching wearily for the knocker she hung on to it until the door finally opened.

An offensively handsome blond man looked down on her, the blue chambray shirt he was wearing a perfect match to his eyes. An angelic white-haired little girl was snuggled up in his arms.

'Bloody locked myself out again,' Calypso said to her brother-in-law. 'Can I come in?'

7

'Who was the chap who dropped you off?' Caro Towey was curled on one end of the Laura Ashley sofa, six-year-old son Milo on her lap. At nearly forty, she was twelve years older than Calypso, and a couple of dress sizes bigger, but both sisters shared the same innate blonde sexiness and beguiling hazel eyes.

Another gust of wind flattened itself against the windows. No. 1 Mill House was a blissful sanctuary from the outside world, the spacious, cosy living room with its flagstone floors and open fireplace bringing much-needed warmth to Calypso's goose-pimpled limbs. 'Oh, you saw him?' In typical Calypso style she'd already rifled through Caro's drawer for a pair of socks, and was wearing a cashmere jumper of Benedict's, fresh back from the dry-cleaners.

Benedict got up from his armchair to throw another log on the fire. 'I think the whole village saw him,' he said dryly. 'Or rather heard him. The kids thought a 747 was about to crash-land.'

Calypso leaned down from the sofa and ruffled Rosie's blonde curls. 'What's that, scamp?' she said. 'You thought your Auntie Lipso was flying in?' She sat back up and coughed dirtily. 'Eurgh, I can't believe I smoked last night. I'm meant to be giving up.'

Caro and Benedict exchanged a wry look. Calypso had been saying the same thing for as long as they could remember. 'Is that new?' Caro asked, looking at the leather jacket, now discarded over the back of the armchair.

Calypso yawned. 'Elliot gave it to me. Dolce & Gabbana, from some shoot he's just done.'

'He's a model?' Caro was very impressed.

'No, he's got a band. The Railroaders. He just does a bit of modelling on the side.'

Trust her sister to hook up with someone cool. 'He did remind me of a young Mick Jagger, actually,' Caro said. 'You know, in that sexy rock 'n' roll way.'

'So you'll be trying to get me into leather trousers next?' Benedict asked.

'Now, that I would like to see,' Calypso scoffed. She lay back on the sofa. 'I can't believe I've got work tomorrow. I could seriously sleep for a *week*.'

Caro wasn't letting her sister off that lightly. 'Did you meet Elliot at this party you went to?'

'Yup.' Calypso had spent all of the previous night—and most of that day—at a country pile that belonged to a friend of a friend. Most of the guests had been the kind of braying, inbred rahs that made Calypso's skin crawl. Thank God for the discovery of the wondrously sexy Elliot.

'When are you seeing him again?'

'I'm not. He's flying to the States tomorrow to tour.'

Caro was an eternal optimist. 'Oh. Maybe you could phone, email. Stay in contact?'

'No point. He'll have forgotten all about me by the time he flies out of Terminal Five.'

'I'm sure that's not true, darling,' Caro started to say as Milo wriggled down off her lap, and ran to the playroom.

'It's all right, I'm not looking for sympathy.' Calypso plonked her feet into the space vacated by Milo. 'It's just what I do, isn't it? Meet men who are about to move to a different country, or have facial warts, or who are total lying, cheating bastards . . .'

Caro knew better than to go *there*. 'You'll find someone, darling.' It wasn't as if her little sister was short of offers. Men (and the odd woman) threw themselves at Calypso on a regular basis.

'In this dump? Not unless I want a fat-thighed farmer or some clapped-out City bloke, fresh from a breakdown and his second divorce.'

'Oh, stop it.' Caro stifled a smile. Benedict came back from the kitchen, now wearing Caro's Emma Bridgewater 'Pink Hearts' apron over his athletic body.

'Suits you, my love,' Caro told him.

He dropped her a wink. 'I might wear it for you later.'

'Oh yuk, you two, I feel sick as it is,' Calypso said lazily. She didn't know a couple more in love after four years of marriage than her sister and brother-in-law.

Benedict chuckled. 'Charming. We're having roast beef, do you want to stay?'

'Oh, wow, yes please.' Calypso's mouth salivated at the thought. Aside from the Veuve Clicquot licked off Elliot's stomach the previous night, she'd had nothing to eat or drink since.

Milo wandered in from the playroom. 'Auntie Lipso, will you come and play racing cars with me?'

'Course I will, gorgeous.' The thumping in her head was getting worse. 'Caro, have you got any Nurofen? My skull is seriously about to split open.'

Caro went to dig some out from the bathroom cabinet. By the time she came back Calypso was spreadeagled on the living room floor with Milo and Rosie, all three of them giggling as they tickled

10

each other. In Benedict's too-big jumper, her hair pulled back off her heart-shaped face, Calypso looked like a child herself—instead of one of the most ravishing women in the Cotswolds.

'Here you go, sweet pea.' Caro handed her the tablets. 'I'll get you a glass of water.'

Calypso shot her a cheeky look. 'A glass of Merlot would be nice while you're at it. Hair of the dog is the only thing that's going to get me through this.' She was only prolonging the hangover, but sod it. She'd deal with the consequences tomorrow morning.

'Good idea, I might join you.' Caro was turning to go into the kitchen when the front doorbell rang. Smoothing her hair down, she went into the hallway to answer it. A dark outline loomed through the frosted glass.

'Calypso there?' The buck-toothed man standing on the doorstep did a good impression of looking down on Caro in her own home. A long green checked coat was wearing him, and not the other way around. The rather incongruous deerstalker hat on his head reminded Caro of Sherlock Holmes.

'Calypso?' she asked, confused.

On closer inspection the man looked no more than in his early twenties. 'Yah, *Calypso*,' he said, as if Caro was mentally challenged. 'We met at PJ's in Cheltenham last week. She said if she wasn't at hers she'd probably be here.' He looked plaintive. 'So is she? I've been to that cottage, and there's no sign . . .'

'Give me a minute,' Caro said hurriedly. 'Sorry, I didn't catch your name.'

'*Anthony*. She'll know who it is.'

11

'One minute,' Caro said, delicately pulling the door to. She raced back into the living room. 'Calypso! Some man called Anthony for you!'

'Eh?'

'*Anthony!*' Caro hissed. 'Apparently you met him in somewhere called PJ's last week? You told him he could find you here.'

Calypso scurried over to the window to have a look. She jumped back, hand over her mouth. 'OMG! The twat in a hat! He was totally pestering me all night.' She shook her head violently. 'You've got to get rid of him.'

'I can't!' Caro implored. 'He'll know something's up.'

'Well, I'm not going out there.'

'Why are you two whispering?' Benedict had come back through from the kitchen.

'There's a man on the doorstep! Go and get rid of him!' Caro said.

Benedict frowned. 'What on earth are you talking about?'

As they heard the front door open again, all three of them spun round. With the brutal honesty only a six-year-old is capable of, Milo's voice rang out from the hallway.

'Auntie Lipso says you're a twat. Go away.'

Moments later the front door was slammed shut. Caro clapped her hand over her mouth and looked at her husband. The armchair creaked as Calypso collapsed in helpless giggles.

'I can't believe he just said that!'

'Nor can I,' Benedict said faintly.

As Milo trotted back in, Calypso got up and hugged him. 'You little legend! You totally saved me!'

His face lit up with pleasure. 'Yay! So what's a twat anyway?'

CHAPTER THREE

Kizzy bounded down the stairs, tying her long highlighted hair into a ponytail. 'Mum, I'm off!' she called. Her mother, Bev, came out of the kitchen in her dressing gown, a mug of tea in her hand.

'Don't you want some breakfast? You can't go out on an empty stomach.'

'I'll get something later.' Kizzy grabbed her turquoise Joules jacket off the bottom of the stairs.

'Are you back for dinner?' Bev asked.

'I'll call you.' The clock on the wall read six o'clock. She'd better get a move on.

Her mum wasn't giving up that easily. 'How about some sandwiches for lunch, then?' she said, following Kizzy into the porch.

'I'm cool, Mum, don't worry! Go back inside.' Kizzy dropped an affectionate kiss on Bev's cheek, and then she was off—a whirling blonde dervish—out of the door.

Kizzy still lived at home with her parents, but she didn't mind. They were a close family, but still gave each other enough space to make for a happy home life. Her dad, Graham, was a fireman at the station in Bedlington, and her mum worked at a printing firm.

Kizzy's older brother, Dan, was in Afghanistan, a captain in the Royal Artillery. Even though he wasn't on the front line, they all knew he could be sent there any time. Bev worried constantly, but

Kizzy and her dad did their best to keep her spirits up. As Dan had told them in one of his rare phone calls home, there was no point getting stressed about something that might not happen. Kizzy always looked on the bright side, and tried to take her brother's advice to heart as much as possible.

It was still dark and cold as Kizzy's Ford Ka pulled out from in front of the modern, identikit houses lining Shakespeare Drive. Most of her mates had been down at pub karaoke last night, smoking, drinking and being chatted up by the local lads, but Kizzy needed to be fresh in the mornings. It wasn't a hardship. Her friends might earn more, not walk around with dirt under their fingernails, or have to get up at the crack of dawn every day, but Kizzy couldn't imagine a better job in the world than hers.

Kizzy had always been different from the rest of the pack. She was an outgoing, popular girl, but while everyone else at primary school had been into pop music and dolls, Kizzy had been madly in love with horses. They certainly hadn't had the space or money at home to keep a pony, so as soon as she'd been allowed Kizzy had been down at the local riding yard helping: mucking out, carrying water buckets, poo-picking the paddocks. Anything in return for a ride on one of the ponies. They might have moved like out-of-kilter shopping trolleys from years of following the tail in front, but when Kizzy rode them, the feeling was magic.

While all her contemporaries were declaring they wanted to be florists or go to university when they left school, Kizzy's ambition had been a little different. She wanted to be the first female jockey to win the Grand National. At the time, she was laughed at and gently patronized, but as the years went on and her focus didn't change, the reaction changed from mild shock to incredulity.

'Why would such a pretty girl want to go into something like that?' her mum's coffee-morning friends would remark within Kizzy's earshot. Only her dad understood, and he'd been the one who'd broken the news to her mum that Kizzy was dropping out of her A levels to go and work at a local racing yard.

That had been seven years ago, and all those sacrifices—not that she saw it that way—had paid off. Because at the grand old age of twenty-four, Kizzy Milton was the proud trainer/jockey of her very own racehorse.

OK, so Nobby wasn't strictly *hers*. He belonged to Kizzy's employers, Angie and Freddie Fox-Titt, who lived in the next-door village of Churchminster. Kizzy had liked the previous yard she'd been at, but it had been a bunfight ever to get a ride on one of the horses. The Fox-Titts were incredibly generous, and let Kizzy treat Nobby as her own.

Now she was down at the Maltings every morning and night, seven days a week. Winning the Grand National was still a long way off, but everyone had to start somewhere. And running in point-to-points—amateur horse-racing, where many of the great jockeys and horses had begun their careers—was a good place. In just under three months, Kizzy and Nobby would have their first race at a meet north of the Cotswolds. Every time Kizzy thought about it, her stomach turned over with excitement.

The Maltings was quiet as her Ka made its way

up the driveway; there was just one lone light on in one of the upstairs windows. The old farmhouse had been lovingly restored by the Fox-Titts and sat in lovely mature gardens opposite the paddocks. It was gorgeous, stuffed full of antiques and countryside watercolours, but it was still a *real* house, full of dogs and people and laughter, with a jumble of Wellington boots kicked off in the conservatory. Kizzy loved coming in from the cold and having one of Angie Fox-Titt's world-famous bacon butties in the country-style kitchen.

The place had become a home from home, but Kizzy's real world existed to the right of the property, in the stables. She drove into the yard and pulled up in her usual space in front of the feed shed. Grabbing the packet of Polos she'd bought from the garage last night, Kizzy got out.

She'd barely got three yards before a soft whinny greeted her. 'Hey, Nobby boy,' she whispered back, making her way down the block. She paused outside one stable to give Angie's horse Stroller a mint and a rub on the nose. Other horses came and looked out hopefully over the door, and Kizzy fed them, too.

Treats all done, she walked down to the end. Nobby was waiting for her, his big tan-coloured face with its white blaze hanging over the door. As Kizzy went up and stroked his ears he blew hot, grassy-sweet breath out, warming the side of her neck. In that moment, as she always did, Kizzy felt intoxicated by the greatest love affair of her young life.

'Hello, beautiful boy. I've missed you.'

*　　*　　*

16

Angie Fox-Titt was on her first strong coffee of the day when she heard the clip-clop of hooves against tarmac. Getting up from the kitchen table, she crossed over to the window. Kizzy was trotting Nobby out of the yard. Wrestling with the sticky latch, Angie pushed it open and stuck her head out.

'Morning, darling!'

Kizzy looked round. 'Hey, Angie! I'm just taking Nobs out to stretch his legs.'

'Good stuff, come in for some brekkie when you've finished.'

Kizzy waved, and she and Nobby trotted off towards the gate to the paddocks, Kizzy's pert little bottom going up and down like a piston.

Angie watched her lean down and undo the latch on the gate. When Kizzy had turned up for the informal interview in the Fox-Titts' large homely kitchen, Angie had assumed there'd been some huge mix-up. With her trendy skinny jeans, dangly earrings and lashings of black mascara Kizzy had looked like she was auditioning for a position in a girl band, not to spend her days pushing wheelbarrows of muck around for very little money.

It had become apparent within five seconds, however, that Kizzy knew her stuff. Any doubts Angie harboured that a girl her age should be out with friends meeting boys had vanished the second Kizzy had hopped up on Nobby. 'Sheer courage mixed with a little insanity,' was how Freddie had described it later. Kizzy was a gutsy, fearless rider who clearly loved being in the saddle, and she'd revved Nobby up beautifully. They'd whizzed round the new gallops track, clearing the brush fences by a mile and arriving back before Freddie had had time

17

to wipe his binoculars. The Fox-Titts had hired her on the spot, and pretty soon the bubbly blonde with the infectious laugh and happy-go-lucky nature had become part of their family.

With her snub nose and wide-apart blue eyes Kizzy had a radiance rather than a classic beauty, but goodness, what a body! Five foot three and neat as a button, she had the kind of curves that made grown men fall to their knees. Angie doubted the racing world had ever seen the likes of Kizzy's chest before. Yet the girl seemed unaware of her sexiness, or at least unaffected by it, hardly noticing the way passing traffic veered off into hedgerows when she rode out, or delivery boys turning up at the house would start stuttering at the mere sight of her jodhpur-clad thigh. Angie thought it was hysterical.

The fact that she and her husband had ended up with their own racehorse in the first place was in itself astonishing. The Fox-Titts ran their estate, two hundred acres of prime Cotswolds land, as a business, leasing it out to farmers, and for shooting and fishing. They also provided livery—and a bit of training—for half a dozen local horses. When Freddie had gone up to the Fur and Feathers Auction in Melton Mowbray his only intention had been to bring back pheasants for the new season, but instead he'd driven back in sheepishly with a borrowed horsebox attached to his Range Rover. Inside Angie had found the most ugly, skinny, pitiful-looking horse she'd ever seen. It turned out Freddie had spotted the chestnut for sale—on a one-way ticket to the knacker's yard—and felt so sorry for the poor bugger he'd snapped it up for a hundred quid.

18

'But what are we going to *do* with him, Freddie?' Angie had asked. She was busy enough with the animals they had already, and the antiques shop she ran down in the village. There was no way they could take on anything else.

'Feed the poor chap up, darling! I couldn't just leave him there.'

Fred had known he had her, and with Angie's care and special horse-feed mixture Nobby had come on astoundingly. It turned out under all that skin and bone was a sadly neglected thoroughbred. With his knobbly knees (hence his name), massive arse and lopsided donkey ears there was no way Nobby would ever win a 'magnificent mount' competition, but he was such an amiable, laid-back character that the Fox-Titts fell completely in love with him.

Then something rather magical happened. When Angie's horse Stroller had gone lame just before the September hunting season, Angie had decided to take Nobby instead. Ignoring the ribbing from her chums about Nobby's unfortunate appearance, Angie had planned to stay at the back, taking things nice and easy. Nobby, on the other hand, had had other ideas. As the Bedlington Hunt had set off, he'd taken off like a Porsche 911, flown past everyone including the hunt master, sailed over a five-foot stone wall, and nearly carried Angie off into the next county before she managed to slow his blistering gallop. When she'd eventually returned she'd been met by stunned silence. Nobby might look like a bumbling carthorse, but it was clear he could jump. The hunt master, who'd never seen anything like it, told Angie she had something rather special there. 'There's some serious oomph

19

in that backside of his. Why don't you have a bash at a point-to-point?'

Angie hadn't been sure. She'd been to a few point-to-points over the years, but more for the socializing and champagne picnics out of car boots. Point-to-pointing, amateur racing that was run by the local hunt, certainly wasn't for anyone seeking glamour or money. Although a few of the great jockeys and trainers had started their careers there, most people did it purely for the love of the sport. Forget the world-famous, wide-open racecourses of Cheltenham and Aintree with their packed stands, point-to-point races were run over muddy tracks and farmers' fields, the riders getting a Styrofoam cup of coffee and a jacket potato from the catering van if they were lucky.

Angie's racing friends had always told her that there was a buzz about it, but she'd been happy socializing on the sidelines. However, as was a recurrent theme with the Fox-Titts, one thing had led to another, and now here they were, with their very own gallops and brush fences borrowed from the local racing yard, about to become one of those mad couples who spent their weekends out in the rain and wind, driving all over the country. With the first race looming, it was surreal and terrifying in equal measure.

A pair of arms wrapped themselves around her waist, and Angie smelt the freshly applied scent of Aramis aftershave. 'Freds, get off my spare tyre!' She laughed.

'I love your spare tyre,' said the deep, rich voice in her ear. It was a voice that belonged to a dark, dashing James-Bond type, but Freddie Fox-Titt was short, round and slightly balding, his friendly face and double chin evidence of a fondness for good cheese and wine. He also had a smile that still made Angie weak at the knees, and was completely in love with his comely, chestnut-haired wife of twenty-seven years.

'What are you doing, my love, standing at the window like Rapunzel?'

'Rapunzel stood at the upstairs window, darling, and I could only dream about having tresses like hers.'

He nuzzled her neck. 'Look good enough to me.'

Angie turned round and smiled affectionately at her husband. 'I was just watching our little team in action.'

'Quite something, aren't they?' Freddie rested his chin on her shoulder.

'Archie is going to think we've properly lost the plot this time, when he comes back and finds out what we've done.'

Archie was Angie and Freddie's beloved only child, currently working on a sheep farm in New Zealand. He wasn't due home until early next year, and Angie was missing him terribly. At least when he'd gone off to university, it had been in the same country.

'I wonder . . .' she went on, and then was silent for a second.

'Wonder what?' Freddie glanced at his wife. 'Oh Christ, you're not going to set him up with Kizzy?'

'I'd be as subtle as an MI5 agent, I promise.'

'No,' said Freddie firmly, showing uncharacteristic disagreement with his wife. 'Archie will kill you if he thinks you're playing Cupid. Not good for a chap's form to have his mother meddling in his love life. Besides, you don't even know if he and Kizzy

21

will like each other.'

'I know I'm terrible.' Angie sighed. 'I just adore a romance.'

'I could give you a romance.' Freddie's hands started to wander over her maturely ripe body.

'Oh don't, I'm far too fat.' She was feeling bloated after that second croissant at breakfast.

'Don't talk such nonsense. Anyway, you know I like my women with a bit on them. Far sexier than some skinny up-and-down thing.'

'Oh, right, how many women do you have, then?' she teased.

Freddie gazed into her gorgeous brown eyes. They might be edged by crows' feet now, but they were as huge and lively as when he'd first clocked his wife-to-be across the dance floor at a young farmers' ball all that time ago. His loins stirred with lust, making him feel like a young man again.

'There's only ever been you, my darling.'

'Oh, Freds.' Her husband really was the most romantic man on earth. 'Shall we go upstairs and do it?'

'No, let's fuck on the floor right now. Like we used to.'

'Fred, your knees. You know what the doctor said.' She screamed with laughter as he pounced and started to pull her down. *'Freddie!'*

CHAPTER FOUR

Caro lay in bed and watched her husband get dressed. They'd just made love lazily, in the half-light of early morning, before Benedict had

22

to get on his way to London. As he reached up to get a shirt from the wardrobe the muscles in his back flexed: taut and prominent as a professional athlete's. While other mere mortals spread and sagged into middle age, her husband somehow remained undiminished. It was most annoying; Caro liked to tease him about where in the house he was hiding his own Dorian-Gray-style portrait.

Her eyes savoured the hard buttocks and long legs. 'Come back to bed,' she said with another sudden rush of longing. This time was so precious: just the two of them, before the kids charged in or he had to leave for work. He looked round at her, as he buttoned up a crisp white Savile Row shirt, and smiled.

'Angel, I would love nothing more.' He sat back down and stroked her hair. 'But someone's got to keep you in your Chablis habit.' He dodged the well-aimed kick, laughing. 'I was only joking.'

'Sod, you'd better be.' Caro settled back down. 'I'd be perfectly happy in a caravan, as long as we were all together. Milo and Rosie tangle-haired and running barefoot outside . . .'

Benedict's eyes sparkled. 'I can just see you as my peasant girl, those lovely legs peeking out from under a long ruffled skirt.' His hands caressed the swell of her full naked breasts. 'Maybe one of those low-cut bodices . . . oh yes.'

'Don't get too carried away!' she laughed. He pulled a regretful face and looked down at his trousers, where a hard bulge had formed.

'Look what you've done to me.'

She reached over and rubbed his hardened cock. Her husband was certainly blessed in all areas.

'I know what I'd *like* to do to you.'

23

He stopped her with a soft kiss. 'That, my darling, will have to wait. I've got a man to see about a two million pound contract today.'

'Is that the Emerald job?' Benedict ran a design agency called The Glass Ceiling in London, and was about to win, fingers crossed, a big contract rebranding Emerald lager.

He went back to the wardrobe and selected a tie. 'Yup, I'm meeting the guy for lunch at the Ivy. If all goes well we should be signing on the dotted line by tomorrow.'

'You are clever, darling.'

He threw a grin over his shoulder. 'I must be, to get myself a wife like you.'

'Flatterer.'

He gave a soft laugh. 'So what are you doing today?'

'Have you forgotten?' Caro nodded towards the window. 'Our next-door neighbours are moving in.'

The other half of the converted mill they lived in, No. 2 Mill House, had lain empty for over a year, ever since the last owners had gone bankrupt before moving. The village was very excited about the new arrivals.

Benedict finished doing up his tie. 'Do we know anything more about them?'

'Only what the estate agent said, that they're a middle-aged couple from Essex. I wonder if they've got kids. It would be lovely for Milo and Rosie to have someone to play with.'

'Well, you must phone me with all the gossip.' Benedict gave a wry smile. 'Although I'm sure your grandmother will get in there first.' Caro's grandmother, known in the family as Granny Clem, lived on the other side of the village.

Clementine Standington-Fulthrope was head of the village committee, and nothing happened in Churchminster without her knowing about it.

'She's already drawn up a list of "suitable"'— Caro made quote marks with her fingers—'clubs they should join. I think the village is a few short on the bridge evening.'

'They're probably moving here for a quiet life.' Benedict fastened his Aspinal cufflinks, a Christmas present from his wife two years ago. 'Poor sods aren't going to know what's hit them.'

*   *   *

As Caro stacked the dishwasher later, she was hit by a surge of contentment. For the first time in for ever, everything seemed right. They'd only been back in No. 1 Mill House for two months, but already London had become a distant memory. The couple had spent the last four years there, so Benedict could build his advertising business up. Their Chelsea mews house had been delightful, and Caro would always have fond memories of it— especially as Rosie had been born there—but there was nothing quite like home.

Caro had been born in this village, like her two sisters, Camilla and Calypso, just as their father, Johnny, had been before them. The girls' parents had retired to Barbados seven years ago, as their mother, Tink, suffered from Seasonal Affective Disorder, but Churchminster was still the place Caro called home. Camilla—when she wasn't off round the world with her travel agency—lived with her boyfriend, Jed, in a cottage two doors up from Calypso, who in turn spent most of her time at

25

Caro's or her grandmother's on the rare night off from her events company. Fairoaks, Granny Clem's house, was the official S-F HQ, as Calypso liked to call it—the Standington-Fulthrope headquarters— and the family loved gathering there for occasions like Sunday lunches, Easter, and birthdays.

Caro put the last plate back on the kitchen dresser and moved over to the window. They were at that lovely time of year when the landscape was a kaleidoscope of fiery fox-reds and burnished golds—before winter moved in and gripped hold. Caro looked out over the garden, a long, wide expanse fringed by chrysanthemums, late-flowering dahlias and, at the bottom, a line of beech trees. In front of them Milo and Rosie's toys lay scattered across the grass like brightly coloured sweets.

It was funny, Caro thought, how unhappy she'd once been here. She'd originally bought the place with Milo's father, her ex-husband Sebastian, but all those years of his cruel put-downs and mood swings had ground her down. Discovering he'd had a mistress had been the final straw, and she'd finally booted him out. Despite what had happened, Caro had been determined to keep things civil for Milo's sake, but Sebastian hadn't made it easy. Any arrangements to see Milo were usually cancelled at the last minute with a phone call from Sebastian's secretary about his workload at the bank he worked for in London. Instead, on rare occasions he'd turn up unannounced at the London mews demanding to see his son. That had *not* gone down well with Benedict, and since they'd moved back to Churchminster they'd heard little from her ex-husband. Caro felt both despair and outrage for her son.

Thank God for Benedict, who'd restored her faith in the human race and embraced Milo like his own. Her family adored her second husband as much as they'd despised the first one. Her unhappy marriage to Sebastian seemed like a bad dream. He was someone else's problem now, probably another poor woman, who he'd be enjoying being perfectly vile to. With a shudder of relief, Caro went to wake Rosie up from her nap.

*   *   *

A few hours later, as she watched a life-size china leopard being carried up the garden path, Caro started to wonder exactly what kind of people were moving in next door. The removal men had been hard at it for the last few hours, and so far she'd seen a cabinet in the shape of the Taj Mahal, a gaudily painted portrait of Sylvester Stallone as 'Rocky' and a vast gilt-gold bed with the initials B & C engraved on the headboard. That was without even mentioning the Versace dining table and chairs set, and the Power Plate machine. Caro was just about to text Benedict details of the extraordinary scene when a baby-blue Range Rover pulled up and a woman jumped out, talking on a mobile phone, and paused to look down in distaste as her five-inch black stiletto boots sank into the grass. Pushing a pair of gold-encrusted sunglasses back on her stiffly sprayed blonde hair, she took a few tottering steps and squinted up at the house.

'Bloody hell, Baz!' she screeched, in a voice that could strip the paint off walls. 'They only haven't put the Sky dish up!'

As the woman skittered up the path, Caro

ducked back behind the living room curtain. She didn't know what she'd been expecting, but it hadn't been *that*. A few minutes later the doorbell went and didn't stop, as someone stood outside and jammed their finger on it.

The noise shrill in her ears, Caro hurried to the front door. When she opened it the blonde woman was standing there, looking out at the green. She whipped round and flashed Caro a smile. At least that's what Caro thought it was; it was difficult to tell through the layers of Botox.

'Hi-ya!' The woman pulled her sunglasses off. 'I'm Cheryl Pike, your new neighbour.'

'Oh, hello!' Caro tried not to stare. Cheryl was so fake-tanned it looked like she'd been rolling in creosote. Lashings of gold necklaces hung around her bony neck, topped off by a pink WAG Juicy Couture tracksuit. 'I'm Caro.'

Cheryl frowned. 'Carol?'

Caro gave a friendly smile. *'Caro.'*

Rosie sidled up beside her mother, gawking at this extraordinary new person. Cheryl's pumped-up lips peeled back into a smile. 'Hello, pretty! Got a smile for your Auntie Cheryl?'

Overcome by the pea-souper waft of Dolce & Gabbana, Rosie started backing away.

'I love kids.' Cheryl nudged Caro in the kidney. 'I just couldn't eat a whole one, ha ha ha ha ha ha!'

Her laugh was like a nail gun firing at Caro's head. 'It's lovely to meet you,' Caro said. 'We've all been really looking forward to you moving in.'

Cheryl looked pleased. 'Isn't that nice? That's why we moved here: slice of village life and all that. We had Balmoral, our estate in Essex, but we was bored, Carol.' She sighed. 'Four acres of paving,

28

and footballer neighbours never there. Me and Baz was bored shitless.'

She let out another rat-a-tat-tat cackle. Rosie put her hands over her ears. 'Would you like to come in for a coffee?' Caro asked. 'I'm sure it must be bedlam next door.'

'Bless your cottons, but my other half will be here any minute. I just wanted to pop over and introduce myself.' A set of pink talons touched Caro's arm. 'Me and you are going to be proper good mates! All those vicar's tea parties and coffee mornings.' Cheryl touched the side of her nose. 'I'll take care of the vodka flask, don't worry.'

In the distance they could hear a whirring noise. It grew louder and louder as it drew nearer, and suddenly it was as if the whole sky was on fire. A huge roar erupted over the village. 'Mummy, I'm scared!' Rosie screamed. Caro scooped her up and watched in shock as a light blue helicopter appeared over the green. Great waves of wind blew out and gusted over them, making even Cheryl's helmet-like waves wobble. The two women could only watch as the aircraft started to descend, flattening the trees and everything else in its wake—until it finally touched down on the grass. A few moments later a figure jumped out and ran across towards them.

Caro had only just wiped the dust from her eyes when a short, tubby man sporting the same radioactive tan as Cheryl popped up in front of her. Caro vaguely noticed his loafers were the same colour as the Range Rover and the helicopter.

The man extended a pudgy hand, dominated by a huge gold sovereign ring. 'Barry Pike, pleasure to meet ya.' He looked at Cheryl and gyrated his hips

29

indecently. 'So, Sexy Pants, we gonna liven this joint up, or what?'

CHAPTER FIVE

Village committee meetings were always a lively affair. Held in the village hall, a long, narrow building which sat on the green next to St Bartholomew's, they were officially for discussing village business, but normally degenerated into a gossip and catch-up, before most people went off to the pub.

The old church was looking rather magnificent that evening, framed by the violet night sky. Calypso, however, wasn't in the mood to admire the local architecture as she stumbled across the green in stiletto ankle boots. 'I really can't be arsed with this,' she grumbled, swearing as her foot stepped in something squashy. 'I've worked every night this week!' All she wanted to do was have a hot bath and a hefty gin and tonic and get in her pyjamas to watch *Emmerdale*.

'It won't take long,' her sister Camilla soothed. The middle Standington-Fulthrope sister, Camilla, was a calm, practical creature who was as clean-living as Calypso was wild. Calypso had lived with Camilla and her boyfriend Jed until she'd bought the cottage two doors down. Even now it was commonplace for her to turn up at their back door and borrow tea bags or loo roll; domesticity was not her strong point.

The Reverend Brian Bellows was standing at the door greeting people as they came in. 'E-evening, girls,' he stuttered, his long, mournful bearded face and black garb making him look like a gravedigger.

'Evening, vicar!' they chorused.

'He does know it's not Sunday service, doesn't he?' Calypso whispered loudly as they walked in. 'Why does he have to stand by the door like that?'

'Ssh, darling,' Camilla said. Her sister's volume control was a little skew-whiff sometimes.

The hall was filling up. Joyce Bellows, the vicar's wife, hurried past with a tray of cups and saucers. 'Hello, girls!' Even though she wasn't that much older than Camilla, Joyce had a jolly, mumsy way of addressing everyone that made her seem a generation older.

'Evening, Mrs B,' Calypso said. 'Loving the sexy boots.'

The vicar's wife blushed slightly, and looked down at the knee-length suede creations. 'Why, thank you, Calypso! I was wondering if they were too much, but Brian loves them . . .'

'I bet he does!' Calypso said and nudged her. Joyce had undergone something of a Carol-Vorderman-style radical makeover in recent years. Her beige cardigans and tights were a thing of the past.

Joyce went even redder. 'Let us know if we can help with refreshments later,' Camilla said kindly.

'Over here!' Caro waved at them. She was sitting in the middle row with Angie Fox-Titt and her new girl, Kizzy. They'd saved two seats beside them.

'*Buongiorno*, peeps,' Calypso said, plonking herself down next to Caro. She kissed her sister on the cheek. 'Have you got anything to eat? I'm beyond starving.'

Caro dug around in her vast handbag and came

out with a bag of Skittles, one of Milo's favourite treats. 'They're a bit squashed, I'm afraid. I'm not sure how long they've been in there.'

'Fine by me,' Calypso said, ripping it open and pouring half the contents into her mouth. 'Aah, dinner.'

'Looking forward to the grand ceremony?' Camilla asked Angie. One of the items on the agenda tonight was choosing an official racing name for Nobby. The whole village were excited about having a resident racehorse: it was lovely to have something everyone could get behind. The Fox-Titts had consulted Kizzy, and decided it would be a nice idea for everyone to write down their suggestions so Nobby's new name could be drawn out of a hat that evening.

'We are rather, aren't we, Kizzo?' Angie smiled at the others. 'Kiz has been doing such a marvellous job with Nobby. We're very proud.'

Kizzy grinned, little dimples creasing up in her cheeks. She was still dressed in her riding gear, but her bright-blonde hair was loose, nestling in the collar of her jacket.

'Where's Freddie?' Calypso said, through a mouthful of sugar.

Angie rolled her eyes good-naturedly. 'Rugby dinner with the boys. He says he doesn't mind what we call Nobby, as long as it's not Guinevere, which was the name of his first love. She dumped him, apparently. Bad memories.'

The others glanced at each other. 'Oh dear,' said Camilla.

'Freds should be over it now, they were only seven at the time.'

'Can we have some quiet, please!'

32

A tall, elderly woman stood at the front, her grey hair pulled back in its trademark bun: Clementine Standington-Fulthrope, Caro's, Camilla and Calypso's grandmother, and matriarch of the village. Despite her advancing years, there was still something very regal about the 82-year-old, from the proud, handsome chin to the straight back and keen eyes. Clementine's sparse frame—maintained by a series of morning exercises she'd been doing since her twenties—was dressed sensibly in a tweed skirt and jumper. Her ever-present glasses hung on a chain round her neck.

'What does Clementine think of the new neighbours?' whispered Angie. The Pikes' arrival two days earlier—especially Barry Pike flying in on his own chauffeured helicopter—was still the talk of the village.

'Once she got over the groove marks on the green, she took it surprisingly well,' said Caro. 'Although I'm not quite sure she approves of the hot tubs.'

'Hot tubs?' Camilla asked. 'In this weather?'

'That's why it's called a hot tub, dear,' Calypso told her.

'There are *two* hot tubs,' Caro said. 'That's one of his businesses, selling hot tubs. "Bubblez", I think it's called. From what Cheryl says, he's a bit of an über-entrepreneur. Made a fair whack of money.'

Angie was fascinated. 'What are they like?'

'I haven't seen much of Barry. He works all over the place, apparently, but Cheryl's very friendly. I popped over with a bottle of wine and some apples from the orchard. You should *see* what they've done to the house. It looks like Jackie Collins's

33

boudoir.'

Angie laughed. 'They sound like fun! Are they coming tonight?'

'I did ask, but Cheryl's got the Sky man coming round. She mentioned having a party, though, to get to know everyone. I think her and Barry are quite the socialites.'

'Good-oh, you know how Freds and I like a knees-up.'

A warning look was shot in their direction and everyone shut up. Clementine turned back to the audience. 'Brenda Briggs has made her apologies for not being here tonight. I believe she left a message with someone?'

'Yeah, her varicose veins are playing up,' called a woman from the second row.

Clementine visibly blanched, and went back to her clipboard. 'Ah yes, the first thing I would like to address is the pothole situation on the Bedlington Road. The council *assure* me they are coming next week . . .'

Forty minutes later they'd nearly finished. Clementine paused and cleared her throat. 'Now we have the rather unsociable *activities* in Foxglove Woods.'

'You mean the dogging,' Calypso interjected cheerfully. She deflected the death stare inflicted back at her. 'That is the official term for it, Granny Clem.'

'Yeah, it's on Wikipedia,' someone else called out.

'Thank you,' Clementine said crossly. She sighed. 'All right then, the *dogging*.' She said it as if she'd uttered the most hideous of profanities. 'I've spoken with the police constable at Bedlington

34

station, and he's doing his utmost to stamp out the situation.'

'What, sitting up there in his patrol car all day?' called out the same woman who'd told them about Brenda Briggs's varicose veins. 'He's probably doing it himself!'

Giggles rippled across the hall. Clementine noticed the Reverend Bellows looking unsettled. 'So that's all,' she said hurriedly. 'I advise everyone to remain vigilant, and if they do see anything, to chase offenders off with a large stick.' She tapped the clipboard. 'And now to the final item on the agenda.' She smiled over her spectacles. 'Would Angie and Kizzy like to come up?'

The two made their way to the front, Kizzy attracting a second look from all the males in the room. Including Reverend Bellows, who went puce when he saw Caro catch him admiring Kizzy's bottom as she went past.

'For those of you who don't know, this is Kizzy Milton, Nobby's trainer and jockey,' Clementine said. A smattering of applause broke out, and Kizzy grinned. 'I'm sure you're all familiar with the incredible story of how Freddie rescued Nobby, and what progress he's made since then,' Clementine continued. 'And I just want you to know, Angie and Kizzy, that the village wish you the best of luck with your racing career, and we're all one hundred per cent behind you.'

'Thanks, chaps,' Angie said, going slightly pink. 'That means a lot.'

'Now for the big moment!' Clementine announced. 'Has everyone put their name in the hat?'

The hat, actually an old ice-cream tub

35

Clementine had brought along, was full to the brim. She offered it to Kizzy.

'You do the honours, my dear.'

Kizzy stuck her hand in and scrabbled around, coming out with a piece of paper. She undid it while the audience held their breath. Her brow crinkled, and she looked at Angie.

'Er, "Calvin Brown"?'

'"Calvin Brown"?' Clementine was perplexed. 'Is this someone's idea of a silly joke?'

'Excuse me, Calvin Brown is like, *the* fittest boy in Bedlington,' said a busty young brunette in the front row. Stacey Turner lived in the pub with her parents, and styled herself on Katie Price, complete with hair extensions and DayGlo fake-tanned skin.

'We can't name a horse after some chap you like!' exclaimed Clementine.

Stacey crossed her hands over her cleavage and glowered. 'Whatever.'

'Have another go, Kizzy,' Clementine said. She rather hoped her own suggestion, Don José, would be picked. It was the name of the dastardly villain in her favourite opera, *Carmen*.

It got worse. 'David Beckham,' Kizzy read out.

Stacey Turner punched an orange hand in the air. 'Yes! Two out of two.'

'We can't have "David Beckham"!' Clementine said despairingly.

'OMG! Excuse me, he is *lush*.' Stacey shot Clementine an evil look. 'You can't keep changing your mind. I totally won it. Mum, tell her!'

It looked like mutiny was about to break out, until someone else called out a suggestion. 'How about "Goldenballs"?'

'He hasn't got any balls,' Kizzy whispered to

36

Angie, making her giggle.

A few people in the audience were nodding their heads enthusiastically. 'What do you think, Angie?'

'I think it's fun!'

'It's David Beckham's nickname, isn't it?' Beryl Turner was trying to placate her daughter. 'What do you think, Stacey?'

Stacey's drawn-out sigh indicated she had better things to be getting on with.

'Clementine?' Angie asked. The name was growing on her by the second.

The old lady gave a sigh of her own. 'Fine.' *Goldenballs. How ridiculous!* she thought.

'Pity Nobby isn't as good-looking as Becks,' Calypso muttered. 'If he gets over the first fence without tripping over his teeth I'll be amazed.'

'Ssh, darling,' said Caro, smiling gaily at Angie.

*   *   *

Afterwards they all congregated in the kitchen, where Joyce and Camilla dished out cups of tea and slices of Joyce's homemade banana loaf. 'This is amazing,' Calypso declared, through another huge mouthful.

'Where do you put it all?' Angie looked at Calypso's sylphlike figure.

'Sickening, isn't it?' Caro said. 'I put on two pounds just looking at cake.'

'Oi, I burn it all off!' protested Calypso. 'I work hard, you know.'

'We know you do, darling,' Camilla smiled. She worked just as hard as her sister—if not longer hours—at the travel agency she'd set up in a barn conversion just outside the village, but they were all

37

used to Calypso's exaggerations by now.

Camilla felt a warm hand on her shoulder, and turned to see the gorgeous green eyes of her boyfriend, Jed. He kissed her on the cheek. 'Hey, babe.'

'Hello.' She looked at him fondly. Jed had come straight from work in his overalls, and the slightly sweaty, masculine smell that he always had after a day of hard physical labour always turned Camilla on. Now estate manager at Clanfield Hall, Jed had moved on from his handyman days, but he still liked to muck in with the lads.

Jed greeted the others in his soft country burr, and turned back to his girlfriend. 'I came to walk you back if you're ready to go.'

'How romantic,' declared Angie. 'And they say chivalry is dead.'

From the look he was giving her, Camilla knew exactly what lay in store for her when she got back. A man of few words, Jed could communicate a thousand feelings in that mesmerizing gaze of his. Most of the women in the district thought he was a complete hunk.

At this moment in time, however, his hands were wandering surreptitiously on to Camilla's bottom. She put her cup and saucer down.

'We might be off, then.'

'They are SO going to bonk,' declared Calypso, while they were still in earshot.

*   *   *

A harvest moon had broken through the low cloud, giving them enough light to get back across the green. A faint tang hung in the air: the rising smoke

38

from nearby wood-burning stoves and from Agas. Jed slipped his arm round Camilla's waist. 'How was your day? Did you get the Nicaraguan trip sorted?'

'Yes, all fine now. I found an eco-lodge that does vortex healing, so the client's happy.' Camilla's agency, Windchimes Travel, was hard work, with demanding customers, but she loved the challenge, and the satisfaction it gave her.

'Vortex healing.' Jed gave a snort. 'These people have more money than they know what to do with.'

She smiled. 'As long as the customers keep coming, I'm not complaining.'

Jed gave her a little squeeze. 'I'm really proud of you.'

Their cottage was the end one of three square, cosy buildings with plump thatched roofs. While Camilla and Jed's garden was neat and well-maintained, two doors down Calypso's had the Spartan whiff of a horticultural phobic's. Outside her gate, an old suitcase and a poster frame missing its glass had been dumped on top of the green recycling bags.

'Calypso's been having a rare clear-out,' Jed remarked dryly.

Camilla sighed. 'I don't know how many times I've told her the bin men won't take all her junk.'

'I'll take it down to the tip tomorrow. I need to go, anyway.'

'The fairy bin man strikes again. What would my sister do without you?' Camilla stopped on the porch and looked up into Jed's beautiful face. The overhead light gleamed on his pale skin and high cheekbones, and the flop of black hair across his forehand.

They'd been together nearly six years now, and

39

living in unmarried bliss for three of them. Even though they'd grown up in the village together, it had taken that long for the shy country lad—who'd always lived with his mother in a house on the Clanfield estate—to pluck up the courage to ask Camilla for a drink. They hadn't looked back since, and Camilla never ceased to wonder at the time she'd wasted on emotionally-retarded public-school boys, when the real thing had been under her nose all the time.

There wasn't any need for words. Camilla started up the stairs, past the framed prints of Victorian flowers and beautifully shot photographs from her travels. Jed followed close behind, hands resting lightly on her rounded buttocks. He'd already turned the bedside lamp on in their bedroom, so it cast a romantic glow over the Cole & Son floral wallpaper and heavy curtains.

Jed started to unwind the pale pink pashmina from round her neck. Next up was her Zara work blazer, joining the scarf on the armchair in the corner. 'I really like your hair,' he told her, holding the ends gently in his calloused hands.

'You do?' A natural blonde like her sisters, Camilla had taken the plunge a month before and had her hair cut shorter and dyed a warm brown. She hadn't told anyone she was doing it, not even Jed. She'd had the same style practically all her life—long, straight and blonde, more often than not pulled back in a ponytail for practical purposes— so no one could believe it when she'd come back from the hairdressers looking completely different. Once they'd got over the initial shock, her family had all agreed it really suited her. The darker tones brought out Camilla's warm brown eyes and clear complexion.

Jed rubbed her neck. 'It's very sultry.'

'Sultry, huh?' she smiled. 'I don't think I've ever been called that before.'

'I don't believe that,' he murmured, lifting her arms above her head. Off came the black Jigsaw shirt, to reveal her 34B breasts in their lacy M&S bra. Compared to Calypso's legginess and Caro's womanly curves, Camilla was the most athletic of the sisters, her healthy figure helped along by her love of long walks and cottage DIY.

Jed ran his hand across her smooth décolletage wonderingly. 'You have such soft skin.'

Every time he said it, it gave Camilla goosebumps. Jed treated her with such reverence— even at the height of passion—and he always made her feel utterly beautiful. Men like Jed didn't notice if you'd put on weight, or your armpits hadn't been shaved, or your underwear didn't match. As handsome and sexually charged as he was, their relationship was more about emotional connection. This potent mix only intensified the way Camilla felt about Jed.

She started to unbutton the front of his overalls. Even in winter he never felt cold, and only wore a T-shirt underneath. His lean, ripped torso was a true man's body, achieved from years of hard, physical graft. As she pulled his top off, Camilla ached just looking at him. She felt an overwhelming urge to have him inside of her.

Making love had a different beat now, ever since they'd found out two years ago that Jed was unable to have children. Camilla had been devastated, but it had hit him even harder. He was such a man's man, so independent and physical and protective of

41

Camilla, that he felt he'd let her down. It had taken her a long time to make him see things differently.

Now, however, wasn't the time to dwell on such matters. As Jed pulled her chinos off and kicked off his overalls, Camilla saw the bulge at the front of his tight black pants. He sat down on the bed, and pulled her on to his lap. They started kissing again, soft tongues and lips, hands running over familiar bodies.

'You want me to take a shower?' he asked in her ear.

'No.' The musky scent of hard work only turned Camilla on even more. Jed laid her down on the bed, peeling her knickers off in one practised movement. His pants were next, revealing his bush of dark pubic hair and rock-hard erection. Camilla hadn't a vast experience of men's cocks, but Jed's had to be up there with the best of them. Not too small, and not too big, it had lovely smooth skin and always smelt clean. A perfect specimen, just like him.

Jed climbed on top, his eyes locked on hers.

'I love you, Cam.'

There it was again, that moment of fleeting regret in his eyes before he pushed inside her. Wrapping her arms round him, Camilla held her boyfriend tight, to let him know everything was all right.

'I really love you, too.'

CHAPTER SIX

In the village hall things were starting to wrap up. Calypso found her grandmother talking to Joyce Bellows in the kitchen. 'Right, you and me are off to the pub, Granny Clem,' she said, linking her arm through the older woman's.

'It's you and *I*, Calypso. Really, where all that good education has gone I just don't know . . .'

'Cool. You and I are off to the boozer, then,' Calypso said cheerfully. 'Jack's lining the shots up on the bar for us this very minute.'

Joyce's eyes widened.

'I do apologize for my granddaughter,' Clementine told the vicar's wife. She shot Calypso a look. 'I am certainly not going to the pub. You spend far too much time in that place already, if you ask me.'

'Oh, don't be like that,' Calypso coaxed. 'Caro's coming, and Angie and Kizzy . . . we've got to wet the horse's head! Well, you know what I mean.' She fixed endearing brown eyes on her grandmother. 'Pleeeease? You only have to stay for the one sherry.'

'No. I've got to write up the minutes for the village newsletter.'

'It can wait until tomorrow.' Calypso nudged her. 'Come on, Clemballs, live a little.'

Clementine sighed. She might have to scold her youngest granddaughter on a regular basis, but she completely adored her. And Calypso knew it.

'Yay! That's settled, then.' Calypso winked at Joyce. 'Are we going to get smashed or what?'

43

The Jolly Boot public house was a long, low-roofed building on the other side of the village green. In the summer the honeycomb walls were ablaze with climbing plants and hanging baskets, and during the winter it was the perfect place to while away the cold, dark hours.

And that was the case tonight—a huge fire was crackling in the inglenook fireplace, and the hanging horseshoes over the bar were glinting in the warm light. The landlords—a fearsome red-headed cockney called Jack Turner, and his buxom wife, Beryl—treated every customer like a long-lost friend. Everything made you feel at home as soon as you walked through the door—from Jack's cheery greeting: 'What can I getcha, ladies and gents?'—to the newspapers on the bar and the fabulous restaurant next door. Unless you'd drunk too much at closing time, that was, and were being a nuisance. Many a lairy young man had found himself being ejected by the collar through the door. More often than not it was Beryl who did the job; she ran her beloved pub with a no-nonsense iron rule.

Champagne was on the house that night, in honour of Nobby, and even Clementine was persuaded to have a little tipple. Kizzy, who was driving home afterwards, stuck to a glass of orange juice.

After toasting the newly named Goldenballs—'Our first village racehorse!' declared Clementine—Caro and Angie started having a catch-up. Caro had the go-ahead to stay out for a few drinks, having rung Benedict on their way over.

'Poor man,' she told Angie. 'He was barely in the door from work when I had to come out. I left him

44

with his jacket half off and Rosie demanding to be taken for a wee-wee.'

Angie laughed. 'That wonderful husband of yours! I'm sure Benedict is coping. Is he finding the commute OK?'

Caro nodded. 'It's a little tiring, but you know Benedict, he never complains. And I do get wonderful goodies brought back from Fortnum & Mason's.'

'Ooh, yum.' Angie looked down at her stomach, protruding through her dark-blue jeans. 'Although the last thing I need to be thinking about is F & M's duck pâté.'

'Nonsense, darling,' Caro said loyally. 'There's nothing there!' She was about to take a sip of champagne, but stopped dead. 'Is Calypso trying to get Granny Clem to neck a *vodka*?'

*   *   *

The pub was getting very lively by the time Kizzy left. She'd had a really nice time, and everyone in the village had made her feel so welcome. Kizzy especially liked Calypso, who had a naughty side and was great fun. The funniest part of the evening had to be when she'd downed five shots one after the other in front of her horrified grandmother—only to reveal to Clementine that she'd actually only been drinking water. The look on the poor woman's face! Kizzy would never have dared pull such a stunt—Clementine was as strict as a boarding-school headmistress—but Calypso clearly had a way with her. Kizzy and Angie had killed themselves laughing.

Her phone beeped as she got in the car. It was

Lauren. *'Few of us going 2 pub, u fancy? Xx'*

It had been sent at 7 p.m.; Kizzy must have been out of reception all evening. If she really wanted she could still go and meet Lauren and the others in town, but Kizzy didn't fancy it. They'd probably be hammered by now, and dressed up to the nines as usual, and there was no way Kizzy was walking in there in her hoodie and her old jeans, with muddy paw prints on them from being ravished by Angie's border collies, Avon and Barksdale. Her friends thought she was a country hick as it was, anyway.

Kizzy had known Lauren since primary school; they'd been in the same class and become best friends. Lauren had been brought up on the other side of Bedlington, in a house with a really big garden, and Kizzy had practically lived there during the summer holidays. They'd been inseparable, and done everything together. As they'd got older, though, they'd started to have less in common. Kizzy became more and more horse mad, and by the time she was fifteen was spending all her time outside school helping out at a yard. Lauren had joined her once, trod in some horse poo in her brand new heels, and never been back. Now she was an account executive for a PR company, driving around in a very cute sky-blue Fiat. A town car for a town-loving girl. Kizzy still thought the world of Lauren but their friendship had drifted. It was sad, but these things happened.

Lauren was still really good, though, texting Kizzy to invite her to things. Most of Kizzy's other mates had given up on her. Kizzy decided to drop her a text tomorrow. Maybe they could meet up for a coffee next week or something.

There were also two missed calls from home.

Her mum was probably wondering where she'd got to. She started to drive slowly down the road towards the crossroads, tapping out a reply. She wouldn't normally have done this, but there were no other cars about. *'10 mins away. Soz x'*

Turning left at the crossroads, she glanced down to press 'send' and didn't see a car coming the other way. There was a blaze of lights and a screech of brakes as the vehicle swerved to avoid her.

Oh shit! Kizzy dropped the phone in her lap. She'd nearly driven into it!

The black Land Cruiser stopped and the driver's window came whizzing down.

'What the hell do you think you're playing at?' She couldn't really see the person inside properly, but it was a man, broad-shouldered, his dark face in shadow.

'I'm so sorry,' she started to say. Her whole body was shaking with adrenalin.

The man cut her off. 'You're half way over the road! Watch where you're going next time!'

'I said I was sorry,' Kizzy said meekly. Dark eyes flashed out of the Land Cruiser at her. They looked vaguely familiar, but before she could remember where she'd seen them before, the man muttered something and the tinted window slid up. There was a loud rev as he pulled away sharply.

Kizzy sat there, gripping the steering wheel. 'Don't ever do that again, you silly cow!' she said aloud. Heartbeat just about returning to normal, she started for home.

CHAPTER SEVEN

Calypso put her foot down on the accelerator and sighed. She'd just had the most trying few hours of her life, sitting through another precocious brat's birthday party. If she saw another helium balloon or soft play area again she'd scream. To make matters worse, one of the other little brats had eaten four slices of the gluten-free birthday cake and promptly thrown up, scoring a bullseye on Calypso's feet with his vomit spray.

The glamour, she thought savagely as she hurtled around a hairpin bend, nearly taking out an old codger on a tractor. This wasn't what she'd moved back to the Cotswolds for, was it? After eighteen riotous months as an events organizer in New York, Calypso had returned full of high hopes. Everyone knew the Cotswolds, with its stunning views, million-pound houses and mix of rock stars, actors and fat-cat bankers, was the place to be. Calypso had visions of eclectic, high-end parties filled with the rich and beautiful, but instead she seemed to spend her life organizing kids' parties, sixteenths and sixtieths, graduation lunches, and corporate dos—full of boring people who wanted bog-standard things.

There was the odd client who wanted something cool and different, and then Calypso always pulled out all the stops. Those were the jobs that gave her a high, and reminded her why she did what she did. But despite the good feedback she'd had, most of her work was distinctly mundane. She told herself it was still the recession, and that she was operating in the countryside now and not the jumping hot spot of New York. It was still really frustrating. Scene Events might be doing all right financially, but if she was still doing work like this in ten years' time, she'd top herself.

The thought that had been running through her mind recently flashed up again. *London*. She could make a killing there. Calypso slowed down as a pheasant ran across the road ahead. She knew the city—and many of the people—like the back of her hand. Unlike her sisters, who had gone to the more traditional St Mary's in Ascot, Calypso's parents had sent her to Vespers, a very hip, expensive girls' school in Holland Park. Her mother had gone there, and Calypso had inherited Tink's love of socializing and cosmopolitan living. She might not have got the best exam results in the world, and had only just scraped into Reading, but boy, had she partied hard.

Fun-loving and exasperating, sharp-tongued and loving, Calypso had always been the most controversial member of her family. Her parents had despaired of her ever getting a proper job, but Calypso had surprised them all when she'd stopped her 24/7 partying and announced she was getting a real job. Events organizing had been her choice of career; after all, it was a home from home. And she was *good*. Enough people had told her.

Yet here she was, driving home with some kid's puke on her Office shoe boots. Calypso gave a wry smile; she might not put that one up on Twitter.

An oncoming car flashed her as she entered the outskirts of Churchminster, but Calypso didn't realize until too late that it had been Angie. With a sudden sigh she pulled the car back to the

49

30 mph limit. Despite her nonchalance about Elliot the rock-star-in-waiting, Calypso had really liked him. It was so her luck that the only person she'd properly fancied for ages had buggered off across the other side of the world. *He's probably shagging some groupie right now*, she thought, a wave of depression washing over her. What was it with her and arsehole blokes? She obviously had some inbuilt radar that got them flocking. Or else she attracted idiots who were full of it, like the twat in a hat.

She'd never had to deal with this stuff before. Footloose and fancy-free, Calypso had gallivanted her way through life, leaving a trail of broken hearts behind her. It wasn't intentional, more careless, but Calypso was drawn to men like a moth to a candle, and as soon as the next one came along she was off, chasing the thrill. Money or status didn't motivate her, and over the years she'd dated a variety of sexy, unpredictable, naughty people, all with that dangerous edge she'd always lusted after. Men— and there had also been a few women—were there to have fun with, shag senseless, and then it was on to the next one, thanks for coming etc. etc. (Excuse the pun.)

That was how she'd felt until two years ago, when she'd met Rafe Wolfe. He was a famous British movie star who had been in Churchminster filming a costume drama, and at first Calypso had been her usual unimpressed self. *An up-his-arse pin-up*, she'd thought, but Rafe had pursued and pursued her, and to everyone's surprise, including her own, Calypso had fallen in love for the first time in her life. After they'd practically moved in together it had been a nasty shock to discover Rafe had had a secret fiancée in Los Angeles. In fact, shock was far too mild a description. It had felt more like someone reaching into Calypso's stomach, having a good old rummage around, and pulling her guts out with a flourish.

Afterwards Rafe had scarpered back across the Atlantic with his cock between his legs, and devastated as she was, Calypso had hoped having three thousand miles between them would help her get over him. It hadn't been that easy. It wasn't like she could delete him and never hear from him again. Just when she was having a good week and was getting back on track, *bang*, he'd pop up on the E! Channel or in *heat* magazine, giving it the big cheese, and it would all come flooding back.

Time was a healer, though. If someone asked her now, she would say she was over Rafe. Nearly. On the surface she was back to her normal self, but inside . . . To give your heart to someone, only to have it stamped into a million little pieces, well, it made you view the world a bit differently. And right now, there was nothing to change Calypso's opinion that her life was stuck in a rut, and that when it came to picking the wrong men, she had a world-class talent.

She drove round the green, and parked up her car outside the cottages. All around her, Churchminster was as serene and beautiful as always. She felt stifled. Here she was at twenty-eight, living in the same village she'd been born in, with only her middle-aged neighbours' house-warming party to look forward to.

How the hell had this *happened*?

CHAPTER EIGHT

Angie was in her antiques shop on the village green. A long, narrow space, it was a treasure trove of old pieces of furniture and paintings, quirky artefacts and collectable china. As usual, there was a big bunch of scented flowers on the front counter. Antiques shops were known for being a little dark and musty, and Angie wanted to make the experience as nice as possible for her customers.

Not that there had been a lot of them recently. Things were still ticking over, but nothing like the heyday of the eighties, when she'd been able to make a fifty thousand pound sale in a day. Most customers went to auctions online now, and then, of course, they were still feeling the pinch of the recession. The couple's business up at the house had suffered, too, although they were starting to get back on their feet again. It was difficult these days, with more and more competition springing up. When they'd first started hiring their land out for shooting and fishing, they had been only one of a handful. Now every Tom, Dick and Harry with more than an acre seemed to be doing it, and cheaper, too. It was hard to keep up.

The doorbell went, and a woman walked in, done up too tightly in a garish red coat. Ignoring Angie's hello, she had a cursory look round and then walked out, as if nothing in there was worthy of her attention.

'Bye!' Angie called brightly. 'Thanks for coming in!' A buzz from her handbag indicated she'd got a text. Putting down a figurine of a woman with no head, Angie went into the back office. Her spirits lifted when she saw who it was from.

'Hey, Ma. How you doing? All good here, just got back from surfing, and sitting on patio with cold beer. Send my love to the old man, speak soon. Ax'

It was like Archie knew telepathically whenever she needed cheering up. Angie reached for her wallet and the photo of her son she always kept in there. It was creased and tattered now, one snapped on his first day as a knobbly-kneed little imp at prep school. Angie looked at the gap-toothed smile; Freddie had taken the picture on the doorstep of the Maltings with their old black Labrador, Bess, standing in shot. The new cap on Archie's head had been found shortly afterwards floating in the pond. Archie had insisted the dog had taken it, but Angie had known better. The little horror had hated being cooped up in his school uniform.

Not that Archie had to worry about being cooped up now. What a time he must be having! He'd decided on a second gap year after gaining a good degree from an agricultural college up North. Now he was on one of South Island's biggest sheep farms, having a whale of a time and gaining invaluable experience. When Archie came back, the plan was to help his dad out for a few months with the family business and then find a job.

Archie had seriously worried his parents for a while. A nice, friendly boy growing up, he'd had a complete meltdown at seventeen, and got in with the wrong crowd. When Angie thought back to the surly, shaven-headed lout who'd, unbeknown to them, had a secret pot habit, it made her shudder in horror. Thankfully, Archie's rebellious stage hadn't lasted long and, at twenty-three, he was a happy, affable young man. Angie smiled as she thought of him; she'd write a nice long text back.

A loud beeping outside interrupted her thoughts. On the other side of the green a huge lorry was reversing outside the Pikes'. 'Parkfields Sand Company' said the logo down the side. 'For all your outdoor needs.'

It was a bit late to be doing landscaping, wasn't it? The party was tonight. Angie watched as the lorry nearly took out the postbox before coming to an ungainly stop. Talking of the party, there were horses to be got in and dogs to be fed before she could even think about what she'd be wearing later. Angie looked at her watch: just past four. The sun was disappearing out of the sky.

Might as well close up. There was nothing happening here. Angie pulled down the blinds and went to get her bag.

*   *   *

The whole village had turned out for the Pikes' 'hot tub house-warming party' with one notable exception: Clementine. She'd hand-delivered a very gracious note to the Pikes saying she had a prior commitment and would, unfortunately, be unable to attend.

'I don't think I've ever heard of your grandmother turning down an invite before,' Angie said, as she and Caro stood in the hallway of the Pikes' house later, clutching glasses of champagne. Angie's horse-smelling jeans and shirt had been exchanged for a floaty floral dress.

'I think that was before invites started turning up in the shape of a pair of boobs. She was rather alarmed by the dress code.' The novelty creations posted through peoples' letterboxes had advised 'swimwear, diamonds and not much else'.

The two women exchanged a look and broke off into peals of laughter. 'Oh dear!' Angie said. 'Poor Clementine must wonder what the village is coming to.'

Down the corridor a man in a shiny boy-band suit was trying to retrieve his lighter from a foxy redhead's cleavage.

'Dave, you dirty sod, you did that on purpose!' she shrieked, as his hand wriggled around comically inside her low-cut silk blouse. Her bosom was so large and voluptuous that Angie wondered if he might fall down it completely, but eventually he surfaced, platinum lighter in hand.

'Bleedin' 'ell, Linda, I think I just saw Lord Lucan down there!'

'Wa-hay hay hay!' Barry was upon them, decked out in red shorts and matching windbreaker, a brown mullet wig over his bald head. He held up the magnum of champagne. 'More Cristal, ladies?'

'I like your costume, Barry,' Angie told him.

He flashed her a grin. 'It's the Hoff. What do you think? Me and Chez like a bit of fancy dress. Livens things up, dunnit?'

'I think you look splendid, very Hoff-like,' Caro said, as he sloshed in more liquid. 'Ooh, just a little one, please.' The Pikes were proving to be most generous hosts. She'd only been there half an hour, and her glass had been topped up five times already.

Barry gave her an exaggerated wink. 'You won't find any little ones in this house, I can tell you.' He turned to fill up Angie's glass. He gave her a

55

flirtatious look.

'There you go, Angelica, my sweetheart, a nice big one for you.'

'Just how I like them, thank you, Barry!'

'I like you, you're naughty,' Barry said. He gave Angie's cheek a tweak, and bustled off down the hall, dispensing champagne to anyone he passed.

'He's rather taken with you!' Caro laughed.

'I think he's fun! It's nice to have some lively types in the village.' Angie looked round. 'And the Pikes know how to put on a good bash.'

Even before they'd reached the front door, the villagers knew they were in for some party. Sports cars of every name and colour were parked on the road outside the house, while a living statue of Michelangelo's David stood in the front garden. The muscular young man was covered entirely in gold paint, with only a fig leaf for modesty, and had already attracted a gaggle of female guests urging each other to go and steal his foliage.

Then there were the Pikes' friends, all as loud and colourful as they were. Jewels flashed at ears, necks and hands—and that was just the men. Everywhere you looked there was a veritable display of flesh: pumped-up cleavages, personal-trained bodies, big lips, frozen foreheads. Everything was supersized or super-thin, flashy, shiny, and glitzy. It was like watching some sort of exotic tribe at play on their very own Serengeti. One where the wildlife were worn as shoes and handbags, and finished off with a liberal dusting of Swarovski crystals.

Waitresses dressed as Vegas showgirls were going round plying guests with shots of Grey Goose vodka, while the Bacchanalian buffet table

56

groaned with caviar and lobster. If the party itself was a riot, the surroundings were something else. Cheryl had had the decorators working round the clock. The neutral colour pattern put in by the previous owners was gone. Save for the zebra-print three-piece and rugs, the whole place was a homage to gold. There were gold-patterned curtains, gold mirrors, gold ornaments; even the downstairs loo had a gilt-gold toilet seat and gold-leaf wallpaper, which Cheryl told Caro had cost a thousand pounds a metre. There was no art, save a twee landscape painting completely at odds with the surroundings and a blown-up photograph of Barry and Cheryl dressed as Bonnie and Clyde above the fireplace in the living room—all three framed in garish gilt-gold, of course. It would take weeks for Caro's eyes to get back to normal.

Calypso was striding towards them, rock-chick sexy in a pair of tight leather trousers and a black faux-fur jacket.

'Groovy trousers,' Angie told her. 'I wouldn't get those past my ankles.'

'Thanks, they're actually Mummy's from the seventies. Granny Clem's got loads of her old clothes in the attic; there's some really cool stuff up there.' Calypso's eyes had a naughty glint, and there was a sexy flush on her cheeks from the alcohol. 'This place is amazing! Have you been out to the back garden yet?'

'We haven't got past the door yet, for people-watching. What's out there?' A giant straw roof had been erected over it yesterday, and Caro was dying to know what was inside.

Calypso grinned. 'Come and check it out.'

The three of them made their way to the back

of the house, picking up a very merry Freddie, who was now wearing someone's grass skirt over his red cords. 'Bloody good bash!' he said, putting his arm round his wife's shoulders. 'Have you been out to the garden?'

'We're just on our way, Freds,' Angie told him. As they reached the French doors out on to the patio, she let out a delighted shriek. 'Oh, I *love* it!'

The hundred-foot-long garden had been turned into a giant beach, complete with sand, sunloungers and a giant straw roof. Caro was gobsmacked. 'We'd better not let the kids see this, they'll be wanting one in our garden.'

The Pikes certainly didn't do things by halves. Plastic matting had been laid down to accommodate the sand, with a line of sunbeds complete with umbrellas on either side. Large outdoor heaters were dotted about, raising the temperature to a Mauritius-style level. On the decking at the back, a *Cocktail*-style bar had been erected, complete with a chisel-jawed bartender, who was showing off his pouring skills to two heavily tanned cougars.

But the real pièces de résistance were the two enormous hot tubs, in which various half-naked bodies were crammed, laughing and necking champagne from the bottle.

'Cheryl's been giving me a guided tour,' Calypso said. She pointed at the nearest one, which had what looked like disco lights on the floor. 'Staying Alive' was blasting out from somewhere in the tub. 'That's the John Travolta one, and that one over there'—she pointed at the other, which had red seats and a black and white chequered flag—'is Formula One. Barry's had them all custom-made.'

58

A man sitting on the edge pressed a large red button and a loud revving noise could be heard.

There was a shout, and Cheryl emerged out of John Travolta. She tottered over, wearing high-heeled flip-flops and a red high-cut swimming costume.

'Pamela Anderson, what do you think?' Gravity-defying globes were straining through the transparent fabric. Cheryl grabbed them, like she was appraising two melons at the supermarket. 'Harley Street, seven grand. I got them off Baz for my forty-second, the other set had gone well saggy.' She noticed Freddie looking agog, and offered one up. 'Go on, love, have a feel.'

Freddie looked like a rabbit caught in the headlights. 'I'll take your word for it,' he spluttered. 'I'm sure they're splendid.'

Cheryl gestured at John Travolta. 'Coming in?'

'I forgot to put my swimming costume on,' Caro lied, thinking hell would freeze over before she'd reveal her mummy-tummy to a garden full of people.

'Go in your knick-knocks, Carol!'

'It's actually . . .' Caro gave up. She'd told Cheryl her name about a hundred times. She tried a feeble joke instead. 'Besides, what would the vicar say?'

Cheryl gave another cackle. 'He's bloody in there himself!'

They spun round to be confronted by the Reverend Bellows surrounded by Cheryl clones in Formula One. The Reverend's milky chest looked like it hadn't seen the sun since he was a choirboy, and his glasses were getting very steamed up as a buxom brunette draped her Page Three curves over him.

'Denise, keep your hands off!' Cheryl shouted. 'Dirty bitch,' she told the others. 'Always wanted to shag a vicar.'

Poor Reverend Bellows looked so helpless and uncomfortable that Angie tried to control her laughter as she went over to see if he needed rescuing. She discreetly averted her eyes as he stumbled out and started dressing hurriedly from the pile of clothes that had been ripped off him.

'I only stopped by for a dry sherry,' he said in a panicky voice, as Angie went to retrieve his dog collar. 'Joyce will wonder what's happened to me.'

'Well, you know what they say.' Calypso started pulling her T-shirt off. 'When in Rome.' To a chorus of wolf whistles, she shimmied over in her lacy underwear and jumped in.

*   *   *

By one o'clock in the morning Caro was ready to go. Granny Clem was babysitting the children at her house tonight, but Caro wanted to be round there first thing to relieve her. She was in desperate need of a few hours of sleep anyway, even if it was doubtful it would be peaceful. The Pikes' back garden resembled something out of a Benny Hill sketch, as a man in a Borat mankini chased a topless woman round in circles. In the far corner, two couples were howling with laughter as they attempted a naked game of Twister. Barry himself was nearly naked, save for a lacy pants and bra set he'd acquired from somewhere.

She found her husband at the far end of the garden, being pinned against the wall by a black-haired woman who looked like Dorian from

60

Birds of a Feather. As Caro walked up she heard the woman say something about her recent vagina-tightening operation.

'Ah, darling, there you are!' Benedict said brightly. *Save me*, his expression said. 'This is my wife, Caro,' he said. 'Caro, this is Gloria.'

'Hello, Gloria.'

Gloria looked Caro up and down and sniffed, before staggering off in search of more pink champagne.

Benedict leant down and kissed her. 'Thank you for rescuing me. Gloria was just getting to the really gruesome bit.'

'Yikes. I think I might make a move.'

'I'll come with you.' He slid an arm round her waist. 'Better make the most of having the bed to ourselves.'

There was a loud crash behind them. A woman, already perilous on six-inch 'fuck me' heels, had just felt the effect of three bottles of £100 champagne and fallen slap bang into the beach bar. Impressively, even as she lay comatose amongst the wreckage, a cigarette still smouldered in her left hand. They all watched, stunned, as the glowing end ignited a piece of straw, and suddenly fire was blazing away within seconds. The barman just had enough time to pull the woman clear before the whole thing went up.

'Hose! Hose!' someone shouted. Barry appeared from nowhere with a fire extinguisher and started spraying. Just as it seemed under control, a cluster of remaining sparks defiantly flew out.

'Shit!' Barry shouted. 'The rockets!' Caro only just had time to dive clear before a whole line of fireworks ignited. There was pandemonium as

61

everyone ran for cover, and, for a moment, the whole of the village was lit up like daylight. There was a ferocious *whoosh*, followed by banging and whizzing, as one rocket after the other went up.

'Sod it, might as well let all of them off now.' Barry pressed a button and everyone jumped as a giant firework screen sizzled into life at the bottom of the garden. Caro found herself staring at the unmistakable outline of a huge cock and pair of balls. Just in case the point hadn't been hammered home, sparks started spurting out of the huge bell-end.

'You always were a dickhead, Baz!' someone shouted. They all collapsed into drunken cheers and laughter.

Beside Caro, Benedict gave a light cough. 'Shall we head home, then?'

CHAPTER NINE

The next day an unearthly stillness lay over the village, save for a blow-up doll bobbing around in the duck pond. Across the green, Calypso woke and had a second of oblivious bliss before the hangover from hell kicked in.

Her mouth tasted like an ashtray. *Rank.* If she didn't have water soon her whole body would go into shutdown. Barely able to focus, she stared at the wall and tried to piece together the evening. How had she got home? The last thing she remembered was a heated debate about whether *Strictly Come Dancing* was better than *The X Factor* these days. And then she had a vague recollection of snogging someone on the front doorstep.

As there was a movement behind her Calypso froze. *Shit.* Who was it? At least she was wearing a vest top and pyjama bottoms, so they couldn't have had sex. What the hell was his name? She'd have to settle with 'babe' and wing it.

'Hey,' said an unfamiliar voice, inches from her ear. 'You awake?'

'Uh, yeah.' She felt a pair of strong arms circle her waist.

'How are you feeling?'

The voice sounded all right, but what did he look like? The last person she could properly remember was the fiftysomething Danny DeVito lookalike who'd offered to take her sailing on his private yacht. He'd had hair plugs, for God's sake; surely it hadn't come to that . . .

Calypso steeled herself and turned over. First reaction was relief, no Danny DeVito. Second thought a few seconds later: *Hello.* Not bad. Not bad at all. About thirty, nice brown eyes, and still wearing the white T-shirt she now remembered from last night. He had wide shoulders, and otherwise a slim, tennis-player physique. A pair of jeans was neatly folded on the chair at the end of the bed; under the duvet he wore a pair of checked boxer shorts, and his feet were encased in a pair of black socks.

He saw her check his feet. 'Not the best look. But this place is freezing. I tried to get the central heating to work last night.'

'The boiler's on the blink.' She sat up and looked at him, trying to make her alcohol-shrivelled brain think.

'I'm James,' he said good-naturedly. 'James

Ward. You did tell me you were so pissed you'd forget it in the morning.'

She grimaced. 'I'm really sorry. I swear it was those tropical cocktails Barry kept giving me.'

'Don't worry about it.' He looked remarkably comfortable in her bed.

'Er, are you one of the Pikes' friends?' He didn't seem their type.

'No, I'd been at the pub with a couple of mates, and when we came out we thought we'd come and see what all the noise was about. Luckily your hosts didn't seem to mind a couple of gatecrashers.' James smiled at her.

'I'm Calypso, by the way,' she said feebly.

'I know. Calypso Millicent Aurora Standington-Fulthrope. Born August the eleventh, 1983. Secretly fancies Simon Cowell, thinks Bruce Forsyth should be put down, is bored "fucking shitless" of the Cotswolds and cheating men, and wants to move to London, where all the fun, interesting people are, instead.'

She covered her face with a pillow. 'Did I really say that? I must have sounded like a complete tit.'

'Not at all.' James put his hand on her leg. 'I thought it was very entertaining.'

She looked at his hand. Sensing her discomfort, he quickly removed it. 'Did we, I mean . . .?' she asked.

'Did we have sex?' He had a nice smile. 'No, don't worry. You asked me to walk you home— putting one foot in front of the other was quite hard for you by then—and asked me in. Then I had to carry you up the stairs, where you proceeded to get into your pyjamas and demand I stayed the night.'

Oh God. It wasn't so much stripping naked in

64

front of a completely random man that made her wince, but the state of her bush. It was spider-leg central at the moment. Calypso was so off men she hadn't got round to booking in for her usual Brazilian.

James seemed to be very good at reading her thoughts. 'I went next door while you changed, so all modesty has been preserved.'

Calypso felt marginally better. ''Er, we did kiss though, didn't we?'

He smiled. 'Yes, outside your front door. It was very nice. You said you wouldn't remember that, either.'

Calypso cringed. 'Sorry. I'm er, not normally like this.' *Ahem.*

'I'll try not to take offence that my technique was that forgettable.'

His voice was pleasantly neutral, a touch of a drawl at the end. Ex-public-school; a nice, well-brought-up chap with a good job and family background. Calypso could spot his type a mile off.

She flopped down on the pillow, pushing her hand into her forehead to try and stem the drumming. 'I feel terrible. And I smoked! I'm meant to be giving up.'

'You were getting through them. Do you remember flicking your butt into that woman's hair?'

'I didn't!' Calypso was mortified. God, she *hated* herself when she got hammered.

'Nothing caught fire, so I don't think we need to worry about a lawsuit.'

Calypso pushed her face into the pillow. 'Aargh!'

James reached over to the bedside table for a pint glass of water. 'Here, drink this.'

'You lifesaver.' She managed to raise her head and take four thirsty gulps as he held the glass for her. 'Why haven't you got a hangover? It's not fair.'

'I was going quite slow on the beers.' He put the glass down and sat up, swinging his legs off the bed. Despite the off-putting socks Calypso noticed his thighs were quite muscular.

'Painkillers, where are they?'

'Bathroom, if there are any.' She squinted up at him through a mascara-clogged eye. 'Sorry, I'm not usually this incapacitated.'

James bent down and kissed her softly on the cheek. 'Hey, don't worry about it.'

She lay back on the bed, the touch of his lips still on her skin. *I think I'm still pissed*, she thought. She needed more water. With a Herculean effort she bent down for the pint glass. It was then that she saw them. The shoes.

Black and too shiny. Clumpy. OK, so they weren't *too* offensive if you went to work in a suit and hid them under a desk all day. Or maybe if you were a policeman. But off-duty with a pair of blue jeans—*urgh*!

The drumming was reaching a crescendo. All Calypso could do was lie back and close her eyes, as next door some bloke called James, with a dodgy taste in shoes, went through her bathroom cabinet.

*   *   *

At No. 1 Mill House, Caro and Benedict had spent the last hour trying to placate two tired, grumpy children over the breakfast table. They'd both been unsettled by staying over with Clementine, and had kept their poor great-grandmother up half the

66

night.

'Eat your cereal, darling,' Caro told her son.

'I'm not hungry,' Milo moaned. 'Can I get down now?'

'I think what these two need is some fresh air,' Benedict declared decisively. 'Shall we go out for a walk?'

Caro leant over and removed the bowl from her son. 'Good idea.' She needed to blow the cobwebs away as well: her head was feeling distinctly fuzzy.

As she and her family left in their wellies and thick coats people were arriving to pick up their cars from next door. In the harsh winter sunlight, they looked orange and lined, the previous night's debauchery—and a lifetime of five-star sunbathing—etched into their faces. One hungover man in a leather flying jacket grinned sheepishly as he climbed into his Lamborghini. Caro thought she recognized him as the Borat mankini guy running round the garden last night. He looked infinitely better with clothes on.

Camilla and Jed's cottage was quiet as they walked across the green. Camilla had been away at an awards ceremony in London last night, and Jed wasn't much of a partygoer anyway. Two down at Calypso's, the bedroom curtains were still drawn.

'Can we go see Auntie Lipso?' asked Milo.

'We'll just knock on the door and say a quick hello.' Calypso had been very much the worse for wear when they'd left last night, and Caro wanted to make sure she was OK.

Leaving Benedict with Rosie in the pushchair, she took Milo's hand and walked over to the row of cottages. She pushed open the gate, picking up an empty cigarette packet lying on the grass, and

67

knocked quietly on the front door.

'Oi!' Milo bellowed. 'Auntie Lipso!'

'Ssh, darling.' When there was no answer Caro bent down and called through the letterbox. 'It's only us! Sorry to disturb your lie-in, I just wanted to make sure you got home in one piece . . .'

The door suddenly opened and a young man stood there, two steaming mugs of tea in one hand. Caro was rather taken aback. 'Oh! Hello.' She looked round him enquiringly. 'I'm Calypso's sister. I just wanted to see if she was in.'

'Who the hell are you?' asked Milo.

'Dar-ling!' Caro reprimanded. 'It's rude to speak to people like that.' Where had he even picked up the word 'hell' anyway? She looked back at the newcomer apologetically. 'Sorry.'

'It's fine, really.' He had a friendly smile. 'I'll just get her.' He called up the stairs. 'Calypso! Your sister's here.'

There was a short pause. He and Caro looked at each other. 'I'm James, by the way.'

'Caro,' she said, taking his hand. 'Lovely to meet you.'

Calypso appeared at the top of the stairs, one towel round her body and another turbaned round her head. Her face dropped when she saw Caro.

'What are you doing here?'

'Just came to see if you're all right.'

'Course I am, why wouldn't I be?' Calypso didn't look very pleased at being disturbed. Actually, 'caught out' might have been a better description.

James smiled at Caro. There was another pause.

'OK, I'll leave you to it,' Caro said. 'Bye, James, good to meet you.'

'Great to meet you, too.' He did have a nice face.

'I'll make sure she calls when she's feeling more human.'

Mindful of what had happened with Anthony, the twat in a hat who'd called for Calypso last time, Caro pulled Milo away before he could inflict any more damage. 'She's got a man in there!' she whispered when she got back to Benedict. 'James, his name is.'

'Is that Auntie Lipso's boyfriend?' Milo asked.

'Er, it's one of her friends. Why don't you take your sister and go for a little walk?' Caro waited until the kids were running off across the green. She turned to Benedict. 'Do you think he was at the party? I don't remember him.'

Benedict thought. 'It might be the chap she was talking to on the stairs. They were being very touchy-feely with each other.'

Caro raised her eyebrows. 'I wonder if it's a one-off, or if she'll see him again?'

Benedict's expression was wry. 'One can never tell with your sister.'

'I know, but it would be nice to see her with someone decent.'

'Give her a chance, darling, they've only just met.'

'I know.' Caro sighed. 'She's just had such rotten luck with men, and I want to see her happy.'

Benedict touched his wife's arm. 'Your sister's fine, don't worry.'

*   *   *

Half an hour later, they were walking arm in arm through green woodland while the kids scampered ahead. Caro's headache, which was more to do with

69

tiredness than excess of alcohol, had finally lifted, and she was feeling like a new woman.

'Good party, wasn't it?'

'Very good. Now we just have to hope your grandmother doesn't hear about the pyrotechnic genitalia.' Benedict shook his head wonderingly. 'I thought we were pushing the boat out with a Catherine wheel last Bonfire Night.'

Caro laughed. 'It must have had some effect; everyone was getting very fruity when we left!'

They walked along for a few moments, watching the children. 'Milo seems happier now, doesn't he?' Caro said. 'I mean at school.' He'd loved his old school in London and taken a while to adjust to the new one, an excellent village primary five miles away.

'Much happier. I knew he'd settle in.'

'It's such a relief, Benedict. You know, I was worried about the kids when we moved back. There's so much to do in London—'

'Too much,' Benedict interjected. 'Whoever heard of a four-year-old going to yoga classes?'

'God, we were in a bubble!' Caro inhaled the air lustily. 'This is how I want our children to grow up. Like I did, with fields and fresh air and nature all around them.'

He kissed the top of her head. 'Talking of fields, I gave your grandmother a call while you were in the shower. The kids want to have a little Bonfire Night at hers, out the back.'

'Perfect, we'll need to think about food. Floating eyeball soup and all that.'

'I'll look up some recipes, fancy dress costumes too.'

'Whose benefit is this actually for?' she teased.

70

'Benny-dict! Come see what we've found!'

'Saved.' Her husband gave her a wink and strode off.

Caro watched him bend down between the children and feign amazement as Milo flicked a horrible dead frog away with his stick. Rosie gave a shriek of laughter, making Caro smile too. This was what it was all about, just the four of them together. She saw her son go over and pick the dead creature up on the end of his stick.

'Milo, don't you dare throw that at me! You little horror, I'm warning you!'

CHAPTER TEN

Nobby flared his nostrils and snorted. Normally the most docile of creatures, today's high winds had put his tail up. Gung-ho herself, Kizzy had to pull back on the reins several times to slow him down.

'Easy, Nobs. Easy, boy!'

Under her practised touch, she felt him calm down. It was starting to rain now, too, great gusty wet slaps across her face, but Kizzy loved this kind of weather. It made her feel alive, as if along with the bowing trees and scudding clouds, she and Nobby were part of something greater. Forget drugs and sex and whatever else it was that gave people their rush, this was it for Kizzy—the rolling, topsy-turvy patchwork of Cotswolds countryside, with its endless fields and big skies—even on a grey day like this. As far as Kizzy was concerned, it was the best place on earth.

The next fence was coming up, a sturdy five-foot

71

brush. Kizzy stood up in the stirrups to let Nobby find his stride, and felt him get it within seconds. In the same rhythm, horse and rider thundered down the track. They were going at a terrific speed, and a more nervous rider would have pulled back with the reins, but Kizzy knew better than to interfere. Giving Nobby his head, hands resting low on his neck, they did a textbook approach to the fence. Hitting the ground perfectly a metre in front, she felt Nobby jump right up into her hands, and they sailed over in a perfect arc. Kizzy had that euphoric feeling she got when it all went to plan; those precious few seconds when she and Nobby were at one with each other, the perfect partnership.

Landing on the other side, they continued round the final bend. They'd covered three-quarters of the track, and were heading for the final stretch. As Nobby fought for his head, Kizzy let him have it and squeezed into his sides with her heels. They were going so fast she could hardly see, excitement and adrenalin coursing through her body.

'Go, boy!' She leant down even lower, hands on his mane. Nobby had never run this well before; it was like he was operating on a whole new level. All at once, they weren't alone, but on the course at Aintree, surrounded by thousands of cheering fans. The announcer's voice came into her head. *It's Goldenballs, ridden by Kizzy Milton, who's going to win by a furlong!*

'Go on, Nobby!' she yelled. She could feel all the muscles in his body working as if they were her own, the power from his behind surging through her. *This is amazing; I could die right now, happy . . .*

Suddenly something white flew straight out in front of them. Kizzy barely had time to register it

72

as Nobby swerved violently. She felt herself lift out of the saddle, and a weird, thrilling moment of freedom as she knew she was gone. Then she was flying through the air; falling, falling, falling . . .

*   *   *

From the kitchen window Angie witnessed the whole thing. Her heart flew into her mouth as Kizzy was flung off Nobby like a rag doll, landing on the ground with a sickening heaviness. Without realizing, Angie dropped the cafetière she was holding, hot coffee splashing against her legs as the glass smashed on the floor.

Get up, darling. Please, get up, she willed frantically. Nobby trotted back and nudged the motionless figure with his nose.

'Are you all right? What's happened?' Freddie came running out of his study, but Angie was already pulling her Barbour on.

'Phone for an ambulance!' she cried. 'Kizzy's had an accident!'

CHAPTER ELEVEN

She could hear a voice, far away. Kizzy felt like she was lying at the bottom of a well and someone was calling down to her.

'Can you hear me?'

With a superhuman effort Kizzy opened her eyes. A figure was bending over her, their features swimming in and out of focus.

Kizzy blinked, the movement as slow and heavy

as two large shutters going up and down. The face standing over her started to clear. Dark, almost black eyes, a strong jaw. She felt a hand gently touch the side of her face.

'You're going to be OK, just don't move. It's very important you don't move.'

'I can't feel my legs,' she said, panicking.

'It's all right,' the man said. He had a deep voice, soothing, yet authoritative. 'The ambulance is coming.'

Ambulance? What had happened to her? *I can't remember . . .* Kizzy tried to fight it, but it was too much. She felt herself falling back into the well. Then everything went black.

*　　　*　　　*

Mr Sherbourne cast an expert eye over Kizzy. 'How are you feeling?'

'Sore,' she gasped. She was lying flat on her back in a hospital bed, her parents' worried faces over her. Even moving a millimetre sent out a searing pain.

'That's to be expected. You've sustained a traumatic soft-tissue injury and the X-rays have shown up a disc protrusion in your lumbar region.' Mr Sherbourne smiled, as if he were giving her good news. With his tan and expensive teeth he looked more like a movie star than a consultant surgeon at Cheltenham General Hospital.

'My what?' She winced.

'The lumbar spine. It's in the middle of your back. A very nasty place to get an injury.'

'Tell me about it,' she gasped again.

'But there's no permanent damage?' Kizzy's dad

asked. Her parents had been at her bedside since she'd arrived in A & E several hours earlier. Angie had called and told them what had happened.

'No, as long as she doesn't try to rush her recovery,' Mr Sherbourne said.

There was only one question Kizzy wanted the answer to. 'When can I start riding again?'

The consultant wrinkled up his brow. 'I'd say six months, if we play on the safe side.'

'Six *months*?' If Kizzy could have sat up and burst into tears she would have. 'I can't, I've got my first race coming up!'

'Your parents explained the situation to me.' The surgeon's tone was gentler. 'But I'm afraid you're not going to be riding competitively any time soon. Another fall like this could be very serious. One of your discs has been pushed out. If we don't take care of it, it could end up pressing on the spinal cord, and then you'd be facing a major operation.'

'Oh my God,' Kizzy's mum said.

'That won't happen if you recover sensibly.' Mr Sherbourne smiled at Bev. 'People can have a disc protrusion for many years, and get on all right. We just need to monitor yours, and let it settle down again.' He gave her a mock-stern look. 'And in your line of work, we don't want to take any chances, do we?'

Kizzy felt the tears coming, and turned her head to the wall. 'How long will I be in here for?'

'Complete flat bed rest for a week,' Mr Sherbourne said. 'And then home to let Mum and Dad spoil you. You need to take life nice and easy for a while.'

She didn't do nice and easy! Everything was closing in on her. 'Can you give me a few minutes, please?'

Her mum sounded worried. 'Of course, babe. We'll be outside if you need us.'

She heard footsteps file quietly out, the door shutting behind them. Kizzy stared at the shiny white wall. Her brain, groggy from concussion and super-strength painkillers, was struggling to take it in. When she'd met Nobby and the Fox-Titts, it was like all her dreams had come true. For the last two months she'd lived, breathed, eaten racing. It was all she was looking forward to: the start of her future.

A single tear rolled down her cheek. The rug had been pulled out from underneath her. For the first time ever, Kizzy Milton gave up hope.

*   *   *

Angie came in a while later to see her. As soon as she sat down, her stricken brown eyes set Kizzy off. The tears started to ooze. 'I'm sorry,' Kizzy choked. 'I've let you down.'

Angie was close to tears herself. 'Of course you haven't!' She took Kizzy's hand. 'The main thing is that you're going to be OK. I've spoken to the doctor, and your parents . . .' Angie had felt somehow responsible, but the Miltons wouldn't hear of it, and had been lovely to her.

'I can't ride! Look at me! The doctor said it will take months!'

'Hush, darling.' Angie took her hand. 'It doesn't matter. It was just an unfortunate accident.' She smiled ruefully after a few moments. 'It was a plastic bag, of all things, and Nobby got spooked. You would have needed Super Glue on your bottom to have stayed on. I saw the whole thing.'

Kizzy had been having weird dreams. A stranger's dark face, just out of focus, the musky scent of his aftershave as he bent over her . . .

'Was there someone else there? I think I remember him leaning over me . . .'

Angie looked surprised. 'Do you really? I thought you were out for the count.' She hesitated. 'It was Javier Hamilton-Scott, darling.'

Javier Hamilton-Scott. Wasn't he . . .?

'The dressage rider,' Angie told her. 'Rode for Britain in the Olympics? It's probably a bit before your time, darling.'

Kizzy had never really been mad about dressage, but everyone who was into horses knew who Javier Hamilton-Scott was. He was a legend in his own field.

'But what? How . . .?' Realization slowly started to dawn. Javier was the man she'd had the near miss in her car with!

'He was driving past just as it happened, and rushed over to help,' Angie told her. 'He doesn't live far from the village, you know, but I've never seen him round here before.' She widened her brown eyes. 'He was marvellous, Kiz, took off his jacket and laid it over you. Completely took control, thank God, because I was in a complete state. I tried to thank him afterwards, but he wouldn't hear of it. As soon as you were in the ambulance he was off.'

'I've met him before,' Kizzy murmured.

'What's that?'

'Him. Javier. My car . . .'

'Hush now, you need rest.' Angie watched as Kizzy slipped off into a dreamless sleep, her sweet face still troubled.

*   *   *

There wasn't much more Angie could do after that, so after speaking to Kizzy's mum and dad, she got in her car and headed home. She felt numb and completely drained. What an awful thing to happen! She just felt so desperately sorry for Kizzy.

As she started the journey back, Angie's thoughts turned to Javier Hamilton-Scott. She wasn't sure what Kizzy had been talking about; the poor girl was obviously badly concussed. Angie had barely been able to believe her eyes when she'd rushed out to find him leaning over Kizzy, like some knight in shining Barbour.

Javier H-S, in our paddock! Wait until she told her female friends! Four times Olympic dressage champion, in his prime, Javier had been the most famous equestrian on the planet. He'd won his first individual gold in Barcelona at the tender age of twenty-three, bagging the title of *Tatler*'s Most Eligible Batchelor at the same time. Pretty soon Javier and his grey stallion, Gypsy King, became the most famous double act since Starsky and Hutch, and crowd attendance surged whenever they competed. The Olympia Horse Show, Hickstead, the German Grand Prix in Arken—Javier had swept the medals board wherever he went.

His looks certainly matched his talent. While most dressage riders had the long, delicate frames of ballet dancers, Javier stood out with his muscular torso and dark, brooding face. In a sport already rife with bed-hopping and adultery, Javier Hamilton-Scott ramped up the sex appeal of dressage single-handedly.

Not that he'd been interested. Despite the legions of women throwing themselves at him— and a fair few men, too—Javier had remained a confirmed bachelor, devoted to his beloved sport and horses. Then one day, millions of hearts were broken across the world when Javier announced his engagement to Sarah Fitzgerald, a beautiful principal dancer at the Royal Ballet. Tall, blonde and willowy, Sarah provided the perfect foil to Javier's exotic ruggedness. A tireless charity campaigner, Sarah had encouraged her reclusive husband to use his popularity and become an ardent fundraiser. Everyone had wanted a sprinkling of the Hamilton-Scott stardust. They had become the most sought-after guests on the black-tie circuit.

Son of the late Lord Douglas Hamilton-Scott, Javier was rumoured to have had a difficult relationship with his famous politician father. After gaining a First in Classics at Cambridge, it had been widely expected that Javier would follow his father into the Conservative Party, and Douglas had apparently been furious that his son had chosen to go into the infinitely different world of dressage instead. It was a conflict that had not been resolved before Lord Douglas Hamilton-Scott's death from prostate cancer a decade ago. Angie couldn't remember much about Javier's mother, except that she'd been a great Spanish beauty Douglas had met over there and married. She had died young, and Lord Douglas Hamilton-Scott had never referred to it publicly. It was all very sad.

Javier's troubles never seemed to have affected his focus, and had perhaps made him more determined, and anyway, he'd had Sarah. But it seemed the happiness he found in his career was not to be carried over into his personal life. Tragedy had struck again three years ago, when Sarah, herself an accomplished horsewoman, had been out riding on the Homelands estate one day and had been thrown from her horse, suffering catastrophic head injuries. Javier had been in Beijing at the time, having won what would be his fourth and final gold, and had flown straight back. Despite him bringing in the best doctors in the world, Sarah had never regained consciousness, and had remained in a coma ever since. Shortly after the accident, Javier had announced his retirement from competing. It was another huge loss to the sporting world.

Christ, poor chap! Seeing Kizzy lying there must have brought it all back. Angie slowed down into third round a hairpin bend in the road. In shock after the accident, she'd hardly registered it was Javier, but he'd certainly lost none of his innate sex appeal. He was in his early forties now, his dark hair greying a little around his temples, and Angie had detected a sadness in those remarkable, hypnotic eyes, but he was still a stunningly handsome man.

The British public would be seeing more of their old pin-up again. Javier ran an equestrian centre out of his family's stately home, Homelands, half an hour's drive from Churchminster. The centre was considered one of the best in the country, and earlier that year Javier had been coaxed back into the limelight to train the great British hope, Oliver Foster, and his horse, Love's Dream, for the 2012 Olympics. Once again the hopes of the nation rested on those broad shoulders. Angie still couldn't believe he'd been driving past as Kizzy had

had her accident.

Kizzy. The poor lamb. Angie spent the rest of the journey fretting. It was dark as she pulled into the drive of the Maltings. Freddie came out of the back door with Avon and Barksdale around his legs. He went over to Angie's car and opened the door for her. 'How is our poor little patient? Thank God she's going to be OK.'

'I don't really think that's helping at the moment.' Avon pushed his wet nose into Angie's hand. 'You know, Freds, I just feel so bad for her. It's a bit of fun for us, really, to see how far we can get with Nobby, but for Kizzy this is her career. It's a huge setback.'

Freddie put a hand on her shoulder. 'Jockeys get injured, it's part and parcel. I'm sure she'll be up and about in time for next season.'

'I know.'

He helped her out. 'Do you want to go and see Nobby?'

Angie nodded and let Freddie take her hand and lead her across the yard.

'Poor chap knows something's wrong,' he said. 'He keeps sticking his head over the door and calling for Kizzy.'

When they got to the stable door a pair of huge brown eyes looked out at them. It made Angie's heart wrench.

'Oh, you poor darling.' Nobby and Kizzy were a team; it was unthinkable to have one without the other.

Nobby's racing career looked doomed before it'd even started.

CHAPTER TWELVE

The residents of Churchminster were very upset by what had happened. Kizzy had only been with the Fox-Titts a short time, but everyone had got used to seeing her and Nobby riding out around the village, always with a cheery wave and smile. Clementine dipped into the village funds to buy flowers from them all, and Calypso dropped round to Angie's a few days later with a stack of magazines and a huge box of chocolates.

'You are a thoughtful girl, I'll take them in this afternoon,' Angie said.

'No worries, I know how bored I was when I had my appendix out. Let me know if Kizzy needs any books, won't you? Camilla passes all her ones on to me, but I never seem to have time to read them.'

'I'm sure Kizzy would love things to read, she's probably pulling her hair out with boredom already.' Angie stepped back from the front door. 'Won't you come in for breakfast? I'm about to make scrambled eggs and smoked salmon.'

Calypso hesitated. 'Ooh, go on then.' Her meeting wasn't for a while, and as usual she'd flown out with nothing but black coffee in her stomach. She went in and followed Angie down the corridor to the kitchen. Angie sat her down at the table as she filled Calypso in on Kizzy's progress as she made breakfast.

'She's putting on a brave face, typical Kiz, but she's dreadfully upset.' Angie bent down and opened a cupboard. 'All Freds and I keep saying is, thank God it wasn't more serious.'

Calypso looked at the Aga, where one of the dogs, Avon or Barksdale, she didn't know which, was snoring gently. One of his eyes flickered open and looked at her, before he went back to sleep again.

Calypso watched Angie at the Aga. 'It must be a massive blow for you guys, as well.'

Angie paused, saucepan in hand. 'Oh, we're OK. I know the racing isn't important in the big scheme of things, but I just had such a good feeling about this. You know, the timing, us finding Kizzy. It felt like a *sign*.'

'Why don't you get someone else to ride Nobby?' Calypso suggested.

Angie looked horrified. 'Oh no, we couldn't do that to Kizzy.'

She started rapidly cracking eggs into the pan and Calypso realized it was probably a bit tactless to be talking about that yet. Her eyes wandered on to a photograph of a freckle-faced boy in school uniform on the dresser. 'How's Archie getting on?'

Angie's face brightened considerably. 'Great guns, from what he tells us. He phoned last week. They're about to start shearing the lambs, which I would imagine is a heck of a task with fifteen hundred of them!'

'Blimey!' Calypso studied the photo: the snub nose and too-big teeth, the sticky-up brown hair. She couldn't imagine how Archie Fox-Titt was surviving by himself on the other side of the world. To be fair, she hadn't really seen him for a few years, but her overriding memory was of an annoying little mummy's boy who'd once thrown frogspawn in her hair on the green. A couple of years younger than her, Archie had just been one of those random boys who hung round the village causing mischief.

Angie spooned the eggs out and bought the plates over. 'You know, I think this whole experience has been the making of him. He sounds like a proper man now, not my grubby-kneed little Arch.'

Calypso found that hard to believe. She forked up a mouthful of creamy mixture. 'Heavenly.'

'How about you, darling?' Angie said. 'What's new in your world?'

'Well . . .' Calypso put her fork down. She'd always found Angie easy to talk to. 'I've kind of met someone.'

'The chap with the nice shoulders?'

Calypso rolled her eyes. 'Has Caro said something?' She knew what her family were like. Before she knew it her mother would be on the phone from Barbados asking when James was coming over.

'Not a peep. I just saw you talking to him as we left. He looked very into you.'

Calypso groaned. 'I was *really* drunk.'

'Darling, we all were. Freddie fell into the hedgerow twice on the way home. His grass skirt is still out there, heaven knows where.' Angie bristled excitedly. There was nothing like a bit of gossip to put a spring back in her step. 'Do tell.'

'There's not loads *to* tell, really. He's called James, he's from Cheltenham . . .'

'How old?'

'Umm, I think he said thirty-two. I don't even know what he does for a living. He probably told me, and I was too drunk to remember.'

'When are you seeing him again?'

84

'This weekend, actually. He's taking me out for dinner to that new place in Bedlington.'

Angie's eyes twinkled. 'How exciting!'

Calypso was determined to play it down. 'I suppose so.' She smiled. 'He does seem really nice.'

In fact, James had been nothing short of perfect that morning. He'd ministered to her with Nurofen, washed down with copious amounts of tea and water. Then, seeing there was no food in the house, he'd gone over to the village shop and bought supplies to make tasty bacon sandwiches, accompanied by fresh orange juice.

Normally with a random pull, Calypso would have been trying to get them out of the house, but James had proved very easy to be around. He'd stayed until lunchtime, and then called a cab to let her sleep off her hangover. Calypso thought it was quite sweet the way he hadn't laid a finger on her the whole time, save for a lingering kiss on the doorstep. And he had nice soft lips, she remembered. He'd tapped her number into his phone and said he'd call her later. And he had, bang on time. So now here she was, going out with him next Saturday.

Maybe there was hope, after all.

CHAPTER THIRTEEN

That Thursday Camilla and Jed had been invited round to Granny Clem's for supper. Camilla's grandmother lived on the far side of the green, down a twisty country road called Bramble Lane. Her home, Fairoaks House, was a large, handsome building with floor-to-ceiling windows and a delightful apple orchard. It had been in the family for generations, having belonged to Clementine's in-laws before, and their parents before that. She'd lived there alone since her beloved husband Bertie had died in the eighties.

Even in the grip of winter Fairoaks looked impressive, stoically holding up against the cold weather and rain. The security lights came on as Jed and Camilla walked up the driveway, illuminating the vast gardens and the flowerbeds scrupulously maintained by Clementine. They walked round to the back of the house and found her in the kitchen, putting the finishing touches to a lamb hotpot.

Buster, Clementine's young chocolate Labrador—who was madly in love with Jed—launched himself across the room as Jed walked in.

'Buster! Calm down!' scolded Clementine. 'Sorry, Jed, anyone would think he hadn't seen another human being before.'

'It's fine.' Jed grinned easily at her. United by a love of the countryside and village life, he and Clementine had always got along extremely well. She thought how handsome he looked tonight in his red checked shirt.

He bent down to pat the dog's big head. 'Hey, boy, how you doing?'

While the pair conducted a love-in on the kitchen floor, Camilla went over and kissed her grandmother on the cheek. 'A little something for you,' she said, holding up half a lemon meringue pie wrapped in cling film. 'I thought we could have it for pudding, unless you've made something.'

'Thank you, darling,' Clementine said, taking it.

'It looks delicious, and I've got a pot of fresh cream in the pantry we can have with it.'

Jed stood up. 'Want me to take a look at the latch on the garden gate?'

'Oh, it can wait for another day. I don't want you traipsing around in the dark.'

'I don't mind at all. Tools in the normal place, are they?'

'Yes, in the garden shed,' she called after him. 'You'll need a torch as well . . .'

Jed closed the door and disappeared off into the garden. Clementine looked back at her granddaughter. 'He's not even wearing a coat!'

'Jed doesn't bother with mere mortal things like that. I swear he can see in the dark as well.'

Clementine matched Camilla's smile. 'Jed seems happy.'

'Yes, he does, doesn't he?'

The fact that Jed and Camilla couldn't have children was common knowledge in the family. It wasn't something that was talked about all the time, but Camilla knew they were there for her if she needed them.

'Good,' declared Clementine. 'Now then, can I get you something to drink? I've just opened a bottle of Merlot.'

'Ooh, heavenly, shall I get the glasses?'

'Please.' Putting the hotpot back in the oven, Clementine fetched the bottle of wine. 'Shall we go through to the drawing room?'

Shutting Buster in the kitchen, they made their way down the green-painted hallway. The drawing room was a lovely space: double-aspect, with big sofas and a side table covered with photographs of the family. Clementine went over and pulled the curtains shut against the black November night.

'Mmm, wine's nice,' Camilla said. 'Very fruity.'

Clementine studied her own glass from the other sofa. 'Benedict brought it over for me a few weeks ago. He and Caro belong to one of these wine clubs.' She took a tiny sip. 'I don't suppose you've heard from your younger sister?'

Calypso would often dip under the radar without a moment's notice. 'I think she's gone up to London for the evening to see some friends,' Camilla said.

'Humph. I've got a spare room filled with her old stuff, and she's been promising all week to come and clear it.' Clementine sighed, not unhappily. 'Has she gone with this chap James?'

'Don't think so. I got a garbled voicemail as she was heading off earlier.'

A wry smile played round Clementine's mouth. 'I did ask if I was going to meet him soon, but I was told to mind my own business.'

Camilla giggled. 'I had my head bitten off as well. I wouldn't take it personally, Granny Clem, I think she's only being cagey because she doesn't want to jinx things.'

'I know, the poor girl's had a rough ride.' Clementine had been the one to pick up the pieces after the whole Rafe Wolfe episode.

They chatted for a few minutes about the Kizzy situation, before Clementine glanced at her slim gold watch. 'Would you mind if I put on *Strictly: It Takes Two*? I've rather got into it of an evening.'

Camilla stifled a grin; from being vehemently anti 'that ghastly reality television', her grandmother had become the world's biggest *Strictly Come Dancing* fan. 'Course not, I catch the end of it sometimes when I come in from work.'

Moments later the television set filled with Claudia Winkleman interviewing one of the couples: ex-England cricketer Chip Mason, and his dance partner Erin. Chip, a beefy fiftysomething man's man, had been a surprise hit on the show.

'He's lost weight,' commented Clementine. 'Doesn't look quite so florid in the face.'

They watched Claudia quiz the couple about their upcoming foxtrot that Saturday. Chip, wearing rather too much panstick under the studio lights, had his arm draped intimately round Erin.

Clementine and Camilla looked up as Jed came in, face slightly flushed from the cold. 'All done, Mrs Standington-Fulthrope, and you had a broken fence in the back field that I've nailed back together for now, but I'll come round this weekend with a new plank of wood.'

'My dear boy, how kind.' Clementine had told him enough times to call her by her first name, but Jed persisted in using the full version. It was a rather sweet, old-fashioned gesture that only endeared him to her more.

There was a rat-a-tat-tat on the front door. At the back of the house, Buster started a frenzied barking.

'Who can that be?' Clementine started to get up.

'Do you want me to go, Granny Clem?'

'No, dear, you sit there.'

Wrapping her cardigan around her, Clementine went out to the front hall. To her surprise Barry Pike was standing on the doorstep, in a long double-breasted coat.

'Oh! Good evening, Barry.'

'Evening, Clementine,' he said, Essex accent gravelly. 'You got a minute?'

'Of course.' She stood aside, wondering what he could want at this time of night. 'Do come in.'

Even in the dim light from the table lamps, Barry's tan glowed orange. He greeted Camilla and Jed effusively, pumping them each with a gold-encrusted handshake.

'This is nice,' he said, looking round. 'Very olde worlde, Clementine.'

'Thank you, Barry. Please, won't you take a seat? We were just having a glass of wine.'

'No, no. I don't want to interrupt your evening. Cheryl's got my gammon steak and chips on, anyway. I only popped round to give you these.' He dug into one of the pockets of his coat and came out with a handful of shiny pink cards.

'These, my love, are for you.' He held them out to Clementine.

'How kind . . .' She looked down, perplexed. The words 'Bubblez Hot Tubz' were printed across the top. 'Er . . .'

Barry beamed at the other two. 'Seeing as you couldn't make our little shindig and missed out on all the hot tub action, I've got you some vouchers.'

'Vouchers?' Clementine repeated.

'We've just bought the franchise for this new model. They've got super-powered restorative jets: pummel the living daylights out of any aches and pains you've got. We've had a few installed in beauty salons round here, and they've gone down a treat.'

'I don't quite know what to say,' Clementine said truthfully.

'Don't say anything at all!' Barry put a chubby arm round her. 'Me and Cheryl have been worried aboutcha!'

'About me? Whatever for?'

'This cold weather must play havoc with the old bones.' He gripped Clementine fondly, as if she were a doddery old aunt at her hundredth birthday party. 'A nice long soak in one of my tubs will sort that. Cheryl's mum swears they cured the arthritis in her ankles in a couple of goes. And you'll have the whole session to yourself, so you can have it in your birthday suit if you want.'

Clementine's mouth opened, then shut again.

'Bless, she's lost for words,' Barry said cheerily. 'Us neighbours look out for each other, don't we?'

Clementine murmured something incoherent.

'Don't you say a word.' He pinched her cheek. 'Anything else, you just give Uncle Barry a shout. Cheryl's got a great girl who comes in and gives her Botox.'

Since her grandmother had yet to regain the power of speech, Camilla stepped in. 'Thanks, Barry, that's really nice of you.'

'Any time.' Releasing Clementine from the over-familiar embrace, he added, 'Don't worry about getting up, I'll let myself out!' He bounced out in a cloud of mints and aftershave.

Clementine looked down at the vouchers in her hand. 'I think I'll go and check on dinner,' she said faintly.

Camilla and Jed managed to wait until the kitchen door had closed again before bursting out laughing.

CHAPTER FOURTEEN

'Look what you've been sent!'

Kizzy didn't know if this was twisted medic humour. The only thing she could look at was the water stain on the ceiling, her entire focal point for the last three days. Mr Sherbourne hadn't been joking when he'd said flat bed rest.

'What is it?' she asked. As Nurse Elaine came over Kizzy got a waft of something exotic. In her arms was a vase with the biggest bunch of flowers Kizzy had ever seen.

'You've got lilies, pink orchids . . .' Elaine took a big sniff. 'Gorgeous! There must be a hundred quids' worth here. I know a bit about flowers.'

'Really?' Kizzy was rather shocked. She hoped Angie hadn't sent them, out of a misplaced sense of guilt. 'Who are they from?'

'Well, that's the thing,' Elaine said mysteriously. 'There was no note.'

No note? Kizzy didn't know what to make of it. Who would spend a hundred pounds on flowers and not sign their name?'

Elaine put the vase down on the bedside table and turned round. 'Hope you don't mind, but I've been doing a bit of detective work. When they arrived, I thought maybe the note had got lost, so I rang the florist to find out who'd sent them. I don't think they're meant to give that kind of information out, but it was a new girl who answered.' She leant closer. 'And guess who she said it was?'

Kizzy wasn't in the mood for guessing games. 'I have no idea.'

'Javier Hamilton-Scott!' Elaine's voice was triumphant. 'I nearly dropped the phone when she told me. Of course I held it together and said thank you, and that I'd be sure to pass it on to the patient in question.'

She grinned at Kizzy. 'So come on, do tell. What's he doing sending flowers to you?'

Kizzy was trying to process what Elaine had just said. Javier Hamilton-Scott had sent *her* flowers? Why? He didn't even know her.

'Er, he was driving past when I fell off Nobby. He came to help.'

'Never! That was a stroke of luck!'

Kizzy wouldn't call being bedridden and out of action for six months luck . . . Elaine's face was right in hers, shiny and eager.

'So go on then, spill the beans.'

'To be honest, I can't remember anything about it.' Kizzy felt like she was being interrogated by MI6. 'So you've heard of him, then?'

'*Heard* of him?' Elaine whistled. 'I used to seriously fancy him! I'm not even into horses, and I used to follow the dressage on telly.' She sighed happily. 'There was all this stuff about how handsome he was, but I loved his bum. Made for jodhpurs, it was.'

Kizzy didn't want to think about Javier Hamilton-Scott's derrière.

'I don't really know that much about him, apart from the dressage stuff.'

'He's a bit before your time, duckie,' Elaine said, putting her fingers on Kizzy's wrist to feel her pulse. 'Ask your mum, I bet she'll know him.' She gave Kizzy a wink. 'You must have impressed him, anyway!'

93

'I think he's just being kind.' The constant chatter was making Kizzy's head hurt. Elaine looked down and studied her face.

'You look a bit peaky. How's the pain today?'

'Pretty intense.' That was an understatement. Every time she breathed her back filled up with white-hot pain.

'Sounds like it's time for the Tramadol.'

'Please.' Kizzy never normally even took paracetamol, but these painkillers were the only things making her situation bearable.

'Won't be a minute.'

Elaine left the room, leaving Kizzy to stare at her normal spot on the ceiling. She thought about Javier. It *was* a bit weird he'd sent her flowers, wasn't it? He had to be nearly as old as her dad. She tried to remember his face, but all she could see were those intense, treacle-coloured eyes.

Kizzy caught another waft of lilies. How had her life ended up like this? One minute she'd been happily ticking along, getting Nobby ready for their first race, now she was stuck in here like a useless lump, with only a stranger's bunch of flowers as company. She blinked, seeing dear old Nobby's face at the paddock gate, wondering where she was. It was a whole new agony.

The door opened again and a new voice greeted her. 'Oh my God, you poor thing!'

Kizzy would have known those dramatic tones anywhere. 'Lauren?'

'I'm here, babe.' There was a clack of heels across the floor and Lauren's bronzed face was looking down at her in concern. She overpowered the flowery scent with a strong gust of Vera Wang.

'You look *really* ill. Does it hurt?'

94

'Just a bit,' Kizzy said wryly. It was actually really nice to see Lauren. In the sterile white hospital environment, Lauren's glossy locks and red mac were a welcome burst of colour.

'I've bought you all the new magazines: *heat*, *Grazia*, *OK!*'

'Thanks, hun,' Kizzy said, knowing she'd probably never read them. There was an awkward moment between them, as if neither was sure what to say, before Lauren's eyes feasted gratefully on Javier's flowers.

'Oh my GOD! They're amazing. Are they from Brett?'

'No, silly, why would they be?' Brett was Kizzy's ex-boyfriend, and ran with the crowd Lauren was in. The same crowd Kizzy used to be on the edge of.

Her friend gave her a knowing look, and went back to the flowers. 'They are stunning, Kiz! Who sent them, then?'

Kizzy wasn't sure how to answer this one. 'Um, Javier Hamilton-Scott?'

Lauren's pretty little brow wrinkled. 'Who?'

'He's a dressage rider, rode in the . . .'

'Oh God, not another of your horsey mates,' Lauren scoffed. 'I'm surprised he didn't send you a bale of hay.' She examined a red nail. 'So, come on, who is he?'

Not more questions, Kizzy thought. She'd have to make up something when her dad came in later; she wasn't going to try explaining this to him! 'It's just this bloke, Laur, I don't really know him,' she said, aware how weird it sounded. 'Besides,' she added lamely, 'that's what you do, don't you? Send people in hospital flowers.'

95

'I suppose so.' Lauren gazed enviously at the bouquet. 'Tell you what, though, Kiz, this guy must be pretty loaded. I'd die if someone sent me a bunch like this.'

Kizzy gave a small smile. They were pretty amazing. If she ever got out of this bloody place, she'd somehow track this Javier down and thank him.

CHAPTER FIFTEEN

When James turned up at Calypso's that Saturday evening, the front room was awash with empty Topshop bags.

'Had a bit of a spree?' he asked.

'You could say that. I was up in London this week.' Calypso had somehow managed to blow three hundred quid in the twenty minutes she'd had to kill before meeting her mates.

'Is that a new outfit?' James said, looking at the sequinned batwing top she'd paired with skinny jeans.

'It's not, actually,' Calypso said, wondering if that sounded a bit bad. She hadn't wanted to overdress; it was only Bedlington they were going to.

'Well, you look very pretty,' James pronounced, leaning in and kissing her on the cheek. 'Shall we go? I've booked a table for eight.'

Grabbing her jacket from the banisters, Calypso closed the front door and followed James down the front path. She was pleased to notice that, even when she was in her heels, he was still taller than her. She'd spotted something else, though, that wasn't so great. The black dress shoes were back, poking out from the bottom of James's jeans like a pair of mutant beetles. The rest of him was all right: blue wool blazer, black jumper, non-offensive straight-legged jeans. So what was it with the dodgy footwear?

As she climbed into James's Saab, Calypso saw the curtain flicker in the living room of her sister's cottage. Calypso bet she'd be straight on the phone to Caro.

'Something funny?' James noticed her smile as he started the engine up. The car's interior was immaculate: clean, shiny, fresh-smelling. Much like James himself.

'I was just reminded about a family thing.' She buckled up. 'So, Bastilles of Bedlington, is it?'

'That OK?' He glanced across.

'Yeah, cool.'

'Apparently the fillet steak is quite something.'

The Saab started out of Churchminster. Calypso, who normally drove like Lewis Hamilton, noticed that in the four miles to Bedlington James didn't once go over the speed limit.

Bastilles was busy—it was a small, cosy bistro, and there was a table in the window waiting for them. The waiter came over to take their drink orders. Calypso studied the list as James ordered a Diet Coke.

'Go on, live dangerously,' she urged, looking up. 'You can have one.'

'Better not, just in case.'

It wasn't as much fun drinking by herself. 'You could always get a cab?'

'From yours?'

'I actually meant from here. You can if you want,

97

though,' she added.

She watched James blush beetroot across the table. 'I'll drive, it's fine, really.'

The waiter was still standing there, a deceptively bland expression on his face. 'I'll have a double gin and tonic,' Calypso said, and sank back in her seat. Oh, how she loved the awkwardness of first dates!

*   *   *

Thankfully, things got a bit easier then, and after ordering their food—potted crab and chicken for her, and carpaccio and steak for him—James leant back, visibly more relaxed. As he put his arm over the chair next to him Calypso admired the nice bicep on show.

'Tell me more about London. Did you go there for work?'

'I wish.' She took a slug of the white wine she'd moved on to. 'I was getting a bit of cabin fever, so I went up for the evening.'

'I was glad to get out of there myself.'

'You lived in London?' She realized how little she knew about him.

'Yeah, for ten years. I used to work for an accountancy firm in the city, but I got sick of the lifestyle. All that "my dick's bigger than yours" stuff.'

'Sorry, did you just say you're an accountant?' she deadpanned.

James's eyes twinkled. 'Sorry. Is that a deal-breaker?'

'Let's wait and find out. You're doing pretty well so far.'

'Am I now?'

98

'So where do you work?' she said, attacking the bread basket. 'You live in Cheltenham, right?'

'Yup, I work for a firm called Armitage's. Have you heard of it?'

'No, sorry.'

'Thought not. Accountants probably don't feature much in your wildly glamorous lifestyle.'

Calypso snorted. 'I wouldn't say that. You should have seen me at lunch recently in a minging conference hall, trying to control forty rowdy businessmen with red-wine mouths.'

Their starters arrived, and Calypso asked for another glass of wine. She had a sudden urge to get properly sozzled. 'Sure I can't persuade you?' she asked James.

'Maybe next time.'

She picked up her knife and fork. 'So, what is it you do at Armitage's? Apart from cuddle up in the stationery cupboards with all those calculators?'

James laughed. 'Cheeky, aren't you?'

Calypso feigned mock-innocence. 'I thought that was what all accountants did?'

'Ha ha, not this one, I'm afraid. I'm a partner there.'

'Sounds very important.'

'Hmm, well.' He was neatly working his way through the carpaccio. 'That's not how my mother sees it. She wanted me to stay at my old firm and get the big salary, all the perks.' James shook his head. 'That's not my thing. Most of my friends are married with kids and have moved out to the country, anyway.'

Calypso took a sip of her new wine. 'What *is* your thing?'

'Working for a nice firm, being able to cycle to

99

work. It's the little things, like being able to get out on my bike at the weekend, get some fresh air in the old lungs.' James put his knife and fork together. 'And of course, it's a great place to bring up a family.'

'You want the whole kids and marriage thing?'

He looked surprised. 'Doesn't everyone?'

His honesty was quite refreshing. 'My older sister Caro,' Calypso said, 'lives over the green—she has it all. Great house, devoted husband, two gorgeous kids.'

'Sounds idyllic.'

'Yeah, I suppose.'

'You don't seem that enthusiastic.'

Calypso picked up her wine glass again. 'Don't you ever think there's more out there? I mean, is that everything decided? Just like that? I keep thinking maybe I should go back to London.'

'Trust me. London's not the be all and end all,' James said confidently. 'Sometimes everything you want is right on your doorstep.'

*   *   *

A delicious main course was followed by a shared chocolate brownie, and James insisted on picking up the bill. The high street was quiet as they walked down it, just a group of teenagers sitting in the bus shelter smoking something rather fruity-smelling and passing a bottle of cider around.

Back in James's car, Calypso buckled up. 'The good old days. When ten quid bought you a packet of Marlboro Lights and two bottles of Blossom Hill.'

''Fraid I was too busy playing sport,' James said.

'Rugby, cricket, hockey. You name it, I played it.'

'Any good?'

'I played county a few times.'

'Check you out. The nearest I got to sport was playing lacrosse for a term at school, before I decided bunking off and going into dirty Camden pubs was more my thing.'

'Bit of a rebel, eh?'

'Yeah, right,' she said dryly. 'At least I thought so at the time.'

The car left the square and turned right back towards Churchminster. James turned on the stereo. 'Clocks' came flooding through the speakers.

'You like Coldplay?' he asked.

'Some of their early stuff.' Calypso looked round the car's neat-as-a-pin interior. There was no way she could ever let James in the cesspit that was her car: empty coffee cups and crisp packets on the floor, piles of random shit on the back seat.

So you're already thinking about seeing him again. Smiling to herself, Calypso looked out the window.

It was past eleven when they pulled up outside the cottage. Two doors up Calypso could see Jed and Camilla's bedroom light on. She wondered if the curtains would start twitching again.

'Well, thanks very much for dinner.'

'My pleasure. I really enjoyed myself.'

They lapsed into silence, but Calypso didn't mind. There was something reassuring about James that made her feel relaxed. This didn't feel like a first date, more like dinner with someone she'd known for years.

Date. She was using the term already. But this was one, wasn't it? She could see how James had

101

been looking at her, even if he behaved like a perfect gentleman.

'Do you want to come in for a coffee?' she asked. 'I've got milk this time, promise.'

'Only if you're sure.'

'Course, come on in.' Maybe it was the double gin and the three large glasses of wine, or the fact that James had great shoulders, but Calypso was suddenly feeling as horny as hell.

He followed her up the garden path, and Calypso had barely unlocked the front door before she started snogging him. She felt a moment of surprised hesitation, before James eagerly kissed her back.

'I think you're great,' he breathed in-between kisses, his hands test-driving her body for the first time. 'God . . .'

As if someone had turned a switch on down there, Calypso was as wet as anything. Her body was craving intimate contact, and James did feel really nice and muscled . . .

'The living room, through here,' she said, pulling him down the corridor.

'Don't you want to go upstairs?' He was silenced by a kiss.

'You, me, the sofa. Now.'

They started snogging their way across the room. Jackets fell to the floor, shoes were kicked off. A small coffee table went flying. Calypso pushed him down on to the settee, pushing a copy of *Vogue* and a Topshop bag out of the way. Sitting astride him, she reached her arms over her head and pulled off her top, exposing her full, upright breasts and flat stomach. The moonlight streamed in through the window, giving her skin a luminous nymph-like

102

quality.

'Oh my God.' James's hands ran over the lacy cups of her bra, squeezing and caressing as if he couldn't believe his luck. 'You have beautiful breasts.'

He was being far too polite. 'Get the bra off, James, touch me!' He tried to undo the clasp, but Calypso got impatient and did it herself. A perfect pair of D cups burst forward. Despite her slim frame, Calypso had a great set that was still defying the laws of gravity.

James groaned in appreciation. He tried to sit up and nuzzle them, but she pushed him down again. 'Now you,' she said, helping him out of his black jumper. James looked up at her expectantly. His torso was toned, without an ounce of fat on it. She ran her hands across his chest, feeling the smooth pale flesh.

'Let's fuck.' She could already feel him hard, under her.

'Condoms,' he panted. 'They're in my wallet. Jacket pocket . . .'

She grinned wickedly. 'Thought you'd try your luck, did you?'

'No . . . I mean yes . . .' He groaned again. 'I don't know what I mean. You're the sexiest woman I've ever met, Calypso.'

She located the johnnies and was back within seconds, kicking her skinny jeans off in a heap on the floor. James was already out of his boxer shorts, a perfectly acceptable cock standing upright and ready. Pulling the gusset of her knickers aside, Calypso positioned herself and slid down on to him. He fitted nicely inside as she began to move back and forth, testing the ride.

'Jesus . . .' His eyes were shut, face contorted with lust. 'You feel amazing.' Calypso reached for his hands and put them on her breasts, feeling him knead and grasp her hard nipples.

A car drove past outside, for a moment illuminating the room, but Calypso didn't care. Faster and faster she went, until she heard him groan loudly. Not wanting him to go soft, she fucked and fucked until the glorious beginnings of her own spasm came. As the final one subsided, she looked down at James. He was lying there in a post-coital stupor.

'Wow,' he managed. 'Are you always like that?'

'If you catch me on a good day.'

CHAPTER SIXTEEN

Caro was stirring a pot on the Aga when a figure popped up in the kitchen window. 'Coo-ee!' It was Cheryl, in a straining-at-the-chest fuchsia silk shirt. Caro went over and opened the back door.

'Didn't mean to startle you, Carol, no one was answering at the front.'

Caro went over and turned down the radio. 'Sorry, Cheryl, I didn't hear you. I'm just making some carrot and coriander soup for lunch, would you like some? I've got fresh bread from the baker's.'

Cheryl patted her concave stomach. 'Not for me, thanks. I do Rosemary Conley during the week, have done for years.' She held up a man's watch with a diamond-encrusted face and stainless steel strap. 'Found this down the back of the sofa earlier;

it must be from the party. Not Benedict's is it?'

'No, sorry. It's very rock star.'

'Never mind, I'll do a ring round later.' She leant back against the work surface. 'Cor, some party, wasn't it? I bet I get a few more stories later.' Cheryl's nose was twitching inquisitively. ''Ere, who was that bloke your sister was chatting up? Baz said if they made it across the green without shagging like rabbits it'd be a miracle!'

'I think they made it across the green,' Caro said tactfully.

Cheryl snorted. 'I see what you did there, Carol!' She readjusted her cleavage. 'Benedict was quite a hit with my mates, I can tell you. You're lucky Gloria didn't throw him in her car and make off with him.'

Caro laughed. 'I'm sure he wouldn't have minded.'

'Oh, that is funny. He is nice, though, your Benedict. Second marriage, is it?'

Caro was rather surprised. 'What makes you say that?'

'No one gets it right first time, love,' Cheryl said sagely.

'How about you and Barry?'

'I was his PA. It was love at first sight. And a few shags over the boardroom table!' Cheryl gave her gun-rattle cackle and then looked a bit wistful. 'I was married to a right shit at the time, ever so unhappy, but then Barry came along and saved me. First thing he did was buy me new boobs. If that's not love for you, what is?'

The doorbell rang. 'Will you excuse me?' Caro said.

'If it's those Jehovah's, tell 'em to piss off!'

105

Cheryl called after her. 'Or even worse, the bloody Avon lady!'

Caro hoped whoever was outside hadn't heard. Wiping a smear of puréed carrot off her jumper, she opened the front door.

'Hi . . .' Her smile dropped like a boulder off a cliff.

'Hello, darling,' her ex-husband Sebastian said, stepping out from behind a huge bunch of flowers. 'Are you going to invite me in?'

*   *   *

Caro took a deep breath. 'What are you *doing* here?'

There he was, standing in the middle of her living room. Except for the new moustache, Sebastian looked the same. Proud, suntanned face, upright posture to disguise the fact that he was four inches shorter than he'd like to be. The blond bouffant hair looked freshly brushed. Sebastian had always been very vain about his hair. When they'd lived in London he had been a regular at Charles Worthington.

Cheryl was sat on the sofa, head swivelling between them like a meerkat.

'That's no welcome for your ex-husband, is it?' Sebastian turned his twinkly blue eyes on Cheryl. 'She was always horrible to me, you know.'

'For God's sake!'

'Darling, I was only joking!' He grinned. 'It's wonderful to see you.'

Caro could hardly say the same.

'We was just talking about you, actually,' Cheryl told him.

106

'Oh really? All good, I hope.'

Caro couldn't stop looking at the moustache. It was a bit like the one Lord Flashheart wore in Blackadder II.

'Like it?' he said, noticing her scrutiny. 'It's for Movember, raising money for testicular cancer. All the chaps at work are doing it.'

'My Barry tried to grow a mooey once,' Cheryl said. 'All he got was bumfluff though, bless him.'

'This is only a week's growth.' Sebastian gave her a winning smile. 'Think what this puppy could do in a month.'

Caro didn't want to talk about facial hair. 'Anyway . . .'

Sebastian adjusted a cufflink. 'Sorry for dropping in like this.'

'Milo's at school,' she told him. Why else would he be here?

'Actually, I came to see you. Benedict not in?' he added mildly.

'He's at work.' Despite the fact that he was behaving himself so far, Caro hated the way she felt so unnerved in her own home. Which had once been *their* home.

'Do you want me to go?' Cheryl asked, even though she was wearing the expression of a Donny Osmond super-fan who'd just won a front-row ticket to his concert.

'Don't leave on my account, please,' Sebastian told her. His gaze travelled round the room. 'I like what you've done with the place, Caro.'

'You do?' She couldn't help but raise an eyebrow.

'Yah. I mean, it's a little too homely for me, darling, but you did always like this sort of stuff.

107

Besides, I can't imagine you had much help from Benedict when it came to any kind of vision.'

'Sebastian . . .' she said warningly.

He laughed, showing off blindingly white teeth. 'Darling, I'm *joking*! Honestly, I wish the old boy all the best.' He flashed Cheryl a conspiratorial grin. 'What does it matter if he stole my family and house off me?'

'Sebastian!'

'He's a one, isn't he?' Cheryl scolded. 'And I've had enough ex-husbands to know.'

Sebastian chortled loudly.

Caro tried to think straight. 'Would you like a drink? If you're staying . . .'

'Perrier, if you've got it.'

'I'm afraid you'll have to do with good old Cotswold tap.' She picked up the huge bouquet of flowers he'd brought. 'Thanks, Seb, they're lovely.'

'French lilies. They're your favourite, aren't they?'

'Uh, yes.' He'd never remembered when they were married. Leaving Cheryl to gabble away in Sebastian's ear, she went through to the kitchen.

Caro filled a vase at the sink, her head spinning. Why was he here? The last time she'd seen her ex-husband was one Saturday morning months ago, when he'd turned up in Chelsea to take Milo out, even though he'd given her no prior warning. When Caro had told him Benedict had taken Milo to the cinema, Sebastian had snarled something about them having a conspiracy against him, and stormed out. Utter, utter madness, the kind of spoilt behaviour Caro wouldn't even tolerate from her own three-year-old daughter. And yet here Sebastian was, larger than life, as if the last five years hadn't happened.

Caro turned off the tap, got the glasses out, and went back through to the living room with a tray. Sebastian was already working his charm on Cheryl, sitting back in the armchair, one leg thrown over the other, as if he still lived there. His smart blue blazer was folded over the back of the chair, and he wore a tailored, striped shirt. He looked good, although Caro could tell from the slight rigidness of his upper body that he still sucked his stomach in when he sat down. Funny she knew such an intimate thing about a man who was now a stranger to her.

"Ere, I've just been telling Sebastian all about our hot tub bash,' Cheryl said.

'Oh yes?' Caro put the tray down on the coffee table.

'We were just having a giggle about it, weren't we, Carol?' Cheryl chortled. 'We were all smashed! Everyone had their togs off by midnight. It was a right laugh.'

Sebastian raised an eyebrow.

'*I* didn't,' Caro said firmly.

He gave her an indulgent smile. 'You always were an adorable little prude.'

What was he doing here? she thought again. The normality of this conversation was ridiculous, but she didn't want to get on to any sticky ground in front of Cheryl.

'Can't say Calypso's backward about coming forward!' Cheryl cackled. 'Bloody 'ell, there was no stopping her!'

'Nice to see nothing's changed,' Sebastian said smoothly.

Uncharacteristically, Cheryl seemed to sense

she'd said too much—and shut up.

A long silence followed. Sebastian got up and went to stand by the window. 'Caro, I haven't been entirely straight with you.'

'About what?' She was unsettled by the way he was looking at her.

'About the reason I'm here. I'm not just passing by.' Sebastian put his hands in his pockets and took them out again. For once there was none of the usual smug bravado. 'I've been doing a lot of thinking lately, about my relationship with Milo. I, er, acknowledge things haven't been exactly perfect.' He at least had the grace to look sheepish.

'So what are you saying, Sebastian?' Caro asked. 'You want to spend more time with Milo?' *Finally, the penny drops.*

'Oh, I can do a bit better than that.' Sebastian gave another flash of ten thousand pounds of Harley Street dentistry at her. 'Marvellous news, darling, I'm renting a place in Churchminster!'

CHAPTER SEVENTEEN

Caro waited until after dinner to break the news to Benedict. It was going to turn their lives upside down. 'We had a visitor earlier,' she said. They were sat in the kitchen, enjoying the remnants of a nice bottle of Chablis.

'Oh?' He smiled at her across the table.

'Yes.' Caro swallowed. 'Sebastian.'

Benedict's face remained calm. 'Oh, right. What was he doing here?'

'He was just passing. Well, actually . . .' She tried

110

a different tack. 'You'll never guess! He's renting a place in the village!'

'Oh.' Benedict put his glass down.

'Bluebell Cottage,' she said, trying to sound jolly. 'You know, the one on the Bedlington Road.'

'Right.'

His lack of reaction was unsettling her. 'Benedict,' she said desperately. 'It was a dreadful shock for me as well. He just turned up on the doorstep with this huge bunch of flowers, and . . .'

Benedict's gaze swivelled to the vase on the dresser. 'I thought you told me your grandmother bought them?'

'I know I should have said, but I didn't want to spring it on you.' *Oh God.* They'd only been talking about Sebastian for thirty seconds, and already he was causing trouble.

Benedict rubbed his hands across his temples. 'Run it past me again why he was here?'

'I know it seems astonishing, but he says he's had a change of heart. He wants to rebuild his relationship with Milo.'

'God, Caro! This is a bit of a bombshell.'

Caro had been thinking of nothing else all afternoon. 'It threw me as well, but what else could I do, Benedict? I could hardly chuck him out when he'd come all the way out here to tell me he wants to make it up to Milo.'

'I know.'

'He did seem genuine,' she offered. 'And if he's going to all the trouble to rent a place . . .'

'It's hardly trouble, making time to see more of your own son,' he said sharply.

She bit her lip. 'I didn't mean it like that.'

Benedict sighed and reached out for her hand.

111

'I'm sorry, I didn't mean to snap. I know how difficult it is for you.'

'And I know how difficult it is for *you*.' Benedict had been the one who'd brought Milo up as his own the past few years.

'You don't need to worry about me, Caro.' His forehead creased into a frown. 'What does he want?'

At least Benedict was prepared to discuss it. 'Well, he's still going to work most of the week in London and keep the house there, but I think he'd like to see Milo on the odd Friday and the weekends. Providing it's all right with us. He was very clear about making the point he didn't want to intrude.'

Benedict raised an eyebrow at this. 'And you're happy with him just breezing back in?'

'I'm not *happy* . . .'

Her husband heard her tone, and checked himself. 'Did he say why he's had this change of heart?'

'The impression I got was that he's had a bit of a wake-up call. I mean, he's still Sebastian, but I don't know, Benedict, he just seemed *different*. Reflective. A tiny bit humble, even.' She tried to make a joke. 'I know the words "humble" and "Sebastian" don't normally go together.'

'Well, you know him better than anyone.'

'He's got this new girlfriend. Suzette, I think he said her name was. She's French.'

'Obviously his reputation hasn't preceded him across the Channel.' Benedict got up and started clearing the plates away. The conversation was over for now. She couldn't blame him; it was a lot to take in.

112

She got up to help him, but he stopped her. 'Sit and enjoy your wine, you've been running round after the kids all day.'

Caro grabbed his hand as he went to walk off. 'Are we OK?'

He dropped a kiss on her head. 'Always.'

He strode off into the kitchen, leaving Caro staring at her wine glass. It had actually gone better than expected. After all, the two men hated each other with a passion. They'd met when Benedict had moved in next door and Caro had still been married to Sebastian. Benedict had thought Sebastian was an unscrupulous arsehole, and despised the way he had treated Caro, while Sebastian had been jealous of Benedict's investments, his London marathon time, his business, everything really, but especially the fact that Benedict was a taller, better-looking version of him. Nothing had happened between Caro and Benedict until Caro and Sebastian had separated, but the men's feelings about each other had added to the friction. Sebastian was the only person Caro had ever seen her husband truly riled by.

He didn't have to say anything—his face had done that—but she knew Benedict thought she was being too forgiving. Her whole family did. But it wasn't like that. Caro had endured too many years of Sebastian's put-downs ever to let him hurt her again. Benedict was right: she did know more than anyone what kind of man Sebastian was, but he was also Milo's father. If Sebastian's intentions really were serious, Caro would put any bad feelings she had aside to make sure his relationship with Milo improved. Besides, she had her own family now, and they were rock solid. There was nothing

Sebastian could do to change that.

Maybe he doesn't want to. Maybe this new relationship of Seb's had made him reassess things.

Caro let out a heavy sigh. No matter what positive spin she put on it, Sebastian's return was seriously going to rock the boat.

CHAPTER EIGHTEEN

'Hey u, heard the bad news. Hope yr OK. Let me know if I can do anything 2 cheer u up. Bxx'

Lauren had obviously been spreading word of Kizzy's accident. Brett had been the nearest thing Kizzy had ever had to a serious boyfriend. He'd been *the* local hunk, with nice big arms and dark, gelled hair. A few years older than Kizzy, he worked for his dad's firm, and, judging by the silver BMW Kizzy had seen him in a few weeks earlier, was doing very well for himself.

She reread the text. Brett was a really nice guy. He'd treated her like a princess in the year they'd gone out: flowers, dinner dates, pretty little dresses she'd never wear picked out by himself from Topshop. No one could understand why Kizzy had ended it six months ago, except Kizzy herself. Brett was lovely, but she felt she was being put in this box she didn't want to be in. He'd always said he understood, but she knew it had pissed him off that the horses had come first.

Kizzy screwed up her face—about the only thing that didn't hurt at the moment—and decided to send a text later. It would be rude not to reply, but she didn't want Brett getting the wrong idea. When

Lauren had dropped in she'd told Kizzy Brett was still in love with her. Apparently he'd said it in so many words. Kizzy really hadn't wanted to go there, and had manoeuvred the conversation on to shopping instead.

*   *   *

After the longest week of her life, Kizzy had finally been allowed home. Her euphoria was short-lived, however, as she could only hobble round like an old lady. Getting up the stairs had been like climbing Mount Everest. Kizzy had to grudgingly admit that Mr Sherbourne had been right; she wasn't going to go from lying flat on her back for a week to jumping back on a horse again.

Her mum and dad tried to reassure her—'It's just going to take time, Kiz!'—and bought her all her favourite foods, and a stack of magazines and DVDs, but Kizzy's sunny disposition was being severely tested. She didn't want to be stuck in this house, feeling more claustrophobic by the second. She should be out on the gallops on Nobby, the wind rushing through her hair, their dream of winning their first race becoming closer every day.

Despite it all, Kizzy was a practical girl and a realist. When Angie came to visit the next day and found her shuffling around the back garden for exercise, Kizzy had a proposition.

'I think you should get someone else to ride Nobby.'

Angie stared disbelievingly. 'Oh no, darling, we couldn't! Nobby is your horse, we said that from the start.'

Kizzy found a smile from somewhere. Angie was

115

so nice. 'I know that, and I appreciate it, I really do. But I'm the one who's injured, not Nobby. It's not fair he should miss out.'

Angie was quiet for a moment. 'What are you thinking?'

'I've been making some calls.' Kizzy managed a smile. 'You know me, Angie, I can't just sit here all day.'

'OK, I'm listening . . .'

'I've found someone. From Penny Benjamin's yard.'

'Really?' Despite herself Angie's interest was piqued. Penny Benjamin was a very well-respected trainer up in Lincolnshire.

'It's this guy called Edward Cleverley,' Kizzy said. 'He's a trainee jockey there, but it's a case of too many riders and not enough horses. I don't know him, but my mate Sally rides at Penny's and says Edward's really good. He just needs a break, apparently.'

Angie stared at Kizzy. 'You really don't mind?'

Kizzy attempted a brave smile. 'Nobby's got talent, Angie, we all know that. There's no point wasting him for another year.'

It was getting cold outside. Kizzy shivered under her hoodie. 'Let's go in, and I'll get you the number.'

'You'll have to vet him first, darling,' Angie said. 'Freds and I won't give the green light unless you say so.'

'It all depends on whether Nobby likes him!' Kizzy's eyes sparkled, a flash of the old spirit back again. 'I have got one request, though.'

'Name it, and it's yours.'

Kizzy hesitated. 'I know I'm not loads of use at

116

the moment, but I am getting stronger. I'd still love to be Nobby's groom. You don't even have to pay me . . .'

'Of course we will! I won't hear of anything else. None of us would be here without you.'

They made their way into the living room, where Kizzy carefully manoeuvred herself down on to the armchair, propped up by several cushions. 'So, what's been going on in the outside world?'

'Well, the big news in Churchminster is that Caro's ex-husband has moved back. I say moved— he's renting a cottage in the village.'

'Oh, right.' Kizzy tried to work out the expression on Angie's face. 'Is that a good or a bad thing?'

'Bad, if previous form is anything to go by. Excuse my French, but judging by that the man is a complete shit.' Angie raised an eyebrow. 'Apparently Sebastian has turned over a new leaf and wants to spend some time with Milo.'

'I thought Benedict was Milo's dad.'

'He is in every other way.' Angie sighed. 'Caro's putting on a brave face, and of course I'll support her. Maybe he *has* really changed.'

'Maybe he's realized what he's been missing out on.' Kizzy thought of how close she was to her own dad.

'Maybe. I won't hold my breath just yet.' Angie smiled at Kizzy.

'So I was thinking . . .' Kizzy slowly put her legs up on the pouffe. 'About sending a thank you card to Javier Hamilton-Scott. Do you think it's a bit random, though?'

'Not at all. It was a lovely gesture.'

Kizzy wasn't sure if there was something else in Angie's eyes.

'I had a look on the internet, he was really famous, wasn't he?'

'Really famous!' Angie laughed. 'And not that long ago.'

'So sad about his wife.'

'Terrible. I knew Sarah's mother from when we hunted together. Sarah was the apple of her parents' eyes, completely beautiful, and a world-class dancer. And such a sweet girl. Since the accident, the family have completely closed ranks.'

'Is she in hospital or something?'

'Private hospice somewhere, I think.' Angie made a regretful sound. 'Such a waste of a life.'

With nothing to do in hospital, Kizzy had often found herself thinking about Javier. It was hard to get away from it, with the massive bunch of flowers beside her. When her mum had finally stopped fussing over her last night, Kizzy had taken the opportunity to go online and find out a bit more about Javier. There were loads of photos of him competing, but it was the few of Javier and Sarah at a red carpet event together that had really piqued Kizzy's interest. They had been such a beautiful, glamorous couple. Sarah reminded Kizzy a bit of Claudia Schiffer: that kind of statuesque physique that mere mortals could only dream of. Kizzy didn't know if it was because of Javier's fame as a horseman or the tragedy of what had happened, but there was something completely fascinating about pictures of the two of them.

Or maybe she *really* needed to get a life again.

'OK, cool. I'll send something then. To Homelands.'

'If you want me to drop the card off, I'd be more than happy,' Angie joked. 'Golly, old Javier hasn't lost his looks! If I hadn't been so worried about you, I might have swooned there and then.'

Kizzy laughed. 'Maybe you should go and hand-deliver the card for me.'

'And tell poor old Freds I'm eloping with Javier Hamilton-Scott? I couldn't do it to him.' She stood up. 'Talking of which, I'd better get back. I'm cooking beef bourguignon tonight, and I need to get to the butcher's before he closes.'

'Hold on.' Kizzy reached over to the table and picked up a piece of paper. 'Edward Cleverley's number. Will you call him?'

Angie looked rueful. 'If you're sure . . .'

'Surer than I've ever been.' Kizzy gave a big grin. 'Nobby isn't going to train himself!'

It was only when she heard Angie's car reverse down the drive that she allowed the tears to roll down her face.

CHAPTER NINETEEN

It had been exactly a week since Calypso and James's shag on the sofa. She'd been really busy at work, but he'd called every day, just to check in and see how she was. He asked the right questions, and was interested without being overbearing. As he'd said when Calypso had joked about never hearing from him again, he was too old to play games. He liked her, so why shouldn't he show it?

Calypso decided she liked him, too. There wasn't much to *dis*like about James. Aside from the shoes, and she was trying to stop herself being so superficial about those. Maybe it was just a blip, and all his other footwear had been eaten by a bad-taste shoe-monster or something. Next time he might turn up in something really cool. Or not. Anyway.

She'd been in back-to-back meetings all day, and it was past five by the time she returned to Churchminster. It was already as black as midnight, a dank smell of winter in the air. Man, this country was depressing! Calypso thought about the only thing that was keeping her going at the moment: the family's Christmas holiday in Antigua. Her parents had hired a beachfront mansion, and they were all flying out to be together. Her dad had emailed the photos over, and the place looked amazing. Calypso envisaged walking down through the palm trees to their private beach, the hot white sand between her toes . . .

Her happy dreaming stopped when she saw the Aston Martin outside Bluebell Cottage. Cockface had landed, then. The brash red car was like an obscene gesture, a giant 'fingers up' to the rest of the village. Calypso had been seething since Caro had told her about Sebastian moving back. She slowed down to have a look; how the hell he'd got that bouffant head of his through the door she'd never know.

Drive on, the little voice said in her head. She'd promised Caro she wouldn't say anything. Resolutely she pushed her foot on the accelerator and drove past, blood rising by the second. Bloody Sebastian, who did he think he was, swanning up like this? After everything he'd done to her sister and Milo . . .

Fuck it. She had to say something.

Slamming her foot on the brakes, she did a hasty

three-point turn and wrenched the car back in the other direction. She'd parked and was up the path before she could stop herself.

Bluebell Cottage was an enchanting little place, with leaded windows and a low thatched roof. Calypso, however, wasn't in the mood to admire the aesthetics as she clanged the bell and stood back, arms folded.

A full minute later, the door opened. Already cross at being kept waiting, Calypso found herself being given the evil eye by a small, skeletally thin woman with Pilates-worked arms and a dark, razor-sharp bob. The woman raised a perfectly shaped eyebrow.

'Yes?' Her voice was strongly accented. French, Calypso decided. Aside from immaculate blood-red nails, the woman wasn't wearing a scrap of make-up, as if her drawn, defined features were above needing any help.

'Is Sebastian in?' Calypso forced a smile on to her face.

'And you are?'

'Calypso Standington-Fulthrope. I'm his *ex*-sister-in-law.'

The woman curled her thin lips. 'Sebastian has told me all about your *family*.' She said the last word as if describing wild animals in the zoo.

'And you are?' Calypso enquired archly. Who did this silly cow think she was, the Queen of Sheba?

'I am Suzette,' she said, as if there were no need for further explanation. She turned and called over her shoulder. 'Sebastian! *Une des soeurs laides est ici.*'

Calypso smiled sweetly. 'We might live out in the countryside, sweetheart, but some of us local peasants can actually speak French. And before you start calling me one of the ugly sisters, you should take a look at that face in the mirror first.'

Two red spots appeared on Suzette's expensively moisturized cheeks. Just then a figure appeared in the doorway behind her, a pretentious new moustache above the beaming smile.

'Calypso, darling!' Sebastian came forward to kiss her effusively on both cheeks, engulfing her in heavy Hermès aftershave. He was as short and smug as she remembered.

'How are you?' He stepped back and gave her a warm once-over. 'I see you're looking as stunning as ever. Would you like to come in?'

Calypso wasn't in the mood for niceties. 'Cut the crap, Sebastian. What the hell are you doing here?'

She watched his fake smile loosen slightly. 'Is it a crime for a man to want to spend time with his son?'

'You've only just discovered that six years on?'

'Look, Calypso, I know we haven't exactly seen eye to eye in the past—'

'That's a bloody understatement!'

Sebastian fixed her with a sympathy-seeking gaze. 'Try and see it from my point of view, Calypso. I always felt like an outsider in your family. No matter what I tried, it was never good enough.'

Calypso wasn't won over that easily. 'You could have *tried* keeping your dick in your trousers!'

To her satisfaction, Sebastian winced. 'It wasn't like that. I was going through a difficult time.'

'*You* were having a difficult time?' Calypso laughed disbelievingly. 'What about what you did to my sister!'

He looked at the floor. 'I know it's hard to hear, but your sister wasn't perfect either. Our marriage was having . . . problems.'

'Don't try and tar Caro with your sleazy antics!'

'Calypso . . .' Sebastian stopped. 'I do understand how you feel.'

'No, you don't.'

'Can't we move on from this?' Putting his arm around Suzette, he looked back at Calypso straight in the eyes. 'All I want is to get to know my son. You can't want to stop that, surely?'

*   *   *

'I still think he's a total bell-end, evil banker who blow-dries his hair,' Calypso told her sister fifteen minutes later. After the stand-off—where she'd begrudgingly shaken a temporary truce with Sebastian, she'd driven straight round to Caro's.

They were in the living room with G and Ts, while Rosie and Milo sat on the other sofa watching a cartoon on the television.

'Darling, I really do appreciate you looking out for me, but please try not to upset anyone,' Caro said. She knew her sister was as loyal as a lion when it came to her family, but Caro couldn't bear more drama.

Calypso took a vengeful slug of her drink. 'I swear he was wearing shoe-lifts. And what's with the dodgy mooey?'

'He's growing it for this Movember thing, for charity. That's a nice thing to do, isn't it?' Caro was desperately trying to avoid a full-scale argument.

'Yeah, right. He's only doing it to get back in people's good books after losing all their money.

Bloody bankers!'

'Please, Calypso,' Caro said despairingly. 'I know it's not ideal, but I am really trying here. I've had enough grief already off Benedict.'

Calypso was about to say he had good judgement, but she saw Caro's face. 'OK.' She sighed. 'I won't throw a manure bomb at Sebastian's head just yet.' She jingled the ice in her drink and shot her sister a look. 'But seriously, after what he's done, doesn't it *bother* you?'

Did it bother her? Of course it did. But Sebastian hadn't always been the monster her family thought he was. Caro would never have married him otherwise. In the early days he'd been good fun: they'd both had their careers, and loved their boozy dinner parties, ski trips to Verbier and sun-filled holidays around the world. It was only after the marriage had settled down, and she'd got pregnant, that it had all gone wrong: the black rages when things weren't going his way, the nasty remarks about her appearance or how useless she was.

Caro had soldiered on, making excuses to herself and to other people. Seb was just tired, he had a lot going on at work, he didn't mean it that way ... He'd always been emotionally distant, but she'd wanted to believe it was because he just didn't know how to express himself or relate to people. It was only when he'd cheated on her—and in effect cheated on Milo—that she'd given up and called time on the marriage. Parenthood had come as naturally as breathing air to her, and she hadn't understood why Sebastian hadn't felt the same. Until now, it seemed.

'This isn't about me, it's about Milo,' she said tightly. 'If Seb wants to spend more time with him

I'm not going to stand in his way.'

'Are you talking about me?' Milo said, not taking his eyes off the TV screen.

'Only what a handsome little chap you are, sweet pea,' Caro told him. She turned back to Calypso. 'What's Suzette like?'

'French, anorexic looking head-to-toe black. She won't last a minute in this place.'

Caro had a mental image of someone unsmiling and fashionably skinny. 'I think they met through work. She's a high-powered lawyer or something.'

'She seemed like a miserable old cow to me.'

'Anyway.' Caro didn't want to get into it. 'On to more important things. How's it going with James?'

'It's hardly a *thing*. I've only seen him once.'

'But you got on well, didn't you?' Caro said eagerly.

'Yeah, he's lovely.' She started to recite his virtues like a lonely-hearts ad: 'He's thirty-two, from Cheltenham, and has all his own hair and teeth.'

'Thirty-two! Good age.'

Calypso shot Caro an irritated look. 'A good age for what?'

'It's just an expression,' Caro said hurriedly. After Rafegate, her sister was still touchy about her love life. 'He seemed very nice when I met him.' She paused. 'Are you seeing him again?'

'Tonight. He's bringing over a takeaway.'

'All the way from Cheltenham?'

'Well, no, obviously he's picking up the curry from the Ghandi in Bedlington, otherwise it would be stone cold by the time he got here . . .'

'You know what I mean.' Caro smiled. 'He must be pretty keen.'

Calypso pulled a funny face at Rosie. 'Yeah well, we'll see. He's probably got a wife and sixteen children tucked away somewhere.'

Caro stifled a smile. Her sister might be being typically sardonic, but she had high hopes. It sounded like Calypso had finally picked a good one.

CHAPTER TWENTY

Angie looked at the clock on the kitchen wall again. Edward Cleverley was due any minute.

'You'll wear that thing out looking at it. I'm sure he'll be here soon,' Freddie told her. It was a grey and blustery day, and he was sitting in the old armchair by the fire, Avon and Barksdale dozing at his feet.

'I hope he hasn't got lost,' Angie said, getting up to look out of the window. 'He seemed a bit uncertain when we spoke.' Her face lit up. 'Ooh, look, Kizzy's here. She probably needs some help getting out of the car, poor thing.'

'Darling . . .' Freddie said, but his wife had already gone. Kizzy was up and about again, but Angie still treated the poor girl like an invalid. Freddie had only known Kizzy a short time, but he sensed that that was the exact opposite of what she wanted.

She was getting out of the car slightly gingerly— Angie hovering in attendance—as he walked over, pulling his quilted waistcoat round his rotund middle. 'What ho, Kizzo! How are you?'

'Better now I've escaped from the private hospital.' She was pale, curves slightly reduced, but the smile was back on her pretty face. 'Bless Mum, but she's driving me mad! It's like I can't do anything for myself.'

'That's the perils of an overprotective mother for you.' Freddie smiled warningly at his wife. 'Although maybe you shouldn't be attempting any five-foot brush fences yet.'

'Ha ha, if only. Speaking of which,' Kizzy looked round. 'No Edward yet?'

'He's a whole two minutes late. Angie is beside herself,' Freddie said, as a car turned into the driveway towards them. 'Hang a leg, though, this could be him now.'

An old, rust-covered Mini started up the long drive towards them. It edged along at a timid pace, as though the driver didn't really know where he was going. Freddie raised his hand in a tentative wave, and the vehicle stopped and then started again.

'Do you think that's Edward?' Angie asked.

Kizzy had a good squint. The windscreen was so mud-splattered it was hard to make anything out behind it. All she knew about Edward Cleverley was what her mate Sally had told her. He was twenty-three—a year younger than her—and a promising jockey. Sally hadn't given much more information than that. 'Tell me what you think when you meet him, Kiz,' she'd said. Kizzy wasn't sure if that was a good or a bad thing.

The Mini bumped to a stop a good distance away from them. As the driver's door opened the two dogs ran to it, and the door was slammed violently shut again. The three of them could see a narrow-shouldered, pale-faced man sitting rigidly in the seat.

'Maybe he's scared of dogs,' offered Kizzy.

'Oh dear,' Angie said. 'That's not a good start.'

Freddie called the dogs to heel. 'Don't mind them,' he called out. 'They're more likely to lick you to death than anything else!'

Grabbing hold of their collars, he held the border collies firm. The door cautiously opened again. 'Sorry about that,' Freddie said, as a thin, ghost-like figure started to climb out. 'They just get a bit overexcited . . .'

His voice fell away as the young man unfolded his frame. He had to be six foot four and barely eleven stone, with a long mournful face too big for his gangly body. Everything about him was sharp, from the tip of his nose to his famished cheekbones to the elbows poking through the cheap-looking windbreaker jacket he was wearing. Colossal white hands splayed out of the end of the sleeves like marble shovels.

'Hello,' he said falteringly. 'I'm Edward C-Cleverley.' He had a soft, quiet voice tinged with a Northern accent. *Yorkshire*, Freddie thought.

'Freddie Fox-Titt.' He smiled. 'Delighted to meet you.' He extended his hand. Edward's cold one closed round it, engulfing it completely.

'Darling,' Freddie called. 'This is Edward Cleverley, come and say hello.' Now they'd had a sniff at the newcomer, Avon and Barksdale lost interest and scampered off.

Angie realized she was being rude and staring. It was just that she hadn't been expecting someone so . . . tall. Edward's skin was so chalky pale, his eyes a strange, almost lilac colour. She wondered if he might be part-albino.

Freddie cleared his throat.

'Hello there!' Angie said brightly. 'I'm Angie. Did you find us OK?'

Edward made a tiny sound and looked away. They all just stood there, until Kizzy's voice broke the silence.

'Bloody hell.' She gave Edward a cheery grin. 'Aren't you a bit short to be a jockey?'

*　　　*　　　*

'He's not exactly what I was expecting,' Angie said tactfully. She had her arm linked with Kizzy's as they walked across the paddock to get a good view of the gallops. Kizzy was still moving delicately, and she knew Angie was only trying to help, but the gesture was making her feel claustrophobic.

'Me neither,' she admitted, 'but I do trust Sally's judgement. Edward is meant to be good.'

'I'm sure you're right. Jump jockeys can get away with a few more inches.' They watched Freddie lead Nobby out of his stable and hand the reins to Edward, who laid a huge hand on the horse's neck, and stroked him as if testing the goods.

Getting a leg up from Freddie, Edward hopped onto the saddle. The action reminded Angie of a praying mantis stepping over a beetle, and the pair looked so incongruous together that when Edward's legs hung down either side—almost to Nobby's knees—she didn't know whether to laugh or weep. This had to be some kind of cruel trick, didn't it? Someone had to have put Edward up to this. They were probably filming the whole thing from a hedgerow somewhere, ready to put it up on YouTube.

Freddie came to join them, slightly bemused.

129

'Edward seems like a nice chap.'

'Yes, doesn't he?' Angie said gaily. She exchanged a quick look with her husband.

Kizzy's gaze was locked on horse and rider as they walked towards the start of the gallops. Nobby was doing his normal ambling, head swaying from side to side as if being pulled by a piece of string. They watched as Edward stopped to adjust the stirrups. His long legs were up so high, his knees were nearly past his ears. *He looks so precarious and unsure*, Angie thought. *One stumble from Nobby and he'll be launched off.*

'I don't have a good feeling about this,' she said anxiously. 'Maybe we shouldn't . . .'

'Just let them go,' Kizzy said. There was something in the way Edward sat in the saddle that encouraged her. The horse's donkey ears were swishing back and forth, alert and listening.

As Edward reached the start, Kizzy got her stopwatch ready. Even from here they could see a subtle change ripple through the young man. He sat up straighter, body focused. Knowing they were for the off, Nobby snapped out of his normal dozy self and started to prance around. Edward didn't fight it, and Angie let out an inadvertent gasp as Nobby took off, the movement seeming to take Edward by surprise. Oh God, he was going to come a cropper . . .

But Edward didn't. Every inch of his tall frame bent low, he seemed to gain strength with each metre they covered. They took the first fence with two feet to spare, landing on the other side with barely a ripple.

'The kid's got something,' Freddie said as they watched the pair speed up down the first straight.

130

Kizzy couldn't take her eyes off Edward. He rode very differently from her, sitting quietly and determinedly, hands not moving on the reins. Kizzy and Nobby had always ridden well together, but it had been a battle of wills as to who was in charge sometimes. Edward was letting Nobby have his head and the horse was responding brilliantly. Kizzy felt a pang of admiration—and jealousy.

Ten minutes later they were back in the yard, watching Edward dismount from Nobby. As soon as his feet were back on the ground all the awkwardness seemed to return. He gave Nobby a quick pat and stepped back, eyes downcast.

'Edward, you rode Nobby beautifully!' Angie exclaimed.

Freddie nodded in admiration. 'Bloody good ride, son. Well done.'

At Nobby's head, Kizzy stood holding the reins. She'd barely said a word since they'd got back, her normally happy face solemn. Angie and Fred exchanged a glance.

'What do you think, darling?' Angie asked. Edward was still staring at the ground, seemingly transfixed by a piece of twine from one of the hay bales.

A good five seconds passed. It felt like a lifetime. Finally Kizzy lifted her blue eyes and looked at Edward.

'I think you and Nobby were made for each other.' She held out her hand. 'Welcome aboard.'

*   *   *

It was all decided pretty quickly. Edward would become Nobby's official new rider, and exercise the

131

other horses, too, while Kizzy would be the groom. They would do a job share on Nobby's training, or as much as was possible when one person could only watch from the sidelines. Angie was sure she wanted Kizzy to have a large role in Nobby's diet and exercise. Kizzy was being typically good-natured about the whole thing, and Angie's fondness for her grew.

Meanwhile, Edward had managed the smallest of smiles at the good news, and after reluctantly being persuaded to come in for a celebratory pot of tea, had folded himself back into the Mini as soon as his mug was empty and trundled off down the driveway. The car was a bit like Edward: scruffy and forlorn, a dent in the back bumper. It was all Angie could do to stop herself running after him and dragging him back in for a home-cooked meal.

*   *   *

Kizzy hadn't hung about, either. The Fox-Titts had been so lovely and sensitive about everything, and Kizzy did really like Edward, but now she wanted to be alone. Her back had started playing up from standing for so long, and the little spasms felt like taunts. She drove down the driveway in a fit of depression. Instead of turning left at the entrance, she pulled up and sat there.

The gallops stretched out to her left, reminding her of her accident. Kizzy sighed heavily. If she hadn't been acting like an idiot, imagining herself winning the Grand National, instead of concentrating on the job in hand, she would probably have been able to hang on. Instead she was now watching someone else taking on *her*

Nobby, and riding him even better than she'd ever done.

Kizzy stared at the hedgerow across the road. She *was* happy—happy that Nobby was getting the chance to run, and that Angie and Fred didn't have to hang around waiting for her to get better. But it didn't stop her feeling like the most pissed-off person on earth right now. Instead of starting her racing career, she was looking at months of physio appointments and medication that made her feel tired and grumpy. The worst thing was everyone asking how she was every five seconds. She hated fussing!

Get over it. People were only like that because they cared. And she couldn't deny that finding Edward had been a masterstroke. Despite that horrible, unfamiliar feeling of jealousy from earlier, she knew Edward Cleverley could give Nobby a real chance. Better than her, maybe; if she was big enough to admit it.

At that moment, Kizzy gave herself a mental kick up the backside. It had happened, and she had to deal with it. She'd be there for Edward, and do her best to get along with him. Maybe his social awkwardness had something to do with the way he looked, but Kizzy didn't care about things like that. Anyone who'd struck up such a rapport with Nobby was doing well enough in her books.

It was nearly four o'clock, the light diminishing by the minute. Kizzy looked across at the passenger seat, where the stamped addressed envelope lay. It was her thank you card to Javier Hamilton-Scott. Not knowing what the hell to buy or write, she'd settled on a countryside scene, and written a few polite words about how kind he'd been to help her and send the beautiful flowers.

It was annoying how much she was still thinking about him. Why *had* he sent the flowers? The extravagant gesture had both surprised and confused Kizzy. What did Javier want from her? Nothing, if the fact he hadn't signed his name was anything to go by. *He was just being kind*, she told herself again. It was only polite to show her gratitude. Kizzy had been brought up to say thank you and she was going to do just that.

She glanced at the card again. What if she just delivered it herself? She knew roughly where Homelands was; there'd been a lot of publicity when the equestrian centre had opened. *Admit it, you're curious.* 'Sod it, I *do* want to know,' she declared aloud. A mysterious married man, who'd come to her rescue and sent her a bloody huge bunch of flowers? Who wouldn't be a tiny bit intrigued?

Don't, said a little voice of warning in the back of her head. Kizzy normally listened to her instinct, but the bit was between her teeth. The sooner she said thank you, the sooner the whole situation would be wrapped up. *I'll just drop the card off and get out.* Javier probably wouldn't be there, anyway . . .

Kizzy started off in the opposite direction to home. The stately home was about fifteen miles away on the outskirts of a hamlet called Badger's Mount. It wasn't an area Kizzy would normally have gone to, but she was sure she'd driven past once or twice.

The further she drove into the night, the twistier the lanes became. Her back was really starting to hurt now, and her painkillers were at home. Kizzy

134

was just beginning to question what she was doing when the sign for the hamlet came up out of the gloom in front. Badger's Mount was down in a little hollow—a collection of pretty houses round a crossroads—and it felt no longer than twenty seconds before she was up and out the other side. Kizzy carried on, thinking maybe she'd somehow missed it, when a large wall appeared in front. There was a big black sign on it, with 'Homelands' written in looping gold writing. Underneath was: 'International Equestrian Centre'.

Kizzy pulled into the large driveway to be confronted by iron gates. They were closed, the black spikes on the top warning her off. Behind was only blackness, a wide strip of tarmac leading off into the dark.

Kizzy felt a stab of disappointment. She'd been thwarted, but what had she expected? To drive straight in and put the card through Javier's front door?

There was an intercom on the wall, with a slot saying 'Post' above it. Kizzy inched the car forward and stopped beside it.

There was no way she could reach from where she was. Kizzy got out slowly, inwardly cursing the inevitable sharp stab of pain as she stood up. She had posted the card when the intercom crackled loudly, frightening the life out of her.

'Hello?' A male voice spoke, crisp and efficient. 'Can I help you?'

'Uh, I was just delivering a card for Mr Hamilton-Scott?' Kizzy felt really stupid, as if she'd been caught doing something she wasn't supposed to. 'This is really random, but I fell off my horse and Mr, er, Javier helped me. I just wanted to say

135

thank you really . . .' She trailed off lamely, realizing how dumb this idea was.

The intercom fell silent. Kizzy was about to turn round when the voice spoke again. 'Mr Hamilton-Scott isn't here at the moment. I'll make sure he gets your card.'

'Great, if you could! He sent me some lovely flowers.' As she said it Kizzy had the horrible thought that Javier hadn't signed his name for a reason. 'Um, and I just wanted to say I got them and thank you.' She leant forward, waiting for a reply. This time the intercom remained silent; she'd been dismissed.

Kizzy got back in the car. That was that, then. Putting the vehicle into reverse, she switched on the radio. Lady Gaga's 'Bad Romance' blasted out into the night as she started back towards the hamlet.

CHAPTER TWENTY-ONE

It was nine o'clock on Saturday morning, and Calypso was dead to the world. She'd only got in five hours earlier from a function and had stayed up with a bottle of wine watching crap telly. When the doorbell went it felt like she was being roused from the dead.

The first time she ignored it, hoping whoever it was would go away, but then it sounded again. 'All right, I'm bloody coming,' she grumbled, reaching for her dressing gown. Trust her first lie-in for like, *ever*, to be disturbed.

It was an ice-blue winter's day, and it took Calypso's eyes several seconds to adjust to the

136

bright sunlight outside. James was standing there in an all-in-one Lycra bodysuit and cycling helmet. He grinned. 'What do you think?'

'You look like a giant condom.'

She watched his face fall. 'I meant the bike.' He was holding on to a lightweight racer that looked top-of-the-range. 'I only got it yesterday, it's a Trek Madone 5.9. Lance Armstrong won the Tour de France on it.' He added somewhat forlornly, 'I thought I'd come and show it to you.'

It was just a bike, wasn't it? 'Lovely.' Calypso yawned. She put a hand over her mouth. 'Sorry, late night. I had a gala dinner for a local architects' firm.'

'How was it?'

'Great, if you like a hundred pissed people banging on the table and throwing bread rolls about.' She looked down at the bike. 'Where are you off to? It must be thirty miles from Cheltenham already!'

'Twenty-four point nine miles, actually. Thought I'd head up to Moreton-in-Marsh and back again.'

She shook her head in admiring disbelief. 'You're mad. And extremely fit.'

He laughed. 'You should come out with me. Nothing like the wind whipping past your ears, nature all around you.'

'I get that when I open the car window.' They were smiling at each other. James leant over the handlebars to give her a kiss. 'So I'll call you later? Have a nice day off.'

'Have fun, Lance Armstrong.' She watched him speed off and went back inside to the comfort of her nice warm bed.

Across the green it was a big day at Caro and Benedict's. Sebastian was coming over to take Milo out for the first time since moving to Churchminster. The night before, Caro had sat her son down and explained that Daddy was back in the village and was taking him out the next day, but she had had no idea if it had actually gone in. Milo had been in a delightful mood all morning, so she hoped that was a good sign.

Benedict was making himself scarce, and taking Rosie out to the farmer's market in Bedlington. Caro knew the two men's paths would have to cross at some point, but at the moment she was just thankful Benedict was going along with everything so graciously. Having to accept a man you hated back into your life and home must be pretty grating.

Caro was in Milo's bedroom getting him dressed when Benedict came up and found her. 'I've got the list, is there anything else we need?'

'No, I think tonight's dinner is pretty much covered.'

'How about I get you some of those chocolates you like? The ones with the pecans.'

'Ooh, you do spoil me! Milo, stand still please,' she said as she tried to get the jumper over his head.

'We'll be back in a few hours, then.'

'Can I come?' Milo's red face popped up through the neck hole. 'Can we see the pigs like last time?'

The two adults exchanged glances. 'Not this time, champ.' Benedict smoothed down a tuft of the little boy's hair. 'You're doing something really exciting today.'

Milo's eyes shone. 'Wow! Is it Dinosaurland?' He was obsessed with the new adventure park on the outskirts of Gloucester.

'You'll just have to wait and find out.' Benedict gave him a wink. 'You promise to behave yourself and be a big grown-up boy?'

'Woo hoo, dinosaurs!' Milo went and leapt on his bed.

Benedict brushed a kiss on Caro's cheek. 'I'm on the mobile if you need anything. We'll bring something back for lunch.'

'That would be divine.' Caro stuck her head out the door. 'Rosie! Are you ready to go and have a lovely time with Daddy?' Benedict gave a supportive smile and left.

Caro wandered round the living room, re-plumping cushions that had only been done minutes earlier. She didn't know why she was so nervous. A better relationship with Sebastian was what she'd wanted for Milo all this time, wasn't it? Caro just prayed Milo would be able to cope; he'd only seen his father a handful of times over the last few years, and it was a lot for a little boy to deal with. Praying everything would run smoothly, Caro went to get her son's jacket.

*   *   *

Sebastian was bang on time, wearing a pristine white scarf that fought for attention with his smile. No Suzette; it had actually been his suggestion it might be too soon to introduce Milo to a new partner. Caro had to admit she was a little disappointed; even after Calypso's less than complimentary observation, she was intrigued to meet the woman who'd apparently had such an effect on her ex-husband.

'All good?' she asked.

'Excellent.' Sebastian patted his blazer pocket. 'Got the tickets for this Dragonland place. I'm rather looking forward to it.'

Caro couldn't help but laugh. 'You wait until you've been dragged on the Goblins and Dungeons ride five times in a row!'

Sebastian smiled. 'I thought no one was home. There are no cars out the front.'

'Mine's in the garage, and Benedict's taken Rosie to the farmer's market.'

'Ah, I see.' His eyes twinkled. 'Is he avoiding me?'

'No, of course not,' she replied uncomfortably, well aware the blush was giving her away.

'It's completely understandable, Caro,' Sebastian said. 'I hope Benedict knows I'm not trying to muscle in.'

'Benedict's fine about it, really,' she lied.

'That's wonderful to hear. You know, I really am so pleased we can all be adults about this.'

'Sebastian?'

'Yes, darling?'

'You're not going to fuck this up, are you?'

There was a thunder of footsteps down the stairs and Milo appeared at the doorstep, minus the jumper Caro had spent five minutes getting him into. Ignoring Sebastian, he looked up at her expectantly.

'Are we going to Dinosaurland, then?'

Sebastian knelt down. 'Hello, son, got a hug for me?'

The child's gaze wandered on to him

140

suspiciously. 'Who are you?'

Caro saw Sebastian's smile falter for a second. 'Come on, Milo!' he said heartily. 'I'm your father. You remember me, don't you?'

'Darling, it's Daddy,' Caro told him.

Her son's face screwed up into an angry red ball. 'I want Benny-dick to take me!' he howled. Bursting into tears, he ran upstairs again.

There was an excruciating silence. Caro pulled an apologetic face. 'It's probably just a bit overwhelming for him . . .'

Sebastian surprised her with a rueful smile. 'I suppose I asked for that, didn't I?'

CHAPTER TWENTY-TWO

It was the first time Calypso had stayed at James's. She had a meeting first thing in the morning in Cheltenham, so it suited her. And she wanted to see him, of course. He lived in a converted apartment in an old factory, ten minutes outside the city centre. It was a nice building, built of burnished yellow stone and with large oval windows looking out on to the street below.

James's was flat No. 6, on the middle floor. It had two bedrooms and was spacious, with exposed brickwork and wooden floors throughout. Generic art hung from the walls, while the colour scheme was a study in neutral browns and beiges.

'Nice pad,' Calypso said, settling down on the sofa. There were a few scatter cushions placed strategically about, their embroidered flowers incongruous against the plain palette. An iPad sat on the coffee table, the Sudoko app still open on it. She bet he did the *Telegraph* crossword as well.

Enticing smells were coming from the open-plan kitchen. James came out and brought a glass of white wine over for her.

'You like it?'

'Deffo.'

He looked pleased. 'I've gone for a boutique vibe, you know. The cushions were a house-warming present from Mum,' he added.

Clearly. Only a mother could love those cushions. 'How long have you lived here?' she asked.

'Two years.' He hesitated. 'I originally moved in with my ex, Claire, but we finished after six months. I bought her out.'

'Uh-oh, the ghost of girlfriends past!'

He looked anxious. 'Have I upset you?'

'I was joking, silly. People have exes, don't they?' She took a sip of wine. 'So why did you break up?'

James shrugged. 'We wanted different things. Last I heard she was working in Australia. What about you?' he asked carefully.

'No one worth mentioning.' *Unless you happen to have heard of the world-famous movie star, Rafe Wolfe*, she thought sardonically.

'Oh, right . . .'

He was clearly fishing, but Calypso changed the subject. 'What's on the menu?'

'Beef with pak choi, mushroom and noodles. That sound good to you?'

'Very good. Can we have a shag for starters?'

James looked a bit disconcerted. 'It's only that timing the stir fry is quite tricky . . .'

'Joking again, James . . .' God, he was easy to

142

wind up!

'Phew.' He smiled. 'I'll make it up to you later.'

As he went back into the kitchen, Calypso got up with her wine glass and went over to look at the IKEA bookshelf. James was clearly a Tom Clancy fan, and there were several Lance Armstrong autobiographies and a book on something called the Alexander Technique.

'What's this?' she asked, waving the manual at him.

He looked up from the wok. 'It's this series of exercises that improves posture and gets rid of muscular tension. I go to a class every week. It's important to, when you've got a desk job.'

She flicked through the pages and saw serene-faced people in various poses being all touchy-feely with each other. It all looked a bit silly and, well, a bit unmanly. 'I can't imagine you have any bad habits,' she said, snapping the book shut.

'I am trying to give up salt,' he said. She shot him a look. He was joking, wasn't he?

'Don't mind if I go for a snoop, do you?'

'Snoop away, I got rid of all the dead bodies down the rubbish chute this morning.'

That was quite funny. Smiling, Calypso made her way into James's bedroom. It was as neat and tidy as the rest of the flat, a *Cycling Weekly* magazine by the bed. She opened the wardrobe to see a line of work shirts lined up. Further along were his casual clothes, a mixture of T-shirts, jeans and jumpers that mainly seemed to come from Next and Topman. At the bottom of the cupboard was a shoe rack, on which stood six pairs of black shoes— of varying styles and ages—all clean and polished. Nothing else. Calypso shut the door and went back into the kitchen.

'Don't you have any trainers? Or boots of any kind . . .'

'I've got running trainers.' He was busy serving up on to two big white plates.

'I mean something a bit more casual. I don't know, maybe they'd look a bit more . . . *comfortable* with jeans.'

He looked up. 'Why, what's wrong with my shoes?'

'Nothing!' she said brightly. 'Nothing at all!'

He picked up the plates. 'Let's go eat.' He shot her a look. 'And then maybe we could have afters in the bedroom.'

CHAPTER TWENTY-THREE

It was fair to say Sebastian wasn't exactly Mr Popular in the area. The last most people had seen of him had been at the Save Churchminster Ball nearly six years ago, when he'd been publicly exposed for his philandering with a society airhead from London. Along with his rude, arrogant behaviour when he'd lived in the village, this meant that everyone had been pleased to see the back of him when he and Caro had split up.

If people had been expecting more of the same when he returned, they would have been pleasantly surprised. Sebastian had been keeping a very low profile. Aside from the sports car parked outside Bluebell Cottage, little had been seen or heard of him since he and Suzette had moved in. Brenda Briggs, who lived in the cottage next door and ran the village shop, was sorely disappointed. She'd been looking forward to a slanging match over the garden fence, or at least throwing a stale ciabatta at Sebastian's head when he came into the store.

The grand reunion with Milo had gone from bad to worse. The little boy had hidden himself under the spare room bed, and despite Caro's attempt at cajoling him with a chocolate digestive, had refused to come out. Caro had half-expected Sebastian to storm off—he'd always had a notoriously short fuse when things didn't go his way—but he'd been amazingly understanding, and instead suggested a dinner at Bluebell Cottage for all four adults, to discuss how best to handle the situation. It was a good chance for Caro and Benedict to meet Suzette, anyway. According to Sebastian she was 'dying' to meet them.

Caro thought her husband would flatly refuse, but to her surprise he agreed. Which is why they were there one week later, pulling up outside in Benedict's Porsche.

The cottage, the middle one of three, was as pretty as a picture as they walked up the front path. Benedict clocked the red Aston Martin. 'Sebastian's obviously doing well for himself.'

'Mmm.' Caro shot him a sideways glance, but Benedict's face was a study in passivity. It had been all day.

As they got to the front door, she turned to her husband. His elegant profile was framed under the porch light. 'Thank you for coming. I know you'd rather be pulling teeth.'

He turned to her, his blue eyes softening. 'Of course I wanted to come, Caro. I'd do anything for you and Milo.'

'Thank you.' She reached up to give him a kiss.

The front door opened so quietly it was several seconds before they realized they had an audience. 'Oh!' Caro felt like a naughty schoolgirl caught in the act. 'We were just . . .'

Sebastian was smiling broadly on the doorstep, as if enjoying his temporary height advantage over Benedict. 'Oh, don't mind us, it's rather sweet.' He turned to the tiny, pin-thin woman standing in the hall behind him. 'Isn't it, darling?'

'Very sweet.' Her voice was husky.

Sebastian threw his arms open in an over-the-top gesture. 'Come on in!'

In the crowded little hallway, Sebastian did the introductions. Suzette was already eyeing up Benedict the way all women did. She gave him a regal double kiss and turned to Caro. Caro got a waft of Thierry Mugler's Angel as her lips brushed Suzette's cold cheek.

'I love your shoes,' Caro said. The Frenchwoman was wearing an amazing pair of black heels, their ankle straps and dangerously pointy toes showcasing her slender legs.

'Louboutin,' Suzette said. She looked down at Caro's L.K. Bennett court shoes.

'Here you go.' Benedict handed the bottle of wine he was carrying to Sebastian.

'Oh, thanks, old boy.' He made a show of examining the label. 'Hermitage Côtes du Rhône! Not our usual tipple, but I'm sure we'll find a use for it.'

Caro was sure her husband muttered 'wanker', but mercifully Sebastian didn't appear to hear. He started to help her out of her coat.

'Darling, would you find somewhere for this?'

146

He handed it to Suzette. 'That's the problem with these chocolate-box places,' he told the other two. 'Cute as hell from the outside, but not enough room to swing a cat indoors.'

'Looks really nice, though,' Caro said, as Sebastian stood aside to let her walk through to the living room. She'd been in this cottage only once, years ago, when old Pearl Potts had lived there, and it had been small and chintzy and smelt of dog. Now it seemed spacious, with an all-white, modern living room and open kitchen-cum-dining room. There were no personal possessions save a flat-screen television built into one wall and a Bang & Olufsen iPod dock on the polished worktop. The place might look like a spread out of *Living Etc*, but Caro would take the madness of No. 1 Mill House any day.

'The place was OK, but Suzette wanted a few, shall we say, modifications.' Sebastian smiled indulgently. 'She does like her things just so.'

Caro raised an eyebrow. 'I'm not sure what she'll make of Milo's sticky little hands everywhere!' she said.

Sebastian chuckled throatily. 'Suzette *loves* children.'

'Have you been together long?' Benedict asked.

Sebastian went through to the kitchen and brought a bottle of Perrier Jouet out of the Smeg fridge. 'We met at work—Suzette's a rather excellent lawyer.' He popped the cork. 'Somehow I managed to persuade her to move in with me three months later.'

'Congratulations,' Benedict said blandly.

Sebastian gave him an engaging wink. 'Thanks, old chap.'

'Congratulations on what?' Suzette had appeared noiselessly behind them.

Sebastian planted a kiss on her pale cheek. 'Benedict was just congratulating me on the stunner I've managed to land myself with.'

'I didn't say that, exactly.' Benedict smiled pleasantly. 'But Caro and I are very happy for you.'

'And Suzette and I are very happy for you both, so it's congratulations all round.' Sebastian handed the flutes out, saving his own for last. He raised it in the air.

'Cheers!'

Suzette did the same, flashing the muscles in her minuscule arms. An antique diamond ring sparkled on her finger. 'Or as we say, "*A la vôtre*".'

It might look like nothing but fresh air had ever passed her lips, but Suzette was clearly a dab hand in the kitchen. The other three sat at the dining table drinking an excellent Burgundy while she whizzed about in the background. Occasionally Sebastian would break off from his conversation to give her an adoring look.

'It took a little persuasion to get Suzette to come out here; she's a real city person.' He leant back in his chair. 'But you love it now, darling, don't you?'

She looked up from her speedy chopping. 'Love what?'

'Here, darling! Churchminster.'

The dark bob swished into a nod.

'Suzette might seem a bit reserved, but she's a doll once you get to know her,' Sebastian confided.

Caro smiled. Suzette clearly wasn't the evil witch Calypso had made out, but she still wouldn't use the word 'doll' to describe her.

Across the table, Sebastian stroked his

148

moustache. 'I noticed the lack of face furniture, Towey. Not doing your bit for charity?'

'We do quite a lot by direct debit every month already, don't we?' Caro answered for her husband.

'I'm not trying to make a contest out of it, darling.' Sebastian flashed Benedict an indulgent smile. 'Worried I'd show up your bumfluff? Never mind, Towey, you've either got it or you haven't.'

Caro saw her husband's hand tighten round his wine glass. *Don't rise to it.* Couldn't he see Seb was only trying to wind him up?

The stand-off was mercifully stopped by the arrival of the first course. 'Gosh!' Caro said, as Suzette put the plate down in front of her.

'Sauté of langoustine tails with beluga caviar and a beurre blanc sauce,' Suzette reeled off.

'The langoustines were sourced especially from Scotland,' Sebastian added.

The portions were small but beautifully presented, the kind of thing you'd get in a Michelin-starred restaurant. Benedict took a mouthful and savoured the flavours. 'Superb, Suzette, really superb.'

'Thank you.' She shot him a grateful look from under her fringe.

'How's work, Sebastian?' Benedict said. 'Still at Harwells?'

Harwells was one of the biggest private banks in London. Sebastian had been there since marrying Caro. The lifestyle, the look—everything about it suited him down to the ground.

'Can't complain, really.' He looked modest. 'You know I've been made a partner?' He looked round the table. 'I mean, one is made to feel like a serial killer if one talks about bonuses these days, but . . .'

149

'Sebastian,' Suzette admonished.

He gave a contrite grin. 'Suzette thinks it's vulgar to talk about money. You're right, darling.' He sighed. 'I guess I'm just one of the lucky ones. We've seen a lot of casualties.'

'What kind of law do you practise, Suzette?' Benedict asked.

'Private equity, but now I'm studying.'

'She's doing a PhD in papyrology,' Sebastian said proudly. 'Suz is giving all those academics something to choke about in their dusty old books.'

The main course was brought out in equal style: a thyme- and garlic-scented supreme of corn-fed poussin, with braised legs and saffron pommes mousseline. Sebastian was the perfect host, asking Benedict all about his business and filling up Caro's glass continuously. She told him and Suzette about Angie and Freddie having their own racehorse, and the hoo-ha over Kizzy. 'Thankfully they've got a new boy to ride it,' Caro said. 'Angie's been really rather worried.'

'I bet she has!' Sebastian enthused. 'At least it's turned out all right in the end.'

The food was too delicious to ignore. As everyone tucked in, the room fell silent, aside from the scrape of cutlery across porcelain and a few approving 'mmms'.

'Planning to stay here long?' Benedict asked. Caro glanced at him. His face wore the same amiable, mildly interested expression that it had all evening.

'Well, we've got this on a six-month basis, haven't we, darling?' Sebastian grinned. 'Reduced winter rate. Even I'm not averse to saving the spondoolies on occasion.'

150

Benedict reached out for his wine glass, and his gaze met Sebastian's. The tension that had been kept at bay so far suddenly flared up. Sebastian sighed loudly and put down his knife and fork.

'OK, look. I know me being back here is a bit of a shock.' He grinned ruefully. 'You know, I had Brenda from next door round earlier, giving me a flea in my ear.' Suzette went to say something, but he put his hand up to stop. 'No, it's fine. I've behaved like a selfish bastard for forty-two years, and only just realized it.'

He turned to Caro. 'I know it seems trite to try and sum it up in a sentence, but I am sorry about the way I behaved during our marriage. And dodging my responsibilities towards Milo. I didn't realize it at the time, but I had issues I wasn't sure how to deal with.' He put on a gruff voice. 'Didn't think it was right for a chap to talk about his feelings like that.'

Suzette squeezed his shoulder.

'I'll just come out with it. I've been having counselling. That's really what the catalyst for all this has been.'

Caro had to stop her jaw from sagging. Counselling? But Sebastian was the least reflective person in the world! She realized he was talking to her.

'I never really talked about my upbringing, did I? I mean, I know you asked at the time, but I just didn't have the emotional tools to deal with it.'

Caro paused. She knew that Sebastian's dad had run off with another woman when he was Milo's age, and that his flighty socialite mother had dumped him at boarding school. Sebastian had had no relationship with his mother: she hadn't

151

even been invited to their wedding. The last Caro heard, Mrs Belmont—or 'the bitch' as Seb had always called her—had been living penniless in Switzerland.

He followed her train of thought. 'I know I haven't been very complimentary about my mother,' he said hurriedly, 'but I had all this anger inside me.' His brow creased into a manly frown and he turned to Benedict. 'Now see here, Towey, I don't expect you to have any sympathy, but I didn't have the best of starts. Money, yes, but I can't say there was much love going round. My father—wherever he is now—wasn't exactly the best role model.' He smiled bravely. 'But it's only since I met Suzette that I've felt brave enough to confront these issues. What was it my therapist said, darling? "You have a fear of commitment, and abandonment issues."' He shrugged. 'Psychobabble cod-speak, I always thought, but it fitted how I felt.'

Benedict had listened to the whole speech without a reaction, but now he lifted piercing blue eyes. 'Do you think it's wise, in the circumstances, then, wanting to spend more time with Milo?'

Caro flushed, but Sebastian acknowledged the comment. 'Your concern is completely understandable, but I can assure you there's nothing to worry about.' He smiled fondly at Suzette. 'I'm out the other side now, aren't I? In fact, that's part of the process my therapist recommends, building my relationship back up with Milo. I realize now that's why I had such a hard time when the little chap was born. Having never really had a father figure, the whole idea terrified me.'

'I'm not having you using a six-year-old boy as

152

part of some pie-in-the-sky healing process.'

'Benedict!' Mortified, Caro turned to Sebastian. 'I'm so sorry . . .'

Everyone stared at their plates uncomfortably. 'No, I'm sorry,' Benedict finally said. 'That was out of line, Sebastian.'

For once, Sebastian wasn't crowing in victory. 'It's fine, old boy, really. I understand it's hard for you, me turning up like this.' He turned to Caro, his expression imploring. 'All I want is for us to work together as Milo's parents. *All* his parents,' he added. 'Please.' A look she'd never seen before crossed Sebastian's face. 'Don't make me beg to be allowed to spend time with my son.'

CHAPTER TWENTY-FOUR

'I have my own apology,' Suzette murmured. She and Caro were standing in the bedroom that looked out on to the back garden. It was to be Milo's room, they'd told her, and he could decorate it any way he wanted.

'Apology?' Caro's stomach was churning, a combination of the stress, too much alcohol and a dinner that, delicious as it was, had been served in such tiny portions that she'd probably only ingested about three hundred calories.

'Yes. I think I got off to a bad start with your sister. Calypso?'

'Ah. The ugly sister?' Caro's tone was humorous, and Suzette turned to her, the faintest smile playing over her shiny lips.

'Yes. That one. It is hard, Caro, when people

are horrible to the man you love. She came to the door and was, well, sour. It offended me, and I said something I didn't mean.'

Caro couldn't help but smile, too. She guessed that was some kind of compliment.

The French woman turned to her. Up close her dark eyes were flecked with amber, the first sign of warmth Caro had seen. 'Good. It is nice to know we haven't enemies here. I am not a lover of the English countryside, it is too cold, too much mud.' She shrugged. 'But I am here for Sebastian, and he wants to be here for his son.'

'How do you feel about having a noisy, messy little boy about?'

'I adore children,' Suzette said. 'I would have liked my own, but it wasn't to be.' She gave a Gallic shrug and stared out the window.

Caro didn't want to pry. Maybe Suzette couldn't have kids. There was a shout up the stairs. 'Darling! Are you two OK? Come back down and join us.'

Another small smile flickered across Suzette's face. 'Sebastian, he always cares for me.' She left the room gracefully, as if being carried by a gust of wind.

Does he now? Caro turned back to look out of the window. Something dark and sleek ran across the garden into the hedgerow. Probably a fox. She stared out into the night; she'd never seen Sebastian act this way around someone before. He'd never been this devoted to her in the early days. He'd been touched by the one thing he'd always scorned.

Love.

*   *   *

Benedict posed the question cautiously. 'Happy with how the evening went?'

'I think so, in the end.' They'd both had a bit too much to drink—on Caro's part out of nerves—and had decided to leave the car and walk back. It was a beautiful night anyway, the full moon bathing the landscape in luminous colour. Suzette had insisted on lending Caro her black Yves Saint Laurent pashmina to wrap up against the cold.

She could feel her husband weighing up his words. 'I'm sorry for the comment about Milo. I behaved like an arsehole.'

'Yes, darling, you did,' she said, but her eyes held a twinkle.

He grabbed her hand, and squeezed hard. 'He does seem . . .' Benedict said the words reluctantly, '. . . all right. About Milo, I mean.'

Caro stopped in the road and looked at her tall, beautiful husband, who would lay his life down for his wife and children. 'Benedict, I get where you're coming from. I really do. I know you and Sebastian are never going to be good friends, but if we can just behave like adults and make the best of the situation, things will be a lot easier.'

He gazed down at her. 'You're a better person than I am, Caro.'

'Of course I'm not,' she said, slightly frustrated. 'It's not about that.'

They walked along a few more steps in silence. 'So you buy that therapy stuff?'

'I'm not saying I *buy* it, but at least he's trying. Despite what you think, a lot of things he said in there did make sense.'

Benedict let out a strangled laugh. 'Christ!

155

Sebastian in therapy. What next, a born-again Christian?'

Caro giggled. 'I hope not. Sebastian as an over-zealous Christian would be truly terrifying.'

They linked arms comfortably. The Bedlington Road was quiet and sleepy, the odd bedroom light on in the houses they passed.

'Suzette's very glamorous, isn't she?' Caro commented.

'Bit thin for me. I'm not a fan of the wasted look.'

'Are you saying I'm a porker?' she said, mock-indignant.

'The complete opposite.' Benedict's hands ran up inside the hem of her coat and wandered on to the lace hold ups. He groaned. 'You didn't tell me you were wearing these. I don't think I'd have lasted through dinner if I'd known. '

Caro kissed him back, feeling his hands cup her buttocks. 'Benedict, we can't!' she whispered, as he started to unwrap her dress.

'We bloody well can. I feel like I haven't been inside you for weeks, and if you will insist on wearing stockings . . .' He started kissing her neck. 'I mean I love our kids, but sharing a bed with them doesn't leave much time for . . .' His fingers were on bare flesh now, pulling her dress open.

'Someone might see us! And I might die of cold.'

'I've got something to keep you warm with.' He pushed her into the old bus shelter by the rectory. Despite her protests Caro could feel her clitoris swell and throb, almost painfully. Benedict was right: it had been far too long . . .

'Christ.' He looked down at her smooth, comely body, swelling out of the lacy underwear. 'I could come right now.'

Caro knew what he meant. Her nipples were stiff, more now through arousal than the plunging temperatures. She sat down on the bench and splayed her legs, giving her best come-hither look. 'Is this what you want?'

Benedict's eyes darkened with lust. He started to unbutton himself with one hand, pulling down her best Rigby and Peller knickers with the other. They were at the point of no return now, Benedict's cock hard and glistening in the moonlight. He lowered himself on to her and Caro felt the delicious shiver of pleasure as he pushed himself in. She wrapped her stockinged legs round his broad back, wanting all nine inches of him.

The rough wood from the bus shelter caught in her hair as she grabbed his shoulders. Caro was so wet he kept slipping out, prompting a moment of sheer longing, before he was back in her again. As he fucked her masterfully Caro's mind started to swim blissfully. She forgot the toy-strewn living room and leaky dishwasher at home, the roll of flesh above her knickers. It was about this moment; God, it could still be so amazing.

She orgasmed sensationally, the sensations shooting upwards through her body. Benedict came at the same time and slumped forward against her chest.

'Jesus!'

Caro put her hands through his thick hair, feeling his heart thudding against hers. They stayed like that for a while, sweaty naked flesh pressed together, until the chill night air started to creep in again. Benedict sat up and gently pulled her dress together, fastening it competently at the side.

'Shall we go home, then? I think I need a cup of cocoa after that.'

Laughing, Caro let him help her up. 'We're getting old.'

'You're only as old as the woman you feel.' Benedict zipped his trousers up. 'And you feel about . . .'

'Watch it!'

'I was actually going to be very complimentary.' Grinning, he held out his arm.

'Were you, now?' Caro nestled into her husband's shoulder, feeling the strong, familiar contours. Giddy as a pair of teenagers on their first date, they started for home.

CHAPTER TWENTY-FIVE

The Fox-Titts were driving back from having dinner with friends in a new gastropub. A cold mist shrouded the landscape, giving it a dreamlike quality.

'Good dinner, wasn't it?' Angie was driving the Jag.

Freddie patted his stomach. 'Bloody good. I think a brisk walk in the morning is called for.'

She glanced at him fondly. 'All that wonderful exotic food, and you went for the steak.'

'It's the simple pleasures for me, my love.'

They were in a contented mood as they drove in past the house, towards the outbuildings beside the stables. Unlike their everyday Range Rovers, Freddie's beloved XJS was only brought out on special occasions, and spent most of its time in the garage.

As Angie pressed the electronic button to open the doors, she frowned and leant forward. 'That's Edward's car!'

Freddie peered into the gloom. Sure enough, the old Mini was parked between the garage and the stable block, as if it didn't want to be seen.

'Odd. Why would he still be here?' The car stopped, and they both got out. Freddie got to the car first. 'Hello?' He had a good look. 'There's no one in here.'

'I hope he's OK.' Angie looked at her watch. 'What if there's been an accident or something?'

'Darling, I'm sure it's nothing like that.' Even so, Freddie had a funny sensation that something wasn't quite right. Intuition made him look towards the stable block. *Nobby*. Without knowing why, he put his finger to his lips and started to walk, very quietly, towards it.

Angie's heart was in her mouth as she followed. Oh God, had something happened to one of the horses? Her stomach turned as another thought occurred. *Edward. They hardly knew him . . .*

The security lights came on, lighting up the ground. A few yards ahead, Freddie stopped at Nobby's stable and looked over the door. The shocked expression on his face made Angie's fears seem justified. *Oh no.* Heart thumping, she steeled herself for whatever was in there.

Thank God. Nobby was still very much alive, sleepy eyes watching them from the far right corner. But as Angie looked over to the other side of the stable, she had the shock of her life.

A tall, thin figure was curled up in the corner, caterpillar-like, in a sleeping bag. A few carrier

159

bags stuffed with things had been placed neatly in a pile together nearby.

'Edward?' she said aloud in astonishment. The figure sat up quickly, like a puppet jerked by a string.

'I'm sorry,' Edward said, his face gleaming white in the weak light. 'I didn't mean to intrude. I'll go now . . .' Immediately, he got up and started gathering his meagre belongings.

Freddie and Angie exchanged glances. 'Edward,' Angie said again. 'Stop, it's OK. What are you doing in there?'

He stopped rolling up the sleeping bag and hung his head. 'Where I was staying, they put the rates up, and I couldn't pay.'

'At your lodgings?' Freddie asked. 'Son, why didn't you say? We could have helped you out.'

'I don't like to ask for things.'

Angie couldn't bear it. *Poor Edward, out in here in the middle of winter!* 'How long have you been sleeping there?'

'Only a few nights.' He swallowed, Adam's apple bobbing. 'I'm sorry, I can pay for anything . . .'

'You'll do no such thing,' she said firmly. 'Freddie, go and unlock the granny annexe, everything's clean and ready in there, anyway.'

In spite of himself, Freddie smiled. His wife's mother-hen instincts were kicking in. 'Yes, darling.'

Edward's big hands were twisting together. 'It's all right, honestly. I was going to find somewhere else.'

'Darling, we've got a perfectly good granny annexe that's not being used,' Angie told him. 'I only didn't offer because you told me you had lodgings. Of course you must stay with us.'

His eyes widened. 'I can pay, but not much.'

'Don't worry about that, just buy Nobby the odd packet of Polos.' She undid the bolts on the door and held it open. 'Come on, darling, let's get you settled in. I can carry some of your bags.'

As he handed her a Budgen's carrier bag filled with what looked like clothes, Edward suddenly stopped. His long face, caught in the shadows, looked even more carved out than normal.

'Th-thank you.'

She smiled at him. 'It's our pleasure. Might take a while for the central heating to come on, though, so you could have a cold bed to get into!'

Out of nowhere Edward's face lifted into a mournful smile. 'Better than a sleeping bag in a stable.'

As he walked out carrying his possessions, Angie felt overwhelmed again. How desperate must his situation be, if he couldn't ask his friends or family for help?

CHAPTER TWENTY-SIX

The Santa outfit was a little premature. 'Ta-da!' Cheryl gave a little twirl on the front doorstep. 'What do you think?'

'Oh! It's er, very festive.' Caro could think of a few other words to describe the red fur-trimmed basque and black stockings.

'Baz bought it for me from Ann Summers.' Cheryl wiggled her hips and a bell tinkled somewhere. 'I thought we might try this.' She held up a wine bottle.

'Oh, I can't really. I've got to pick Milo up from school in an hour or so.'

Cheryl winked. 'You'll be all right, then, it's non-alcoholic.'

A few minutes later they were ensconced at the kitchen table. Caro poured out the wine while Cheryl told her about her friends Lesley and Mike, who ran a chain of off-licences across the South West.

'It's called "Fizzles", I don't know if you've heard of it.' Cheryl readjusted her little red hat. 'They've done ever so well, sent me a box of this stuff to road-test this morning.'

Caro looked at the label. It was very pretty, but she had never really seen the point of non-alcoholic wine. Either you drank or you didn't.

'I wondered who liked a tipple and I thought of you, Carol!' Cheryl said. 'I'm not really keen on wine myself.'

'Really? I had you down as a Pinot Grigio girl.'

'Nah, me and Barry aren't actually big drinkers. Baz likes to keep his head sharp for business, and I'd rather spend the calories on a strawberry cheesecake.' Cheryl readjusted her cleavage. 'We love entertaining and all that, but we're just as happy on the sofa watching *Corrie*. Baz likes me to Sky Plus it so he doesn't miss an episode.'

Well, well. Some people were full of surprises. Caro had a funny image of the Pikes on the zebra-print three-piece, curled up in their matching dressing gowns.

The wine actually smelt quite palatable. She took a mouthful and tasted tropical fruit. Bit sweet for her, but not bad. 'It's very authentic. I'd never know the difference.'

'That's what Lesley said. Apparently this non-boozy stuff is getting really popular.'

'I must admit, it's nice to take the weight off my feet.'

'Bless you, Carol, you do look a bit tired. That ex of yours giving you gyp?'

It was hard not to look at Cheryl's rock-hard cleavage. 'He's actually been very well-behaved.' Caro raised her eyebrows. 'For a change.'

'What does Benedict make of it all? Must have set the cat among the pigeons.'

Caro picked up her drink. 'I won't pretend it's been plain sailing, but we're getting there.'

'Kids, eh, must make you wonder why you bother. Barry had terrible trouble with his first wife and their daughter. When they split, the old bag wanted full custody, even though she'd never shown Joanne a blind bit of notice. Course, she didn't have a leg to stand on.'

'Barry's got a daughter?' Caro hadn't known.

'Yeah, she's studying at Southampton University, wants to be a marine biologist.' Cheryl sighed. 'It's a terrible disappointment. What does she want to go and work with smelly old fish for?'

Caro tried not to smile. 'Do you get on with her?'

'Joanne's a nice girl, Carol. Just *plain*, you know. I did talk to her about getting a nose job, but she wasn't having any of it. Said she'd rather have the money to go travelling. Travelling!' Her kohl-rimmed eyes widened. 'Why would she want to go off to all these horrible smelly countries when we've got a perfectly good yacht in Marbella?'

Cheryl was a one-woman show. By the time she'd got on to something called 'vajazzling'—'You know, Carol, when you stick crystals on your lady bits'—

163

Caro was in fits of laughter. Wiping her eyes, she caught sight of the clock. 'I need to go and get Milo in a minute.' Her stomach was aching. 'Oh dear, I haven't laughed so much in ages.'

'Get yourself vajazzled for Benedict's Christmas present!' Cheryl urged. They both started giggling.

'Don't set me off again . . .' As Caro stood up the blood rushed straight to her head. She blinked. 'It must be my imagination, but I do actually feel a bit light-headed.'

'Now you come to mention it, so do I! I thought the menopause had started, and I was having one of those hot flushes.'

Caro frowned. Something wasn't right. Picking up the bottle, she studied the label again. It definitely said 'non-alcoholic'. 'You don't think your friend has played a trick on you or something?' she said, only half jokingly.

'What, and given us real booze?' Cheryl's false eyelashes widened. 'No! I'll ring Lesley right now.' She got her pink iPhone out and dialled up a number. 'It's gone straight to voicemail.'

'Hmm.' Either Caro had had an allergic reaction—and completely coincidentally Cheryl had, too—or there was alcohol in that wine.

'I really don't know if I should drive.' She looked at Cheryl. 'What am I going to do about Milo?'

'Can't someone else pick him up?'

'Everyone's at work.' Caro rubbed her face, not quite believing the ludicrousness of the situation. 'I can't even ask Granny Clem, she's gone to a Beatrix Potter exhibition with the WI.'

'What about Sebastian?'

'No way! He'll have a field day.'

'Come on, it's not your fault. This is mad, Carol,

164

he'll piss himself!'

Sebastian had texted her about Milo that morning, so she knew he was in the village. She really, *really*, didn't want to ring her ex-husband and explain she'd accidentally got herself over the limit and couldn't pick up their child from school, but the minutes were ticking by. Any longer and Milo would be left in that classroom by himself.

'Christ!' She went to get her mobile.

*   *   *

Thirty minutes later Milo had been deposited home.

'Seb, I don't know what to say. Thank you so much.' Caro had eaten a whole pack of mints, worried her breath might smell of alcohol.

'It's fine, darling, he only had to wait fifteen minutes! Luckily the teacher was there to look after him.'

Caro cringed. 'What must Miss Ekins think? You didn't tell her, did you?'

'Of course not, I just said you'd had a little mishap.' The luxuriant moustache made him look rakishly handsome. '*Are* you OK, darling?'

'I wasn't *drunk*, Seb,' she said defensively. 'Cheryl managed to get hold of her friend, and, would you believe it, there'd been a mix-up with the labels. Apparently we were drinking a fifteen per cent Californian chardonnay.' She gave a forced laugh. 'Someone else is going to be having a very sober dinner party!'

'Quite.'

'Don't look at me like that.'

'Like what?'

'Like you don't believe me.' Caro was feeling bad enough as it was. 'I know it sounds ridiculous, but I'm not making it up.'

'Of course you're not.' Sebastian removed his foot from the doorstep. 'Milo's home safely now, that's all that matters.'

'Thank you again,' she said stiffly.

'Don't mention it.' He treated her to a crooked grin. 'That's what ex-husbands are for.'

CHAPTER TWENTY-SEVEN

Angie and Kizzy were having a cup of tea at the kitchen table, talking about Edward moving in.

'It makes much more sense having him here,' Kizzy said, dunking a chocolate HobNob. 'Where was he living before? I don't think he ever told me.'

'Er . . . well, that's the funny thing.'

Kizzy looked inquisitive.

Angie dropped her voice, even though it was just the two of them in the house. 'Freds and I found him sleeping in Nobby's stable the other night.'

Kizzy's blue eyes widened. 'He's been sleeping rough?'

'Apparently the B & B he'd been staying in put their rates up, and Edward couldn't afford them. The poor thing had nowhere else to go.'

'That's terrible. You'd think his friends or family would help out, wouldn't you?'

'Edward never talks about his family.' Angie had only managed to get out of him that he came from a small village near Harrogate. 'Has he mentioned anything? He'd be more likely to speak to you than

166

me.'

'I only know what my mate Sally said. He hasn't been on the racing scene long; I think Penny Benjamin was his first yard. Sal said he kept himself to himself, was only interested in horses, and didn't socialize.'

Angie tutted regretfully. 'He just seems so lost.'

'He might just like his own company,' Kizzy reasoned. 'You get a lot of people like that in racing; they prefer the horses to the people.' She nibbled on her biscuit thoughtfully. 'Maybe Edward was too proud to ask for help from anyone.'

'You won't say anything, will you, darling? We don't want to embarrass him. If anyone asks, he's moved into the granny annexe because it's easier for him with Nobby. It's the truth, anyway.' She smiled ruefully. 'At least now I can keep a proper eye on him and make sure he's eating properly.'

Kizzy took another HobNob and Angie debated whether to do the same. 'I forgot to ask, did you manage to thank Javier in the end?'

She watched Kizzy flush. 'Uh, yeah. I dropped a card off.'

'You drove over there?'

Kizzy was blushing properly now. 'I was passing anyway.'

'Fair enough!' Angie said brightly. Kizzy was normally the most open of people, but Angie felt this was one subject she couldn't stray on.

*   *   *

When Kizzy went out again it was getting dark. She found Edward in the tack shed, cleaning a harness under a bare light bulb.

'I can do that that, you know,' she smiled. 'I am your groom, after all.'

She was rewarded with a shy grin. 'It's all right. I like doing it.'

He went back to polishing a bridle. Kizzy remained in the doorway. 'Hey, Edward . . . if there's ever anything you want to talk about, or if you just fancy hanging out, give me a call. It must be a bit weird, being in a new place and everything.'

'Thanks.' He kept his eyes firmly on the bridle this time. Kizzy dug in her pocket for her car keys. 'Well, I'd better be going, anyway. I'll just go and say goodbye to Nobby.'

'Kizzy.'

She turned round. 'Yeah?'

'How's your back?'

'Uh, it's OK.' She looked round the tack room and sighed. 'I just want to get back to normal, you know?'

'It must be really hard.' Edward's cheeks were going pink. 'Thanks. I mean, for letting me be here.'

'Hey, I'm not in charge.' She grinned. 'We're a team, remember?'

Edward was a strange one, Kizzy reflected on the way back. But she did really like him, and the progress Nobby was making was amazing. They'd done their quickest time ever on the gallops that week.

She leant forward and started twiddling with the radio, anything not to dwell on the fact that it could have been her riding out there. Her conversation with Angie came to mind instead. Angie had only been asking about Javier, why had Kizzy overreacted like that? It felt like her secret had been found out, that, despite all Kizzy's best

168

efforts, she'd developed a full blown crush on Javier Hamilton-Scott. Kizzy found herself daydreaming about him constantly, like a teenage girl. It was ridiculous; she was never going to see him again!

You need to sort it out. It was only because she wasn't feeling herself at the moment.

Just then, the car gave a funny little shudder and started to slow down.

'What's going . . .' Kizzy pumped the accelerator but it was loose and floppy. 'Ah, come on!' she wailed. 'Don't do this to me!'

Her luck was out. Twenty metres down the road the car rolled to a complete stop. Kizzy stared at the dashboard in disbelief. This was not happening!

'Come on,' she urged, trying the ignition again. Her eyes caught sight of the fuel gauge. The arrow was pointing to empty.

Oh, you muppet! All the medication she was taking must be making her brain funny. She picked up her phone and looked at it; no signal. Kizzy banged her head softly against the steering wheel. She was about three miles from the Fox-Titts', and a mile and a half from the petrol station outside Bedlington.

Bedlington it was, then. Easing herself out of the car, Kizzy traipsed round to the boot to get the petrol can out. If anyone she knew saw her, she'd seriously never live it down.

Kizzy wasn't the type to get easily scared, but it was lonely out on that dark country lane. She pulled her jacket collar up and shivered.

A few minutes later a car's headlights appeared from the other direction. The driver switched their lights on full beam as they approached, almost blinding Kizzy. She squinted and put her hand up to shield her eyes. What, were they trying to make her feel even worse about the situation she was in right now?

The car didn't speed off with a shouted taunt as she'd expected, but stopped a little way down the road. Kizzy turned round to see if it was someone she knew. It was a black Land Cruiser, with a private number plate. The letters were just about visible in the tail lights: JHS 77.

Kizzy's anxiety started to build. She was in a dark country lane, with no other witnesses. Just as she was wondering whether to go up and front it out, the driver's door opened. A man in a long waxed jacket and riding boots got out.

'Do you need any help?'

'I was just walking to the garage . . .'

Kizzy's voice faded as the man approached. It wasn't just his tall frame and powerful neck and shoulders. There was something really familiar about his dark, sensual features. As he got closer, it hit her like a hammer. The face that had occupied her mind these past weeks.

Oh. My. God. Kizzy clutched the petrol can nervously. Forget the fantasy she'd built up in her mind, Javier was really *standing* there in front of her! He was even more gorgeous in the flesh. Kizzy cursed herself for feeling so attracted to him.

'I said: do you need any help?'

He didn't seem to recognize her. Even in this winter darkness, Javier oozed magnetism. With his broken nose and the deep lines running either side of his mouth, he wasn't classically handsome, but there was something utterly compelling about him. And those eyes! A boulder-sized lump grew in Kizzy's throat. She swallowed painfully.

170

'I, er, ran out of petrol.' She held up the can. 'Playing up to the stereotype of a dumb blonde.'

He frowned, not sharing her smile. 'Can I drive you somewhere?'

Kizzy gestured down the road. 'I was just walking to the garage.'

'Let me drive you,' he said, and turned on his heel.

It was a command, not a question. Kizzy hesitated for a moment. She didn't know the bloke, what should she do?

It's cold and dark and he's throwing you a lifeline. Hoping Javier wasn't secretly a serial killer, Kizzy started to follow.

His car's interior smelt of leather and money. Hearing movement behind her, Kizzy turned to see two large black dogs sitting watchfully in the boot.

'Gorgeous dogs. What are their names?'

'Salvador and Pablo.' He was showing absolutely no sign of knowing her.

Kizzy was completely thrown. 'We've met,' she blurted out. 'You probably don't remember, I was riding—'

He interrupted. 'Of course I remember.'

'You do? Oh, right.' When nothing more was forthcoming, Kizzy looked out of the window. This was awkward.

They drove along in silence for a few moments before Javier spoke again. 'How's the recovery going? I noticed you're quite stiff when you walk.'

Had he? 'Er, yeah. I've got a disc protrusion on my lumbar spine.' Kizzy tried to make a joke of it. 'It's amazing how you pick up the lingo when you've spent enough time round doctors.'

'So you're not riding at the moment?'

171

'Not for six months,' she said gloomily. 'It's so rubbish.'

'It's not the end of the world,' he said matter-of-factly. 'You'll be back again before you know it.'

Kizzy could have kicked herself. Here she was moaning, and Javier's bloody wife was in a coma from her riding accident! She quickly moved the conversation on.

'Thanks so much for the flowers. I did send a card . . .'

'I got it.'

'Oh,' she said again. 'That's good. It was a really nice thing to do.'

'It was my secretary's idea.'

Kizzy felt crushed. 'Well, it was really nice of her,' she said brightly.

'Him.'

'Sorry?'

Javier shot her a glance, and for that second it felt like Kizzy's skin was on fire.

'My secretary is called Nigel.'

There was no hint of amusement on his face. In fact there was no sign of any emotion at all. Kizzy drummed her fingers on her lap and desperately tried to think of something to say.

'What breed are your dogs? I don't think I've ever seen ones like them before.'

'Pondenco Canario. Spanish hunting dogs.' Javier's pronunciation was perfect. 'You don't see them very often in the UK.'

'Yeah, I suppose it's more black Labrador territory round here,' she said, making a bad joke.

Javier's eyes remained fixed on the road ahead. 'You have dogs?'

'I'd love one, but my mum's really house-proud.'

172

Kizzy caught the spicy tang of his aftershave and crossed her arms uncomfortably. She'd been helping Edward muck out earlier, and probably smelled vile.

The glow of the petrol station appeared up ahead. Javier pulled in and glided to a stop in front of one of the pumps.

'Give me the can.' He looked at the shop rather than her.

'It's cool, I can do it.'

Javier gestured impatiently. 'The can.' Kizzy bent down to her feet and handed it over. There was a rush of cold air as he got out. Kizzy watched the tall, supple figure stride across the forecourt.

Her heart was going like the clappers. She couldn't believe this had happened again! Javier probably thought she lay in wait for him, hoping to be rescued. Kizzy turned round and looked at the two pairs of black eyes staring at her.

'Hello, you two. This is a bit weird, isn't it?'

*　　　*　　　*

A few minutes later they were driving back down the lane.

'I'm really sorry, I haven't got any money on me.' Kizzy felt mortified. 'Of course I'll repay you.'

'Don't worry about it.'

'No, seriously. I'll send you a cheque or something. You've been really kind.'

He gave a shrug. 'Whatever you want.'

They continued in silence. Kizzy looked at the elegant, deft fingers resting on the steering wheel. Javier wasn't wearing a wedding ring.

'I've seen you ride before,' he suddenly

announced.

Kizzy tore her eyes away, mouth open. 'You have? Where?'

'I was at a party at Clanfield Hall earlier this year. You were on a big bay.' Javier paused. 'Correct me if I'm wrong; you have a very distinctive style.'

'Oh my God! Do you mean that stately home outside Churchminster?' Kizzy was so surprised she forgot her nerves. 'I can't believe you saw that! I had no idea I was on private property.'

She turned back and caught the generous mouth ever-so-slightly curling at the corners. Was it a smile or a sneer?

'You were quite the talk at dinner.'

'Oh don't say that! I hope I didn't do too much damage to their lawns.'

'I think everyone was more taken with you jumping the five-bar gate.'

'Really?' She pulled a rueful expression. 'It's a bit of a bad habit of mine. Put an obstacle in my way and I have to jump it.'

'You're a jockey?'

'Amateur. It's my first point-to-point season.' Kizzy corrected herself. '*Was* my first season. I had a horse down at a yard in Churchminster, Nobby.' She sighed. 'My accident's written that off now. We've got someone else to ride him.'

Javier didn't comment, and Kizzy wanted to kick herself again. He was an Olympic medal winner, with one of the most important jobs in, like, the country, right now: training other Olympic competitors! He certainly didn't need to hear about her trials and tribulations. Kizzy looked out of the window again, resisting the urge to turn her head.

There was something about Javier's rugged profile that made her want to gaze at him for ever.

All too soon, and yet not soon enough, the headlights picked out her car up ahead. 'Thanks again, it was really kind of you,' Kizzy said as they pulled up. 'I'll send you a cheque in the post.'

He threw his seat belt off, making her jump. 'Your car keys?'

'My what . . . oh, right.'

Javier got out and went over to her car. After a hesitation, Kizzy got out herself. He was bent over her little Ka, filling it up from the can intently. Kizzy hovered self-consciously on the verge until he'd finished.

'Honestly, thank you so much,' she said. 'I'll write that cheque out as soon as I get home. Has Homelands got a website? I'll get the address from that.'

'If you must.'

They stood there for a moment, before Javier gave the tiniest nod towards her car. Kizzy got the hint.

'I'd better be going, then.'

'Your mother will be getting worried.' He didn't move, so Kizzy turned round and got in the car. Her hands were shaking so much she stalled the first time. The second attempt worked, thank God. Glowing with embarrassment, she wound down the window.

'Thanks again.'

Javier's face was shrouded in darkness. 'Come and visit Homelands some time, if you like, Kizzy. I can show you round.'

She gaped up at him. 'Are you being serious?'

He didn't answer immediately and Kizzy worried

175

he was regretting the decision. She jumped in before he had time to change his mind. 'Oh my God, that would be amazing! Er, do you want to give me your number?'

'The main number is on our website.'

Javier was giving her nothing back. Kizzy blushed. She was being way too keen! 'Yeah, of course.'

He stepped back, ending the conversation. 'You'd better get going.'

All the way back down the road Kizzy didn't dare look in the rear-view mirror in case he was still standing there. What had just happened? Javier was a lot older than her, married, and yet she'd never felt so attracted to someone.

Calm down, she chided herself. *It just took you by surprise.*

Next thought: *He invited you to Homelands!* The voice of reason wasn't finished. *They probably do lots of tours, nothing to get excited about.*

He invited you personally though, didn't he? With a little fizz of glee, Kizzy continued the journey home. It wasn't until she pulled into the drive that something else hit her. Javier had remembered her name.

CHAPTER TWENTY-EIGHT

The inexorable slide into Christmas began. That evening Calypso was at James's office party, in an overpriced bistro in Cheltenham. She'd come straight from work and the little black dress she'd pulled off the hanger that morning was now looking rumpled. As James's boss droned in her left ear Calypso caught sight of herself in the mirror opposite. *Gross.* She looked as if she'd been dug up: there were dark circles under her eyes and her complexion was pale. Bring on Antigua; it wouldn't be long now until she was stretched out on the beach, cold beer in one hand, Jackie Collins book in the other . . .

Her idyllic daydream was interrupted by another wave of Mr Armitage's breath. Calypso subtly shifted her chair back a few inches and took a drink from her wine glass, hoping the physical barrier would fend off the stench of his stomach gases.

'So, it's getting serious between you and young James, then?' He manoeuvred his fat gut round to face her.

Calypso smiled politely. Over the other side of the table James had been listening attentively to Mr Armitage's wife—a snooty battleaxe with fat ankles—for the last half hour, no doubt boring on about how fantastic her husband was.

'We haven't been seeing each other long,' she said sweetly, 'but yes, James is very nice.'

Mr Armitage took a long slurp of claret. 'Young Jimbo reminds me a lot of myself, you know.'

'Does he?' Calypso said in alarm.

'Of course.' Mr Armitage gave her a leery wink. 'I was quite the athlete in my day, you know.' He surveyed his prodigy across the table, before turning his attention back to Calypso. 'Do you want children?'

Don't hold back, mate, will you? 'Er, yeah. Some day . . .'

'Word of advice: don't leave it too late. That's the problem with you girls these days: think you

177

can go off and have a career, when you should be at home bringing up your children.'

Calypso gritted her teeth. *What a horrible old dinosaur. How did James put up with him?*

'Yes, James is a fine boy,' he continued. 'Hardworking, ambitious, good family values. He and I sing from the same song sheet. Or should I say spreadsheet?' Mr Armitage looked for her reaction. 'It's an accountants' joke.'

'Ha ha,' she said half-heartedly.

*   *   *

'Everyone loved you.' James put an arm round her shoulder as they walked back to his later.

'Really?' Apart from one lovely lady who'd had to leave early to go and breastfeed her baby, she'd thought the whole lot of them had been boring, small-minded and smug.

James had let go on the drink for once, and his eyes were slightly glazed and dreamy. By contrast she felt tired, and sober as a judge.

'Samuel—Mr Armitage—thought you were *fantastic*. In fact I think he was quite jealous.' He kissed her on the cheek. 'And so he should be, I was very proud to show you off.'

'I'm not some sort of show pet,' she said, a touch irritably.

He gave her a loose smile. 'Hey, I wasn't saying that.'

She felt his full body weight sagging on to her. 'Mr Armitage doesn't believe in women having careers, does he?'

'Don't mind him, he doesn't mean it. He's just a bit old-fashioned.'

178

'You're definitely his golden boy.'

James smiled. 'Did he say that? I do look up to him. That's where I'd like to be in twenty years: my own company, a family, a beautiful house in the country.' He waved his arm round. 'What more could anyone want?'

'James, you're suffocating me,' she protested, pushing him off.

'Whoops, sorry.' He stood back smiling at her, his brown hair ruffled like a schoolboy's, an untied dicky bow hanging round his neck. She couldn't help but soften; he was really quite sweet.

The droopy eyes flickered. 'Shall we go and find an alleyway? Be really naughty and do it outside?'

'Come on, lightweight, we're going home,' she said, catching him as he swayed.

'Do you like me?'

'Of course I do.'

'Really?'

'Yeah!' She lowered her voice as a couple walked past.

He smiled dreamily. 'Cos I really like you . . . And when I get home I'm going to do things to you. Wonderful things . . . really *naughty* things.'

Half an hour later she was rubbing his back as he threw up in the loo.

CHAPTER TWENTY-NINE

'What are you so engrossed in?' Kizzy's mum smiled at her from the doorway.

Kizzy quickly pulled the laptop screen down. 'Nothing.' She could feel her cheeks blushing, but

179

Bev didn't seem to notice.

'Just came to tell you dinner's in fifteen minutes. Have you done your exercises today, by the way?'

'Yes, nurse.'

'And sit up straight!' Bev called, walking back down the stairs.

With a furtive look at the door, Kizzy opened her computer up again. She'd made a pact with herself not to look Javier up on the Internet any more, but since their chance—or was it fate?—meeting in the lane two days ago, Kizzy had found it too hard to resist. She'd been left wanting more of him, although photographs and the odd jerky footage was no substitute. She savoured the delicious snapshots running through her mind; Javier's rich voice, the spicy tang of his cologne (men like Javier always wore cologne) and oh, those eyes! Kizzy felt like she could stare into them for ever.

Kizzy had been back and forth from the Homelands website like a nervous twitch, and she knew the number off by heart by now. How long did she leave before calling? The last thing she wanted was to appear over-keen, but Kizzy didn't know if she could wait for long.

Tucking the thought away to joyfully ponder over later, Kizzy went back to the webpage she'd been looking at. She had read up so much about Javier, it was like she knew every small detail of his life. For example, it was not generally known that he was a concert-level pianist, that he'd set up his own sanctuary for abused horses in Egypt or that, since his wife Sarah's accident, he'd ploughed millions of pounds of his own money into stem-cell research. His generosity had funded and helped medical science all over the world, with several eminent surgeons remarking on the significant contribution he had made to their work, and how they hoped it would help coma patients in the future.

One thing had really made her sad: a mention on Wikipedia about Javier's mother. Lord Douglas Aubrey Rawden Hamilton-Scott had married Elena Mendoza in 1967 and Javier had been born two years later. In 1975, aged thirty-one, Elena had died giving birth to a second son. The child, Fraser, had also not survived. No reasons were given aside from 'complications'.

Two lives lost, the destruction of a family reduced to a two-line entry. Kizzy couldn't believe it when she'd read it, how much bad luck could one bloke endure?

Kizzy went back on to YouTube. After a moment's hesitation, she typed in 'Sarah Hamilton-Scott' and 'Royal Ballet'. A whole page of clips came up. Scrolling down, she went on to one from 2005. Kizzy knew nothing about dancing, but she was mesmerized as Sarah floated across the stage. Her long limbs were perfectly controlled, her beautiful face filled with emotion. As the orchestra faded out Sarah came to rest, head bowed, on the floor. Flowers rained down on the stage, and there were shouts of 'Brava!'. The camera panned to the black-tie audience, on their feet and clapping wildly. It zoomed in on one of the boxes, where Javier stood, clapping harder and louder than any of them, a rapt expression on his face. As the camera moved back to Sarah, she glanced up to where her husband was sitting. The two shared an electric look, and for a moment it was just them alone, in a theatre with a thousand cheering people. The film ended abruptly, a fuzzy frame on Sarah's radiant face.

Kizzy pushed the laptop away, suddenly disgusted by herself. What the hell was she doing? Javier had never given her any sign he was interested. He'd probably only invited her to Homelands out of politeness, and because she'd been standing there like a gawping idiot. What must he think? She must have come across as some kind of sad, desperate groupie.

She thought back to Sarah: tall, elegant, a natural beauty. Kizzy looked down at her hands, red and scrubby from working outside, her nails bitten down to the quick. Javier would never go for someone like her in a million years. Why was she even thinking like that? He had a *wife*, who'd suffered the most terrible ordeal, and here Kizzy was, snooping through their lives like a dirty little voyeur.

The light which had been dancing through her for the last forty-eight hours faded. She'd been kidding herself about a man she would never know. Heart bleak, Kizzy switched off the laptop.

CHAPTER THIRTY

'Rosie, not again!' Caro looked in despair at her daughter. 'Will you please put your clothes on?'

The blonde moppet glowered up at her. 'Shan't!' Rosie's latest thing in the morning was to take all her clothes off when Caro had got her ready, and climb back into her pyjamas.

Caro was losing patience. 'Right, missy, I've had enough. We're leaving to take Milo to school in five minutes, and if you're not ready, I'll take you as you are.'

'Shan't!'

'Fine.' Caro sighed. 'Suit yourself.'

They ended up leaving ten minutes late, Rosie still in her pyjama bottoms and Milo stressing because he hadn't been able to go for a 'number two'.

'You'll have to go when you get there, darling.' Caro concentrated on the frosty road in front of her. She hoped no one would stop to talk to her at the school gates. She was wearing Benedict's too-big walking jacket, and hadn't had time to brush her hair yet.

'Mum, stop!' Milo shouted from the back seat.

'What now?'

'We're supposed to take something in today. Miss Ekins said.'

'God, Milo! Like what?'

'Stuff we use . . . in the house. We have to go back! I'll get told off.'

'Isn't there something in the car you can use?' Her son was wriggling around in the back seat, agitated. 'No! We have to bring something and tell a story about it. Harry will have something gooder than me!'

'All right.' She sighed, looking for a turning place. They were going to be so late.

*   *   *

'In, quickly.' She opened the front door and stood there, keeping an eye on the car.

'What do I get?' Her son looked panicked.

'Anything, darling! The remote control?' She

183

watched him scoot through into the living room. 'Nothing sharp from the kitchen!'

'I can't find anything!' He was running round like a headless chicken.

'What about something from upstairs?' Her mind had gone blank. 'How about our alarm clock?'

'Good idea.' He panted and pelted up the stairs. It all went quiet. 'Milo!' she called. 'We have to go!'

'I'm *coming*!' he screamed. 'I can't find anything.' She heard him running from one room to the next. Moments later he came skidding back down with his school bag.

'What did you get?' She closed the door behind them.

'The pink toy,' he shouted, running off down the path.

'Not Rosie's new Mermaid Barbie? Oh, Milo, she's only just got that.'

'You were shouting at me!' Her son's little face was hot and cross. 'Come on, Mummy! We're going to be late!'

*　　　*　　　*

Caro was having the day from hell. After dropping Milo off ten minutes late, she'd rushed to get Rosie to nursery, and come home to discover the washing machine had flooded the entire kitchen. The repairman had been very nice, but he had wanted to talk, and by the time Caro had got rid of him and looked at her watch it had been lunchtime. After collecting Rosie, the afternoon had disappeared in a whirlwind of floor-mopping, sorting dinner and hanging out wet piles of laundry. The next time Caro looked at her watch again it was nearly time to pick up Milo.

Christ. Where did it all go? Caro sat down on the upstairs toilet and put her head in her hands. She couldn't remember when she'd last had five minutes to herself. Life seemed to be an endless round of school runs, nursery, swimming practice and ballet lessons. Somehow in-between she had to fit in the food shopping and housework. It didn't help that she kept picking up winter bugs from the kids and never had the chance to recover from them. She felt as if she was running on empty, always in a mad rush to get from one thing to the next.

Benedict kept telling her to get a nanny or a cleaner, but Caro refused. She somehow felt that would be an admission of failure: plenty of women managed to juggle a career and a family, so surely she could manage. Her husband helped as much as he could, but he was busy at the moment. The creative director at his design agency had just resigned out of the blue and left him in the lurch, so Benedict was flat out until they could replace him. During the week Caro was pretty much on her own from breakfast to bath-time. She felt bad asking for help from her sisters, as both were busy with work, and although Clementine always offered, she was eighty-two now. It wasn't fair unleashing two hyperactive monkeys on her.

At least they were going on holiday soon, with the rest of the family. Caro was looking forward to Antigua, but just the thought of getting everyone packed and to the airport on time was overwhelming her at the moment. Her head was pounding down one side. She wondered if she was coming down with something again.

185

The grandfather clock by the front door chimed three times. Milo finished school in ten minutes; they needed to get a move on.

Her daughter was playing next door in her bedroom. 'Rosie!' she called, getting up and taking a look at her bedraggled face in the mirror. She was just pressing the last out of her Touche Eclat when the front doorbell rang.

God, what now? The bell rang again. 'All right, I'm coming!' she yelled. Kicking a pile of dirty laundry out of the way that she hadn't got round to washing yet, she ran down to answer it.

Her ex-husband stood there holding a plush purple envelope. 'Christmas card from Suz and I.'

Caro flushed at the memory of the recent wine debacle. 'Thanks, Seb, how nice of you. I'm afraid I haven't got round to writing mine yet.'

She noticed his clean-shaven face. 'Got rid of the moustache?'

'Yup, raised over thirty thou. Hammered all the boys in the office.'

'Still competitive to the last,' she teased.

He chuckled. 'Darling, I haven't changed completely!'

They stood there for a moment, smiling at each other. She was glad they were on good terms, no accusations or recriminations flying about.

'Is Milo around?' he asked.

'I'm just about to get him from school.' Caro turned and shouted again. 'Rosie! Come on!'

Sebastian took in her harried appearance. 'One of those days?'

'Just having a minor breakdown,' she sighed. 'No worries.'

'How about if I came along? I could help with

186

the children.'

Caro was a bit surprised. 'Er yes, all right.'

'Excellent. I did enjoy going last time.'

If he brought up the wine, she'd bloody kill him. 'Shall we go in mine or yours?' he asked.

Caro looked at the gleaming Aston Martin parked outside. 'It's probably safer to go in mine.'

Eagle Crest Primary was an adorable little school in the nearby village of Cottersham. It had a 'Santa's Grotto' this year, and the place was festooned with homemade cards and decorations. They made their way down to Milo's classroom, where they found him dealing Top Trumps on one of the desks with a friend. Miss Ekins, Milo's teacher, was talking to another parent at the front. She smiled at Caro and Sebastian when they walked in.

Sebastian greeted his son and got ignored, so he went to look at some paintings on the wall. Caro got Milo's things together. She was packing his lunchbox away when Miss Ekins broke off her conversation and came over.

'Hello, Mrs Towey.' She saw Sebastian. 'Hello again, Mr Belmont.'

He strode up, hands in pockets. 'Now then, Molly. I told you to call me Sebastian.'

Miss Ekins flushed. A dumpy little thing with a pleasant face, her patient classroom manner worked wonders on her unruly charges.

Caro smiled. 'I was just telling Seb about the household object task you set them. It sounds like a jolly good idea.'

Miss Ekins glanced round. The classroom had emptied out now, and Milo was off showing his sister some paintings in the corner.

'I was wondering if I could have a word with you about that.'

'Of course! I'm so sorry Milo didn't get something more suitable. He didn't tell me until I was driving him in this morning, and I'm afraid it was a bit of a mad rush back to the house. He grabbed the first thing he could lay his hands on.'

'I see.' Miss Ekins had a funny expression on her face. 'Mrs Towey, do you think it's appropriate for Milo to bring an adult toy in?'

'No, he had one of my daughter's toys.' Caro wasn't quite sure what she was talking about.

Miss Ekins had gone bright red. 'I'd like to show you something.' She went over to her desk. 'If you could come here.' Caro shot Sebastian a puzzled look. She knew a Barbie doll wasn't the most appropriate thing for a six-year-old boy to take in to school, but she'd just explained why it had happened.

Miss Ekins unlocked the drawer and slid it open. Caro had a brief glimpse into her working day: there were pens, Tippex and a packet of Polos there, and someone's misplaced Jelly Cat snuggled up in the corner. Caro looked at the object in the plastic bag lying in the middle of it all. She frowned, not able to place it at first. Why did it look familiar? Then she had a gut-clenching moment as the penny dropped.

It was her vibrator.

'Oh my God!' Caro had never felt horror like it. 'Miss Ekins, I had no idea. Milo was upstairs in my bedroom, I thought he had my daughter's Barbie!' She didn't even want to look at Sebastian.

'OK,' Miss Ekins said uncomfortably. 'I don't think Milo knew what it was, and I took it off him before the other children saw.'

Caro wanted the classroom floor to swallow her up. 'Really, I'm so sorry.' She watched as Miss Ekins produced a pair of surgical gloves and put them on, as if about to handle toxic waste. She picked up the bag by one corner and handed it to Caro.

'I don't want to patronize you by telling you to keep certain things in a safe place . ...'

Glowing with shame, Caro took the offending item and stuffed it deep in her coat pocket. She didn't even know when she'd last seen the damn thing; Milo must have rifled through her drawers.

Miss Ekins cleared her throat. 'But there was something else I wanted to talk to you about. We're having a few problems with Milo's language.'

'His language?' Sebastian spoke for the first time.

'A few months ago Milo started using a swear word. I don't know where he picked it up from'— she looked at Caro—'and I managed to stop him, but now it's started up again.'

Sebastian took a step closer. 'Well, what is it?'

Miss Ekins lowered her voice. 'Twat.' She didn't look like the sort of person who used it very often. 'He's called me it a few times—and Henry, one of his classmates. Then yesterday he shouted it across the lunch hall at the headmistress. Luckily, it was rather noisy . . .' Seeing the aghast look on their faces, she added, 'And she didn't hear. But I am rather concerned.'

Sebastian tutted. 'Caro, do you know where Milo got this disgusting language from?'

Caro knew exactly. Calypso. 'Erm, I really couldn't say,' she said, aware her cheeks were flushing. She was a terrible liar.

'I won't stand for this.' Sebastian called his son over. 'Milo, what's this about you using naughty words?'

'What naughty words?' He stood before them, a picture of innocence.

'You know very well,' Sebastian said sternly. 'The word beginning with T. It rhymes with cat.'

Milo grinned, sensing an opportunity. 'Mummy taught me!'

'Milo, I did not! I think, er, he might have overheard another member of the family use it,' she said hastily.

'I thought you didn't know where he got it from?' Sebastian asked mildly.

'I didn't! Well, not really. He wasn't meant to overhear . . .' Miss Ekins was looking at her as if she was a child murderer. 'I'll have strong words with Milo, I promise.'

'Just make sure they're not swear words.' Sebastian smiled benevolently. 'I *am* sorry, Molly. I'm sure my ex-wife will do her utmost to rectify the situation.'

He was unnervingly quiet until they got back to the car. Still reeling, Caro buckled the kids up and shut the door.

'Darling?' He was looking at her over the roof.

'What?' The last thing she needed was him being sanctimonious again.

He flashed a wolfish grin. 'You were never into vibrators when we were married. Benedict not satisfying you, then?'

'Oh, piss off!'

CHAPTER THIRTY-ONE

It felt like Jack Turner had barely put his head on the pillow before he needed to get up again. He squinted at the clock beside the bed and groaned. It was three in the morning. Trying not to wake his sleeping wife, he climbed out from under the floral patterned duvet and made his way across the chintzy room.

Beryl stirred. 'What's up, love?'

'Just visiting the bathroom, go back to sleep.'

He opened the door and walked out into the corridor, cursing the state of his bloody bladder again. If he only had to get up twice in the night, he was lucky. *You're getting old, my son.*

Finishing his business, Jack flushed the toilet and headed back to bed. He was just passing the landing window looking out on the green when a black shadow moving outside caught his eye.

Jack stopped and frowned. What was going on here, then? The electric lanterns they kept on outside the front door threw some light on to the frosty grass. A second look revealed nothing out of the ordinary.

Just as Jack was wondering if his eyesight had packed up as well as his waterworks, the black shape moved again.

Jack's fists automatically tightened; there'd been a spate of car thefts round the district recently. This bugger looked big, though. Just as he was debating whether to get his baseball bat, the intruder moved out of the darkness towards him. Instead of a prospective car thief, Jack found himself staring into the long ugly face of Nobby.

'Bleeding 'ell!' He watched as Nobby started to walk off down the road, hooves gently clip-clopping.

'Horse, wait!' he hissed. 'Come back.' Jesus Mary, what was he going to do now? The closest Jack had ever got to an animal was a budgerigar called Frank Sinatra he'd had as a pet when he'd been a boy. There was no way he was going to go down there and put himself in front of half a ton of heaving beast.

'Nobby!' He banged on the window, as if the horse would trot over and ask to be let in. 'Over here, son!'

There was a creak at the end of the corridor, and Stacey came out in a pair of fleecy patterned pyjamas. Her cross little face was squashy and criss-crossed with sleep patterns.

'*Dad*. Oh my God, what are you doing? You've totally woken me up.'

Jack gestured frantically out of the window. 'Angie and Freddie's bleedin' racehorse has escaped! It's wandering round out there, happy as Larry.'

Stacey gave a momentous sigh. 'Is that it? Can I go back to bed now?'

'What do you mean? I can't go out there, Stace.'

'Well, I'm not going out there, am I? I haven't got any make-up on, someone might see me.'

'It's the middle of the bleedin' night!'

'What's going on, love?' Beryl called from their bedroom.

'Nothing!' Jack turned back to his daughter imploringly. 'Please, Stace, help me out. You know I'm scared of animals.'

'Don't be such a loser. Take a carrot out there

192

or something.' She shot her dad a pitying look and walked back into her bedroom.

The door creaked at the other end and Beryl came out, her hair in rollers. 'Jack, what are you doing?'

'I didn't want to wake you, love, but that bloody horse of Angie's is wandering round out there! It must 'ave escaped.'

'What are you talking about?' His wife came over to the window. Luckily Nobby had stopped on the green a bit further down. They watched as he put his head down, nose travelling like a metal detector across the ground as he searched for a strand of sparse winter grass.

'Nothing for it, I'm going to have to go out there, aren't I?' Beryl said.

Jack looked down at his wife's short satin nightie, which barely contained her enormous bosoms. 'Bez, you can't go out like that! You'll catch your death.'

'That horse ain't gonna catch itself, Jack. What if he gets out on the main road? Angie and Freds would never forgive us.'

There was nothing for it. 'You're right, I'll go and phone 'em.'

'Better get me coat, then. And a length of rope to catch the bugger.'

As she marched off towards the stairs Jack could only watch in admiration. This was the woman who'd single-handedly ejected two strapping blokes from the bar last night for being too drunk. A seventeen-hand racehorse was going to be a piece of cake.

*   *   *

193

The following lunchtime was Clementine's annual Christmas drinks party at Fairoaks. It was a dark and gloomy day, the sunlight fading early, but the twinkling lights stretching through various trees and bushes in the garden were a cheering sight as guests arrived. Inside it was just as welcoming, with every downstairs room decorated, and the smell of mince pies and mulled wine floating through the house. Nobby's audacious escape was the hot topic of conversation.

'Honestly, Caro, you should have seen it.' Angie was feeling rather bleary eyed, after being woken up in the middle of the night by a frantic Jack. Her first thoughts on hearing the telephone ring were that something terrible had happened to Archie. It was a relief to discover it was only their prize racehorse rampaging round the village green.

'Freddie says that to his dying day he'll never forget the sight of Beryl Turner in her nightie, running after Nobby with a honey-glazed carrot.' It was only after Nobby had cleared the previous vicar's memorial bench by a good three feet that they'd managed to catch the little bugger.

'I can't believe we didn't wake up!' Caro ran her tongue round the inside of her mouth. She was sure she had an ulcer coming.

'I never knew Beryl had such a pace on her, but apparently she was athletics captain at school.' Angie took another sip of her Kir Royal. 'Fred went straight down to B&Q and bought a sooper-dooper new latch for his stable. Houdini back home will have no chance of getting out now.'

'All's well that ends well, I suppose. At least Nobby didn't hurt himself.'

Angie looked at her friend. 'You still feeling

under the weather?' she asked sympathetically. Caro had been laid up the last few days with a vomiting virus she'd caught off Rosie.

'I'm just a bit weak, I'll be OK.' She still had a million and one things to do before they went away.

Benedict came up, holding a plate piled high. 'Your grandmother has given me strict instructions to make sure you eat this.'

Caro looked down at the French onion tart, still warm from the oven. It looked lovely, but she didn't have much appetite.

'At least I've lost a few pounds,' she told Angie. 'I was dreading getting into a bikini.'

Benedict kissed his stressed-out, tired wife. 'Everything's going to be fine, darling. We're going to have a wonderful holiday.'

*   *   *

By three o'clock the house was packed with people from the village, and most of Clementine's bridge friends. One of them, a recent widow, caused quite a stir when she turned up with a very attractive Italian man half her age. Apparently they'd met on a painting holiday in Umbria, where she'd gone following the death of her husband. The bridge circle was scandalized.

'I'm sure he's only with her for the money,' Angie overheard one of them say, as she went to find Freddie. 'You know Percy's art collection went for two million at Sotheby's? And that's without even thinking about the town flat in Chelsea.'

After a search, Angie found Freddie in the snug with Jed, watching a rugby match. The commentary was blaring out excitedly.

195

'*And here come Gloucester. Just listen to that crowd! For the first time, Ben Mason leads out the team as captain. Carrying on a famous sporting family dynasty, his dad Christopher "Chip" Mason recently came third in BBC1's show* Strictly Come Dancing . . .'

'Why do they clog the bloody commentary up with this stuff?' Freddie grumbled. He looked up as his wife came in the room.

'Freds, there you are! Reverend Bellows was just asking after you.' Angie handed him the plate she'd been carrying. 'I've brought you a few goodies from the buffet.'

'Super.' Eyes fixed to the screen, Freddie took it off her.

'Well, are you coming out?'

'Don't deny a chap his rugger, Angelica! This is one of the most important games this season.'

Angie rolled her eyes and left them to it. Outside, she found Calypso and her new chap, James, in the corridor. He looked very smart in his neatly pressed shirt and polished shoes.

'I'm hammered already!' Calypso announced. Her mouth was red from the mulled wine she'd been sneaking from a pan in Granny Clem's kitchen.

Angie was feeling a little tiddly herself. Although a most generous hostess in every other way, Clementine had a rather abstemious approach to alcohol. Angie and Fred had brought three bottles of Billecart-Salmon champagne, and she was sure she'd nearly worked her way through one already. She held a hand out. 'Hello, I've heard lots about you.'

James grinned. 'All good, I hope.'

196

'Soz, I should do the introductions.' Calypso waved her glass. 'James, meet the gorgeously sexy Angie Fox-Titt.'

'Ah, the racehorse owner.'

Angie laughed. 'That makes it sound a lot more glamorous than it actually is.'

'Calypso tells me you've got your first race coming up.'

'Yup, up north of Worcester. Chaddesley Corbett?'

James nodded. 'I've done a few cycle rides up there.'

'Have you really?' Angie was impressed. 'It's fifty miles away. You must be super fit.'

'*Super* fit,' Calypso drawled. 'James thinks nothing of fitting in sixty miles before breakfast.' She pulled on his hand. 'Come outside for a fag with me.'

'I thought you were giving up.' His tone was mildly disapproving.

'I am!' she pleaded. 'But it's Christmas, and I've been working so hard.'

'I'll leave you to it.' Angie laughed as James was dragged off towards the back door. 'Lovely to meet you.'

'You, too!'

*   *   *

It was getting dark by the time Benedict came in from the garden with Rosie. Caro touched her daughter's cold cheek and smiled at Benedict. 'Where's Milo?'

'Milo? I thought he was with you.'

Caro went cold. 'No, I thought he was with you.'

197

She put her drink down. 'He must be upstairs somewhere.'

A quick search through the bedrooms revealed nothing. He wasn't even hiding in the attic. With a sense of unease, Caro turned to Benedict.

'God, where is he?'

She could see her husband was trying to keep calm. 'I'm sure he's just wandered off up to the orchard or something, you know how he likes exploring.'

Asking Angie to keep an eye on Rosie, they slipped away from the party and out to the back garden and the apple trees beyond. 'Milo!' Benedict shouted. 'Can you hear us?'

No answer. Caro was actually feeling sick now. 'Milo!' she shouted. *Christ, what if he'd gone wandering off near the road?*

'I'll go down to the green,' Benedict said. 'He might have gone there to see the ducks.'

They hurried back inside and were accosted by a very jolly Freddie. 'Gloucester trounced Bath twenty-two to nine! I think celebrations are in order.'

Despite his slight inebriation, he noticed their strained faces. 'What's wrong?'

'Milo's missing,' Caro said.

'Hang on, we don't know that,' Benedict said, trying to keep a lid on the situation.

'Where the hell is he, then?' Several people looked round at her raised voice.

Freddie put his glass down. 'I'll go and get Angie, and we'll help you look.' He patted Caro on the shoulder. 'I'm sure he's just off playing somewhere, you know how small chaps are.'

Caro felt sick. Call it mother's instinct, but she

198

was sure it was more than that.

*   *   *

Word quickly spread, and before long Jed had taken a search party into the surrounding fields. Benedict ran back down to the house in case Milo had wandered home, but he was nowhere to be seen.

'Do you think we should call the police?' Camilla said quietly to Jed.

He frowned. 'Let's give it another fifteen minutes.'

Every nook and cranny of the house was searched again. The pond, surrounding ditches and even the fields backing on to the house were investigated, but to no avail. People started to trail back inside, defeated. In the kitchen Caro was clutching Rosie for dear life. The little girl had picked up on the tension and started to grizzle.

Benedict's face was devoid of colour. 'I think we should call the police.'

Caro nodded numbly. If her son had come to any harm she would never, ever forgive herself . . .

'Caro!' someone shouted. 'Look!'

'I think you might be missing someone,' a voice said. Suddenly, like a beautiful vision, Sebastian and Suzette were standing in front of her with Milo between them.

Still holding Rosie, Caro bent down and grasped him. 'Oh, darling, where have you been?' He wasn't even wearing his coat. The little boy squirmed, completely unaware of the drama he'd just caused.

'We found him on the Bedlington Road,' Sebastian said. 'He was making his way over to see us.'

The Bedlington *Road*? 'Milo, what on earth were you doing?'

'Bored. Wanted Zette to make me her special hot chocolate.'

Weak with relief Caro stood up. 'Thank you so much. I just don't know how it happened.' The guilt was starting to rush in: how could she have taken her eye off him?

'Not at all,' Sebastian said. 'It was just lucky Suzette and I were driving past.'

Clementine arrived at Caro's side. She glanced at everyone uncertainly.

'Seb and Suzette found Milo. He was on his way to their cottage,' Caro explained.

'What?' Clementine was horrified. 'Milo, you shouldn't go off without telling people!'

'No one was playing with me.'

'It's all right, Milo,' Sebastian patted his head with a driving-gloved hand. 'You're back now, no harm done.'

Clementine looked rather awkward. Despite Sebastian being back in the village, she had gone out of her way to avoid him. She hadn't seen her former grandson-in-law since the acrimonious divorce.

'It was very kind of you to bring Milo back,' she told him.

'Honestly, not a problem,' he said graciously. He and Suzette looked very smart, as if they'd been for a nice lunch somewhere. 'Having a party?'

'Just a few drinks.' Clementine suddenly felt embarrassed. Sebastian was Milo's father; maybe she should have invited him. 'Would you like to stay for a drink?' she asked.

'That's very kind of you, but we wouldn't want to impose.'

There was a painful silence.

'Well, now,' Sebastian said genially. 'You all have a splendid Christmas in Antigua.'

'I don't want to go!' Milo suddenly shouted. Everyone looked down at him.

'Milo,' Benedict warned, but the boy clung on to Sebastian.

'Want to stay here with Daddy and Zette. They're taking me to Disneyland!'

Sebastian gave the others an apologetic grin. 'Ah yes, we did mention taking him. Sorry if it's put ideas in his head.'

'Want to go on the rides there!' howled Milo. He was getting hysterical. Caro went to calm him but he pushed her away. 'You don't want me, anyway! I hate you!'

'Milo!' Benedict said again, more sharply.

Caro felt like she'd been kicked in the stomach. 'It's all right, Benedict.' She spoke to her son again. 'Darling, what on earth are you talking about?'

To everyone's surprise Suzette suddenly bent down and started muttering soothing entreaties into his ear. Her words seemed to have the right effect, as Milo's cross little face started to calm down.

'Milo, apologize to your mother,' Benedict said. 'You can't talk to her like that.'

The devil child had instantly transformed. 'Sorry, Mummy.' He did his best to look contrite. 'Can I have some more cake now?'

'I think it's time we took you home,' Benedict said. He turned to the unlikely saviour. 'Thank you.'

Sebastian accepted the outstretched hand.

'Really, it was nothing.' He took Suzette's hand. 'Come on, darling, we'd better be off. Happy Christmas, everyone.'

CHAPTER THIRTY-TWO

Kizzy brushed the last stubborn clump of mud out of Nobby's tail and stood back. In the dim light of the stable she could see the sinewy, gleaming contours of the horse's body. Even with his obvious shortcomings, there was no disguising the new strength that lay beneath. Nobby had turned from a knock-kneed horse with a bit of potential to a lean, mean, jumping machine.

Edward knew his stuff; there was no doubt about that. Every day, come rain or shine, he was out on the gallops building up Nobby's stamina. Kizzy and the Fox-Titts could only stand with their stopwatch as the horse pelted round the course, jumping the fences without even breaking his stride. Edward was a gifted rider, knowing when to hold the horse back and when to let him go, and, as seconds continued to be shaved off the timings, a real sense of hope was starting to build in everyone. What had once been a pipe dream really could turn into something.

Despite their best efforts, Edward had kept to himself since he'd moved in. He was up at dawn, and out all day in the stables; by evening he would retire to the granny annexe, close the curtains and shut out the world. No friends came to visit, and he didn't seem to have any to go and see. Offers to join the Fox-Titts for dinner were turned down with a polite smile. As Freddie kept pointing out, Edward seemed perfectly happy being self-sufficient, and they should give the young chap some space. Eventually Angie had laid off, even though she still took Edward a cup of coffee every morning. A dash of milk, no sugar—it was about the only bit of information about himself he'd volunteered.

Edward and Kizzy's situation could have been awkward, but they'd forged a relationship that worked. He didn't seem to mind her cheery chatter, even if he didn't contribute much back, and in turn she appreciated the fact that he still let her play a big part in Nobby's training. Edward respected her closeness to the horse and that she had been there from the beginning, and in turn she respected him back.

Tonight it was her turn to get Nobby in, brush him down and give him his sugar beet. Kizzy picked up Nobby's night rug from the stable door and carefully slid it over his body, taking time with all the straps. Nobby was munching on his hay net and she gave him a kiss, taking in his warmth and the sweet smell of the hay. It was one of her favourite times of day.

'Night, Nobs, see you soon, babe.'

It was bitterly cold outside, the cloud-covered night sky hanging low. Kizzy was heading to the car when she noticed the living room light in the granny annexe was on. She wanted to remind Edward that the farrier was coming in the morning. But as she walked back across the yard and approached the building, she was surprised to see the front door slightly ajar. That was strange; maybe he hadn't closed it properly on his way in.

'Edward?' She felt awkward, like she was

invading his private space. She'd never been here before, and he'd never invited her in. She looked through the crack in the door and saw the small living area, the L-shaped kitchen at the other end of the room.

'Edward?'

Tentatively Kizzy pushed the door open and stepped in. Despite the homely touches Angie had added, the stuffed cushions, dried flowers and cheery rug, there was no evidence Edward actually lived there, save a stack of *Racing Post*s on the coffee table, and an empty milk carton left out on the side.

Kizzy was painfully aware of her own breathing. It was too quiet in here. Walking carefully on the tiptoes of her wellies so as not to leave any mud, she made her way towards the staircase.

'Anyone home?' She paused at the bottom, unsure what to do. Maybe he was asleep. Someone as private as Edward would not appreciate her barging in. Kizzy turned to leave, but a strange sound from upstairs made her stop dead.

She strained her ears, trying to figure it out. A low muttering was coming from above. Was it the telly? *Leave. Now,* a little voice urged her, but concern and curiosity took over. Kizzy put one foot on the bottom step and started up.

As she got closer, she realized the muttering was some kind of chanting. It was Edward's voice, but it was different, his normal quiet whisper replaced by something feverish, almost possessed. Knowing she could still turn back, Kizzy steeled herself and peered round the doorway. The bedroom was surprisingly large, the king-sized bed sitting comfortably in a space that probably ran the whole length of the downstairs.

Room proportions were the last thing on Kizzy's mind. Edward was stood at the end of the room with his back to her, looking in a full-length mirror. She had a double take as she saw he was wearing the silks Angie and Freddie had bought for him, the glossy purple and black a startling contrast against his chalky skin. Shoulders rigid, he was staring fixatedly at his reflection, a black riding crop in his right hand.

'I can do this, I *will* do this!' *Thwack.* He brought the crop down sharply on his skinny thigh. Kizzy winced, but Edward didn't even seem to register the pain.

'You can do this!' The crop came down again, as Edward repeated his mantra, lilac eyes blazing into the mirror.

Kizzy started to back away. She knew she shouldn't be there, that she had stumbled on something she shouldn't be seeing. Terrified of being heard, it was only when she was sat in the car, hands shaking, that she realized she was still holding her breath.

She thought about what she'd just heard. What was Edward hoping to do? Ride Nobby out to be a winner? Maybe he was just psyching himself up before the race, but it had seemed more than that. He'd seemed totally lost inside himself.

She switched on the ignition and crawled past the granny annexe, not daring to glance up at the window. Whatever it was, she had seen something passionate and tortured in Edward that none of them had known existed.

She didn't know whether to be worried or scared.

By the time Kizzy had got home, her dad was sitting in the living room watching telly. As she opened the door he automatically took his feet off the coffee table, but then saw who it was and put his slippers back up again.

'Thought it was your mum,' he said, his eyes settling back on the rugby game.

Kizzy went over and dropped a kiss on his forehead. An unexpected spasm shot through her back and she winced. The cold weather had made it worse today.

'How many cats did you get today, then?'

It was a long-standing joke between them that Graham Milton really spent all his time on shifts drinking tea at the fire station and rescuing the odd moggy from a tree.

'Loads,' he said, eyes still on the screen. 'Thinking of starting my own animal sanctuary, actually.'

'Oh, Mum would love that. Where is she, anyway?'

'Out delivering cards.' He nodded at the mantelpiece. 'You've got one of your own up there.'

There was a large black envelope propped up next to the clock. It had swirly gold writing across the front, and when she picked it up, whatever was inside felt heavy.

'What is it, then?' her dad asked.

'Give me a chance to open it.' Kizzy racked her brains, but couldn't think of any major parties going on. She was intrigued.

Inside the envelope was an equally plush-looking piece of card with the same gold lettering. Kizzy pulled it out and read it. It took a few seconds to register, and then all thoughts of Edward dropped out of her mind.

Javier Hamilton-Scott and sponsors request the pleasure of your company for a Christmas drinks reception on
Wednesday, 23 December, at
Homelands International Equestrian Centre,
Badger's Mount, Gloucestershire
Time: 7 o'clock until 9 o'clock
Dress: Formal

Kizzy stared at the card, and back at the front of the envelope. It was definitely addressed to her, wasn't it? 'Ms Kizzy Milton, 6, Shakespeare Drive.' How had Javier known where she lived?

'Come on then, what is it?'

Kizzy made her voice deliberately casual. 'It's a party invite from Javier Hamilton-Scott. You know, the dressage rider?'

'Who?'

'He was the one who came to help me when I fell off Nobby.' At least that was the truth.

'The bloke that was passing in his car?' Her dad frowned. 'How does he know where you live?'

'Er, Angie might have mentioned it . . .' Kizzy said, hoping Angie wouldn't mind her name being used.

The ruse seemed to work. Her dad raised his eyebrows. 'And now you've got some invite to a swanky party? That's a bit of a leap.'

'It's a horse thing.'

'Are the Fox-Titts going?'

'Probably,' she lied. 'It's an official drinks party.

207

"Javier Hamilton-Scott and sponsors",' she read out. 'I bet there'll be loads of important people there.'

'Hmm.' Her dad gave her a hard look. 'No offence, Kiz, but why are you going?'

'Oh, cheers! I already told you, it's because I'm into horses.' Kizzy was amazed at how easily the stories were coming. 'Javier's one of the trainers for the GB team, Dad. I might even get to meet the team!'

Her dad sighed and settled back in the sofa. 'Suit yourself. It's not like you're going to listen to me, anyway.'

Kizzy went straight to her room to RSVP. Her laptop seemed to take for ever to come on. She went straight into her emails, ignoring the spam about penis enlargements and a message from her friend Emma. Her hands were shaking. *It's only an invite*, she told herself. *Like I said to Dad, there's probably hundreds of people going.*

It didn't calm the little frisson of excitement that had reawakened inside her.

From: KizzyMilton99@hotmail.co.uk
To: admin@homelandsinternational.com

She didn't know who she was replying to. Probably one of his team. What had his secretary been called, Nigel? After staring at the screen for a good minute, Kizzy started to type.

Hi! Got the invite. Love to come. Thanks, it sounds amazing!

Delete. *Much* too overexcited. They would think

she was a deranged fan or something, and not let her through the gates. In the end, after several more attempts Kizzy decided to go for the straightforward approach.

Hi there,
Thanks very much for the invite to the drinks reception. I'd love to come.
Best Wishes,
Kizzy Milton.

In a daredevil moment she added her mobile number and pressed 'send' before she could change her mind.

CHAPTER THIRTY-THREE

Balls and shitbags! They were leaving for the airport in less than thirty minutes! Calypso stared at the wet G-strings on the radiator, willing them to dry. As usual, she'd left her holiday packing until the last minute, and had forgotten to take her washing out of the machine overnight. Now here she was, with a pile of wet underwear and a half-empty suitcase. With perfect timing her boiler had chosen to pack up again, and after an emergency shout for Jed's handyman skills, the radiators were only just flickering back to life.

There was no point standing here, as if the heat from her eyeballs was going to make her knickers dry any quicker. Sighing, Calypso headed back into her bedroom and started throwing clothes in the suitcase. String bikinis, flip-flops, cowboy hats, denim cut-offs. It wasn't like she needed much, anyway. As she bent down to pick up a stripy boob tube, Calypso caught a flash of something white under the bed. She reached down to retrieve it and came out with a pair of James's boxer shorts.

Calypso studied the pants: clean-looking, size medium, from Next. Just like all his underwear. He must have brought a spare pair with him; there was no way he'd have driven home commando. Her thoughts turned to last night, when he'd come over for dinner, their 'goodbye dinner' as he called it. Calypso had thought that was a bit over the top: she was only going away for ten days. But they'd had a chilled evening: she'd managed not to burn the lasagne, they'd watched the Woody Allen DVD he'd brought over, and, after a bit of rolling around on the rug, he'd taken her upstairs and given it to her, missionary style. After their first dirty shag on the sofa, it had quickly become clear James wasn't the most adventurous lover. He was a great kisser and very complimentary about her body, but Calypso wanted to be thrown round the bedroom more, and given a good seeing to. Last night she'd spent most of the shag thinking about the work emails she had to answer. She'd even started to amuse herself by seeing how loudly she could fake an orgasm, porn-star style, before James noticed. That wasn't right, was it?

Maybe she was being unrealistic. Calypso had always had a strong sex drive and enjoyed herself in bed, but she could have been lucky up till now. It wasn't always shag heaven. One of her friends was infamous for Tweeting while her lump of a boyfriend shagged her over the bed from behind. At least James was sweet and thoughtful and always called when he said he would. There was no being given the runaround or 'feeling-sick-waiting-for-him-to-text-back' stuff with James. Most women would probably find his transparency attractive. Calypso was starting to find it really suffocating.

She stared into the suitcase, still holding the boxer shorts in her hand. James had been a big hit at her grandmother's party: helping in the kitchen, talking to everyone, joining in the search party when Milo went missing. Everyone had said how nice he was and, really, she couldn't disagree. That was the problem, he was just *nice*. Her stomach didn't flutter every time his name flashed up on her phone, like it had with Rafe or any of the others.

Grow up, she told herself. Bad boys did not make for a happy girl. Rafe had done the dirty on her, and men like Elliot would never commit. James was the perfect man. Everyone kept telling her so.

She just wished he had a bit more *spontaneity* about him.

It took a moment for her to realize her mobile was ringing. Locating it under her wash bag, Calypso looked at the caller. Speak of the devil. 'James!'

'Are you in?' His voice was echoey, like he was standing in a Portakabin.

'Yes, where are you?'

'On your front doorstep.'

She went to look out of the window. It was one of those perfect winter days, a clean blue sky looking down on the frost-covered green. Sure enough, James's Saab was parked on the verge outside.

'What are you doing here?' she asked. 'Shouldn't you be at work?'

'I'm on my lunch break. I've got something to

211

give you, can you let me in?'

'You drove all the way out here?'

'Yes,' he said amusedly. 'So can you come down and let—'

'Shit, yes. Sorry.' Still on the phone, she ran downstairs and pulled the door open. Sure enough James was there, looking very professional and smart in his grey suit.

'Hello,' she said, kissing him on the mouth. 'I wasn't expecting to see you again.'

'Thought I'd surprise you.'

Calypso looked at her watch; James always took his lunch between one and two. 'Isn't it a bit of a slog over here? You're going to be late back.' She was sure Mr Armitage wouldn't like that.

'I got an extended lunch break.' He put his arms round her waist. 'I suppose you're wondering what I'm doing here.'

'I was thinking.' She pulled back. 'Isn't it a bit *daring* to break free from the office like this?'

He laughed. 'I told you, not all accountants are boring.' Reaching into his pocket he brought out a small black box, gift-wrapped with a taffeta bow. 'I was hoping it would turn up yesterday so I could give it to you, but it only arrived this morning.'

Calypso looked down at the box. Hadn't they given each other their jokey little presents last night?

'Go on, it won't bite,' he told her.

A sudden panicky feeling flooded over her. This wasn't what she thought it was, was it? In trepidation she pulled off the ribbon and opened the box. There, nestled in a pile of expertly arranged tissue paper, was the most exquisite pair of black and gold drop earrings.

212

'Oh my God!' she squealed, as she saw the name on the label. 'Lola Rose! She's my favourite jewellery designer.' She picked one earring up and studied it. 'How did you know?' she asked. 'James, they're lovely.'

'You mentioned it once.' He was watching to see if her reaction was real. 'After I'd made dinner at mine, you were flicking through your copy of *ASOS Magazine* and you mentioned it.'

Calypso had a vague recollection. She was suddenly quite overcome. 'I can't believe you *remembered* something like that.' The weak sunlight caught the earring, making it glitter and sparkle like a Christmas bauble. She held it up to her ear, the jewels draping down her long neck. 'What do you reckon? Does it suit me?'

'I think you look beautiful,' he said softly. 'I think you always look beautiful.'

'Calypso!' The romantic moment was broken by a voice. Camilla was standing by the garden wall, and for once her placid demeanour looked slightly ruffled. 'Calypso, have you got any of my sarongs? I've been looking for them all morning, and I can't find one.'

'Whoops!' Calypso said. 'Caught out. I'll pack them in my case!' she shouted back at her sister.

'You have to be ready, we're leaving in fifteen minutes.' She caught sight of James. 'Hello there!'

'Hi, Camilla, I just came to see your sister.'

Camilla gave a distracted smile and disappeared back to her cottage. Calypso looked at James with a funny warm feeling in her stomach she'd never had before. 'I'm really touched, James. Seriously. And with you driving all the way over here to give them to me.' She wrapped her arms round him.

213

'You like them, then?'

'They're gorgeous. *You're* gorgeous,' she declared. She pressed herself into him. 'Come inside quickly,' she whispered.

Regretfully, James extricated himself. 'I don't want to be responsible for you missing your flight.' He stroked her hair. 'Go and finish packing.' He looked into her eyes. 'I'll miss you.'

'Yeah,' she said. 'I'll miss you, too.'

PART TWO

CHAPTER THIRTY-FOUR

While the Jolly Boot was heaving with Christmas trade, the rest of the village was decidedly quiet. Caro and family had flown off for the balmy climes of Antigua, while the Pikes had left for their Barbados holiday ten days earlier. Even village stalwart Brenda Briggs and her husband Ted were on a festive break in Lapland, the flashing Santa on her roof turned off and barely visible against the thatched roof. When Angie locked up the shop at lunchtime and headed home the green was disconcertingly quiet.

It would just be her and Freds at home for Christmas dinner, and even though they had strung up the lights in the trees at the end of the drive as usual, and decorated the house, she was feeling a bit flat about it all. It wouldn't be the same without Archie, who wasn't due back until at least February. Even the usual midday drinks at the Jolly Boot would be quieter than normal, with so many people away.

Thank God then for Nobby's imminent debut, to keep them busy. The maiden race, for horses who had never been placed first before, was on the twenty-seventh, seven days away. Aside from the usual Christmas preparation, Angie could barely think of anything else. She and Fred had done the paperwork: paid the British Horseracing Authority for Edward's Riders Qualification Certificate, and made sure all his medicals were up to date. Edward had turned up with barely a penny to his name, so they'd bought a new pair of boots to replace his worn-out ones, a body protector, and the black and purple silks he would race in. They were barely paying him anything anyway, so Angie was happy to help out.

Angie wondered if Edward's racing career would even have got off the ground if he hadn't had someone to do the 'admin' side of everything. It was as if he were entirely unaware he had to actually do anything but turn up and ride. He spent every second with Nobby: exercising, making sure the horse had the right amount in every feed, fretting the ground was too muddy/dry/hard/soft whenever he was let out in the paddock. At least Kizzy was there to calm Edward down, and Nobby played his part by being as laid-back as ever. Except out on the gallops, when his ears pricked up and the rocket inside him revved up and took off.

The riding weight for Chaddesley Corbett was twelve stone six, but Edward looked like he'd lost even more weight recently. Like all good jockeys in the making, he was scrupulous about his diet, but Angie thought he looked positively emaciated at the moment. Tired, too. At least Edward was going home for Christmas. It would only be for two days but the break would do him the world of good. Edward had been reluctant to leave, but Angie had told him they'd all be there to look after Nobby while he was away. It was sweet and yet rather heart-wrenching how dedicated Edward was, as if there had been nothing before to direct his love and passion towards.

*   *   *

That evening Angie was in the kitchen watching

a *Strictly Come Dancing* Christmas special as she prepared dinner. Her favourite Holby boy had won, and was now twirling his partner round the dance floor to a funky version of 'Jingle Bells'. Angie took a glug of the G and T Freddie had made her, and stared wistfully at the dancers' glamorous outfits. Maybe if she took up dancing she'd lose a bit of weight off her thighs so she could wear short skirts. Although Freds always told her she was perfect already.

The sound at the back door was so soft she thought it was the wind at first. Then she realized someone was knocking. Edward. She went over and pulled the door open. He loomed there, waxed jacket hanging over his skinny frame.

'Dear boy, you must be freezing!' she exclaimed. 'Come in.'

He looked down at his cheap wellies, wet with fresh mud. 'I'd better not.'

'That's what the boot jack is there for,' she said cheerily. 'Leave them there, next to mine and Freddie's.'

His long bony feet were encased in thick stripy red and white socks. They looked rather incongruous on such a sorrowful person.

'I do like your socks,' she told him.

Edward looked down at his huge feet. 'They were a Christmas present from my mum.'

It was the first time he'd mentioned any of his family. 'You must be looking forward to seeing them. Your parents, I mean.'

Edward didn't reply. 'Will you come in, then?' Angie asked. She was getting used to him not replying to most of her questions. She pulled out a chair for him. 'I was just watching a *Strictly* special, do you watch it?' What Edward got up to by himself every night in the annexe was anyone's guess.

He folded himself down and looked at the screen, where Samantha Janus was tackling a very steamy paso doble. 'I don't watch much telly.'

'Fred tells me I spend far too much time watching these shows.' Angie went over to the fridge. 'What can I get you? Wine, beer, a G and T?'

She had to ask again. Edward seemed miles away, still looking blankly at the television.

'Drink, Edward?

He started. 'Oh, a cup of tea would be nice, thank you.'

Angie went to put on the kettle. Edward was so pale she wondered if he was coming down with something.

'You must be excited about going home!' Angie said. The only information she'd been able to prise out of Edward about his family life was that he came from a village called Haxby.

'Yeah.' He looked anything but.

'Will it just be you and your parents?'

'Um, my brother's going to be there as well. Angie, could I ask you a favour?'

'Of course, what is it?' She poured a cup of sugary tea and gave it to Edward, trying to think what there was in the fridge that she could give him to eat.

'I was wondering if it would be OK with you— well, you and Freddie—if I stayed here. For Christmas, I mean. I wouldn't bother you,' he said hurriedly, seeing the surprise on her face. 'I'd just feel better being here with Nobby: you know, with the race coming up.'

'Won't your parents mind?'

'Mum might be a bit upset, but I'll explain.' His hands were twisting round the mug. 'Honestly, you won't know I'm here, I'll not get in your way.'

'I *want* you to get in my way!' she exclaimed. 'Edward, of course you can stay here. You know that's perfectly fine with Fred and me.'

He looked relieved. 'Great.'

'There's one condition. You must have Christmas lunch with us,' she said, mock-sternly. 'I'm not having you out there eating one of those horrible microwave meals.'

For the second time since she'd known him, Edward smiled. *It made such a difference*, she thought. It softened the sharp angles, the purplish wary eyes. He suddenly looked rather sweet.

'OK then. Thanks.' He jumped as Avon shoved a wet nose on his lap. A big pink tongue came out and took a lick of his jodhpurs.

'I think you've got a fan there,' Angie said. 'Avon is very particular who he slobbers over.'

Edward looked rather pleased.

CHAPTER THIRTY-FIVE

It was the fifth dress that clinched it. Kizzy had bought it from ASOS in the summer, but hadn't had the chance to wear it. Cobalt-blue and above the knee, it had frilled cap sleeves and a V-neck that showed just enough. Next up, accessories. How about her big Topshop gold hoops? Kizzy smiled. Probably too ghetto for the likes of Javier Hamilton-Scott and co. Instead she picked out a

221

delicate wishbone necklace, a twenty-first present from her parents. Her blonde locks were loose around her shoulders, extra-shiny from the Aussie hair pack she'd put on in the bath. In an ideal world Kizzy would have booked herself in for a manicure, but she'd forgotten; too involved with Nobby again. She'd just have to put on a few layers of Barry M nail varnish and hope it distracted people from seeing the scrubby bits.

She was scrabbling around in the back of her wardrobe for her only clutch bag when her mum called up the stairs.

'Kiz, your mobile's going!'

'Coming!' she yelled. She met Bev on the top step and took the phone. 'Ta.' It was a private number.

'Hello?' she said as she walked back into her bedroom.

'Am I speaking to Kizzy Milton?' The man's voice was precise, familiar.

'Yes, that's me.' She sat down on the bed, careful to avoid the dress laid out on her rumpled duvet.

'This is Nigel Bennett, Javier Hamilton-Scott's private secretary.'

'Oh,' said Kizzy. She suddenly found it hard to breathe.

'Mr Hamilton-Scott would like to know if you have transport arranged for this evening.'

'Transport? Er, I was going to drive over. If that's all right?'

'That won't be necessary. We can send a chauffeur to pick you up.' He recited her address. 'Is that correct?'

'Yes, that's correct,' Kizzy said, struggling to take it in. Javier Hamilton-Scott was sending a chauffeur

222

to pick her up!

'Excellent. Thomas will be with you at six thirty, on the dot.'

Kizzy hung up and flopped back on to her bed. OMG! She felt like a celebrity. Javier must be spending some money on this party.

She lay there for a moment, imagining herself stepping gracefully out of a limousine on to the red carpet, where Javier waited, dark and dashing in a dinner jacket, to take her arm.

This was swiftly followed by a big reality check. *What has got into you?* she said to herself. She had to get her head screwed on properly for tonight, because right now the swarm of butterflies in her stomach was threatening to rise up and overwhelm her.

*   *   *

Her tight-covered legs were sliding all over the silky leather seats. She'd never been in a Bentley before, and the car was as vast on the inside as it had seemed when it had pulled up outside her house. She'd been surprised to see that Thomas, the chauffeur, only looked her age, but he had impeccable manners and had been there with the passenger door open as she'd walked down the path.

Kizzy checked her clutch bag again for her mobile phone. She knew it was there, but suddenly she was in need of something familiar, something that kept her close to home. Her dad, already antsy about Kizzy going to this party, had *not* been happy about the new development. Her mum, on the other hand, had been as excited as a schoolgirl.

223

'You must text me as soon as you get there, tell me what it's like. Oh, Kiz, you look absolutely beautiful.'

Even her dad had agreed on that one. Kizzy usually found compliments awkward, but she had to admit, she felt good. The dress brought out the blue in her eyes perfectly, her hair lying like a sheet down her back. She crossed one shapely leg over the other, and hoped to God her pointed stilettos didn't give her blisters, like they had the last time she'd worn them.

Ahead of her, Thomas was handling the car seamlessly. Wanting a bit of human contact, she leant forward.

'Do you work for Javier full-time, Thomas?'

'Only when Mr Hamilton-Scott needs me.' His accent was local. 'I'm at college.'

She noticed that none of Javier's employees seemed to refer to him by his first name. She made a mental note not to be overfamiliar when she spoke to him herself.

'What are you studying?'

'Equine dentistry.'

'Hoping for a job with Mr Hamilton-Scott afterwards?' she asked a bit cheekily.

Thomas's eyes met hers in the rear-view mirror. 'I bloody hope so!'

Kizzy settled back and tried to enjoy the ride. After all, it wasn't every day you got driven around in a Bentley. It was only when they approached the hamlet of Badger's Mount that she began to feel anxious. She leant forward again.

'Big do, is it?'

'Pretty big. When Mr Hamilton-Scott does things, he doesn't do them by halves.'

Great. Now she felt even more nervous. What was the matter with her? Normally you could put her in a room and she could talk to anyone.

She suddenly remembered Javier's rugged face, the charisma so potent you could bottle it. *Oh God.* Maybe she shouldn't have come. She didn't belong here. But it was too late to back out now: they were turning into the entrance. Thomas pressed a button on his key ring and the gates slid open. She could see nothing ahead, except a smooth winding road leading into darkness.

Around the first bend there were lights marking the way, and pretty soon Kizzy could see the glow of Homelands laid out in front of her. It was even more impressive than she'd imagined. On the left stood the stately home, a huge square-shaped building with a flag flying from the pole on the roof. It was a masterpiece of golden stone, the two rows of long wide windows giving the place an imperious symmetry. The front porch was the size of a small house alone, with two large white pillars flanking its flight of steps. The whole thing was stunning, but Kizzy couldn't imagine living there. She'd feel swallowed up.

To the right of the house, down a rolling slope, was something Kizzy found more appealing. The world-renowned equestrian centre. Even from a distance it looked like some set-up. A white American-style ranch sat in the middle of the complex, complete with arched entrance and clock tower. Sprawled round it were long, low-roofed buildings and immaculate paddocks.

Thomas broke his placid silence. 'Something else, isn't it?'

Kizzy could only nod as they glided down the

drive. There were lots of cars already parked to the right of the house, and a man in a black outdoor jacket directing drivers into spaces.

'Didn't everyone get picked up, then?' she asked. 'Just you.'

Then they were pulling up in front of the house. Up close, Homelands was even more intimidating. People were milling about on the steps: two men in evening wear and a woman in a long black dress. Kizzy noticed how the woman's dress fell ever-so-elegantly off the edge of the step. Feeling more self-conscious than ever, she tugged at her hemline. She should have stuck to black.

Thomas was already at her door, opening it. Trying to remember what she'd read in celebrity magazines about making a dignified exit from a car, Kizzy clamped her legs together and turned sideways on the leather seat. Thomas offered a hand as she got out.

'Thanks.' Kizzy looked up. 'Wowzers,' was all she could muster up to describe one of the most stunning homes in Gloucestershire. *Nice one, Kiz, great command of the English language you've got there.*

'Kizzy Milton?' A small, neat man materialized beside her, looking as dapper and sleek as a baby seal in his dinner jacket. 'I'm Nigel Bennett.'

'Nigel, hi!' Kizzy took his hand and in her nervousness enthusiastically pumped it.

He allowed himself a small smile. Despite his reserve, Javier's secretary had kind eyes. 'Please, come with me.'

She followed him up the stairs, aware on every step just how much her dress rode up, exposing toned thigh. At the top Nigel turned to her just as

226

she was giving it another surreptitious tug. As if it could miraculously grow two inches longer!

Nigel stood aside. 'After you.'

Lifting her chin high, Kizzy walked in.

First impressions: the ceilings were *high*. She was in an entrance hall with a wide sweeping staircase going up to the first floor. Doors led off everywhere; through the one to Kizzy's left she could see a drawing room filled with the sort of furniture you saw in those costume dramas on telly. Guests stood around chatting and laughing while discreet waiters passed through, topping up champagne glasses. Kizzy did a quick scan of the crowd, but there was no sign of her host. He must be meeting and greeting somewhere.

She took stock of her surroundings. The place was beautiful, if a little forbidding. Those soaring arched ceilings dwarfed even the enormous chandeliers. Kizzy noticed that all the gold-framed paintings on the walls were of animals: beautiful horses and proud hunting dogs.

Aside from the tall, well-dressed tree by the stairs, the house didn't have much else in the way of Christmas decorations. But what the place lacked in sparkle, the crowd made up for. The dressage lot clearly liked their bling. There were acres of legs and cleavage on show; the girls wore big jewels and the boys glittery stock-pins. Several of the men were wearing white tie; one tall guy had even accessorized with a diamanté bow tie. Was it real? Kizzy couldn't think how much it had cost. Mistaking her astonishment for something else, the man gave Kizzy a wolfish grin. She recognized him as one of the Great Britain dressage team, and managed a polite smile back.

The GB rider dropped her a suggestive wink. Just then a furious-faced battleaxe of a woman in unfashionable tartan taffeta barged over and started bending the man's ear. Kizzy turned away. The last thing she wanted to do was get dragged into a domestic.

The babble of voices was deafening: an incongruous mix of clipped upper-class vowels and peaty Yorkshire tones. Two men next to her—one sporting the ruddy face of a life spent outdoors—were talking loudly about a horse someone had just bought from Holland.

'. . . he got them down to seven million. I still think he paid over the odds, if you ask me.'

'Yes, but think what they could make if they breed from him . . .'

Kizzy raised an eyebrow. Seven million quid for a horse! She felt a light hand on her arm; Nigel was there with a champagne flute. Nerves made her take a bigger gulp than she'd meant to. For one terrifying moment the bubbles threatened to go down the wrong way.

'I've got some people I think you'll find interesting.' Kizzy felt a little twitch of excitement. She'd already spotted Oliver Foster, Javier's protégé and Olympic hope, across the room. It would be amazing to meet him.

For the next half hour Nigel took her on a whirlwind tour of the room. It was an intoxicating mix of sporting legends, and not just from the horse world. In one corner was the Olympics lot: 2012 chairman Sebastian Coe was looking sleek in a dinner jacket as he chatted to Dame Kelly Holmes. Kizzy was introduced to Oliver Foster, whose elfin looks were more suited to a choirboy than to a great dressage hope; a famous racing commentator; an Olympic silver medallist for three-day eventing; and a tall, raffish-looking man who turned out to be Javier's personal physio. Amazingly, he seemed to know all about what had happened to Kizzy, and he even gave her his business card with instructions to call if she ever needed to. From the flirty look in his eye Kizzy wasn't sure if his interest was entirely professional, but she was flattered, anyway. Nigel had been discreetly watching from the sidelines and came over as the conversation wound up. He put a light hand on Kizzy's arm again. 'I'd like you to meet Sandy Powell now. I think you two will get along.'

Kizzy's eyes widened. Sandy Powell was a legendary jockey. After twice winning the Grand National, and four times the Cheltenham Gold Cup, he'd had a bad fall two seasons ago and retired. He was still a big name, and about as close to an idol as Kizzy could get.

'I can't!' she said. 'What am I going to say to him?'

'Why don't you start by comparing battle wounds?' came the dry reply.

It was easy to spot Sandy: he was five foot nothing and wearing a jaunty red and green bow tie. Kizzy thought he might be a bit arrogant, but he turned out to be lovely, and forty minutes later they were still deep in conversation. As well as being a supreme jockey Sandy was also a world-class gossip, and he had her in fits of laughter by telling scandalous stories about the people in the room: like the sixtysomething trainer fresh out of rehab for cocaine addiction, and the two (married) male dressage riders who'd been having it off for years.

229

As Sandy started on another funny anecdote, she cast another surreptitious look round the room. Where was Javier? A few times out of the corner of her eye she thought she'd seen his dark head, and occasionally she was certain she'd smelt his distinctive aftershave. But then she'd turn and he wouldn't be there, so she assumed she was imagining things or that what she'd seen had been a trick of the light.

Maybe she *was* seeing stuff. Sandy had been grabbing the champagne guy every time he'd passed and Kizzy was starting to feel a bit drunk. Any more alcohol, and she'd trip in her heels and make a complete idiot of herself.

By now there were several people circling Sandy. Excusing herself, Kizzy went off to find the toilet. The place was thinning out now, as everyone started to leave. She checked her watch. A quarter to nine. The party finished in fifteen minutes. She felt dismayed: the possibility that she'd talk to Javier was diminishing by the second.

'Do you know where the Ladies is?' she asked a passing waitress. The girl smiled and pointed to a door two feet away, clearly marked 'Ladies'.

'D'oh!' Kizzy said. 'Thanks.'

Pushing it open she found herself in a long corridor stretching away to the back of beyond. The first door on the left was open, and she could hear female voices.

'What does he do, rattling round here by himself?'

'God knows. Poor Javier. Tell you, though, if I wasn't happily married . . .'

A screech of laughter. 'Pippa, you are dreadful!'

The two women in front of the mirror stopped as

230

Kizzy walked in. 'Do excuse us,' said the nearest, a stocky sort with an ample bosom, as she hustled her friend out.

So she wasn't the only one wondering about Javier. Kizzy looked at herself in the mirror. Her cheeks were slightly flushed from the alcohol, her eyes heavy-lidded and glittery. Gulping down a few restorative mouthfuls of water from the tap, she reapplied her lipgloss. Deliberating whether her hair looked smarter up, Kizzy decided it was a lost cause and left it as it was. Grabbing her bag, she walked out.

She was so busy trying to shut the dodgy clasp that she banged straight into someone coming the other way. Balance already off-kilter, Kizzy felt her feet go from under her and toppled forward, straight into a side table on the other side of the corridor. She bounced off it against the wall and could only watch helplessly as a porcelain vase on the table wobbled and fell, smashing into a thousand pieces on the ground.

Shit, shit, shit! It was probably a priceless family heirloom. Kizzy looked up, ready to beg the person's silence while she tried to work out what to do. This was a disaster!

Instead she was confronted by the implacable black eyes of Javier Hamilton-Scott.

CHAPTER THIRTY-SIX

Time stopped as Kizzy stared at the man who'd invaded her thoughts over the past few weeks. The man whose precious possession now lay smashed to smithereens between them. It was an apt metaphor for her ability to mess things up.

In one movement he was reaching down. 'Are you all right?'

Kizzy tried to catch her breath. Her hand was more sore than anything, from where she'd put it out to stop herself falling.

'Yeah, I think . . .' She felt herself being pulled up effortlessly to standing.

'Your back?' He still had hold of her arm.

Kizzy shifted gingerly. 'I think it's all right.'

As soon as she said it, Javier stepped back. His eyes flickered down to the pieces of patterned china on the floor.

'Oh God, I'm so sorry.' Kizzy had never been more mortified. 'I'll pay for that, of course.'

His gaze held her prisoner. Javier's thick dark hair was brushed back, showing off his strong nose and face. Even in a smart tuxedo there was something wild about him, the powerful shoulders untamed. Like a lion dressed in silk clothing, Kizzy thought. *Or a wolf.* A shiver rippled through her. Just sharing the same physical space was electrifying.

The dark pools were still, assessing her. 'It's fine.'

'It's not. God!' Kizzy had completely sobered up. '*Is* it expensive?' she asked, hoping for a no.

'Very. You've done me a favour, I've always hated it.' He didn't look too cross. 'I can claim it back on my household insurance. Perfect timing, really, I've got my eye on this new horse.'

Kizzy remembered reading somewhere that Javier's last acquisition had cost him eight hundred grand. Eight hundred *grand*! She glowed like a light bulb with shame.

'Would you like to take a walk?'

'What?' He changed the subject so fast it was hard to keep up.

'I need some fresh air; I was wondering if you'd like to join me.'

'Er, your chauffeur is meant to be taking me home in a minute.'

Javier picked up her bag and handed it to her. 'He'll wait.'

*   *   *

The corridors were so wide they could walk comfortably side by side. Not that comfortable was a word Kizzy would have used to describe how she was feeling right now, as Javier strode out beside her, on the long muscular legs that made him look so good atop a horse. It felt like they walked down a mile of mahogany wood hung with paintings, the occasional feel of soft rugs under her feet, before they came to a back door.

'Do you have something to put on?' His gaze flickered over her bare arms.

'You mean a coat? I don't have a smart one, my mum's always on at me to get one, but I don't see the point, as I'd never have the chance to wear it much. I know it's stupid, in this weather . . .'

She was rambling, her mouth a jumble of nerves. *Shut up, you idiot.*

He turned to a coat rack by the door and pulled out something. 'Try this.' Kizzy took the wool blazer; it was moss green, a faint smell of expensive aftershave lingering on its silk collar. It swamped her diminutive frame, and she immediately felt warmer.

'Thanks,' she said shyly.

He pulled the door open, making her start. 'This way. Mind your step.'

They passed through a walled garden area with a very professional-looking vegetable patch, to another door on the other side. Beyond it was open parkland, a rolling canvas stretched out across the countryside. The lights from the equestrian centre glowed in the distance.

Javier gave a low whistle, and out of the darkness his two dogs came bounding up. Pablo and Salvador. It was as if they'd been waiting for him. They circled Kizzy and Javier protectively, as lean and muscular as their master.

'Don't you worry about them running off?' she asked. They were hunting dogs after all, designed to track and search.

'They wouldn't.'

The two hounds ran off ahead, their ears flattened, like black devils. Javier started after them, his hands in his pockets. Kizzy had to watch her step; heels and dark fields were not a good combination.

'Did you have a good time tonight?' she asked, swearing silently as her heel sank into another muddy clump.

'I could think of better ways to spend my evenings, but with the Olympics so near, the sponsors were keen. After all, they have a say in all this.' He made an elaborate hand movement towards the centre.

'Are you nervous?'

He swivelled his head, hawklike. 'About what?'

She quailed under his stare. 'The Olympics. It must be pretty mental competing in them.' *God,*

234

why did everything coming out of her mouth sound so stupid?

'I don't get caught up in that. Sport is all about politics these days.' He looked at her again. 'Do you have tickets for anything?'

'No, I didn't apply in time. I would have loved to have seen some of the athletics.'

'Leave it with me, I might be able to sort something.'

'Really? Oh, wow, that would be amazing . . .' *All I seem to do to this man is apologize to him or thank him.*

'What are your plans for Christmas?'

She was just beginning to get her head round the random turns the conversation was taking. 'I'm spending it at home with my parents. My older brother Dan is away in Afghanistan, a captain in the Royal Artillery.'

'Front line?'

'No, but he could be sent there any moment.'

'Bravery obviously runs in the family.'

What did he mean by that? She glanced across, but Javier was staring fixedly ahead.

'That must be very hard,' he said.

'Mmm, yeah.' She tried not to dwell on the subject. 'Mum worries, but you've got to be positive, haven't you? Dan doesn't need us adding to his stress; he's got enough going on out there.' Her words melted away into the night.

'How is the training going?'

'Training?'

Javier cocked a dark eyebrow. 'Your horse. You are still training him, aren't you?'

'Oh, sorry. We've—I mean Edward and Nobby—have got their first race up at Chaddesley Corbett

235

on the twenty-seventh.'

'Are you worried this Edward will replace you?'

'Of course I am,' she replied stiffly. That fear lurked constantly at the back of her mind, no matter how lovely Angie and Freddie were being. And Javier had just come out and articulated it.

'I've offended you,' he said.

'No, you haven't.' She sighed. 'It's happened, anyway. Edward's doing amazing things with Nobby.'

'I'm afraid I've rather lost my manners.' He gave a brief smile. It transformed his granite features, and Kizzy saw a glimmer of the man he must once have been. 'I spend too much time with animals these days,' he told her. 'You can be as rude as you want, and they don't answer back. It's probably why I prefer being around them.'

Kizzy grinned. 'I know what you mean!'

The tension started to ease. 'What are you doing for Christmas?' she asked.

'I'm away.'

Kizzy pushed her hands deeper into the pockets of the coat, feeling the silk lining. Who would Javier be having Christmas lunch with? He couldn't be short of offers.

They'd reached the main road into the equestrian centre now. To the left and right were the white-railed paddocks: flat, even and green even in winter. Javier carried on towards the entrance arch under the clock tower.

'Come on,' he told her. 'I'll show you round.'

*   *   *

The yards Kizzy was used to were dirty, loud, smelly

236

places but this was straight out of the pages of a glossy magazine. It was utterly immaculate: there were no telltale pieces of hay or horse droppings to suggest that animals were even being kept there. Javier showed her the wash-down bay for the horses after they'd exercised, which looked like a giant shower, and the solar room, where big red lamps were played on the animals to dry them and warm their muscles. The feed shed contained so many supplements and vitamins that it made Holland & Barrett look inadequate. As they walked round, Javier pointed out the rubber matting covering every walkway and surface. 'So the horses never have to stand on concrete,' he explained. 'It's better for their legs.'

It reminded Kizzy of going on those travelators at Heathrow airport. This place was a byword for luxury and glamour, where horses were treated like kings and queens, never destined to tread on anything as mundane as concrete or grass.

The indoor arena was just as impressive, with mirrors adorning each wall so a rider could check his or her position, and a viewing gallery. Then there was the office, the head groom's cottage, the gleaming eight-seat Oakley horsebox Javier used as a 'runaround', as he told Kizzy. The sheer opulence of everything was dazzling.

The biggest building was the huge barn where the horses were stabled. It was a vast, airy place with a line of stalls running down each side. The lights were turned down low as they walked in. Kizzy looked up and her mouth dropped open. There, hanging from the ceiling, fifty foot up, was the biggest chandelier she'd ever seen.

'Oh my God, what is that?'

Javier followed her gaze. 'I must admit I had my reservations, but the Americans love that kind of thing. It all helps the business.'

'You've got a chandelier in your stables?' Kizzy laughed out loud. 'That's hilarious!'

Immediately, she worried she'd gone too far, but Javier's lips twitched subtly. 'It is a little over the top.'

There was the sound of a big body moving in the nearest stall, and then a gold-coloured head appeared over the door. Javier walked across and rubbed the horse's pale pink nose.

'This is Morning Sun, or Deirdre, as the grooms have named her.'

Kizzy went over and stood by him. 'She's really beautiful.'

'She's a warmblood, Hanoverian. Fantastic breeding potential.'

Kizzy could immediately see the difference between her and a thoroughbred. Racehorses carry all their power in their behinds, their necks long and low. Deirdre was the opposite: all her power and muscle was in her shoulders and high neck. Kizzy remarked on this to Javier.

'That's because the mechanics are different. You ride for speed, whereas with us it's all about here.' He patted the horse's front. 'For dressage, they need to be able to engage and collect, for rounds at a time. Their energy is in the absolute control of movement.'

Javier was like a different man down here: his defences were down, and he was relaxed and animated. It was clearly where he felt at home. Like everything else, the stables were spotless; their occupants were warm and toasty in thick night

238

rugs, big hay nets hanging from the walls. Although it was undeniably beautiful, Javier's stately home lacked the love and care that had been poured into this place. Kizzy thought she would prefer being down here, as well.

There were eleven horses in total, including Javier's old stallion, Gypsy King, who was just as impressive in retirement—and a poor knackered-looking piebald called Arthur. Javier had found the terrified horse tethered at the side of a main road and rescued him.

In one of the stalls towards the end was a gorgeous Arab mare with a fine head. She was resting on a back hoof, and even in the dim light Kizzy could see the scars on her swollen front knees.

'Aphrodite, Sarah's horse,' Javier said. 'She was riding her when the accident happened. Aphrodite broke her knees, but we got the best vet on board and managed to get her sound again. She can't be ridden any more so we've put her out to pasture.'

It was said very matter-of-factly. Kizzy suddenly had an awful vision of Aphrodite stumbling and going down, Sarah being catapulted over the horse's head . . .

A low whinny sounded from the end stable. Javier smiled. 'All right, Dream, we're coming.' As they walked down, a gleaming unicorn-white head appeared imperiously over the metal door.

Kizzy exhaled. In the flesh, Love's Dream was even more gorgeous. Eighteen hands of sheer muscle, the stallion could have been carved out of marble if he hadn't had such a haughty look in his big dark eyes.

'He is seriously gorgeous. Oh, wow, Javier!'

He seemed happy with her delight. 'He's quite something, isn't he? Vain as hell. We were thinking about putting a full-length mirror on the wall for him.'

'You might as well,' she said cheekily. 'The Americans would love it.'

Javier grinned, the sudden vivacity in his face making Kizzy's heart quicken. Bored of his audience, Dream manoeuvred his huge body round and shifted to the back of the stable.

They continued to stand and look.

'He comes from an impeccable bloodline,' Javier remarked. 'His sire is Bismarck III, one of the best breeding stallions in the world.'

Kizzy had read all about Love's Dream, but the knowledgeable questions she'd planned to ask faded away. She could see the rise and fall of her own chest: she was taking short, sharp little breaths. Javier's arms were resting on the top of the door, his right elbow a millimetre from hers. As he shifted slightly, Kizzy allowed herself a sideways look. His bow tie was now undone—when had he done that?—and hanging down either side of his collar. Kizzy caught a flash of brown skin, a glimpse of the solid chest underneath. She turned away quickly. Her heart was banging so hard it felt like a drum beating in the darkness. Surely he could hear . . .

'Thank you for coming.' He directed the words into the horsebox.

'Thank you for inviting me.'

'You're a breath of fresh air; believe me. You've no idea how much I hate things like this. Nigel will be furious I'm not there to wish everyone on their merry way, but I don't care.'

240

His voice turned brittle. 'I see it, you know: how everyone looks, the panic in their eyes when they're left alone with me. No one knows what to say. If I was a widower, or even a divorcee, it would be easier. At least people could mutter their commiserations or offer words of encouragement.'

'I'm sure people do care.' Kizzy couldn't believe Javier was opening up to her.

'They don't want to know. In the last three years barely one of these people, my so-called friends or business associates, has asked after my wife. They don't dare mention Sarah's name, as if she's some sort of bloody ghost.'

'It must be really difficult for you,' Kizzy said softly. She hesitated, wondering how far to push it. 'How is she? Sarah, I mean.'

Instantly she knew she'd said the wrong thing. Javier's face darkened. 'She's in a bloody coma. What do you think?'

Kizzy went bright red. 'I didn't mean to pry.'

An excruciating silence followed. Javier sighed and shook his head. 'You weren't prying. Forgive me, Kizzy. It's been a long night.'

The air had gone flat, the sexual tension evaporated. *If it had even been there in the first place.* Was this just some stupid schoolgirl crush, was she just imagining he felt something for her?

Javier looked round. 'Let's go and find Thomas and get you home.'

Kizzy watched him stride off towards the entrance. She felt utterly miserable. What must he think? She'd just made a really stupid remark to someone she barely knew, who had suffered a loss she couldn't start to comprehend.

Pulling the jacket tighter, Kizzy trailed after him.

241

CHAPTER THIRTY-SEVEN

The next day, Kizzy dragged herself out of bed with a thumping headache and had to cope with Slade's 'I Wish It Could Be Christmas Everyday' blasting out of the radio in the kitchen. Her mum wanted to know all about the evening: what Javier's house had been like, what famous people had been there.

There were more questions at the yard. Angie wanted to hear everything.

'Did you talk to Javier?'

'For a bit. He was pretty busy, though.'

'I can't believe you met Sandy Powell! I've heard he's a complete hoot.'

'He was pretty funny.'

'Did you tell him he's got competition with our Nobby?'

Kizzy smiled wanly.

'Are you all right?' Angie studied her. Despite the fact she'd been to one of the most exclusive Christmas parties in the country, Kizzy seemed rather subdued.

'Yeah, I'm cool. A bit hungover.' She changed the subject. 'Is Edward out with Nobby?'

'Yes, they went off a while ago.'

'I'll go and start mucking out, then.'

Angie watched her trudge across the yard. 'Come over for a drink later, won't you? It is Christmas Eve.'

Kizzy managed a smile. 'Great, see you then.'

*　　　*　　　*

242

'I think there's something going on with Kizzy.' Angie brought up the subject that evening as she sat with Freddie in the living room, sharing a festive bottle of bubbly. Three dogs snoozed happily on the rug in front of the fire. They were looking after Buster for Clementine while she was away in Antigua.

'Hmm?' Freddie had one eye on the television, watching a documentary about the North Pole.

'Kizzy. She's definitely not herself.'

'Mmm.'

'Do you want the lap-dance now or later?'

'Mmm.'

'Freddie!'

Her husband reluctantly dragged his eyes away. 'What's that, my love?'

'Kizzy. Don't you think she was a bit flat earlier?'

'I thought she just looked tired, that's all.'

'Maybe.' Angie weighed up the situation. 'I wonder if it's getting to her: the first race coming up.'

'Our Kizzy's an optimist. I'm sure she'll be OK.'

Angie bit her lip, wondering whether to say anything about Javier. Freddie would only say she was reading too much into everything. Abandoning her husband to his programme, she got up and went next door. The kitchen looked like a Red Cross food station: every surface was covered with poultry, game, cheeses, charcuterie, bread, chocolate logs, and a full-to-the-brim fruit bowl. Used to Archie and his mammoth appetite, Angie had overspent hugely on the food bill this year. They'd be eating pigs in blankets and pheasant for months to come.

Her thoughts had just returned to Kizzy when

there was a shout from next door. 'That was a bloody knock-on, ref!'

The dogs started barking. Moments later there was a crash.

'Freddie? What's happened?' God, she hoped it wasn't the Victorian rosewood table she'd just put in there . . .

'Nothing, darling!' her husband called back. 'Buster just got a bit excited and caught the bottle with his tail. Lucky we'd finished most of it . . .'

Sighing, Angie went to get a cloth. Maybe Christmas wouldn't be that quiet after all.

CHAPTER THIRTY-EIGHT

Christmas Day

Angie woke early. It was still dark in the bedroom, and Freddie was snoring gently beside her the way he always did when he'd had too much cheese and port. She gave a yawn and looked at the alarm clock. Six thirty. Time to get up soon, anyway.

'Merry Christmas, darling,' she whispered, dropping a kiss on his head. He grunted contentedly and muttered something about algebra. They'd had two rather large nightcaps after getting in from Midnight Mass, and Angie's head was fuzzy as she made her way into the en suite. Sitting on the loo, she looked out of the window.

It all looked rather magical. Dawn hadn't yet broken, the beginnings of colour starting far away on the horizon. There had been a heavy frost overnight, and the garden and fields beyond were blanketed in dense white as an ethereal morning mist rose up from the ground.

Angie's hangover felt less painful already. Savouring the view a few moments longer, she flushed the chain and went back through to the bedroom. Freddie started to stir as she was putting on her dressing gown.

'Merry Christmas, my love,' he said sleepily.

'You, too.' She went over and kissed him. 'I'm just going to let the dogs out.'

'Be down soon.'

'It's fine, have a lie-in,' she said, opening the door. At the other end of the hallway was Archie's bedroom. Angie liked to keep the door open; even though Archie hadn't really lived there since he'd gone off to college, seeing his possessions made her feel close to him.

But the room made her melancholy today. Normally there would be a big lump under the duvet, and clothes scattered over the floor from Archie's boozy Christmas Eve out with his friends. She felt an unexpected lump in her throat.

You silly woman. Archie had his own life now, and it was perfectly understandable that he wanted to do his own thing. She was just going to have to get used to it. Besides, they were speaking to him later. Feeling brighter at the thought of hearing all about his day, Angie went down the stairs. At the bottom she was about to turn left as normal when something caught her eye in the living room. She turned to look.

'What the *hell*?'

*   *   *

'At least he didn't actually eat anything,' she said

245

later, as they sat surrounded by presents. Buster had somehow got out of the kitchen in the night and decided to open the gifts under the tree himself. Angie had come down to a sea of wrapping paper and a very sheepish Labrador.

'He's obviously been taking escape tips from Nobby,' Freddie said. He picked up a small object in the shape of an aeroplane. 'What's this?'

Angie looked up from the Crabtree & Evelyn bath set Clementine had given her. 'Oh, that's just something silly for your office, Freds. You don't have to use it.'

'Of course I'll use it, darling! A Red Arrow fountain pen is just what I need.'

Angie smiled at her husband across the living room. They'd promised not to spend too much on each other this year, but Freddie had been as thoughtful and generous as ever with his presents. Along with a facial at the hugely expensive spa at Daylesford, he'd bought her a lovely French bra and knicker set. Freddie had always had excellent taste in underwear.

He gave her a white envelope. 'I've got one more little thing for you,' he said.

'But I've had all my presents!' She slid her thumb under the back flap. 'You spoil me far too much.'

It took a moment for her to realize what the tickets were for. 'Oh my God!' she shrieked. 'How did you get these?' The dressage for the Olympics had sold out months ago.

'They're the right ones, aren't they?'

'They're absolutely perfect. And they're for the last day!' Tickets for the prestigious Grand Prix individual freestyle and victory ceremony were the rarest of all. Angie leapt up and jumped on her husband's lap. 'A million, billion thank yous! How on earth did you get hold of them?'

He kissed her shoulder. 'Let's just say I have friends in high places.'

'You really are the best husband in the world. Am I squashing you?'

'Only a little, but I like it.' He nuzzled his face into her chest. 'How about a preview of my Christmas present?'

She kissed him fervently. 'Later, I promise.' She climbed off; there were a million and one things to do. 'I must go and say Happy Christmas to Edward.'

'Tell him from me as well. I'll go and start peeling the parsnips.'

*   *   *

When Angie returned from taking a Buck's Fizz to Edward, the kitchen was empty. A pile of untouched parsnips lay on the kitchen sink. Freddie must have gone for his morning constitutional. Angie was about to start on them herself when she heard Fred's voice, low, coming from the hallway. She caught the tail end of a throaty chuckle as he stood leaning against the doorway of his study, his back to her.

'Freds?' It wouldn't be Archie he was talking to; they hadn't planned to speak until later.

Her husband whirled round. For the first time in their marriage Angie caught a glimpse of something in his eye. Guilt.

'Thank you, then. Put me down for a dozen,' he spluttered, and hung up.

'Who was that, Freds? You just cut them off!'

He was looking anywhere but at her. 'Oh, just

one of the rugby lads. I was, er, just asking him to, er, get me some tickets.'

'On Christmas morning?'

'These games get booked up super-quick!' Planting a hasty kiss on her cheek, he hurried past her. Angie followed him back into the kitchen and watched as he put the French maid apron on, the one that always made her laugh.

'Freds,' she said, half-smiling. 'Are there any more presents I should know about?'

'What's that? No, I'm afraid that's your lot there.'

'Oh.' What on earth was it all about, then?

Freddie whacked up Frank Sinatra on the CD player and went over to the sink, humming. Feeling her eyes on him, he looked up and smiled evasively. 'Are you all right, darling?'

'Perfectly.' It was clear she wasn't going to get any more out of him. 'You're not having an affair, are you?' she asked jokingly.

He stopped mid-peel and started spluttering. 'Good Lord! Why on earth would you say that?'

Angie hadn't been expecting such an over-reaction. 'Freds, I was only teasing!'

'I should think so, too!' He still wouldn't meet her eye.

Something was definitely up. Angie opened her mouth, and then thought better of it. It was Christmas. Casting a final curious look at her husband, she went upstairs to get changed.

*　　　*　　　*

By the time the horses had been given their Christmas puddings made from bran and molasses

248

and put to bed, it was past 4 o'clock. It was already dark again as the three of them sat in the living room enjoying an aperitif.

'Thanks for my plant, Edward, it's so pretty,' Angie said. She'd been rather touched when he'd presented her with a potted hydrangea from the local garden centre, done up in a festive red bow. Freddie had been given a bottle of Tesco's own-brand rum, which he'd accepted so graciously one would never have known he hated the stuff. He was gallantly working his way through a glass of it now, with a long dash of soda.

'That's OK.' A shy blush. 'Thanks for my stocking.'

Angie smiled at Edward. 'It's only full of the silly little things I get Archie, but you might find something useful in there.'

Edward had turned down the offer of joining them for an alcoholic beverage, and Angie had fixed him a Virgin Mary instead. Buster, no longer *canis non grata*, was sat with his head on Edward's knee. Once he'd realized he was only in danger of being licked to death Edward had relaxed, even reaching down occasionally to pat Buster. When he did, his hand covered the dog's entire head.

'When's Clementine back?' Freddie asked. 'I bet the little sod's not as badly behaved with her.'

'Tomorrow. She told me she doesn't want to miss the big race. I don't think Clementine likes being away from her garden for too long, anyway. You know how older people are.'

Freddie looked out at the black windows. 'They're probably pulling crackers on the terrace right now.'

'Archie seemed well when we spoke, didn't

249

he?' Angie said. Their son had phoned earlier as promised, on a very crackly line from some house party. He'd sounded more than a little merry.

'Time of his life!'

'Oh well.' Angie sat back with her drink. She smiled at Edward. 'Arch is really looking forward to meeting you. I've told him all about the wonderful work you've done with Nobby.'

She watched him look down into his drink. Meeting new people wasn't Edward's forte, but Angie wasn't too worried. Archie was so easy-going he could get on with anybody.

They sat there for a few minutes, listening to the hiss and crackle from the fireplace. 'They say we might get snow.' It was probably only the third time Angie had heard Edward open a conversation.

She raised an eyebrow. 'Do they, darling? Heavens, I hope it keeps off before the race!'

'Nobby can run in anything.' It was true: hard going, soft ground, even wet and boggy. Nothing seemed to stop those dinner-plate hooves of his.

Angie laughed. 'All the same. We don't want any extreme weather.' Heaven forbid the race got cancelled after all this!

The smell of goose was mouth-watering. 'Not long to go now, chaps,' she told them. 'I'd better go and put the rest of the veggies on.'

Freddie patted his stomach. 'Oh, I'm looking forward to this! I've been practically starving myself all day.'

'What about the smoked salmon you polished off about half an hour ago?' Angie teased.

'A mere appetizer!'

'Can I help?' Edward asked.

'No, darling, you sit there and relax.' It was just

250

nice to see him there, warm and content.

Angie noticed her husband look at his watch again. He'd been checking it like a nervous twitch. 'Everything OK, Fred?'

'Yes, yes,' he said distractedly. 'Tell you what, I'll go and chuck another log on the fire in the dining room.'

'You've only just stoked it.'

'You never know.' He leapt up. 'I'll make sure we've got enough crackers out, as well.'

'I think you've *gone* crackers!' Rolling her eyes at Edward, Angie went to put the sprouts on.

*   *   *

An hour later they sat down to eat. The dining room looked magical: the fire was roaring away in the inglenook fireplace, and Christmas candelabras were glowing in both windows. They all took their places at the beautifully dressed table, Freddie at the head, Angie to his left. On the other side Edward was sitting in Archie's chair. All three were wearing their sparkly hats from the crackers, Edward's askew on his head as if it had just blown there by accident.

Angie looked across the huge mound of food. 'Heavens, we're going to need a week to get through this lot!'

Freddie was busy carving into the goose. 'Try a piece of this skin, Edward. It's jolly good.'

'Edward, help yourself,' Angie said. 'We've got roast parsnips, glazed carrots, oh, and that's pancetta and chestnuts in with the Brussels, in case you were wondering . . .'

Minutes later they were good to go. 'Freds, is

that all you're having?' Angie commented. It was odd that, after his initial enthusiasm her husband was suddenly dragging his feet, barely filling half his plate.

'Ah, yes,' he said. 'Just deciding what to go for first.'

'It'll get cold, darling, just dive in.' She watched him pick up a few more roast potatoes.

'Well?'

'Well, what?' he asked.

'Aren't you going to do the toast like last year?' He was acting all strange again.

'Of course, of course! Everyone got drinks? Good.' He raised his glass. 'Well, I'd like to welcome Edward to our table this year . . .'

'Hear hear!' interjected Angie.

'We wish you the best of luck for the race on Tuesday, son. Angie and I are very proud of what you've achieved with Nobby. Aren't we, darling? Why, when I first laid eyes on you . . .'

Two minutes later he was still going. Even Edward was starting to look a little baffled at this homage to him, especially when Freddie started going on about Patch, the first pony he'd ever had, and how it used to sail over seven-foot muck heaps.

Angie gave her husband a subtle nudge under the table. 'Darling, this is all very interesting, but do you think we could save it for after the toast?'

Freddie stopped. 'Sorry, got a bit carried away reminiscing.' His glass went up so slowly, it was like raising the Titanic. 'Well, I suppose really, then . . .'

'Oh, for heaven's sake!' Angie laughed. 'Just spit it out, Freds.' She held her glass up. 'Merry Christmas!'

'Starting without me?' drawled a deep voice from

the doorway.

CHAPTER THIRTY-NINE

Angie was in complete shock. Was this really her darling Archie standing in front of her, tall, shaggy-haired and disgustingly brown?

'You little horror!' she said, leaping on her son. 'I can't believe you didn't tell me!'

Her son grinned. 'Did you like my impression of being pissed at a party in Mangawhai? I was actually en route at Hong Kong airport.'

Angie couldn't believe it. 'How long have you known?' she asked Freddie.

'Only a few days. It's been bloody hard work keeping it from you!'

Angie looked up at her son. 'But why are you here? Has something happened?'

Archie rolled his eyes comically. 'Typical mum reaction, think the worst.' He kissed the top of her head. 'I just changed my plans, that's all. Decided I couldn't live without your Christmas dinner after all.'

She gave him another squeeze. 'This is the best Christmas present ever.'

'Hang on, you said that about my Olympic tickets!' teased Freddie.

Archie grinned at his father. 'Sorry, Pa, didn't mean to steal your thunder.'

Angie stepped back to look at her son again. God, he'd changed! Of course, he was still her Arch, but he was so much bigger and positively indecent with good health. The easy confidence he'd developed over the past few years was more than evident on his handsome face. His tan made Angie feel like a complete ghoul.

Archie raked big hands through his mop of brown hair. 'Excuse me if I look a bit of a mess. I've been travelling thirty hours straight.'

Angie hugged him again, barely able to get both arms round the newly broad torso. 'You look wonderful.'

In all the hullabaloo and dogs barking, Edward had been sitting quietly. 'I should go,' he said, getting up. 'I don't want to intrude.'

'No! Of course not!' Angie and Freddie chimed at the same time.

'I'm terribly sorry. How rude we've been!' Freddie said. 'Archie, this is Edward Cleverley. Edward, our son Archie.'

As Archie went up to Edward, Angie noticed how he held his own physically. Archie wasn't as tall as Edward—no one was—but he made up for it in width. Her son had certainly filled out doing all that manual labour.

'Pleased to meet you, mate,' he said, shaking Edward's hand. He got a faltering smile in return.

'Y-you, too.'

'Where's all your stuff, Archie?' Angie asked him. She'd already spotted the surfboard in the hallway.

'I dumped my rucksack in the kitchen.'

'I'll put a wash on later.'

'You'll do no such thing,' Freddie told her. 'It's Christmas Day! I'll go and get you a plate, Arch.'

'Perfect timing,' Archie said, rubbing his hands together. He went to sit in the spare seat. 'Wait until you've tried Mum's roast potatoes, Edward,

254

you'll never want to leave.'

The house had come alive again. Still recovering, Angie watched Archie sit down and nick a glazed parsnip from the serving dish. It was like he'd never left.

Freddie came back in and put a plate down in front of Archie. 'I put it in the microwave to warm up for a few seconds.'

'The same can't be said for our food. Eat, everyone, eat!' Angie urged.

'First, a toast.' Freddie raised his glass. 'Here's to making it four, and Archie coming home!'

'Hurrah!' They all clashed glasses. 'Merry Christmas!'

*   *   *

At Kizzy's everyone was slumped on the sofa watching television. 'Another Guylian?' her gran asked, offering the box from the other end of the sofa.

'Thanks, Nan, but I'm stuffed!' Kizzy seriously couldn't move. Why did her mum's homemade Christmas pudding have to be so good?

She stretched her feet out, the new stripy thermal socks a present from Angie. She'd had a really nice day: eating, playing board games with her dad, and chilling. Dan had even Skyped them from Afghanistan wearing a Santa hat, which had brought a smile to all of their faces. It was so lovely to see her big bro again.

An hour later Kizzy was getting twitchy. 'I might go for a walk.'

'Do you want me to come with you?' her dad asked. He looked very comfortable, with a plate of cold meats and a mince pie on his lap.

'I'll be fine, Dad. You stay there.'

She was in the hallway cupboard when she heard a new text beep on her phone. Putting her jacket on, Kizzy went into the kitchen to look at it. *'Hey, babe, just wanted to wish U a Merry Xmas. U going to NY? :) Bxx'*

Brett. She'd had a funny feeling her ex would text. Venue, a wine bar in town, was putting on a big fancy dress party. Lauren had got her a ticket, but she hadn't decided whether to go. She hadn't realized Brett would be going as well.

Kizzy put the mobile back on the kitchen table. She needed time to think how to reply to that one.

'Do you want me to take the rubbish out?' she yelled.

Her mum called back. 'Thanks, babe. Just watch your back!'

It had been twingeing a bit today. Probably all the lying around. Taking more care than usual, Kizzy carried the bin liner out to the front of the house. She'd have to do the exercises the physio gave her when she got back. They might be tedious, but there was no way Kizzy was hobbling around like an old lady on Edward and Nobby's big day.

Shakespeare Drive was quiet as she set off on her walk, identical scenes to her family's being played out in each living room window. It was a wonderfully clean, crisp night, with the kind of air that made you draw in deep, lung-clearing breaths. High above, the sky was a smooth velvet cloak, and Kizzy could make out the Plough, each star etched as clear as she'd ever seen it. *I wonder if Javier can see this.* He'd said he was going away, but she didn't know where. He might even be abroad, staying in some amazing city apartment or a five-star beach villa. A million miles away. What did it matter, anyway? She wasn't going to see him again.

It was nearly an hour later when Kizzy looked at her watch. The lawns and verges were already crunchy with frost, and that deep silence that you only got on Christmas Day hung over the town. Her mum would be getting worried. Taking the quick route back across the playing fields, Kizzy started for home.

As Kizzy approached her front door along the sleepy close she noticed a black shape in the porch. It was a large flat rectangular box, standing against the wall as if someone had placed it there.

Kizzy frowned. Was it discarded wrapping from a present? She couldn't remember anyone being given something in a black box. There was a little label in the bottom left hand corner. Kizzy bent down to read it. It had her name on it!

Picking the box up, she tested its weight. It felt like there was something substantial inside. She turned it over, looking for a sender's address, but there was nothing. The top of the box slid off easily and Kizzy found herself looking at a beautifully wrapped package. There was a logo on it, reading 'Air and Fire'. She knew that boutique, she'd been in there once on a shopping trip to Cheltenham. It was seriously expensive. Desperate to see what was inside, Kizzy tore at the paper.

And suddenly she was holding up the most exquisite wool trench coat. Midnight blue, it had two fashionably large pockets on the front, and a belted waist. It was the kind of coat you'd normally see in the pages of *Vogue*.

'Oh my God!' The beauty of the thing

overwhelmed her. Giddy with excitement, she pulled off her old Joules jacket and slipped the coat on. It fitted like a glove. Kizzy could feel the luxury melting into her. She did a little spin, checking out her reflection in the porch window.

Who would send me this? Hardly daring to hope, Kizzy looked inside the box. She couldn't see any card. Bemused and slightly disappointed, she was about to stand up when she noticed a small white square, lost in the wrapping paper at the bottom. She reached for it, heart in mouth. The simple message took her breath away.

Merry Christmas.
J

Kizzy closed her eyes, savouring the feel of the fabric. It was almost as if Javier had draped the coat over her himself, as if he were there now with his arms round her.

It was crazy, she hardly knew him. He was forty-two. He was married.

But there and then she knew she was in love.

CHAPTER FORTY

26 December
'I've missed you.'
    'I've missed you, too.'
    He nuzzled her fondly. 'Say it like you mean it.'
    'What are you going on about?' Calypso said.
    James's hand trailed over her honeyed shoulder. 'I'm only teasing. I wouldn't have missed me, either,

if I'd been in Antigua.'

'I can't believe you think I'd pick a tropical palm-fringed beach over the muddy fields of Churchminster.'

He chuckled and leant over to kiss her. They were in Calypso's bed, having completed the post-holiday, welcome-back shag. Her tan and her sun-streaked hair were radiant against the white duvet.

'Your eyes look amazing,' he told her.

'Do they?'

'Yes.' He propped himself up to have a better look. 'I mean, they're lovely anyway, but they've gone this amazing hazel colour. I can't stop staring at them.'

All these compliments were making her head spin. James had been looking at her like she was some sort of goddess since he'd got here, when in reality she was knackered and had a pot belly from scoffing down carb-heavy plane food. He was sweet, though.

'Oh, that reminds me. I bought you a present.' She slid out of bed and went over to her suitcase. Feeling guilty that she hadn't given James anything more for Christmas than a pair of comedy boxer shorts, after the lovely earrings he'd got her, she'd stopped in Duty Free on the way home. 'What the . . .? The little fucker!'

'What's happened?'

Calypso waved a remote control in James's face. 'It's the one for Mum and Dad's telly! Milo must have put it in my suitcase when I was packing. I knew he was up to something.'

'Uh-oh. Can you send it back?'

'It's probably cheaper to buy a new one.' Calypso

started laughing. 'Oh God, I bet they're looking for it right this moment. Daddy goes wild when he can't find things.'

She found what she was looking for, and came back to the bed. 'Happy belated Christmas. Sorry it's not wrapped.'

'You didn't have to get me anything.' He unwrapped the big bottle of Tom Ford aftershave and sprayed it on his neck. 'It's really nice, thanks.'

'Mmm, it is nice.' Elliot the rock musician had worn something similar. It was making Calypso feel a bit horny. She snuggled down beside James and wrapped one leg over his body.

He stroked her thigh. 'Tell me more about your holiday.'

'There's not much to tell, really. Everyone was on great form; the house was stunning. I just chilled out, sunbathed, slept, ate and drank loads. Watching Granny Clem learn to waterski was probably the highlight.'

'She's a bit old to be doing that, isn't she?'

'Don't let her hear you say that. She actually rocked it.'

'Wow. But no other gossip?'

Calypso got the distinct impression James was fishing. Did he not trust her or something? 'OK, then, I got ravished by a big Antiguan with a ten-foot dong.'

She watched his face drop. 'Don't say that.'

'Seriously? I was winding you up!' Oh God, he really didn't get her sense of humour!

'I just don't like you saying things like that.'

'OK, I was really writing love letters to you and sending them out to sea in a bottle.' Calypso grabbed the sports watch round his wrist and checked it. 'In fact, there should be one popping up in the village pond any time now.'

He couldn't help smiling. 'You're something else, you know that?'

'Is that a good or bad thing?'

'Good, I think. Hey, I've got something to ask: are you free this Friday? Mum and Dad are dying to meet you. I've told them all about you.'

She put her hand on his cock. 'Not everything, I hope.'

'Is that a yes?'

'It's a yes from me.' She felt him swelling and started to caress him with her fingers.

Blimey, meeting the parents. It must be getting serious.

*   *   *

At No. 1 Mill House, Caro and Benedict were collapsed on the sofa after a seriously long day that had started that morning in Antigua. With the tiredness from the time difference and the long journey, the kids' bedtime had been rather fractious.

'I hope Milo's speaking to me in the morning,' Caro said. When she'd eventually got her son into bed he'd turned to face the wall and refused to say good night.

'They'll be all right once they've had a good sleep and are back in their routine.'

'I hope so.' Rosie was behaving better, thank God, but Milo had acted up on holiday: telling Caro he hated her, and running off. Her family had kept telling her it was just a stage, but they didn't have to live with the stage twenty-four seven.

261

Benedict got up. 'There's a nice Merlot in the wine rack, do you fancy a glass?'

'Ooh, yes please. Benedict?' Her husband turned round, his handsome bronzed face glowing with health.

'Yes?'

'You don't think it has anything to do with Sebastian, do you?'

'In what way?' He had remained stoically reticent on the subject.

'Not in a bad way, just that Milo might be feeling a bit more unsettled than we thought. I mean, I have made a point of talking to him about it.'

'Little boys are amazingly resilient. As long as he's happy and feels secure with us, I'm sure he'll be fine.'

'You're right.' She worried too much.

Benedict gave her shoulders a quick rub and went into the kitchen. He came back a few moments later with a bottle and her mobile.

'You've got a text message.'

She read it and frowned. 'It's from Mummy. Why would I know where the remote control is?'

'Maybe it's your mother's sense of humour again.' He poured out two large glasses. 'Here, to our holiday.'

'Chin chin.' Caro took a sip. 'You know, I do feel like a new woman. I think it all just got on top of me before Christmas.'

'I'm sorry I haven't been here. You've done brilliantly.'

She smiled at him fondly. 'I'm not asking for a prize. Millions of women do what I do *and* work full-time.'

He took her free hand and kissed it. 'I know the

way things have been is not what we moved out here for, but it'll all be much better in the New Year, when the new creative director starts. Things will get back to normal.'

'I know.' She moved her hand to cup his face. 'Talking of New Year, I must go and pick up our tickets for the ball. Don't let me forget.'

One of Gloucestershire's biggest social events that year was being held at Clanfield Hall, a stately home on the outskirts of the village. The owners, Sir Ambrose and Lady Fraser, were putting on the ball to raise money for WaterAid. Anyone who was anyone was going.

Benedict put his arm round his wife. 'What time's Sebastian coming over?' As part of Milo's Christmas present Sebastian and Suzette were taking Milo to the pantomime in Cheltenham.

'Eleven, which gives us just enough time to get up to the race, and watch Nobby.' Caro rubbed her eyes. She could have done with staying at home and getting everything straight, but supporting their friends was important.

'Tired?' Benedict's hand brushed over her full breast.

'A little.'

He squeezed gently. 'Fancy going to bed?'

Caro smiled lazily. 'What did you have in mind?'

He leant in and whispered something, making her laugh. 'I'm not sure I've got the energy for that!'

'I'll do most of the work.' He got up. 'Let's make the most of the peace and quiet. I want to see that lovely naked body of yours.'

Caro let him pull her up. His hands felt hot and hard, deliciously tanned.

'Did I happen to mention how much I love you?' he murmured, kissing her deeply. 'Because I really do.'

He pushed the back of Caro's shirt up, touching soft, sun-kissed flesh.

'Mmm. I'd like to see more of that.'

A tan always made Caro feel thinner and sexier. 'If you play your cards right . . .'

'Oh yes?' One hand moved round to touch her warm bush.

They never made it past the fourth step.

CHAPTER FORTY-ONE

Race day dawned, cold and frosty. By seven o'clock everyone was up at the Maltings, the horsebox parked and ready out the front. Edward had already been out with Nobby when Angie had let the dogs out at six. Her attempts at cheery conversation had fallen flat: Edward was withdrawn, preoccupied. Angie's nerves had been jangling too, since seeing their names in the *Racing Post* pull-out section the previous Wednesday, along with the other entries. It had just been basic information—the name of the horse and its owners—but Angie's stomach had still heaved at the sight of it. It had all suddenly become very real.

Kizzy was there by seven thirty, looking smart in tight dark-blue jeans, jodhpur boots and a jumper and shirt. Even in the dark of the yard she radiated sunshine: pink and white complexion, blonde hair gleaming under the stable lights.

'You're glowing!' Angie told her. 'The break's

obviously done you good.'

Kizzy felt herself going red, and bent down to pick up a feed bucket. She didn't want to tell Angie she'd been floating on a secret cloud of euphoria the last few days. She couldn't eat, couldn't sleep, and felt the happiest she'd been for a long while. It was only slightly tempered by the fact that she'd heard nothing from Javier since getting the present. Was he expecting her to make the first move? Kizzy didn't want him to think she was being rude, but another thank you card seemed a bit silly. There was no way she was emailing the main Homelands website, either.

She felt like she had to wait and see what he did next. Her lack of control over the situation was both exciting and unsettling.

*   *   *

By ten o'clock the horsebox was on the road, Freddie behind the huge wheel. Their race wasn't until one in the afternoon, which gave them plenty of time to get there and get Nobby out to stretch his legs. Nobby had loafed up the ramp after Kizzy, looking more like he was off for an amble at the seaside instead of the first meet of his racing career.

'Is everyone all right?' Angie said, turning round to look at the little sitting area behind the front seat. Archie had his long legs up and was drinking coffee out of a hip flask.

'We're fine, Ma.'

Angie smiled at her son. She was pleased he'd come along. Archie's laid-back demeanour would be good at calming any fraught nerves. Angie had rather hoped he and Kizzy would hit it off

265

immediately, but Kizzy had just huddled up in her big jacket, and been unusually quiet. A few times Angie had said something to her, and Kizzy hadn't heard, as if she were off in her own little world. It was hardly surprising. This was a big day for them all.

It was eleven thirty by the time the navy horsebox trundled down the hill to Chaddesley Corbett. The sprawling point-to-point course sat in the middle of farmland, the rolling Malvern Hills in the background. A weak sun was thawing the last of the frost. A long wooden building, little more than an outbuilding, housed the changing rooms and the place where Edward would weigh 'out' and 'in'. It was already busy, people milling about amongst the marquees and car parks. Angie's stomach turned over. Funny how everything seemed so much bigger and scarier when it was your horse running.

A steward stood by the entrance, directing traffic. As they moved towards the horsebox park, Kizzy seemed to snap out of her trance; she got up, moving towards Nobby's stall at the back of the lorry. In the park, activity was at a high already. One big grey was refusing to go back in its box, while a groom was hauled past on the end of a lead-rope, trying desperately to control her overexcited horse.

Freddie parked up next to a big red horsebox and cut the engine.

'We're here, chaps.' Angie smoothed down her Jaeger wool coat, bought especially for the occasion, and reached into her handbag for her leather gloves. By the time she'd climbed down from the cab Freddie and Archie were already letting the ramp down at the back of the lorry.

266

'All right, boy.' Kizzy started to lead Nobby carefully down the ramp. Hooves scraping and sliding, he made it in one piece. Then he took a leisurely look round, lifted his plaited tail, and let out an enormous wet fart. Goldenballs had arrived.

*   *   *

The next hour was taken up with admin. They had to register Nobby with the hunt secretary, and get Edward into his silks so that Angie could take him off to get weighed in. The commentator's voice blared out through the loudspeakers, giving the crowd an update on the conditions.

'Well, folks, I've just heard back from the clerk of the course, and all the frost is out of the ground. The official going is good; good to soft in places.'

Back in the horsebox Kizzy was busy checking Nobby's plaits. For once, thoughts of Javier were pushed to the back of her mind as she focused on the job in hand. Nobby had been walked round to stretch his legs out. All his tack was ready to go on. There was nothing to do but wait.

Kizzy was sharing a coffee with the groom from next-door's horsebox when Edward came back from the weigh-in carrying his saddle. Against the strong black and purple colours of the silks his face was paler than ever.

'Blimey, is that your jockey?' the other groom said. Even Kizzy had to admit Edward stuck out like a sore thumb. He had to be twice the height of everyone else, and even compared to his featherweight counterparts he was rake thin, his wasted thighs and sharp elbows clearly visible under his silks.

267

'Everything go all right, Edward?' Kizzy called out. He dragged his eyes off the ground.

'Yes.'

Kizzy watched him disappear up the ramp. 'I'd better go and tack up.'

'Christ, me too,' the other groom said. She smiled at Kizzy. 'Well, good luck.'

'You, too!' *Not too much luck, though*, Kizzy thought wryly.

'Hey, Kizzy.' Archie was walking up with two hot drinks in his hand. 'Do you want anything from the refreshments tent?'

'I'm fine, thanks.' She liked what she'd seen of Archie so far. He was big and friendly; what her mum would call 'hunky'. He grinned; he had the same lively brown eyes as Angie.

'Give me a shout if you want anything.' He held up the paper cups. 'Mum's fifth of the day. She's heading for a serious caffeine overload.'

'Maybe we should put her out to run instead.' Kizzy laughed and walked up the ramp. Edward was on the bench seat inside, frantically rubbing a stain off his boot. 'You're going to work off the leather there!' She cast a quick look over the partition at Nobby. 'You OK?'

Edward's Adam's apple bobbled. 'A bit nervous.'

'Just go out there and enjoy it,' she said. 'The Nobster won't let you down.'

'Yeah.'

Kizzy studied him, remembering the strange episode in the granny annexe. 'Edward, I know now's not the time, but if you ever want to talk about . . .'

'Hello, chaps!' Freddie stuck his head through the door. 'Are we ready to roll?'

*   *   *

Sitting on the bonnet of Benedict's 4×4, Calypso took a swig of Moët and surveyed the proceedings. They had a good vantage point up here on the hillside, and Calypso had spent the last half hour watching everything going on. The place reminded her of a cross between a kids playground and country fair. Stalls and refreshment places stood in a wide semi-circle away from the track; there was a 'Fursty Fox' real ale tent, a wine bar, and tack shops selling saddles and waxed jackets. In one corner was a bouncy castle and pick 'n' mix stall, where children were cajoling their parents to load up on goodies for the day.

The people-watching was *brilliant*. At centre stage were the smartly-dressed professional trainers with an eye on Cheltenham, the flat-capped old farmers with their know-how and racing cards, the bowler-hatted race officials rushing round, and the gaggles of horse-mad teenage girls in Topshop hoodies and Dubarry boots. Adding an element of glamour were the Kate Middleton wannabees in blazers and tight jeans, tossing their long brown tresses at the pint-sized jockeys strutting through the crowds.

The Churchminster gang were up amongst the county set, with their shooting sticks and black Labradors, and rows of Volvos and Range Rovers, their boots groaning with food and booze. As far as she could make out, it was more about the socializing and who had the biggest Fortnum & Mason hamper than racing with this lot. The loud-voiced jolly sorts in the car next door had just

269

produced oysters on ice from their cool box.

Calypso took another sip of champagne and decided there were worse ways to spend a winter's day. Aside from Camilla and Jed, who both had to work, and Milo, who was spending the day with Cockface Sebastian, her whole family had come along. There was a good turnout from the village: the Turners minus Stacey, a couple of locals, and even the Reverend and Joyce Bellows, the latter startling in a PVC plastic mac. Brenda Briggs was also there, a stone heavier from her week in Lapland—'It was an all-you-can-eat buffet every night,' she kept telling people. 'Ted had to wheel me out of there in the end.'

They'd all been down to the bookies to put some money down. Calypso hadn't got a clue how the odds worked, but Nobby was running at fifty to one, which was apparently standard for a first-time entry. Back up on the slope, the alcohol was starting to flow freely now, and Calypso watched Jack Turner give the Reverend Bellows a surreptitious nip of whisky from his hip flask.

Clementine was next to Calypso, looking very dapper in a checked tweed coat and a felt hat with pheasant feathers. She had her binoculars trained on the starting post.

'What's going down?' Calypso asked. 'Can you see Nobby?'

'Yes, he's wearing the black and purple colours. Walking around at the back.' Clementine handed Calypso the binoculars. Sure enough, there was Edward astride Nobby, knees up round his ears. He was completely rigid, like a frozen praying mantis.

'Edward looks like he's about to shit himself.'

Her grandmother tutted. 'Must you be so gross?'

270

Calypso flicked one of her grandmother's feathers. 'Only round you, Clemballs. Don't worry.'

*   *   *

Down at the start line the eighteen horses were jostling round. The jockeys walked them up to look at the first fence and came back. As the grey-haired starter climbed on to his rostrum an expectant hush rippled through the onlookers.

Calypso trained the binoculars closer. The owners and trainers were all gathered together. Angie's face came into view, twitchy with tension as she said something to Freddie. Kizzy was to the left of them: a blonde sex-bomb in the sea of brown and olive-green outfits. Calypso's lenses swung on to the man standing next to Kizzy. He looked vaguely familiar, his hands shoved deep into his coat pockets. Calypso's eyes travelled over the broad frame and tan, the shaggy surfer haircut.

'Who's that bloke with the Fox-Titts?' she asked her grandmother.

Clementine took a look. 'Archie, darling. I told you he'd come home.'

'No way.' Calypso grabbed the binoculars back and took a second look at the face. She gave a disbelieving laugh. Was that Archie *Fox-Titt*?

The starter was getting out his flag. 'Horses under order!'

He lifted the flag up. Everyone held their breath. The horses quivered, jockeys holding them back. A few seconds passed, before the white flag swished down like an axe.

'*And they're off!*' shouted the excited commentator.

271

CHAPTER FORTY-TWO

Down on the track, Angie's heart was in her mouth. The field cleared the first fence without any mishaps, and were galloping on to the second. She could see Nobby's big bottom bobbing up and down, Edward perched precariously on top of him.

'What's that riding number eleven?' someone said. 'I didn't know Peter Crouch had gone into jump racing.'

'Ugly bastard, isn't it?'

'What, the horse or rider?'

'Ignore them,' whispered Freddie, as there were loud chortles behind. He held on to Angie's arm tightly. The pack was disappearing up the hill towards the third fence, a few runners already breaking away in front. Angie was dismayed to see Nobby in last place. He was cruising along as if out on a gentle hack, instead of running in front of a capacity crowd at his debut. All the horses managed to get over the next fence, and Nobby overtook the one in front as it landed awkwardly.

'*Small mistake by Sunshine Boy,*' the commentator said. '*Goldenballs moves up from the back of the field.*'

'Come on!' Angie shouted, as if Edward would somehow hear her, and find that extra gear from somewhere. Kizzy was on tiptoe, straining to see as the horses came round the next bend.

By the time they were back in full sight again, they had strung out completely. Nobby had moved up a couple more places, but Bladerunner, the odds-on favourite, was leading the front three.

272

Angie's heart sank. There was no way Nobby could catch up.

'Where's that oomph?' Freddie urged. 'We know he's got it!'

'He's still got eight fences,' Kizzy said. 'Edward's a tactical rider, he knows what he's doing.'

She didn't sound convinced.

The commentator was in full flow. *'Dancing Diva is coming to have a look at leader Humdinger . . . Hold up, he's lost an iron! Ouch—I imagine certain parts of him are twitching slightly.'*

The crowd guffawed as Dancing Diva's jockey fought to retrieve his loose stirrup. It gained a precious few seconds for the middle runners to make some ground.

As they came down the final straight Angie saw Nobby's huge donkey ears flatten against his head. Edward was crouched forward so far Angie was worried he might be about to topple off. As they approached the third from last fence, Edward seemed to panic, and instead of letting Nobby go, hung on to the reins. There was a gasp from the crowd as Nobby misjudged his stride and hit the fence hard.

'Nasty moment there for Goldenballs.'

Angie put her hands over her eyes. Why had she ever agreed to put them through this?

'Bloody hell, look at that chestnut tank coming from behind!' someone shouted. Freddie nudged her. 'Darling!'

She looked up to see that, somehow, Nobby had ramped up from first gear into fifth, and was now zooming past the horse in front of him. He was striding out, huge great hooves churning up clods of earth behind him. He passed another horse and

273

then another. There were only two fences to go . . .

'And Goldenballs is making progress through the field . . .'

'Come on, Nobby, come on!' she shrieked. Beside her Kizzy was hopping up and down with excitement. 'Go, Nobby and Edward!' The first three horses were past the post now, and amidst thunderous applause they watched Nobby fly over the last fence and speed down the final furlong to finish fourth.

Freddie punched the air. 'Yes! Way to go, lads!' The winning horse's trainer was celebrating beside them, but they barely took any notice. Angie threw her arms round Kizzy. 'I can't believe it!' Unlike a lot of the horses there, Nobby had never run a race in his life. To come in fourth in a field of eighteen was beyond all their expectations.

They rushed over to congratulate him and Edward. Nobby's tail was high in the air, and his nostrils were snorting. From the way he was bouncing round, it was clear he'd loved the whole thing. They might not have won, but Angie swelled with pride. From the huge, stunned smile on Edward's face anyone would think he'd won the Lottery.

*   *   *

The Churchminster gang found the happy team in their horsebox opening a celebratory bottle of champagne. 'Well done, chaps!' said Clementine, who'd uttered a most unseemly word as the pair had charged down the final straight. 'What a thrilling race.'

They congregated on the grass outside to crack

open more bubbly. Edward was slapped on the back and praised, while Nobby was inundated with pats and Polos. He'd been washed down and was now back in his rug, sleepy-eyed, and as if he'd never even run a race.

Angie took a long drink from her plastic glass. 'That was a bit nerve-racking!'

Caro laughed. 'You should have heard us at the end! I think Calypso's lost her voice.'

'I don't think I've seen her yet, where is she?' Angie looked about.

'Popped to the loo.'

As a young man came round from the back carrying a cool box, Caro did a massive double take. 'Archie? Don't you look great! Your mum said you were back.'

He came up and surprised her with a hug. 'How are you doing?'

Caro remembered him as a gawky, awkward teenager; he'd certainly grown into those big shoulders of his. There was a new air of confidence about him, too. 'Did you have a marvellous time in New Zealand?' she asked.

'Awesome, thanks.' He put an arm round Angie. 'It's good to be back, though. I've missed Mum's cooking.'

'And now you're staying at home and going to work with Freddie?'

'Yep, thought I'd try my hand at the family business.'

'Howdy, guys, congratulations!' It was Calypso, looking very fashionable in skinny jeans and camel cape. 'My God, I don't think my heart could have stood much more of that.' She flicked her hair back. 'Hey, Arch. Nice tan.'

275

He treated her to a winning grin, showing nice white teeth. 'Same to you.'

If she hadn't known him, and he hadn't been, like, twelve or something, Calypso would have said Archie was looking extremely hot.

But she did, and he was, so it didn't matter.

CHAPTER FORTY-THREE

Caro phoned Sebastian as they were heading back on the M5.

'Darling, how was it?' he asked effusively.

'Nobby came fourth!'

'Did he, really? How marvellous!'

'We're on our way back now, probably about an hour away.'

There was a loud cackle from the back seat. They'd been invited into the hospitality tent by some of Angie's racing chums, and Calypso and Brenda had got stuck into the vodka. They were now working their way through the last bottle of champagne in the icebox.

'We've been having lots of fun, haven't we, Milo? It's your mother on the phone.'

'Can I say hello to him?'

'Milo, come and say hi to your mother . . . Sorry, he's run off again.'

'No matter.'

Calypso leaned forward between the seats. 'Is that Bouffant-head?' she shouted, making Brenda cackle with laughter again. 'Hope he got a nice new hairdryer for Christmas!'

'Sssh!' Caro turned round and shot her sister a

cross look. Clementine, who was sat next to a sleepy eyed Rosie on the middle seat, turned round and took the champagne bottle off her granddaughter.

There was a pointed cough on the other end of the phone.

'Calypso's only joking, Seb,' Caro said hurriedly. 'She's got a bit too carried away celebrating.'

'It's fine, darling,' he said smoothly. 'We all know how she likes a drinkie.'

'Speaking of which, we're going to drop her at the pub with the others, and come round to pick Milo up. Is that OK?'

He wouldn't hear of it. 'You must go and celebrate with your friends! You probably want to catch up anyway, after being away.'

'I suppose that would be nice.' She'd stuck to Diet Coke all day, and a glass of something would be nice. 'OK, we'll pop in for a quick one. We need to get Rosie back, anyway.'

Hanging up, she turned to Benedict. 'Seb's going to hold on to Milo for a while longer, so we can go for a quick drink.'

He raised an eyebrow. 'Great.'

*   *   *

Calypso was at the bar when someone tapped her on the shoulder.

'My shout, what do you want?'

It was Archie, rather hunky in a navy jumper and white T-shirt that accentuated the tan. The ubiquitous country-boy Timberland boots were adorning his feet.

'Cool, thanks very much. I'll have a gin and tonic.'

'Coming right up.' He leant on the bar, trying to catch Jack's eye. 'Mum tells me your business is going well. It's an events company, isn't it?'

'Yeah, if you can call an eightieth birthday lunch an event.' She was beginning to get a headache from all that champagne. 'Can you get me a glass of tap water as well?'

'Sure.' He looked sideways at her. 'What do you call an event, then?'

'Oh, I don't know. Something fun. An orgy, maybe.'

'You haven't changed,' he said, grinning.

'What does that mean?!'

He was saved from answering by the arrival of Angie. 'My two favourite people!' She hugged Archie.

'Nobby OK?' he asked.

'All tucked up in bed. I did invite Edward and Kizzy down, but I think they wanted to do their own thing.'

'Edward seems like a "do his own thing" kind of guy,' Archie said. 'Shame Kizzy didn't come down, though, she seems like fun.'

'Does she?' Angie asked hopefully. 'I mean, of course she is.'

She looked back at Calypso. 'Is James coming tonight?'

'Who's James?' Archie asked.

'Calypso's new chap. He's very nice.'

'Er, no. He's got his Alexander Technique class tonight.'

She saw Archie raise an eyebrow. 'Alexander who?'

'I've read an article about that,' Angie said. 'Jolly interesting. All the top ballet dancers do it to help

278

their fitness.'

Archie seemed to be finding it rather amusing. 'So he's a ballet dancer?'

'*No*. He's an accountant,' Calypso said defensively. 'The Alexander Technique is really good at helping with posture and stuff. James sits at a desk all day and, you know, that can really mess your back up.'

'Posture.' Archie's brown eyes twinkled. 'Right.'

'I do miss Darcey Bussell,' sighed Angie.

*   *   *

The pub started to get decidedly raucous. When Calypso, in the middle of an animated story about travelling in Thailand, accidentally knocked Caro's glass of wine all over her, she and Benedict decided it was time to leave. They had to feed the kids and put them to bed, anyway.

'Not long now, Roso,' Caro said, as they pulled up outside Bluebell Cottage.

'I'm tired!' Any second now that voice was going to turn into a wail. Caro unbuckled her seat belt and turned round. 'I'll be one minute! Then we can go home and have your favourite mashed potato.'

Benedict waited in the car as she knocked on Sebastian's front door. She waited for thirty seconds and tried again. Moments later he appeared.

'Sorry, darling, I didn't hear you. We're all out the back in the TV room. Suzette's been wowing us with her world famous *chocolate chaud*.' He pronounced it dramatically. 'An age-old family recipe, apparently. She's loath to tell anyone the ingredients.'

279

A picture of domestic bliss greeted her. In front of the blazing fire Suzette and Milo were curled up in an armchair reading *The Cat in the Hat*.

'Hello, Caro.' Even lounging at home, it looked like Suzette had just stepped off the Rue Faubourg Saint-Honoré: she was wearing a silky black pantsuit and a big statement necklace.

'Is it raining out there?' Sebastian enquired mildly.

'No, why do you ask?' Caro followed his gaze to the big wet stain across her left boob. 'Oh, Calypso knocked a glass of wine over me on our way out.' She pulled her coat across herself self-consciously. Something like that would never happen to Suzette.

Milo glanced up from his book. 'Hi, Mum.'

'Did you like the pantomime?'

'Yeah.'

'Thanks so much for looking after him,' she said to the two adults.

'Our pleasure,' Seb told her. 'Would you like to stay for a drink?'

'Thanks, but I'd better not. Benedict's got Rosie in the car, and it's getting past her bedtime.'

Sebastian nodded. 'Of course. We'll get Milo's things together.'

Suzette placed a bird-like kiss on the little boy's cheek. 'Up you get, *mon petit*.'

'Pub good?' Sebastian asked, as Suzette took Milo off to get his coat and things. 'Aside from people drenching you with alcohol.'

'Very busy! Lots of people celebrating.' She could see the lights from Benedict's car outside. Rosie's tantrum was probably starting just about now. 'Well, I don't want to take up any more of your evening.'

280

Milo was in the hallway having his coat buttoned up by Suzette. 'Where is Milo's scarf, Sebastian?' she asked him.

'I think I saw it in the kitchen, won't be a jiffy.'

Suzette finished doing Milo's coat up and touched him on the cheek. 'But I want to stay here,' he moaned.

'Milo.' Caro shot an apologetic look at Suzette. It was his new thing: kicking up a stink whenever they had to leave somewhere.

'Want to stay with Zette.'

'Darling, we're going now. Say goodbye to Daddy and Suzette.'

'No! Staying here! You don't love me, anyway.'

'Milo!' Caro was shocked. 'Why do you keep saying these things? Of course Mummy loves you. We all do.' She looked at Suzette. 'Sorry, Suzette.'

Suzette made an insouciant gesture. 'It is not a problem. Milo is just tired.'

'He certainly is,' Caro said as Sebastian reappeared with the scarf.

'There you go, son!' he said. He wound it round the little boy's neck and stood up. 'Are you and Benedict doing anything nice for New Year?'

'We're going to a charity ball, up at Clanfield Hall.'

'Ah, of course.'

There was an awkward moment. It had been at a black-tie do at the same place that Caro had discovered Sebastian had had the gall to bring his mistress along.

'Excellent!' he said heartily. 'Have a wonderful time, and send my love to the old man.' He leant down again and put his arms round Milo. 'See you soon, darling. Daddy loves you.'

Caro was rather touched by this display of emotion. As Suzette kissed Milo she smiled at her ex. 'Thanks again, and have a great New Year.'

He smiled broadly. 'Oh, we intend to!'

CHAPTER FORTY-FOUR

The Pikes arrived home on New Year's Eve, and promptly invited Caro and Benedict over for a pre-ball bottle of champagne.

'What do you think of our new addition, Carol?' They were in the hallway looking at a huge canvas of a luridly painted sunset. Cheryl had just pointed out a blobby shape in the corner, which was apparently an elephant.

'Very dramatic,' Caro said, thinking she'd never seen an elephant in Barbados before. Barry and Cheryl looked pleased enough with the painting. Their layers of gold jewellery gleamed against their Ronseal tans.

After a few more reverential remarks about the canvas, Cheryl led them back into the living room. 'You must tell me all the goss.'

'Yeah, who's been shagging who?' Barry slapped Benedict on the back and guffawed.

'None of that, I'm afraid.' Caro smiled. 'Well, not that I know of, but I am a boring housewife these days. Oh, but Nobby did come fourth in his first race.'

'Did you hear that, Baz? Aww, I'm a bit gutted we missed all the little gee-gees.'

Barry pinched his wife's Lycra-clad bottom. 'No worries, Toots. We'll make up for it with a fun

282

time tonight.' He sloshed more champagne into everyone's glasses. 'I'm telling you, Benedict, I hope that dance floor's ready for me.'

'Ooh, yes!' Cheryl said. 'He's my very own John Travolta!'

Barry dropped his wife a wink and raised his glass. 'A toast! To new friends and old.'

'New friends and old,' they all chorused. Barry did a revving motion with his left arm. 'We gonna get out of our trees, or what?'

*　　　*　　　*

'What gives, Miss Moneypenny?' Calypso looked up from doing up her bracelet. James was standing in front of her, looking very pleased with himself in a dinner jacket and bow tie.

'That's a terrible Sean Connery accent.' She went back to fiddling with her wrist. James laughed and came to sit down on the bed next to her.

'Sorry, I always go all James Bond when I put a tux on.'

'Don't you mean James Ward?' she said distractedly. 'Bloody thing, I can't do it!'

'Here, let me.' He caught her arm.

'You won't be able to.'

'We won't know until I try,' he said, and took her wrist. Calypso stared at the pink scalp shining through his new neat haircut as he bent his head in concentration. It was hard to believe he'd come out of such a vile old trout.

Dinner with James's parents last night had been an unqualified disaster. His mum, a snide, sharp-featured little woman, had spent the whole evening delving into Calypso's family and

283

background: what her father did, where she'd gone to school. At one point Calypso had been tempted to get her debit card out to see if she wanted a good look at her bank account. Mrs Ward was the worst kind of snob—a middle-class social climber—while James's downtrodden dad had escaped to his study the minute the port was over. Married to such a horror, Calypso didn't blame him.

'Last night went well, didn't it?' James was still fiddling.

'Uh, yeah. Lovely.'

'Mum phoned earlier. She'd like us to come to their annual golf club dinner.'

Calypso automatically searched for an excuse. 'I might be working.'

He looked up. 'I haven't even told you the date yet.'

'I'm just not sure I'm really a golf person, James,' she said half-heartedly.

He grinned. 'That's because you haven't tried it. I'll take you to the driving range. Trust me, you'll love it.' He took her wrist and kissed it. 'There!' The cringey Scottish accent was back again. 'May I say how ravishing you look, Miss Moneypenny?'

Calypso smiled weakly, and tried to block out her growing sense of claustrophobia.

*   *   *

At the Maltings, Freddie was being shoehorned into his tuxedo by Angie. As she heaved the lapels together he groaned loudly.

'I feel like I'm being put in a bloody straitjacket!' He looked down at his belly mournfully. 'Have I really put on that much weight?'

'It's just a bit of Christmas excess.' Angie didn't want to remind him they'd had the same problem last time he'd worn the tux. She was going to have to get Fred on some kind of healthy eating plan in the New Year; it wasn't good for him to be putting all that pressure on his heart.

'It's no good, I'll have to leave it undone. It's that or a corset.'

Archie came into the kitchen. 'Nice threads, Freds.'

'Your father's having a bit of trouble fitting into his dinner jacket,' Angie said tactfully.

Archie grinned. 'Never mind, Pa. You're still a fine figure of a man.'

'If only there wasn't so much of the figure.' Freddie cast an eye over his son. 'Well, well, well! Don't you look the man about town!'

Motherly bias aside, Angie had to agree. The new dinner jacket they'd bought in Cheltenham yesterday fitted perfectly, showing off Archie's broad back and shoulders. Even under the harsh overhead light his face was full of colour, his eyes fresh and clear. His shaggy brown hair, not yet subjected to the barber's scissors, still sported blond tips from the southern hemisphere sun.

He wandered over to get a glass of water from the tap. 'You look nice, Ma,' he said, downing half of it in one gulp. 'Is that new?'

Angie looked down at the flattering floor-length gown, an impulse buy from Coast in the summer. 'Thank you, darling, the Spanx are holding it all in.'

Freddie grabbed her round the waist. 'You look gorgeous. All the other chaps are going to be utterly jealous I've turned up with such a stunner.'

'Oh, Freds!'

Archie averted his eyes out of the window as his parents nuzzled like a pair of teenagers. 'When's Kizzy getting here?'

'Any minute now,' Angie said, untangling herself. 'Has Edward gone out?'

'Can't see his car.'

'I hope he's having fun!' She'd asked Edward to join them at their table, but he'd said he was going to a party with some friends. Angie hadn't pushed him on the details; it was just so nice to see him getting out for once.

'Talking of fun,' said Freddie. 'I'll get the Dom Pérignon out.'

*   *   *

Kizzy was driving at half the speed she did normally. Why hadn't she bought a pair of flat shoes to drive in? The silver heels with diamanté ankle straps had looked perfect when she'd been standing in front of the mirror in her bedroom. Now they had turned into death traps, and were probably covered in mud.

Her headlights picked out the glint of a fox running across the road up ahead, and she slowed down even more. The country lanes were pitch black tonight, a faint outline of the moon struggling to break through the cloud cover. Maybe they were in for snow.

On the radio the DJ was revving up his listeners. *'And now on our New Year's Eve one hundred best party songs EVER, we have the Black Eyed Peas.'* As 'Let's Get This Party Started' came on, Kizzy whacked up the volume. She needed something to get her in the mood.

She'd had the late invite yesterday from the

286

Fox-Titts, when one of their friends had dropped out. Angie had wondered why Kizzy was reluctant to say yes, until Kizzy had confessed about galloping across the lawns at Clanfield Hall on a horse from her old yard all those months ago. Angie had thought it was hysterical, and said she was sure the owners, Sir Ambrose and Lady Fraser, wouldn't remember her.

So now Kizzy was going, although rather sheepishly. She still didn't feel much like celebrating, but a charity ball at stately Clanfield Hall was more appealing than being in a rammed bar in town.

The blaze of happiness she'd felt since finding the coat on the doorstep had steadily dwindled. She'd convinced herself she wouldn't hear from Javier, and that he was probably away, yet every time her mobile had rung, or someone had knocked on the front door, her heart had jumped into her mouth. But as the week had gone on, and he hadn't contacted her, Kizzy had started to feel confused and frustrated.

People just didn't go around leaving expensive hand-wrapped gifts on other people's doorsteps. Kizzy was so tired of the questions going round in her head. She almost wished she hadn't worn the new coat. The longing to see Javier was starting to drive her mad. She just didn't *do* this: this obsession, one person taking over her head. It was making her feel more strung-out by the minute.

I'll leave it a few more days. He might get in touch; it hadn't been *that* long. The time between Christmas and New Year always seemed longer because there wasn't much going on. If Javier didn't contact her soon, she really would do something.

She's send a thank you email or another letter, or whatever was expected of her in this bizarre situation.

Kizzy gave herself a mental shake. She had to stop acting like a love-struck teenager. Tonight was going to be really good fun, and just what she needed to take her mind off things. *But what if you never see him again?* The thought came from nowhere. Kizzy was shocked at how gutted it made her feel.

Reaching across, she turned the radio up even louder, as if it would drown out the pandemonium in her head.

CHAPTER FORTY-FIVE

Clanfield Hall or 'The Shack', as it was affectionately known locally, was *the* place to get an invite to. The owners, Sir Ambrose and Lady Fraser, had a knack of pulling together the perfect mix of people. At any social function they organized (normally in aid of charity), there would be aristocracy, farmers, the horsy lot, council bigwigs, local entrepreneurs and fund-raisers; basically anyone who had *something*— and it didn't have to be a title.

This year the theme of the ball was 'Winter Wonderland' and the charity was WaterAid, which Lady Fraser was super-hot on after going out to work on sanitation projects in Africa. As well as donating all the proceeds from the ticket sales, they were holding a fabulous auction hosted by Felicity Kendal. Lady Fraser was always careful to inject fun into her gatherings, along with a 'message', and as guests drove in that night they knew they were in for something special. Eight-foot-high Swedish fir trees, especially imported by the local garden centre, lined the long sweeping drive, their trees' fairy lights guiding the way. Outside the Hall itself, a nineteenth-century Regency masterpiece with links to Queen Victoria, carpets of fake snow had been put down on the vast front lawns. Two snow cannons stood on each one, firing drifts of white into the night air.

'Frances has really pulled out the stops this year,' Caro said. She and Benedict had driven up with the Pikes, squashed into the back of Barry's Ferrari.

'It's like Buckingham Palace!' Cheryl said. Readjusting her boobs, which were barely contained in a Julien Macdonald split dress, she stared up at Clanfield Hall's own frontage. ''Ere, Baz, we should get this Lady Frances to come and do one of our parties.'

Cheryl's red dress was so tight it looked like it had been shrink-wrapped on her. She was dripping with jewellery, including a huge new sparkler on her right hand that had been a Christmas present from Barry. In his white jacket and trousers, he stood out like a rotund exclamation mark against the sea of black tuxedos. As Caro and Benedict climbed out a loud revving noise was heard, and a quad bike came roaring out of the dark, driven by a cross-faced older man in a dinner jacket. There was a border collie sat on the back, its tongue lolling out.

'That's Sir Ambrose Fraser,' Caro whispered to Cheryl. She put her hand up as he screeched up outside one of the big windows and climbed off. 'Hello, Sir Ambrose!'

Sir Ambrose grunted and disappeared round the

back of the house.

'He's not a big party person,' Caro said apologetically.

Calypso came towards them looking sensational. She was wearing the highest pair of heels Caro had ever seen on a human being, and a backless black dress that showed off her tanned skin. 'Yo, yo.'

'Where are the others?' Calypso and James had driven to the Hall with Camilla and Jed.

'Just parking the car. I got them to drop me off. I can't walk far in these things.'

Barry couldn't take his eyes off her. 'Cor, Calypso, you look like one of them supermodels!'

'So, we're finally going to meet the famous James?' Benedict said. 'You've picked the perfect night to show him off.'

Calypso's smile dropped. 'Don't be a knob.' Shoving her clutch bag under her arm, she stalked off.

'Was it something I said?' Benedict asked bemusedly.

Caro shook her head. 'Don't worry about it.' Her sister had had a bee in her bonnet about something ever since they'd got back from holiday.

*   *   *

The first thing Kizzy had seen when she'd driven up with Freddie and Angie was the sweeping green lawn she'd thundered across with Juno. *Cringe!* The grand entrance hall was no less spectacular. It was full of dry ice, with all-white stilt walkers striding about; there was even a man dressed up as a snake charmer, thrilling a couple of female partygoers with the huge boa constrictor wrapped round his neck. A fifty-foot Christmas tree stood in the centre of the room, stainless steel icicle decorations the size of chandeliers hanging down over it. Smaller-sized icicles dotted the rest of the ceiling, sparkling and twisting as the light bounced off and caught them.

Beautiful voices from a gospel choir soared up into the eaves, singing a spine-tingling version of Sting's 'Every Breath You Take'. Partygoers were standing round listening, being attended to by a succession of nubile young champagne waiters. On the far side of the room was an ice sculpture in the shape of a rearing horse, and beside that, a cordoned-off area where a brand new Land Rover stood on a platform. Two stunning girls selling raffle tickets were wowing their enraptured male audience as they detailed all the perks of the vehicle, and why it was the most eco-friendly model to hit the road.

*   *   *

Kizzy had been hoping to avoid the hostess, but as they walked in, a blonde woman was standing by the door greeting people. Kizzy plastered a smile on; it was definitely the same person who'd shouted at her that day.

Dressed in a stunning floor-length gown, Lady Fraser gave Angie and Freddie a kiss on both cheeks. 'Delighted you could make it.'

'We wouldn't have missed it for the world, Frances,' Angie said. 'It looks spectacular.'

'That's very kind.' Frances looked at Kizzy. 'Hello.'

Freddie made the introductions. 'Frances, this

291

is Kizzy. She's the one who's done all the brilliant stuff with our Nobby.'

Kizzy smiled gratefully at him. 'Er, hi, Lady Frances.'

'Of course!' Frances exclaimed. 'I hear you had a good result at Chaddesley Corbett.'

'Frances is a bit of a racing fan,' Freddie told Kizzy.

Their hostess smiled again. Thank God, she seemed not to recognize Kizzy as the heathen who'd carved up her lawn. Unless Lady Frances was too well bred to bring up such a thing.

A sweet-faced brunette came up, accompanied by a young Paul Newman lookalike with the most piercing blue eyes. 'Hallo, chaps!' It was Harriet, Lady Frances's daughter. Hugging Caro and Angie, she turned to her mother.

'Sorry to intrude, Mummy, but one of the delivery people has blocked Cook's car in, and she can't get out. Daddy is making rather a fuss about it.'

Lady Frances rolled her eyes. 'Do excuse me.' Bidding them farewell, she swept off.

*   *   *

By eight o'clock the hall was buzzing, the volume of noise making it hard to have a conversation. In one corner, Camilla and Harriet were catching up. Best friends from when they were little, they'd rarely seen each other in the last year, what with Camilla starting up her business, and Harriet working in London. Beside them Jed and Harriet's boyfriend, Zack, were clutching beers and making easy conversation.

Calypso was standing with Caro in another corner. She'd positioned herself by one of the entrances so she could grab the drinks waiter when he went past. She was already halfway through her third champagne flute.

'God, I need this.' She took another slug.

'Is everything all right, darling?' Caro asked. 'You seem a bit on edge.' She'd noticed that her sister seemed to be avoiding James.

'Who, me? I'm fine. Why do you say that?'

A bell started tinkling in the middle of the room and everyone turned round to listen. A man was standing there in a black tie holding a microphone. 'Ladies and gentlemen, dinner is about to be served! Will you please make your way through to the ballroom?'

There were oohs and aahs as guests walked in. Fifty tables, each sitting ten, were spread out round a large dance floor. Each table had been laid beautifully with a thick white tablecloth, gleaming cutlery and an extravagant flower and glass display in the middle. More icicle decorations hung down on special wire contraptions from the ceiling, while a silk-draped stage stood at the far end. On it a giant cinema screen had been erected, and was flashing up the WaterAid logo.

Caro and Benedict were on a table with the Reverend Bellows and his wife Joyce, as well as the Pikes. Calypso was in-between James and the reverend, who had already blanched several times from the amount she'd said 'fuck'. As the wine waiter came round to fill up her glass, James put his hand over the top of it.

'Don't you think you've had enough?' he said.

Several of the people on the table looked over.

293

Calypso felt humiliated. 'What are you, my keeper?' She pulled the glass out of his grip and held it up to the waiter. 'I'd love some, thanks.'

On the next table Angie was keeping an eye on Kizzy. She was sitting with Archie, and the pair had been chatting, but Kizzy was a bit flat and distracted.

'Are you having a nice time?' Angie grabbed the chance to kneel down by Kizzy's chair on the way back from the loo.

'It's amazing!' Kizzy smiled at Angie. 'Thanks for inviting me.'

The waiter was hovering to collect the coffee cups. The auction would be starting soon. Angie tried once more. 'You just seem a little quiet.'

'Do I? Sorry, I'm probably just a bit tired, that's all.'

'You take it easy and have fun.' Angie patted her arm and got up. As she made her way back to her chair, a thought struck her. She had seen that expression before. *Lovesick.* Oh God, it wasn't something to do with Javier Hamilton-Scott, was it?

As the music started up everyone swivelled their heads towards the stage expectantly. There was a burst of dry ice, and seconds later Felicity Kendal walked on, looking every inch the mature sex siren in a glittering blue gown.

A few people wolf-whistled, and the actress took it all with her customary grace. She then brought the audience close to tears with an impassioned speech about the work WaterAid did and how every one of them could help. At the end she introduced the auctioneer, an enthusiastic little man called Belvedere Radley, who was a dead ringer for David Suchet.

People looked through their catalogues as Belvedere explained how the auction worked.

James put his hand on Calypso's knee. 'Have I done something?'

She glanced up. 'What do you mean?'

'You seem a bit off with me.'

'I don't appreciate being told how much I can drink.'

'I'm only looking out for you.'

'I'm old enough to look after myself, James!'

Jed glanced across at them. Calypso lowered her voice. James was looking at her with a hurt expression on his face. She sighed. 'I'm sorry, I didn't mean it. I'm just a bit knackered, that's all.'

'You sure?'

'I'm sure.'

He smiled at her. 'Don't worry, I'll look after you.'

James's hand was still on her knee, warm and slightly sticky. Calypso had an insane urge to flick it off. God, what was *wrong* with her tonight? Every time someone opened their mouth she bit their head off.

Up on the stage, Belvedere Radley was getting everyone excited about the auction items. They had a dazzling array: golfing lessons with Colin Montgomerie, a week on Necker Island, even a Hermès Birkin handbag once owned by Victoria Beckham. Belvedere started with the Birkin, and after a fierce battle between two men who owned rival chains of hairdressing salons, it went to one of them for fourteen thousand pounds. The victor flicked a very unsporting finger at his enemy and immediately started transferring the contents of his man-bag.

Next up was a portrait session with David Bailey, and his and hers customized wedding rings from Wright & Tigue. When Lot 7 came up, a Vegas-inspired bar, complete with a mermaid, that had once stood in the home of a famous US rock star, Cheryl sat up in her seat. 'Oh my God, Baz, we've got to have it!'

'What my lady wants, she gets.' A sovereign-encrusted hand went up.

'Do I see ten thousand pounds?' Belvedere said. 'Ah yes, to the fellow in white!'

Hands were raised around the room, but Barry held firm, and eventually got the bar for a colossal twenty-one thousand, five hundred pounds. When Belvedere brought his hammer down, the table erupted into cheers.

'Well done, Barry!' Caro exclaimed. 'How generous of you!'

He looked modest for once. 'I like to do me bit. That speech Felicity did really teared me up.'

'Ah, Baz.' Cheryl sighed. 'My hero.'

After that the auction flew by in a haze of noise, the audience being regularly topped up by the attentive wine waiters. One husband and wife had a huge bust-up when he blew all their money on golf lessons with Colin Montgomerie and not the villa on Necker she'd had her heart set on. Hissed exchanges containing the words 'divorce' and 'selfish bastard' were heard coming from their direction before they settled back in their seats, glowering.

By the penultimate lot they'd raised over a hundred and twenty thousand pounds, and the atmosphere was jubilant. The audience, drunk enough to get restless, were starting to look around for the next slice of entertainment. Belvedere Radley had to speak into the microphone three times to be heard above the rising noise levels.

'Ladies and gentlemen! If I could just have some quiet! You've all been fantastically generous, and I want you to keep on giving, because last but by no means least is our mystery item!' He paused, building up the drama. 'Oh, this is the stuff of dreams. Lot 21: the individual gold medal for dressage won by Javier Hamilton-Scott in the 2008 Beijing Olympics.'

The crowd chattered excitedly. Dozens of women started begging their other halves to bid for it. Sat on the table behind the Fox-Titts was a well-known tabloid newspaper editor.

'Fucking hell!' he exclaimed. 'That's the medal he won straight after his wife's accident, isn't it?' He was already tapping into his mobile phone. 'We have to get this, it's a great tear-jerker for Monday.'

A few feet away Kizzy was aware that Archie was talking to her, but a strange sensation had gripped her body. All she'd been thinking about the whole evening was Javier. And now, just hearing his name paralysed her.

Archie's words were floating in and out. Kizzy looked down and saw her hand clutching the tablecloth.

'Do you think Javier's here?' Angie said across the table. 'Ooh, Kiz, I bet he remembers you.'

'I don't think he's here,' one of Angie's female companions said. 'A man like Javier Hamilton-Scott doesn't walk around unnoticed.'

'You're probably right.' Angie sighed. She smiled at Kizzy, oblivious to her crashed hopes. 'What an incredible gesture, though! I bet it goes for *thousands.'*

The bidding had started, attracting a frenzy of both females and males, all trying to outdo each other. The newspaper editor was instructing the person beside him to do the dirty work. Ten thousand, twenty thousand; it kept going up and up. Belvedere Radley raised his eyebrows.

'One hundred thousand, do I have one hundred thousand pounds?'

The initial flurry of participants had fallen by the wayside. They were playing with the big boys now. By the time the bid got to a hundred and thirty thousand, there was only the newspaper editor left, and an unknown person over the other side of the room. They were going up by five thousand now, everyone's heads swivelling between each bidder.

'One hundred and fifty thousand.' Belvedere sounded like he could hardly believe it himself. Everyone on Angie's table looked at the newspaper editor. He sighed loudly. 'Who *is* this fucker?'

'Sir?' Belvedere was pressing him. 'Do I have a hundred and fifty thousand?' The editor shook his big red head, slumping back in his seat.

'For the last time, anyone?' The crowd were silent. 'No? Lot twenty-one, going, going, gone!' His hammer came down. '*Sold!*' He looked across at the mystery bidder. Thank you, sir.'

The newspaper editor was not a man accustomed to losing. He stood up, wanting to know who'd trumped him. His mouth dropped as he clocked the person.

'It's only fucking Javier Hamilton-Scott! Bastard's bought his own medal back!'

There was an excited rustling around him, as other people rose out of their seats to look.

'Did you hear that, chaps?' Angie whispered excitedly. 'The other bidder was Javier!'

Kizzy didn't realize it, but she'd stood up, too. Following the whispers and finger pointing, she looked across at a table on the far side, right in front of the stage. All Kizzy saw at first was the radiant brunette in a red dress, head bent intimately close to the man next to her. As Kizzy's eyes shifted right she suddenly went wobbly.

Even from this far away, she could feel his presence. Javier's thick hair was swept back off his face, showcasing the rugged profile. As if aware of her scrutiny, he broke off his conversation and looked in Kizzy's direction. His eyes settled on her like heat-seeking missiles. She smiled hopefully. They gazed at each other for a brief moment, before Javier turned back to his companion.

Feeling like she'd been kicked in the stomach, Kizzy slumped back down. Javier had looked right through her as if she were nothing.

CHAPTER FORTY-SIX

With an hour to go until midnight, the salsa band had everyone up on their feet. Revved up by drink, husbands were dirty-dancing with their friends' wives, while Felicity Kendal and Belvedere Radley twirled round in the middle doing a fierce fandango. At the edge of the dance floor Calypso was pouring out her woes about James to her sisters.

'James is really, really, *really* nice,' she slurred.

Caro knew her sister too well. 'But?'

'It's just *wrong.*' Calypso made a funny little

sound, between a wail and a cry. '*Everything*'s wrong.'

Caro glanced at Camilla, and, putting an arm round her youngest sister, led her off to the nearest empty table. 'Come on, what is it?'

Calypso looked round in vain for a discarded drink. 'It's James. No, it's me. Everyone keeps telling me what a catch he is. And he is really nice to me . . .' She trailed off.

'With the best will in the world, sometimes it's not there,' Caro said gently.

Calypso rubbed her face. 'I'm being such a cow to him tonight.' She watched a young couple stagger past, locked in a laughing embrace. That's what she and James should be like; they were only a few months in.

'I just feel *trapped*. Like, James has got it all worked out, y'know. He was even talking about what we'd call our kids!' Calypso shuddered. 'I mean, get *off* me.'

'What are you going to do?' Camilla asked.

'Talk to him, I suppose.' Calypso looked up at the soaring arched ceiling. 'God! This is a cheery conversation for New Year's Eve.'

'Do you think it's wise to say something now?' Caro asked. Her sister wasn't in the best shape.

'No, I'm pissed. I'll wait until tomorrow.'

'He's coming over,' Caro said in a low voice. She smiled brightly. 'James, there you are! Having fun?'

'Awesome.' His face was flushed from dancing. 'Do you want to dance?' he asked Calypso. 'This band are amazing.'

She grinned and stood up. 'Deffo.'

The other two watched her link arms with James and skip off. 'That's one thing about our Calypso,'

300

Camilla said. 'You could never accuse her of being a party pooper.'

'I know, poor lamb. But it's better if she finishes it now. She's too honest to put up with second best.'

'No wonder she was so cagey about introducing him. I knew something wasn't right.'

It was the first time for ages that the two sisters had had time alone together. 'Good night, isn't it?' Caro said.

'Really good.' Camilla looked down at her lap. 'Although I've lost count of the number of times tonight that people have asked when Jed and I are going to start a family.' She gave a rueful smile. 'It's amazing how when you get to your mid-thirties, your private life suddenly becomes a free-for-all.'

'Oh, darling! People can be bloody rude, can't they? You should tell them to mind their own business.'

'It's OK, really. Compared to some people, I've got a lot to be thankful for.'

They watched Barry pretend to take Cheryl from behind on the dance floor.

'Anyway,' Camilla said. 'There's no point in getting upset about it.' She brightened up. 'Dare I ask, are things still going well with Sebastian?'

Caro put her hand briefly on the table. 'Touch wood. To be honest we haven't really seen that much of him, what with Christmas and us being away.'

'Milo seems happy about seeing more of his dad, though.'

'Yes.' Caro smiled. 'He does, doesn't he? You know, Cam, I never thought we'd reach this place, but it's working out so well. Hats off to Sebastian, he really is making the effort.'

Camilla gave her sister an encouraging smile. Maybe Sebastian really was capable of redemption.

*   *   *

Kizzy felt dazed. She barely registered conversations, and she'd forgotten all about watching the countdown to midnight. Javier being present had sucker-punched her. She'd hoped he might come over, but to her disappointment he'd completely disappeared. He wouldn't have left, would he? The dance floor was heaving. Everywhere she looked people were dancing and laughing, spilling their drinks. Normally at the centre of any party, Kizzy felt totally out of sync. She stood on the edge, as if looking in from another planet.

Someone tapped her on the shoulder. It was Archie, tall and boyishly handsome, with his bow tie undone, and shaggy hair. The music was so loud she couldn't hear what he was saying, but he grinned and passed her the Moët bottle he was holding. Wanting a hit, Kizzy drank from it thirstily. The alcohol mainlined straight into her veins.

'Ten minutes to go, folks!' shouted the lead singer from the salsa band. 'Shake your stuff!'

There was a loud shout as one couple, attempting a rather ambitious twirl, got their legs tangled and went flying. They took several people out with them, and would have caught Kizzy, had it not been for Archie stepping in and grabbing her by the elbow. He shouted a query about her being OK. Kizzy nodded and watched him being whisked off by the girl next to him.

The crowd, momentarily split by the melee, flowed back together like glue. The next thing Kizzy felt was a hand on her arm. As she turned her heart stopped. Javier.

She stared up at him. Under the disco lights his face was carved into shadows, his treacle eyes fierce.

'Would you like to dance?'

Even through the music his rich voice was clear. Kizzy nodded and felt his warm arm slide round her waist. She had a brief moment to become aware of his body next to hers before they were off, as if she'd just been jerked on to the most breathless ride of her life.

It quickly became clear that Javier was an accomplished dancer. Kizzy had suddenly developed two left feet and could only let herself be carried by him. All she could feel was the steel of his arms and chest. Every time they came apart she felt vapour trails come off her like white heat. She didn't dare look up into his face.

'Just relax,' she heard him say. His breath was like a cool caress on her neck. Kizzy could literally *feel* Javier's energy soaking into her, uncoiling her muscles. It was a sheer chemical reaction. Not that she knew anything about taking drugs, but she thought this was what they must give you: this incredible surge of elation and energy. Kizzy had an almost vampire-like desire to feed off him.

Their chemistry was not going unnoticed, as other couples nudged each other and stared at Javier Hamilton-Scott locked in a dance of passion with a ravishing young blonde. Ten feet away Angie could only watch the scorching heat of their embrace, and the way Kizzy was utterly spellbound in his grip.

Dancing with his wife, Freddie noticed her

303

expression. 'What's wrong?'

Angie shook her head. For some reason, she had the most terrible sense of foreboding. There was only one way this could end, and it wasn't happily.

*   *   *

The lead singer's voice boomed out through his microphone, 'Ten, nine, eight, seven . . .' As the music stopped, the whole ballroom started chanting: 'Five, four, three, two, one. Happy New Year!' As the room exploded into sound and light everyone started kissing and hugging, and hundreds of balloons floated down from a giant net in the ceiling.

Kizzy was oblivious, as she gazed into Javier's eyes. Taking her hand, he turned and led her off the dance floor.

CHAPTER FORTY-SEVEN

Kizzy could only feel Javier's warm hand on her back, guiding her through the crowds. As they got to the front door he took off his tuxedo and draped it over her shoulders.

'Let's go for a walk. If that's all right with you?'

She wanted to get away from the stares and be alone with him.

'Yes please.'

They walked out into the cold night air. Javier pointed across the gravel to a path leading off to the right. 'Let's go down here.'

He seemed to know where they were going, as

they left the sounds of the party behind. All Kizzy was aware of was the thumping of her heart.

They reached the top of some stone steps, the lawns spread out in front.

'Is it OK if we go across on foot tonight?' Javier asked.

The teasing note in his voice unlocked some of Kizzy's nervous stupor.

'Don't,' Kizzy said. 'I met Lady Frances earlier. I'm surprised she didn't chuck me out!'

Javier laughed softly. 'Frances wouldn't do that.'

'You're friends?'

He nodded. 'I've known her for a long time. I used to come here a lot.'

They continued to walk round towards the back of the Hall. On this side, away from the party, the building was dark and silent.

Kizzy plucked up her courage. 'I got the coat.'

He gave her a keen glance. 'Did you like it?'

'It's really beautiful.'

Javier heard her hesitation. 'But what?'

'I, er . . .' Kizzy couldn't look at him. 'It's just that I'm a bit confused. About what it means . . .' She trailed off.

He didn't answer for a moment. 'I'm sorry if it was the wrong thing to do.'

'No, it really wasn't. I just . . .' *I don't know what to say to him*, she thought.

Javier didn't speak. Kizzy wondered what he was thinking. The air felt heavy to her, full of a thousand thoughts and questions.

Around the back of the Hall was another set of wide steps, descending down into a beautiful circular garden landscaped with rose bushes and giant topiary trees.

They started down them.

'How did the race go?'

'Race?' It was the last thing she was expecting him to talk about.

'Yes.' The amused look was back. 'You told me Edward and Nobby were riding at Chaddesley Corbett.'

Kizzy couldn't believe he'd remembered. 'They came fourth. It was great.'

Javier raised an eyebrow. 'That is good.'

There was an unearthly shriek up above, and Kizzy nearly jumped out of her skin.

'It's only an owl, don't worry,' Javier told her.

Kizzy put a hand on her chest. 'Sorry. I don't know what's wrong with me.'

'Do I make you nervous, Kizzy?' Javier looked at her with a funny mixture of curiosity and sadness.

She couldn't hold his gaze. 'N-no.'

They carried on, as if walking round a rose garden in the early hours was an everyday thing. Javier was so silent Kizzy was sure she'd offended him.

'That was pretty cool, buying your own medal back,' she offered.

'You think?' He put his hands in his pockets. 'I know that editor. He's run a few stories on me. I wasn't too keen on him getting it; he'd probably have ended up doing a mawkish giveaway in his paper.'

Kizzy wasn't entirely sure what he was talking about.

'Your back seems better,' he commented.

'Yeah, it is.' She sighed. 'Not bloody better enough to ride a horse, though.'

He sounded amused. 'Give it time, Kizzy. You

just have to be patient.'

Her skin prickled as Javier used her name. It felt like an actual caress.

'You like to dance, then?' she asked, warming up. 'You were really good at that salsa.'

Javier shrugged. 'I suppose it's in my blood. My mother, Elena, was a professional flamenco dancer.'

'Really? That's pretty cool!'

He raised an eyebrow. 'I suppose it is. Do you know where flamenco comes from?'

Kizzy shook her head. 'Sorry.'

Javier trailed his fingers over a passing rose bush. 'It's the music of the gypsy people, a protest against the persecution they suffered. My mother used to dance the *cante jondo,* the "flamenco singing". They say it is the deepest and most soulful of the flamenco.'

'Was your mum a gypsy?'

'She was.' There was a sardonic twist to his mouth. 'Hardly the most auspicious heritage for the first son of Lord Douglas Hamilton-Scott. And he never let either of us, my mother or me, forget it.'

Kizzy could sense the sudden tension. 'Did your mum dance when she came over here?'

Javier gave a dry laugh. 'In private, as if it were some dirty little secret. The very things that had attracted my father to my mother in the first place were the same ones he ended up despising her for. Back in Seville, he was entranced by her; she was an exotic beauty to show off.' He made a derisive noise. 'The novelty wore off when he brought her home. A free-spirited flamenco dancer didn't make for a *respectable* enough wife for the seventh earl of Homelands.'

'I'm sorry.'

'There's nothing for you to feel sorry for.' He gazed ahead. 'Who are you here with tonight?'

'Angie and Freddie, they're my employers. Well, they're more like friends, really.'

'Sounds like a good set-up.'

'Yeah, it is. How about you?' She was encouraged by the way their conversation had become less tense.

'Some old friends. In fact,' Javier looked down at his wristwatch, 'we're flying to Monte Carlo in thirty minutes.'

'You're what?' Surprise mixed with disappointment; she felt it in her stomach.

'As one does,' he said dryly. 'Arkie, one of our party, is a racing driver. He's got a big race tomorrow. I said I'd go along to keep his wife company, but now . . .' He stopped, his voice soft. 'Now, I don't know.'

'Javier!'

Kizzy turned round, heart in her mouth. A tall blonde woman was standing at the top of the stone stairs. The lights from the house fell on to her white gown, giving her an ethereal, luminous quality.

'Hold on, Pan,' Javier called up.

'You go,' Kizzy managed. 'I'll stay here.' Her legs were actually shaking. What had Javier been about to say?

Javier seemed very relaxed about it all. 'Come and meet Pan, please. I've told her about you, anyway.'

'You have?' Kizzy followed him, still reeling from what had just happened. The woman stood waiting at the top of the stairs, and, as Kizzy got closer to her she stopped dead. Pan had a fine bone structure, and a long swan neck. It was like looking at a ghost.

'Pan, this is Kizzy Milton,' Javier said. 'Kizzy, Pandora Guillory.'

'Hello.' Pan's voice was like silk.

'Hello.' Kizzy was trying not to be unnerved by the spitting image of Sarah Hamilton-Scott standing in front of her. 'Nice to meet you.'

Pandora's cobalt eyes rested not unkindly on her for a moment, then she turned back to Javier. 'I'm afraid we have to go. Are you coming?' They exchanged a look, and then Javier nodded. 'I won't be a minute.'

'Arkie's round the front, in the car.' Pandora turned back. 'It was nice to meet you, Kizzy. Happy New Year.'

'You, too,' Kizzy said as Pandora floated off.

Javier watched her go. 'Pan is . . .'

'Sarah's sister?' Kizzy smiled at his surprise. 'They look identical.'

'You're right, they do.' Javier looked after Pandora. 'Pan is Sarah's younger sister. Sarah and her were extremely close, and Pan and Arkie have been very good to me. I don't know what I would have done without her. Pan's the only one who really understands what it's like.'

It was the first time he'd spoken about what he'd suffered. He and Pan had an unbreakable bond, just as Javier had with Sarah. Kizzy dropped her eyes. What was she doing here?

'Kizzy.'

She looked up, ready to take whatever was coming. 'Would you do me the honour of having dinner?'

'What?' she said stupidly.

309

His gaze settled on her. 'I mean, when I get back. At Homelands. Or we can go out, if you like.'

'No. I mean we don't have to go out . . .' She took a deep breath. 'Homelands would be great.'

His olive-skinned face was still unfathomable. 'I'll call you.'

'You don't have my number.' Shit, she'd left her bag inside. 'If you wait a minute, I can run in and grab my phone . . .'

'I have got your number, you wrote it on your email, remember?'

Of course, when she'd RSVPed for the party. So he had read it after all. Kizzy started as Javier raised his hand and lifted it to her cheek.

Their eyes met. Kizzy was breathless; it was like seeing an old master for the first time: every exquisite feature laid out in stunning, unfettered detail. Up close she could see gold flecks around his irises, and his long silky eyelashes. His skin was thick, yet clear, and Kizzy wanted to run her hand over it, touch the perfect Cupid's bow of his upper lip.

Ever so quietly, the first snowflakes of the year started to fall round them. Just as gently, Javier leaned down and put the softest kiss on her cheek.

CHAPTER FORTY-EIGHT

Calypso woke to a raging hangover.

'Here.' James handed her a glass of water and two paracetamol. 'You probably need this.'

'Thanks.' She drank thirstily. Actually she didn't feel that horrific. Spending the last two hours on the dance floor last night had sobered her up a bit.

'Happy New Year,' he said with more than a touch of sarcasm.

She rolled over and looked at him. 'What's wrong with you?'

'I might ask you the same.'

'What do you mean?' she asked, knowing full well.

'I might as well have not been there last night. You hardly talked to me, and when I tried to dance with you, you virtually pushed me away and went off with a total stranger. Do you remember getting on his shoulders?'

'No! Did I really?'

James reached for his iPhone. He pressed 'play' and a fuzzy sound of music and shouts started up. Calypso looked at herself on the packed dance floor, astride the broad shoulders of Archie Fox-Titt. Her dress was pulled up, her long, tanned legs dangling. She saw Archie put his arm round one of them as he passed up a bottle of Moët with the other. She took a huge swig and bent down and said something to him. Both of them had expressions full of mischief.

Calypso started laughing. 'OMG! I don't remember that!'

James didn't share the joke. 'That's probably best, it was really embarrassing. You had your dress hitched right up, and everyone could see your knickers. It's not how ladies behave, Calypso.'

She was rather taken aback. 'It was only a bit of fun!'

'Well, *I* was embarrassed, Calypso. You're my girlfriend, and you were . . .'

'Yes?' she said challengingly. *Don't you dare.*

'Nothing.' He put the phone down and folded his arms, clearly waiting for an apology.

Calypso couldn't believe this! All she'd done was have fun. That's what people did at parties, wasn't it? It was time to face the facts. James was as boring as hell.

She sat up. 'We need to talk.'

'I wanted to talk last night.'

She put her hand on his arm. 'Please.'

He was looking at her like she was the biggest disappointment ever. 'OK, Calypso. Tell me what's really bothering you. Because no matter what I do, you always dismiss me.'

'No I don't!' She was surprised. 'I'd hate to make you feel that!'

'Well, you do.' He eyed her balefully. 'Like I'm some big joke, or something. Everything's a big joke with you, isn't it? Or you're out to try and shock people and cause controversy. It's really embarrassing.'

The character assassination was a bit much. 'Whoa, where did that come from?'

'Well,' he said sulkily. 'It's how you make me *feel*.'

'James . . .' Calypso paused, wondering how to word it. 'You knew what I was like when we met. I don't set out to shock people, the way you say. It's just me.'

'That's not how it seems to me.'

'Look, I'm sorry if I've offended you, but it wasn't intentional.' *Stop being such a drip*, she wanted to add.

A suffocating feeling overwhelmed her. James kept his arms crossed and stared out of the window, obviously trying to prolong his wounded-victim role

312

for as long as possible. Calypso wasn't going to give him the chance.

'James.'

'What?'

She shifted on the bed. 'I don't think this is working.'

He eyed her pompously. 'It's only not working because you're not putting any effort into it.'

'That wasn't my intention.' She might as well come right out with it; they were at the point of no return. 'If I've come across as detached, I guess it's because, if I'm really truthful, my heart has never really been in this relationship.'

James opened and shut his mouth. 'Oh.'

'I'm really sorry.' She could only think of the oldest cliché in the book. 'It's not you, it's me.'

He looked crestfallen. 'That's what Claire said to me.'

'Claire?' For a moment Calypso couldn't remember who Claire was. Then she said, 'Your ex?'

'That's what she said to me before she told me she was going off travelling.'

There seemed to be a pattern here. Calypso tried again. 'James, you're a lovely, lovely guy, and I know you're going to make someone very happy.'

'Haven't I done everything right?' He sounded baffled and hurt. 'You just said what a special person I was.'

'Yes, you are,' she said, going off him by the second.

'Do you want to think about it?' he asked. 'You might change your mind.'

She shook her head wearily. 'I won't, James. I'm sorry. I don't want to lead you on.'

He shook his head and got up. Calypso watched him dress from the neat pile on the chair. *I feel nothing*, she thought.

'So this is really it?' He stood by the end of the bed.

'I guess so. I am sorry. I mean, for this to happen on New Year's Day.'

She thought he was going to walk out without another word, but James stopped in the doorway. 'You know, you don't want to hang around much longer.'

'Sorry?'

His mouth was tight and mean. 'You're not getting any younger.'

'Excuse me?'

'Men like me don't come along very often. I could really have given you something.'

Calypso laughed in disbelief. 'Are you for real?'

'Girls like you are full of it. You might think you're too good for anyone, but who'll be the joke in twenty years' time, when you're a childless spinster?'

'Goodbye, James,' she said icily.

'Goodbye, Calypso.' The condescension was breathtaking. 'I hope your life isn't too unhappy.'

Speechless, she watched him walk out. A few moments later the front door closed downstairs. 'I *am* happy, you twat!' she yelled. 'Happy I never have to see those hideous shoes again!'

Calypso slumped back on the pillows, reeling. Who knew James could be such a cock? *You've had a lucky escape.* She still wasn't quite sure what had just happened, but one thing was for sure. She was free. And off men for life.

Freaks, she muttered to herself. *The lot of you.*

CHAPTER FORTY-NINE

Later that day the Toweys and Standington-Fulthropes were due at Fairoaks for a New Year's Day lunch. A light frosting of snow still lingered from the night before, coating the bare trees and prettifying the drab landscape.

Calypso arrived last as usual, and found everyone in the sitting room having a drink and talking about Kizzy's dance with Javier Hamilton-Scott. She launched straight into what had happened between her and James.

'He was probably just hurt, darling,' Clementine said. 'Some men take rejection very badly.'

'Did he have to be such a knob about it?'

Clementine's eyes strayed to Milo and Rosie, but they were playing happily on the window seat.

'I mean, telling me I was going to be left on the shelf!' Calypso was outraged. 'As if I'd want to have kids with him! He's probably firing blanks, anyway.'

Everyone looked away. Calypso went white. 'Guys, that was a really dumb thing to say. I'm so sorry.' She looked at Jed. 'I was just having one of my rants. I so didn't mean it to come out like that.'

No one spoke for a moment, and then Benedict got up. 'Anyone for a top-up?'

'Ooh, yes please,' Caro said, holding her glass up. She turned to Jed. 'Have you been up to the Hall today? I hope there's not too much damage.'

Calypso got up too, and followed her grandmother out to the kitchen. 'I hate myself!' she groaned. 'What did I have to go and say that for?'

'Just try and think before you speak,' Clementine

315

told her. 'I know you're upset about James, but . . .'

'I'm *sorry*!' Calypso went and flopped down at the table. 'God, I was feeling shit enough as it was.'

Clementine let the language go for once. She looked down at her tangle-haired granddaughter, who was tired and upset. Her heart softened.

'Oh, darling. I know you're the one who finished things, but it's never nice, is it?'

*   *   *

After a late lunch of roast pork, roast potatoes, and apple sauce made with Bramleys from the orchard, everyone was in a happier, more contented mood. The sun had set through the dining room windows while they were eating, turning the walls deep hues of pink and orange.

While the adults cleared the table, Camilla took the kids next door to put *The Snowman* DVD on for the umpteenth time.

'Anyone for a game of Monopoly?' Clementine asked. 'I've got some homemade sloe gin if anyone fancies a tot.'

Caro nodded. 'Sounds like a good idea.'

'Actually, I might take a rain check,' Benedict said. He looked at his wife. 'I've a few work emails to send.'

'On New Year's Day?' Clementine asked.

'I just want to get ahead on a few things. I won't be long.'

'Who's up for getting smashed on sloe gin, then?' Calypso asked.

*   *   *

Caro was in the kitchen getting squash for Rosie and Milo when the phone rang. 'I'll get it, Granny Clem!' she called, going over and picking it up.

'Churchminster 592.'

'It's me. Can you come home?'

'I thought you were coming back here.'

'I really need you to come here now.'

Benedict didn't sound like himself. Caro got a horrible feeling in her stomach.

'Is something wrong? What's happened?'

'I'd prefer to talk face to face.'

'OK, I'll get the kids.'

'No, leave them there, darling. It's best you come by yourself.'

Caro was home in five minutes flat, kicking the snow off her boots at the front door. 'Darling? Are you all right?'

Benedict called out from the study. 'I'm in here.'

Caro rushed through and found him standing behind his desk. 'Thank God! I thought something dreadful had happened to you.'

He had a letter in his hand. 'I found this on the doorstep when I got back. Promise me you won't get upset. It's completely ridiculous, and there's no way he can do this.'

'Do what? Who?' Benedict's expression worried her.

He came round and handed the letter to her. 'It's from a lawyer, acting on behalf of Sebastian.'

'Why's he writing to us?' Confused, she started to read.

Patrick Carver & Associates
32, The Strand
London

317

WC2N 6JL

Caroline and Benedict Towey
No 1, Mill House
Churchminster
31 December
Dear Mr and Mrs Towey,

Our client: Sebastian Belmont

We have been instructed by Mr Sebastian Charles Belmont, in relation to your son Milo. We understand from our client that he has regular contact with his son, and has become concerned for Milo's wellbeing. Our client has a number of concerns about Milo's home environment, including Milo being exposed to inappropriate sexualized behaviour and excessive alcohol consumption, resulting from your failure to fulfil your parenting duties towards Milo.

In addition Milo has expressed on a number of occasions that he is not happy at home, and has become upset and clingy when he had to leave our client and his partner and return to you.

In view of this, our client feels it would be in Milo's best interests for him to live with our client and to see you regularly. Our client understands Milo has found it difficult to adjust following a recent house move, and proposes to take Milo back to London and reinstate him at his previous school. We should be grateful if you would take legal advice in relation to the contents of this letter, and we look forward to hearing from you or your legal advisor.

318

We hope matters can be agreed, but in the event that they are not we are instructed to make an application to Court for a residence order in favour of our client.

Yours faithfully,
Patrick Carver & Associates

Caro stared dumbly at the letter. 'I don't understand . . .'

Benedict's beautiful features were tight with fury. 'That outrageous bastard. He's going for custody of Milo.'

CHAPTER FIFTY

Benedict had the car keys before she knew it. 'I should have *known* he'd try something like this!'

'Benedict, please!' Caro followed her husband to the front door. 'There has to be some misunderstanding . . .'

'For God's sake, Caro!' He looked at her. 'Wake up and listen to yourself! He's been planning this from day one! I never bought the redemption crap.'

'But why would he *do* something like this?'

Benedict's face was grim. 'That's what I'm about to find out.'

Caro stared at him. 'I'm coming with you.'

Thirty seconds later the Porsche screeched off in the direction of Bluebell Cottage. 'Surely he'd never say such horrible things?' Caro was in complete denial. 'He was there, Benedict, he knows what really happened!'

'Exactly. And now he's trying to make up allegations to try and smear you.' His hands tightened on the steering wheel. 'Jesus! I thought I'd seen it all from that pond life, but this scrapes the bottom of the barrel.'

Caro gazed out at the snowy landscape and had an insane urge to laugh. This was ludicrous! *When we get there Seb will tell us it's all a wind-up. And I'll bloody kill him.*

It seemed an age before Sebastian's voice sounded from behind the front door. 'Hello?'

'It's us, Belmont,' Benedict said. 'Open up and tell us what the hell this letter is about.'

For a horrible moment Caro thought Sebastian wouldn't respond, but then they heard the sound of the lock. The door opened and he stood there, in a chunky knit cardigan that looked oddly domesticated. 'You received it, then?' he said solemnly.

Benedict took a menacing step forward. Caro pulled him back. 'Yes, we got it, Seb.' She looked him in the eye, still not really believing what was happening. 'I don't understand, why would you say such things? You're not really serious about going for custody of Milo?'

His lips moved, as if he were about to smile.

Tell me it's not true, she thought.

'I'm afraid you've left me no choice,' he said smoothly. 'I've become increasingly worried about Milo being under your care. Suzette and I both think it's better if he comes to live with us.'

There was a stunned silence, before Benedict lunged forward. 'You duplicitous son of a bitch!'

'Benedict!' Caro screamed, as he grabbed Sebastian by the shoulders and pushed him back

320

into the hall. There was a brief tussle before Sebastian broke free, his smugness momentarily ruffled.

'Suzette!' he shouted. 'Are you getting this?' Caro's eyes swerved upwards to see Suzette at the top of the stairs filming with a camcorder.

'What is this about?' Caro said furiously. 'Why are you *filming* us?'

Sebastian started retreating back up the stairs. 'Because your *husband*'—he emphasized the word—'has shown aggressive behaviour towards me on a number of occasions in the past, and I was worried about my and Suzette's safety.' He adopted a righteous expression from the safety of the fifth stair. 'Not without good reason, it turns out.'

Caro looked at Suzette, hoping she'd be more reasonable, but was met by a blank stare.

'You can't be bloody serious!' she snapped. 'How dare you make out I'm an unfit mother? I explained to you what happened with the wine!'

'Oh, come on, darling. You were drunk! Drunk—and about to get in a car and go and pick up our son from school!'

'I would *never* jeopardize Milo's safety! That's why I called you!'

'Suzette and I have both witnessed your drinking, Caro!'

'What?' She choked out a laugh. 'You're questioning *my* abilities as a mother? You're the one who's barely seen his son for the last five years!'

'That's because you haven't let me.' A weary note entered Sebastian's voice. 'Don't carry on this charade any longer, Caro, I beg you.'

'Caro.' Benedict took her arm. 'Let's go.'

'No!' she said angrily. 'I want to know why he's

321

doing this.'

'He's going to use anything you say against us,' her husband said quietly in her ear.

'Because a son should be with his father,' Sebastian said self-righteously. He shot a look at Benedict. 'His *real* father. Milo has suffered long enough without me, Caro.'

'You *bastard*!' For a split second she wanted to fly up those stairs and scratch his eyes out. It took a superhuman effort to keep herself calm. 'You're right, Benedict, we need to leave,' she said.

In silence they turned and walked out of the door. It clicked shut behind them like a gunshot. Neither said a word as they got in the car. It was only when Benedict pulled up abruptly a hundred metres down the road that Caro let rip.

'He can't do this! He can't!' The thought of her baby being taken away to live hundreds of miles away made her want to physically retch.

Benedict's earlier fury had been replaced by resolve. 'Of course he can't. He won't, Caro. Everyone knows he hasn't got a leg to stand on.'

She barely heard. '*Is* Milo unhappy?' She was thinking desperately. 'He's said a few things, but I just thought he was playing up.'

'Caro, Milo is the happiest little boy I've ever met. I wouldn't put it past that lowlife to try and put things in his mind, but it's not going to work.'

'We did let him wander off, though! He was on the main road, Benedict. Anything could have happened!' Caro still tortured herself about the incident.

Her husband leaned over and put his arm round her. 'Darling, listen to me. You're a wonderful, loving mother, and that deluded bastard hasn't got

322

a leg to stand on. He'd get laughed out of court.'

She burrowed her face in his chest. How could one human being do this to another, let alone the father of her own son? 'What do we do now?'

Benedict stroked her hair. 'We call my lawyer.'

CHAPTER FIFTY-ONE

Oblivious to the drama unfolding, Calypso finally finished the last of her holiday unpacking. She shoved her suitcase back into the already rammed spare bedroom wardrobe, glumly wondering when she'd get the chance to wear her bikinis and thong sandals again. The sunny climes of Antigua already felt like a lifetime away.

Camilla had asked if she wanted to go back with her and Jed to the cottage, but Calypso had told them she was cool. She probably wasn't Jed's favourite person right now, anyway. Camilla had told her not to worry, but Calypso could still kick herself. Why did she *say* things like that?

It had been weird, going back to her house as a single woman. This time yesterday she and James had been getting ready together and sharing a glass of champagne. This morning they'd been in bed together. Now she'd never see him again.

As she walked back into her bedroom, Calypso could faintly smell the Tom Ford aftershave she'd bought James still hanging in the air. She sat down on the bed, and looked round the room.

She was feeling strangely OK. A bit wrung-out and knackered from the heavy conversation earlier, but definitely fine. There was none of that horrible gut-wrenching devastation she'd felt when she and Rafe had finished. And at least, this time, she hadn't had to deal with the double whammy of finding out she'd been cheated on.

The thing that had probably upset her the most was how nasty James had turned. Of course Calypso understood how horrible he must have felt, but did it warrant such a vicious attack on her? The whole thing had made her even more certain she'd had to end it.

The bed was unmade, the dent in the pillow on James's side still visible. *His side.* Well, there was going to be no more of that. She could have it all to herself again. Sleep like a starfish whenever she wanted! Eat toast in bed again! James had hated having crumbs on the sheets.

Three minutes later the bed linen was going round in the washing machine, the smell of James gone for ever. Calypso leant back against the cupboard, listening to the hypnotic 'chug chug' as the machine went round. She kept waiting for her stomach to drop, for the moment to hit when she realized it was actually over, but there was nothing. It was an exhilarating feeling.

Beyond the kitchen window it was black. Calypso looked at the clock on the cooker. Just after seven. She had a stack of films on Sky Plus, and a space with her name on it on the sofa, but she was strangely restless.

She had her head in the fridge wondering whether the bottle of opened Pinot Grigio was too old to drink when her mobile went. She ran into the next room to get it.

It was the Maltings, Angie's number. 'It's me, Archie.'

'Oh.' That was a bit random. 'Hi, Happy Newzy and all that.' Calypso stifled a yawn.

'You, too. Have fun last night?'

'Apparently I was on your shoulders?'

'Yup. You remember the leapfrogging?'

'No?!'

'Or begging to be allowed to jump over Felicity Kendal's back?'

Calypso sat down on the sofa. 'I didn't!'

'You did. It was the best entertainment of the evening. I had no idea you were so athletic.'

She remembered what James had said about everyone seeing her knickers, and changed the subject. 'So, what are you up to? Trying to get rid of a hangover, like me?'

'Actually, I wondered if you felt like a jar at the pub.'

'Me and you?'

'Yeah. Fancy it?' He sounded relaxed. 'Ma and Pa are passed out on the sofa, and I'm going a bit stir-crazy.'

Calypso thought how tired she was, how all she was good for was a night in front of the telly. But that yearning for human contact washed over her again.

'Why not?'

*   *   *

'Cheers.' They clinked glasses, his pint against her wine. Despite them being virtually the only customers in there, Jack had still lit the fire. It made up for the slightly droopy Christmas tree looking a bit forlorn in the corner.

'Thanks for coming out.' Archie was annoyingly

fresh-faced, all clear eyes and tanned skin. 'My parents are cool, but after being cooped up with them all day I fancied seeing someone my age.'

'Actually, I'm not your age,' she said.

He looked surprised. 'How old are you, then?'

'Twenty-eight. Way older.'

'I'm twenty-three,' he said amusedly. 'Five years is nothing.'

'It is from where I'm standing.' Calypso thought back to what she'd been doing when she'd been twenty-three. Off round the world, partying.

'I spoke to James last night, he seemed like a nice bloke.'

'Actually, we broke up this morning.'

Archie put his glass down. 'Sorry, I didn't realize.'

'Nothing to be sorry about.' She didn't mention that it was her being on Archie's shoulders that had sparked the whole thing off.

'Are you upset?'

Calypso pondered his question. 'You know what, I really don't think I am. Does that sound bad?'

'Not at all.' Archie's eyes twinkled. 'He was a bit serious.'

'That's one way of putting it.'

Archie didn't question her sarcastic tone. 'Oh well,' he said philosophically. 'At least now he's got more time to practise his Alexandria Technique.'

'It's Alexander.' Calypso threw a beer mat at him. 'Stop taking the piss, you cheeky sod!'

Pleasantly relaxed in each other's company, they started talking about old times. 'How about when you got grounded at school for sneaking out of your boarding house?' Archie asked her. 'I remember your mum coming round and telling my mum.'

'Yes!' Calypso started laughing. 'Olivia Barton and I went to an over-twenty-one night at the Café de Paris when we were fourteen. Someone dobbed us in to the dorm mistress, and she actually came down and marched us out.'

'Didn't you take your dad's car out joyriding once, as well?'

Calypso covered her face. 'Yes, and burnt the clutch out! God, I was awful. Although that time I was only about two weeks off my seventeenth birthday, so *technically* it was nearly legal.' She picked up her drink again. 'I can't believe you remember this stuff. I'd forgotten all about it.'

''Course, you were the glamorous wild child. Me and my mates always used to fancy you.'

'Archie, shut up!'

He laughed. 'Especially when you wore those denim dungaree shorts.'

'Hey, those would be seriously retro now.' She looked at him. 'I must have been fourteen when I wore those shorts, which made you nine. Nine-year-olds don't think about stuff like that, do they?'

'You'd be surprised.' He lifted his pint, his gaze meeting hers over the glass. Calypso looked away. Was the cheeky little monkey giving her the *eye*?

It was nearly midnight by the time they walked out. Archie was actually quite good company, if you liked things on a funny random level. It had been a nice way to while away the evening.

'I'll walk you home,' he said.

'Don't worry.'

'I insist. Mum would never let me hear the end of it if I didn't.'

'Seriously, I don't think anyone's going to jump

327

me between the pub and my front door.'

'I'll watch from here, just in case.'

'If you insist.' She went to high five him. 'See you, loser.'

He caught her arm. 'See you, deadbeat.'

She was more pissed than she'd realized. Concentrating on putting one foot in front of the other, Calypso reached her gate. She turned back and saw Archie still outside the pub.

'See ya!'

He shouted something back, but she didn't catch it. Calypso shivered, her thoughts already on her warm bed. It was only when she got inside that she realized her sheets were still wet, and in the washing machine.

CHAPTER FIFTY-TWO

Kizzy could still feel the touch of Javier's lips on her skin. It sounded totally cheesy, but she knew what screaming fans felt like now, when they were kissed by their idol and declared they were never going to wash again.

OK, so she wasn't *that* bad, but she'd been a happy mess these past few days. She couldn't sleep, eat, or concentrate—even on Nobby. She kept replaying every moment of her conversation with Javier: poring over his words, and analysing what the inflections in his voice might have meant. She'd been so flustered at the end that she hadn't even asked Javier how long he was going away for. Was it days, or even weeks? Kizzy doubted it would be that long with Javier's training schedule, but it was still a delicious kind of agony, not knowing. How much longer could she keep hanging on?

Unbeknownst to her, Kizzy was being kept under a watchful eye. Angie knew that everyone was talking about the electrifying dance between Javier and Kizzy, and she'd seen him lead her away somewhere afterwards. She knew if she told Freds he'd tell her to stay out of it, but Angie just had this *feeling*. 'Ominous' was too strong a word, but it wasn't every day that a man like Javier Hamilton-Scott came into a young girl's life. He was fine as a sex symbol, a semi-mythical figure for Angie and millions of women worldwide to fancy, but to be swept up into his world . . . Angie couldn't even start to grasp the complexities Kizzy would have to face: there was a wife in a coma, an eighteen-year age gap, and all the press attention a new relationship would surely bring . . .

Freddie would kill her. But she didn't care. She needed to make sure Kizzy knew what she was getting herself into.

*   *   *

She chose a moment when she and Kizzy were in the feed shed, making up the horses' dinner. A muddy Barksdale lay between them, gnawing on a pilfered carrot.

'Would you mind passing me the feed scoop?' Kizzy looked up from where she sat on an upturned water bucket, making up Nobby's bran and nuts.

'What was that?'

'The feed scoop.' It was the third time Angie had asked. Kizzy reached behind her and handed it over.

329

'You were miles away,' Angie smiled. She saw Kizzy's cheeks darken.

'Sorry.'

'No need to apologize.' Angie dug a pile of nuts out of the feed bin and cut to the chase. 'Javier looked very enamoured with you at the ball.'

'Did he? Oh, right.' Kizzy started mixing furiously.

'You looked rather taken with him, as well.' She watched Kizzy's whole face turn red. 'I didn't mean to embarrass you.'

'It's all right, you're not.' Kizzy brushed a strand of hair away with the back of her hand.

'It's just that . . . well, I want to make sure you're all right, Kizzo,' Angie said gently. 'Javier's a terrifically handsome chap, and I can totally understand why you might be attracted to him.'

Angie wondered if she'd gone too far, but then Kizzy's pretty face creased up into anguish. 'Angie, I'm so confused!' She sat up. 'I mean, I *know*, of course I do, about Sarah and everything, but when I'm with him . . .' She searched for the words. 'Nothing else seems to matter. Do you know what I mean?'

'Oh, sweetheart. Life is complicated sometimes, isn't it?'

'You're telling me.' It was a massive relief for Kizzy to let her feelings out in the open. 'I think I'm going mad, I really do. I keep telling myself it won't work, so why do I feel breathless every time I think about him?'

'Has he told you how he feels about you?'

'Not in so many words, but he looks at me in this way . . .' Kizzy didn't want to mention the kiss, in case Angie disapproved. 'I sound so stupid. I've

330

only ever met him five times.'

'Once is enough, if you feel a real connection with someone.'

Kizzy nodded eagerly. 'That's what it is, Angie, a *connection*.' She looked hopeful. 'Do you, I mean, do you reckon anything could ever happen?'

'I don't know, Kiz. You can feel all sorts of connections with people, even when you're happily married.' Angie's smile was meaningful. 'But it's not always enough to start a life with someone.'

'You're right.' Kizzy's face dropped. 'I've been kidding myself.'

'Darling, I'm sure that's not true.' Angie was dismayed she might have upset her. 'Just go into this with your eyes wide open, won't you?'

Barksdale's ears pricked up, and moments later Edward walked in, his nose bright red from the cold.

'Freddie said to tell you he's gone to watch the rugby.'

It was so quiet it almost came out as a whisper. Angie laughed, trying to lighten the mood. 'That means he'll roll into bed at midnight!' She smiled at him kindly. 'Do you follow the rugger, Edward?'

'No.' He fixed his eyes on the floor. 'I'll go and get the horses in.'

Angie watched him scuttle out. 'Was it something I said?'

Kizzy shook her head. 'That's just Edward. Anything other than horses, and he dies of embarrassment. It was hard enough getting out of him what music he was into.'

'I wish I knew what to do to bring him out of his shell.'

Kizzy wondered whether to mention what she'd

seen in Edward's bedroom. Angie would only worry even more.

'I'll go and give him a hand,' she said, getting up.

'Kizzy.' Angie stopped her. 'If you ever need to talk . . .'

'Thank you.' She gave Angie a grateful smile and walked out into the yard. Her head was all over the shop. If Javier did ring, was it really worth them meeting up again? Up, down, hope, despair: she ran the whole gamut of emotions in half a second. *I can't live like this*, she thought.

A piece of scrap paper fluttered across the yard. Kizzy went over and picked it up. It was a credit card receipt for the cinema in Bedlington at eight o'clock in the evening, for the new Matt Damon film. Eight o'clock. It was dated from two days ago, on 31 December.

Edward came out of Nobby's stable, holding his lead-rope.

'Is this yours?' she asked. It couldn't belong to anyone else, they'd all been at the ball.

Edward took the receipt and stared at it. 'Er, thanks.' Blushing violently, he hurried off in the direction of the field.

Kizzy frowned. Edward had told Angie he was going to a party on New Year's Eve with friends. Why would he lie? A horrible thought struck her. What if there had been no party and no friends?

'Oh, Edward,' she said sorrowfully.

CHAPTER FIFTY-THREE

Camilla and Jed were babysitting Milo and Rosie at theirs. Caro had rung the night before to ask if they would, as she and Benedict had a financial meeting to go to they'd forgotten about. Camilla wasn't due back at work for a few more days anyway, so she and Jed had gladly agreed.

Milo and Rosie had only been there an hour that morning, and already the cottage looked like a bomb had hit it. Milo had decided he wanted to pull all the cushions off the sofa in the living room and jump on to them from the armchair. Camilla watched from the other chair with Rosie on her lap, as Jed helped Milo climb up again.

'That's it . . . put your foot there . . . careful.'

'Wheeeee!' Milo said, as he leapt off the arm of the chair and scored a direct hit. Shrieking with laughter, he got up. 'Can we do it again, Jed?'

'Maybe give it a few minutes.' Jed shot a crooked grin at Camilla. 'I'm not sure Auntie Billa's cushions can take it.'

Milo went over and wrapped his arms round Jed's long legs. 'I love you, Uncle Jed,' he said blissfully. 'I really do.'

Camilla's heart swelled as she watched Jed lean down and kiss Milo on the top of his head. 'I love you too, mate.'

'Can we watch *Rastamouse*?' Rosie asked.

'For a little while, sweet pea, then how about we go for a nice walk?' Camilla gently put Rosie down and stood up. 'Now then, who wants a drink?'

The two children sat transfixed in front of the television as Camilla and Jed tackled the mess in the kitchen. Despite putting newspaper down, Milo and Rosie had still managed to get paint everywhere. Someone's little hand had even found a fluorescent pen and done a very impressive scribble on the right-hand corner of the tabletop.

'Never mind,' Jed said. 'I think it looks quite artistic. You could probably sell that for a couple of thousand quid on eBay, and say it's modern art.'

Camilla laughed. 'You think?'

Their eyes met over the table. 'You've got paint on your cheek,' Jed said.

He walked up to the sink and got a bit of kitchen roll. Dampening it under the tap, he came round and started to dab Camilla's cheek.

'My little warrior princess.' His touch was gentle.

Camilla smiled up at him, enjoying the feel of his breath on her face.

'This is nice, isn't it? I mean, having the kids here,' he said.

'It's lovely. It always is. The house feels good with them in it.'

'I agree.'

Was he giving her a cue? This was the most they'd talked about children for a long while. 'Maybe now is a good time to look into adopting,' she offered up.

Jed carried on wiping her cheek, even though the paint had to have gone by now. 'What if I'm not good enough?'

'Of course you're good enough!' Camilla exclaimed. 'Jed, you're the most . . .'

She stopped as Milo walked in.

'Yuck. Are you two kissing?'

'Might be,' Jed said, winking at him. He squeezed Camilla's shoulder and let her go. The little boy walked round the table, trailing his hand on the top. 'Can I come and live here?'

The two adults exchanged a look. 'Why would you want to do that, Milo?' Camilla asked. 'You love living with Mummy and Daddy, don't you?'

He nodded. 'Yeah, I suppose. But Daddy said . . .'

'What did Daddy say?' Camilla asked, as her nephew started picking at the fruit bowl. Milo pulled off a banana.

'Milo, what did your daddy say?' she asked again. 'Do you mean Benedict?'

It was too late; Milo's attention had wandered. Gripping the banana like a gun, he skipped back off into the living room.

Jed shrugged and put the tissue down on the side.

Camilla hesitated. 'Jed . . .'

There was a bellow from next door. 'Jed, come and watch telly with me!'

He touched her face. 'I love you, babe. Let's talk about this another time, OK?'

*   *   *

Caro and Benedict were waiting in the reception of Stonewall's law firm in Cheltenham. A friend had recommended it as the best family law firm outside London.

'Are you sure you don't want to tell your family?'

'The Third World War will probably kick off if

335

we do. You know Calypso. Before we say anything, let's just see if we can sort it out . . .' Caro trailed off. It was true, she didn't want to worry anyone unnecessarily, but there was another reason too: telling people would make what was happening real.

'Besides,' she said determinately, 'Sebastian's not going to get custody of Milo, so there's no point stirring things up.'

Benedict squeezed her knee. 'That's my girl.'

The raw fury he'd initially displayed had been replaced by calm, and a gritted-teeth determination. Benedict was an organizer, a doer who always wanted to solve any problem. Now they'd taken the first steps and got the ball rolling he was a lot more rational about things.

Caro, on the other hand, was a pile of nerves. She'd barely had any sleep since they'd found out what Sebastian was up to. She was angry about what he was doing, and furious with herself. What a fool she'd been, to be taken in by the nice guy act! She should have known. She'd been over and over why he'd do this to her, and come to the only logical conclusion. Sebastian always got what he wanted. And now, after five years, he'd decided to swan back in and claim Milo as his own. Caro stared miserably at an abstract painting on the wall. It wasn't just the utter unfairness of Sebastian's accusations that hurt so much, it was his insinuation that she wasn't a good mother. And that Milo was anything other than the very centre of her world.

*   *   *

Louise Rennison was a strong, capable blonde in

336

her late thirties. After her secretary had brought in freshly made coffee and shortbread she sat back and scrutinized the letter.

'I take it you are refuting the allegations your ex-husband has made?'

'We certainly are,' Caro said emotionally. 'This whole thing is a nightmare.'

Louise surveyed her through trendy black-rimmed spectacles. 'Mrs Towey, I appreciate how upsetting this is for you. If you could take me through the history of your situation, and how we've ended up here today, I'll do my best to help you.'

She had a calm authority that was reassuring, but it was still mortifying for Caro, having to explain to a complete stranger how her six-year-old son had ended up taking a vibrator to school. Caro also told her about Milo saying she and Benedict didn't love him any more, and explained how she was convinced Sebastian had been bad-mouthing them to him. It didn't produce the result she'd hoped for.

'The problem is, small children say things sometimes that they don't mean,' Louise said. 'If it's a one-off, we'll have a hard time proving it.'

She returned to the copious amounts of notes she'd been making, and added another point.

Benedict's hand tightened round Caro's. 'He hasn't really got a case, Louise, has he?'

The lawyer paused for a moment and looked up. 'My first impression is no.'

Caro felt the first flicker of hope as Louise continued.

'We have evidence to prove his claims otherwise, and of course the fact that Caro has been the primary carer throughout Milo's life.

Despite repeated attempts by you, Mr Belmont has barely played any role in his son's life bar the maintenance payments. Now, quite audaciously in my opinion, he has applied for a residence order, and unfortunately we have to follow procedures.' Louise cast Caro a keen look. 'Aside from the claims he's making, do you have any idea why Mr Belmont would now want Milo to live with him?'

'Is he doing it just to spite me?' Caro shook her head. 'I've been asking myself the same thing.'

'Hmm.' Louise considered it. 'Retribution is a common factor in these cases. How about any monetary gain? His maintenance payments are on the generous end of the scale. Could he think it's more economical for Milo to live with him?'

The couple looked at each other. 'That's unlikely,' Caro said. 'Sebastian has a very well-paid job.'

'Milo does have a substantial inheritance from Caro's grandfather, but I can't see that has anything to do with it,' Benedict said. 'It's very well-protected.'

'Can I ask how much?' Louise asked.

Caro gave Benedict the nod. 'Just over one point two million pounds,' he said. 'To be released to Milo on his twenty-first birthday.'

'And who are the trustees?'

'I am,' Caro said, 'along with my father and grandmother.'

'Are you allowed access to any of the funds?'

Caro nodded. 'But only small sums, for things like Milo's schooling and upkeep. We're also allowed to invest a percentage of it in property and stocks and shares, to add to a portfolio for Milo, but it's all strictly regulated. Sebastian doesn't have

338

a say in any of that.'

Louise nodded and sat back. 'Is there a possibility Mr Belmont really might believe Milo would be happier with him?'

Benedict made a derisive noise. 'That man only thinks about one person, and that's himself.'

'Caro?' Louise was studying her. 'What do you think? No matter how unreasonable his demands are, Mr Belmont obviously feels very strongly that Milo should be with him.'

Caro hesitated. 'I don't know.'

Benedict gave his wife a long look. 'What happens now, Louise?'

'Well, we will write back to Mr Belmont's lawyer, as I said, refuting the claims. The court will then notify us with a date for a conciliation appointment. It sounds far more frightening than it actually is.' Louise smiled. 'It's really just a talk between the parents, in a neutral environment away from everything, with a court-appointed mediator present. You'd be amazed how many parents can sort their differences out. Sometimes all that's needed is a bit of time and space.'

'Is this mediator appointed by the court?' Benedict asked.

Louise nodded. 'They're called Cafcass officers—which stands for "Children and Family Court Advisory and Support Service". They're only there to look out for the child's best interests, not to take sides.'

'What happens if Sebastian refuses to play ball, and carries on with this ridiculous charade?'

'Then we'll have to go before the judge, who will probably advise a Cafcass report.'

'What's that?' Caro asked.

'Basically a report about the child's life, so the court can assess whether to keep the child with the existing parent, or if he or she would be better off being placed with the other one. A Cafcass officer interviews both parents, and comes to the child's home to see them. As it's quite extensive, they'll speak to other relevant authorities: teachers, doctors . . .'

It sounded very invasive. Caro thought what Miss Ekins might say about Vibratorgate and cringed. Still, it wasn't enough to take Milo away from her, was it? She focused on what Louise was saying.

'The report normally takes anything from six weeks to three months, depending on the Cafcass officer's workload.'

'And if it comes back in favour of Sebastian?' Caro had to know everything.

'We'd refute it, of course. There would be a bit more toing and froing, and then a final hearing would be set by the court.'

'To decide who gets custody of Milo?' It didn't feel like Caro was having this conversation.

'That's not going to happen,' Benedict told his wife. Caro was somewhat reassured when Louise didn't contradict him.

'I know it's hard, Mrs Towey, but please try not to worry,' Louise said. 'I'll do everything I can to make sure this situation is resolved happily. In the meantime'—she flashed Benedict a wry look—'please try to avoid any more altercations. We don't want to give them any more ammunition to fire back at us.'

Louise Rennison was a good woman to have on their side. *Everything's going to be OK*, Caro told herself.

It had to be.

CHAPTER FIFTY-FOUR

Kizzy was watching a DVD on her laptop when her phone starting ringing. She snatched it up from where it lay beside her. Private number.

Her heart started jumping. She let it ring twice more and answered. 'Hello?' Her voice was astonishingly steady, considering the brass band going off in her chest.

'Is that Katrina Milton?'

'Yes.' Her heart sank on hearing a woman's voice.

'This is Bedlington Dental Surgery, I'm just ringing to remind you that you're due for your six-monthly check-up.'

Gutted. Kizzy fobbed the receptionist off with an excuse about calling back, and sat glumly against the wall. That was it; Javier was never going to call. Her back ached from where she'd been sitting, rubbing salt into the wound.

Her phone went off again. What now, the bloody doctor's? Kizzy caught her breath as she saw it was another number she didn't recognize. *Don't get excited.* Javier would definitely have a private number.

'Hello?'

There was nothing for a moment, and then a deep voice spoke. 'Kizzy?'

She sat bolt upright, not caring if it was painful.

'Javier?'

'How are you?'

'Good. Really good!' She took a breath. The brass band had started thumping away again, making it difficult to breathe. 'How was Monte Carlo?'

'I'm still here, actually.'

'Oh, right.' Kizzy felt a stab of disappointment.

'We're flying back soon, and I was ringing to arrange that dinner you promised me.'

Kizzy gripped the phone delightedly. 'Great!'

'Would you like to come over to Homelands for say, seven o'clock tomorrow? I can arrange for a car to come and collect you.'

'That's really nice, thanks, but I'll probably drive.' She didn't want her dad reading her the riot act.

She heard Javier pause. 'Up to you. Well, I'll see you then, Kizzy.'

'Bye,' she managed to say normally and put the phone down. *Oh my God, he rang!* She gave a squeal of excitement. It really had happened! Javier had actually called, and she was going to Homelands for dinner! The thought of seeing him again made her feel sick with nervous excitement.

*   *   *

How she got through the next twenty-four hours Kizzy never knew, but Homelands was a darkened castle as she drove up the winding drive the next evening. Nigel had answered the intercom, and buzzed the gates open for her, and as she parked the security lights came on, flooding into the car. Squinting slightly, she got her handbag off the passenger seat and climbed out.

Without all the other cars and people from the

342

party, the place seemed even bigger and more intimidating. Now she was closer, she could see light shining out of several of the ground-floor windows, although she still couldn't make out any sign of life. Should she just go up and knock on the front door? It seemed too big and important for everyday use. Kizzy was wondering whether there was some smaller side door she should be using when there was a crunch on the gravel behind her. Javier walked out of the darkness, his long waxed coat billowing out behind him. Salvador and Pablo followed at his heels.

'Kizzy, how are you?'

'Great! You?'

He nodded, and there was an awkward moment when they both stood there. Then Javier leant forward and kissed her on each cheek, making her skin burn.

'Sorry I'm a bit early,' she said.

'Not at all, I was just down at the stables.' He looked up at the house. 'Shall we go inside?'

He took her round the side, through an archway. Then he led her past the vegetable patch to the back door they'd walked out of at his party. A door off the corridor inside opened on to a long wide kitchen. It looked more old-fashioned than Kizzy had expected it to, with no microwaves or any mod cons like that, but the well-scrubbed table was huge, and there was an impressive array of utensils hanging from the walls and ceiling. Javier hesitated for a moment, as if he were unsure how to introduce it.

'This is the kitchen, obviously. The most important room in the house, according to Mary, anyway.'

'And we both know Mary knows best,' a voice said. A stout, elderly woman stood in the doorway, grey hair pulled back into a neat bun.

'What are you up to now, Javier, bringing your guests in through the back door?' Mary had a strong Irish accent.

Javier smiled, his face relaxing. 'Mary prefers our guests to enter more formally.'

Mary came forward and held her hand out. 'Whatever must you think of us? I'm Mary O'Gara, housekeeper here at Homelands. It's a pleasure to meet you.'

She had a motherly air about her that instantly put Kizzy at ease. 'Hi, Mary, I'm Kizzy Milton.'

'Kizzy's a pretty name, where's that from, then?' Despite the wrinkled skin, Mary's eyes were clear and keen.

'It's a nickname, my real name's Katrina. My dad said I was always whizzing about when I was younger. Whizz, kizz . . .' She smiled. 'Bit random, you know how nicknames are.'

'Well, you look like a Kizzy to me!' Mary declared. She glanced at Javier. 'I've made up your dinner and it's keeping warm in the oven. You can have it whenever you want.'

'What would I do without you?' There was an affectionate familiarity between them, that was more than just member of staff and employer.

'Starve, probably! I'm off up to my room. My friend has just sent me the new Joanna Trollope and I'm itching to start it.' Mary nodded at Kizzy. 'Make sure he looks after you properly. I'll be upstairs, Javier, if you want anything.'

She disappeared off down the corridor, little feet carrying her along at a fair old pace.

344

'Katrina,' Javier said. 'It really is very pretty, Mary was right.'

'Er, thanks.'

There was another, not entirely comfortable, pause. Javier cleared his throat. At that point Kizzy had a major revelation. He was as nervous as she was!

The knowledge somehow made her feel better. 'Has Mary been with you long?'

'Since before I was born. She's the real boss of this place, not me.' His dark eyes shot a sideways look at her. 'Even my father knew not to press his luck with her.'

He took her coat—the one he'd bought her—and complimented Kizzy on her outfit. At least her A-line black dress and opaque tights didn't seem too out of place for dinner in a stately home.

There was a cloakroom near the kitchen. Javier carefully hung Kizzy's coat on a hanger and put his waxed jacket on one of the hooks. Kizzy took the opportunity to see how the fine knit jumper he was wearing showed off his heavily muscled back and shoulders. The sight made her shiver involuntarily.

He came back into the kitchen. 'What can I get you to drink?'

'Uh, squash if you've got it.'

'Nothing stronger?'

'I'll probably wait for dinner, thanks.'

Javier nodded. 'I think Mary made up some lemonade in the pantry, if you'd like that?'

'Sounds great.'

He came back with two tall glasses filled with a cloudy liquid. Ice-cold, it was packed with flavour. The sharpness made Kizzy's eyes water.

'Is it all right?' He sounded almost anxious.

'Really good.' She smiled. 'It's just a bit stronger than the supermarket stuff I'm used to.'

Javier inclined his head towards the corridor. 'Would you like to sit down?'

From the little Kizzy had seen so far, this part of the house was very different from the formal rooms she'd seen at the party. Even though the proportions were still the same, it had a cosier, more domestic feel, with everyday bits of furniture, and pots of flowers on the windowsills.

The next door down the corridor led into a small space dominated by a squashy sofa and a sagging bookshelf filled with romantic novels. The grate in the fire was pulled out, as if someone was about to clean it.

'Mary's sitting room,' Javier said. He remained in the doorway after Kizzy had gone in, as if he didn't want to share such a small space with her. Kizzy hovered awkwardly in the middle of the room. Her eyes searched for something to look at and she fell gratefully on a large silver-framed photo on the mantelpiece. Her stomach dropped as she realized it showed Javier and Sarah on their wedding day. The bride's hair was pulled up off her thoroughbred face, and she had her arm draped round her groom in an intimate gesture. Kizzy hastily averted her eyes, but not before Javier had seen her do it.

He put his hands in his pockets and took them out again. 'Would you like me to show you round? I don't know how much you saw at the party.'

'I'd love that.'

He smiled, seemingly relieved. 'Great, follow me.'

*   *   *

346

'How old is Homelands?' Kizzy asked. They quickly left behind the east wing, and were back in the more formal spaces of the west one.

'It was built in 1792 by a great architect of the time, Sir John Butterworth. My great-great-great grandfather bought it in the mid-eighteen hundreds. The Hamilton-Scotts have been here ever since.'

Kizzy detected a mocking note as Javier stopped through a pair of double doors. He pushed them open. Beyond was the biggest room Kizzy had ever seen. It was empty save for miles of carpet, and lavishly decorated walls.

'The unimaginatively named Great Hall.'

Kizzy peered in. The domed ceiling was so high she had to crane her neck to see it properly. Everywhere she looked was gold and pink. There were six huge windows at the far end of the room, with a balcony running across them.

'It has some of the finest examples of baroque plasterwork in the country,' Javier told her.

'Wow.'

'Ridiculous, isn't it?'

Kizzy giggled. 'No! It's very grand. What do you use it for?'

'We hire it out for functions and conferences.' Javier put his hands back in his pockets, rocking on his heels. 'I think it would be better as an indoor riding school, but I don't think the National Trust would be too happy if we turned it into one.'

She laughed again. 'No, I don't think they would.'

Away from that sitting room and Sarah's photo, Javier warmed up. He was a confident and knowledgeable guide and seemed to know every little bit of history about the place. It felt like they walked for hours, through drawing rooms with fireplaces the size of Kizzy's house, a grand old library chock-a-block with leatherbound books, and endless reception rooms.

'I'd get lost living here,' she said as they proceeded down yet another wide, sweeping corridor, this one decorated with a long row of busts.

'People have. When my grandfather Augustus lived here, guests would leave a trail of confetti from their rooms, so they'd be able to find their way back after dinner.'

'No way!'

'Way,' Javier said dryly. 'Although I suspect it was more to do with the amount of port they sank at dinner. My grandfather was fond of a drink.'

Kizzy smiled, wondering if Javier would mention any other members of the family. In all the formal rooms she'd seen, there had been few feminine touches to show Sarah had ever lived there. Maybe Javier was only showing her what he wanted to. Even the ground floor was so massive Kizzy doubted she'd even seen half of it.

They stopped in a long wide gallery, with polished wood on the walls and floor. Gilt-framed portraits hung in a row on each side. Javier pointed to one, of a stern-looking grey-haired man in a tartan kilt and tweed jacket, a gun dog at his feet.

'My father, Douglas. He was extremely proud of his Scottish heritage.'

That same mocking note. Kizzy studied the picture. Lord Douglas Hamilton-Scott had had the same upright bearing and wide shoulders as his son,

348

but his eyes were grey and cold. Kizzy remembered what Angie had said about him and Javier falling out, and imagined it must have been very hard being Douglas's child.

Javier chose not to linger at the portrait and walked down to another one, several down. 'My mother, Elena.'

Kizzy followed him and gazed up at the exotic, dark-haired woman in the long red gown. She could instantly see where Javier had got his good looks from: the full lips and dark, sensuous eyes. Elena was gazing slightly off-centre, into the distance. She looked slightly wistful, as if dreaming of a far-off place.

'She's really beautiful, Javier.'

'Isn't she?' His voice came alive again. 'This was painted when she first came to Homelands.'

Kizzy looked at the entrancing face. 'What was she like?'

'She was the best, Kizzy.' Javier smiled. 'She had such a passion for life, running round barefoot like a child, hair tumbling down her back. The staff had never seen anything like it. We'd spend every summer out in the grounds exploring. I remember once we found a blackbird lying under the hedge; the poor thing looked like it had broken its wing. My mother carried it all the way home in the palm of her hand, but as soon as we stepped inside the house, it suddenly flew off. Mary was screaming, my mother was bent over laughing as this thing swooped and squawked all over the place . . .' Javier laughed himself, at the memory. 'My father was in his study, entertaining another lot of his important friends, and he came charging out, furious . . . Of course, he didn't see the funny side. He never did

349

when it came to his wife.'

Kizzy thought about Elena, a young girl alone in a foreign country. 'She must have missed Spain.'

'Very much.' Javier touched the portrait. 'At least she's back there now. She'd always wanted to be buried at home; it was about the only good thing my father ever did for her—and I think he acted more out of shame than anything. My mother dying must have been a relief to him.'

Kizzy tried not to show her shock. 'I'm sure that's not true.'

'Perhaps I'm being a little harsh, but it's more likely than people would think.'

'Do you mind if I ask what happened?' Kizzy said. 'We don't have to talk about it if you don't want to.'

'It's fine. I get little chance to remember her these days.' Javier was still staring at the wall, eyes fixed on his mother's face. 'There were a myriad of reasons. She became very ill during her pregnancy, and never really recovered. I was only young at the time, but I remember her being very worried shortly before the birth.' He leaned out and touched the picture's frame. 'All I can recall is her being taken to her room, and not being allowed to see her. It seemed to last a long time. I was out with my dog in the garden when Mary came to tell me there had been complications, and they'd both died.'

Kizzy tried to imagine a small boy, wandering round the vast lawns alone, waiting to see his mother again. It was heartbreaking.

'My father was distraught. He'd already given up on me by then: I was too much like her, and he made that very clear. He hoped Fraser would be the saving grace, the kind of son he needed.' Javier made a derisive sound. 'My mother knew that Fraser had died inside her, and that she was dying, too. She begged my father to bury them together, but he sent her body back without him. Fraser was given a very proper English funeral here. I think it was the only time I ever saw my father shed a tear.'

Kizzy didn't know what to say. 'I'm so, so sorry.'

'I'm sure worse things have happened to families.' Javier turned to her and made a conscious effort to smile. 'Listen to how morbid I sound. I'm sorry, Kizzy, this wasn't what I brought you here for.'

'It's fine, really.' She smiled back. 'I like hearing about your mum. She sounds like an amazing woman.'

Javier acknowledged her remark with a tiny nod. 'Shall we carry on the guided tour?'

They walked through another maze of corridors and more rooms. At the back of the east wing was an orangery with six large sash windows facing out on to the gardens. The place had a restful quality that was absent from the rest of the wing. Kizzy admired the fountains and pillars, the citrus trees flourishing as well as in any Mediterranean grove. 'It's lovely in here, I think it's my favourite room so far.'

He didn't answer for a moment. 'It was Sarah's favourite, too. She spent hours in here.'

Kizzy swallowed. Trust her to put her foot in it.

'Sorry, I didn't mean to . . .'

Javier turned on his heel abruptly. 'Let's have dinner.'

*   *   *

351

They didn't eat in the vast dining room she'd seen, but back in the kitchen, opposite each other at the table. Javier took an enormous earthenware dish out of the oven and placed it between them. Inside was a hearty lamb casserole, enough to feed ten.

While she'd sat at the table, Javier had put together a winter salad with leaves picked earlier from the garden.

'Are you sure you don't mind slumming it in here?' he asked, as he brought an open bottle of wine over.

'Not at all, it's really nice.'

'Apart from outside, I tend to spend most of my time in this room.'

She watched as he dished up a big portion and gave it to her. 'I'm sorry if I was abrupt earlier,' he said. 'I didn't mean to be.'

'It's all right, really.'

Their eyes met. Javier seemed to be about to say something, but instead he picked up the salad and handed it to her. 'Please, help yourself. Mary will never forgive me if she thinks I've let you go hungry.'

Javier filled Kizzy's wine glass, and asked if she was really comfortable sitting on a stool. They started to eat quietly, with the only sounds an occasional comment about the food or the scrape of cutlery against a plate.

It was a delicious stew, robustly flavoured, with large chunks of tender meat, but Kizzy had no appetite.

Javier noticed her barely touched plate. 'Is something wrong?'

'No, it's really lovely. I guess I'm not that hungry,' she admitted.

He pushed his plate away. 'Me, neither.'

Kizzy bit her lip. 'I'm not sure whether I should ask you about Sarah, but I want to.'

She'd been anxious about his reaction, but he just nodded his head. 'I'm glad I showed you the orangery. I haven't been in there for ages, and it reminded me of such happy times.'

'You don't go there any more?'

'One of the few benefits of living in a place this big is that there's enough space to avoid entire wings if you wish to.'

He got up quickly, but not before Kizzy caught the bleak look on his face. He cleared the plates and took them over to the sink. As he started to scrape the food off, she got up and went over to him. She put a tentative hand on his arm.

'I know this must be really weird for you, having me here.'

There was a long pause. Javier didn't move. Kizzy was just thinking she'd overstepped the mark, and that this was all horribly awkward, when he turned to look at her.

She gazed into his eyes. Up this close, they were a deep, warm brown, flecked with gold. His striking face was a mix of masculinity and vulnerability. Her heart quickened as he raised a hand to caress her cheek.

'Why do I feel as nervous as hell?' He searched for answers in her face. Kizzy could barely speak as his fingers continued to stroke her cheek. Her nipples were stiffening through the thin fabric, the heat building between her legs.

'God, Kizzy.' Suddenly his mouth was on hers. They kissed deeply, hungrily, and the space that Javier had kept between them closed as he pulled her into his body. He felt more wonderful than she'd ever imagined. Kizzy sighed as she felt his hands run over her back and ribcage, and brush tantalizingly across her breasts. Instinctively she pushed her groin into him, felt the hardness through his trousers. She knew if he even touched her between her legs, she would orgasm immediately.

I'm yours, Javier, she thought. *I couldn't resist even if I wanted to.*

His hands moved over her dress, gripped her pert buttocks. She heard him moan, and in one easy movement he had her up against the kitchen table. Dizzy with lust, Kizzy spread her legs, reaching for his zip. She wanted him so badly . . .

'Kizzy, no.' He pulled away half-heartedly.

'Why? Don't stop, you can't.' His mouth was inches from hers. Kizzy started kissing him again, running her hands through his thick smooth hair. She felt his erection grow.

'No . . . Kizzy . . . STOP!' This time he pulled away roughly, held her from him at arms' distance. 'We can't do this.'

Kizzy's face burned. She felt like a complete harlot. Javier was a married man. 'I'm s-sorry,' she stuttered. 'Don't get the wrong idea about me.'

'The wrong *idea*? Oh, Kizzy.' He dropped his head. 'You should be out having fun, not stuck in this mausoleum with me.'

'I want to be here!' She had never felt so certain about anything. 'Look, Javier, I know . . . I know you love Sarah.' *There, I've said it.* 'I wouldn't ever dream of trying to change that. But please, just let me *be* with you. It's enough, I swear it is.'

He took her face tenderly. 'You deserve better

than this. Someone who can give you a future.'

'*I'll* be the judge of that. I'm old enough to think for myself, Javier.'

Javier suddenly gave a low chuckle. His big white grin made the corners of his eyes crinkle. They weren't a flat black any more, but treacle-coloured and full of humour.

'You've certainly stirred things up for me, Kizzy.'

'In a good or bad way?' She wasn't sure how to take it, but Javier's smile was reassuring.

'Come here.'

He bent his head and kissed her again. His earlier raw passion was replaced by something lighter and less intense, like a sun-filled walk through a summer meadow.

CHAPTER FIFTY-FIVE

Nobby's sixth birthday was marked by a party in his stable.

'He's done so well, he deserves a bit of spoiling,' Angie said. Freddie poured the Bollinger and handed a glass to Archie and Edward.

'Cheers, everyone! To Nobby!'

'To Goldenballs! May your nonexistent balls remain big and golden,' Angie added. They raised their glasses to Nobby, who looked quizzical and snuffled round in Edward's pocket for another carrot.

Freddie adjusted his party hat. 'No Kizzo then, tonight?'

'It's her mum's birthday, I think they're going out somewhere.'

'Anywhere nice?'

'Bastilles,' Edward ventured. 'That new place in Bedlington.'

'Really, darling?' Angie said. 'You know, Freds, we must try it there.'

'You been then, Ed?' Archie had finally gone to the barber's, and his newly shorn locks showed off his handsome face perfectly. Angie thought so, anyway.

'Yes. My brother came over and took me.'

'Your brother?' Angie said. 'Edward, you should have brought him in! It would have been lovely to meet him.'

'He was just passing through.' A panicky blush was starting at the edge of Edward's cheeks. This was a long conversation for him.

'Well, you must let us meet him next time,' Angie said.

As the dogs started barking Freddie stuck his head out the door. 'That's Calypso's motor, isn't it?'

Angie looked, and saw the sporty Audi pull up. A slim figure got out, blonde hair shining under the security lights. Angie called, 'Yoo-hoo, we're in here!'

Calypso looked as glamorous as usual. She was wearing chain mail ankle boots that clanked as she walked, and her endless legs were encased in a pair of wet-look leggings, topped off by a funky fur jacket.

'Evening all.' A gust of hairspray and perfume floated into the stable. 'What's this, then?'

'It's Nobby's birthday,' Angie told her. 'We guessed when it was, and now we're having a little bash.'

'I love it!' Calypso said, looking up at the

balloons and 'Happy Birthday' sign across the stable door. 'Maybe I should start doing stable parties.' She sighed. 'Gotta be a lot more interesting than putting on a curry buffet for a bunch of IT analysts.' She smiled at the two younger men. 'Hi, guys.'

'Hey, Calypso,' Archie replied.

Edward mumbled something, and took a step back, apparently unnerved by this wild-haired beauty who looked like she'd just swaggered off a rock video.

'Can I interest you in some fizz?' Freddie asked.

'Thanks, Freds, but it's only a flying visit.' She looked at Angie. 'I've got that jam in the car Granny Clem's made for you. She'd kill me if she knew it had been sitting in my fridge for a week.'

'Darling, you're a busy girl!' Angie said. 'That's very sweet of you to drop it over. Are you sure you won't stay? We're about to order a Chinese.'

As usual the inside of Calypso's fridge resembled a nuclear landscape. 'I can't,' she said, 'you're always feeding me.'

'I like feeding you!' Angie exclaimed. 'We always order far too much anyway. You'd be doing us a favour.'

Calypso had only had a vegetable pakora since lunchtime, and was starving. 'You're on, sounds amazing.'

They ate in the kitchen, Avon and Barksdale circling under the table like a pair of hopeful seagulls. After two starters and a plate full of Peking duck, Angie was beat.

'Oh, dear,' she said, sinking back in her chair. 'Why don't I have an "off" button when it comes to Mr Woo's?' She picked up her white wine. 'How's the family, Calypso?'

'Everyone's cool. Getting back into the swing of things.' Caro had seemed a bit more stressed than normal when Calypso had popped round earlier, but she'd said she was just tired.

'Probably battening down the hatches like us after New Year,' Angie said. She watched Freddie offload the last of the deep-fried prawns on to his plate. 'Freds, don't you think you've had enough?'

He looked rather hurt. 'This is sustenance! I need it with this cold weather.'

'Fine.' Angie sighed. She really was going to have to think about signing them both up to the local gym.

Calypso wiped her mouth with a napkin. 'That's me done, as well.' Her leg accidentally brushed Edward's and he jumped like he'd been poked with a cattle prod.

'Sorry, Edward.' She turned to look at him. 'Looking forward to your next big race?'

All the blood seemed to rush to Edward's face in an instant. He made a gargling sound and gazed at his plate.

'Heythrop Hunt, end of the month!' Freddie said heartily. 'Isn't that right, Edward? We've all got high hopes. Nobby's running like an absolute beauty at the moment.'

'You know, you rode Nobby so well last time,' Calypso told Edward kindly. 'I thought you were amazing.'

He turned crimson and started eating furiously. Angie stifled a smile. If Edward sat there any longer next to their ravishing dinner guest, he might actually fatten up a bit.

*   *   *

358

Archie leant against the back door and watched as Calypso started up her car. 'Well, cheers, then,' she said through the open window.

'Cheers.' He looked at her meaningfully.

'What?' she asked. He'd been making annoying eyes at her all night.

'Nothing.' The smile broadened into a grin.

God, he was cocksure! Ignoring him, Calypso started putting her seat belt on.

'Has your engine been making that noise long?' he asked.

Her car had been producing a funny clattering sound recently. 'What, this?' she said, revving up the accelerator. 'A couple of weeks. I've been meaning to take it in . . .'

'I think I know what the problem is. Turn it off a minute.' Calypso did as she was told. He walked round to the front. 'Open the bonnet, I'll have a look.'

'Oh, for God's sake,' she grumbled, secretly pleased that the problem might be about to get sorted. It would save her a trip to the garage. Fumbling round the side of her seat, she realized she hadn't a clue where the bonnet catch was.

'Have you done it?' Archie called.

'I can't find it,' she muttered, feeling like a complete bimbo.

He came round and poked his head in the window. 'That's because it's under the dash,' he said cheerfully. As he leant across Calypso was treated to his arm and shoulder in her face.

'Watch it!' she protested, as a faint scent of Issey Miyake filled her nostrils.

'Sorry.' He came up, his face inches from hers.

His eyes were warm and fringed by long, soft lashes. Even this close his complexion was clear and fresh, without even a hint of an open pore.

Their eyes locked. 'Do you mind?' Calypso said haughtily, trying to regain control. Archie Fox-Titt had her pinned against the car seat. 'I can't breathe.'

He grinned again and stepped back. Calypso smoothed her hair down, her heart beating rather more quickly than she would have liked. Archie went round and pulled the bonnet up.

'What is it?' she called, as he bent down over the engine.

'Thought so. The fan shroud's come loose. The cooling fan was hitting it. Also, you're running low on oil.' He stood up and showed her. 'Look, it's way down the dipstick.'

'You're the dipstick,' she muttered. He was enjoying this.

'Sorry?'

'Nothing!'

He winked. 'I think we've got some oil in one of the sheds.'

'Thanks.' She gave a sarcastic smile as he passed. If he thought he was helping out a damsel in distress, then what did she care?

Three minutes later it was all done. 'There,' he said, closing the bonnet and walking round. 'I've topped up your water as well.'

'Since when did you become a mechanic?'

He shrugged. 'I've been driving four-wheel drives around here since I was twelve, and in New Zealand we had to know our stuff. They operate with some pretty big machinery out there.'

Was that meant to impress her? 'Well, thanks

360

very much. Now I know where to come when I need my MOT done.'

'Why don't you come before that?' Before she knew it he'd put his head through the window and kissed her full on the mouth.

Calypso felt nice soft lips for a second, before coming to her senses.

'What the hell are you doing?' she gasped, recoiling back in the seat.

'Kissing you.' Archie seemed totally unfazed.

Calypso was in outraged shock. 'You can't go around trying it on with random girls!'

'Yes, but you're not random, are you?' He brushed something out of her hair. 'I like you, Calypso, and I think you like me.'

She gave a snort. 'Oh, do you?'

'Yeah.' He stood up. 'I think we could have fun together.'

'Fun! Archie . . .' She stopped. 'We are not even having this conversation.'

'Call me.'

'*Call* me . . . oh, I've heard it all now.' Shaking her head, she started up the engine again. 'Archie, dear?'

He grinned. 'Yes, Calypso?'

'I'm not into cradle-snatching. Sorry.'

CHAPTER FIFTY-SIX

Caro was pushing her Henry round the living room when she realized the phone was ringing. Switching the vacuum cleaner off, she rushed over to get it. 'Hello?'

'Caro, it's Louise Rennison.'

'Louise, hello.' Caro had been on tenterhooks waiting for this call. She was terrified of what Louise might say.

'I've heard from the court.'

'Yes?'

'The date for the first hearing is the first of February.'

Only two weeks away. Caro didn't know if that was a good or a bad thing.

'Please try not to worry too much,' Louise reassured her. 'Nothing will happen that day. As I said, it is just a conciliation appointment to see if both parties can come to an agreement. You'd be amazed how many parents I've seen at complete loggerheads that manage to put their differences aside. Sometimes all that's needed is a bit of time and space.'

Caro didn't respond. She didn't want to think about what might happen if they didn't sort the problem out.

'Is your husband there with you?'

'No, but I'm fine, Louise. In all honesty it's a relief to get the date so we can get this thing over with.'

'OK, I'm going to get on with the paperwork, and you'll need to send your statement over. Are you clear on what you need to do?'

'Yes.' Caro stared out of the kitchen window. Statements, court hearings; it seemed like such an alien world.

After they'd said their goodbyes she sat down at the kitchen table. With both the kids at school the house was unnervingly quiet. *Is this what it would be like without my baby?* Caro stared at the back

362

door, where a pile of little shoes lay in a heap. She tried to imagine just Rosie's muddy wellies there, one small toothbrush in the holder instead of two, empty spaces round the bath where Milo's frogman and submarine usually lay.

Don't do this to yourself. She knew she should call Benedict and tell him the news, but she couldn't face talking to anyone at the moment. Maybe a bit of fresh air would help. Pulling her coat off the back of the chair, Caro went out for a walk.

*   *   *

'My dear, come in. It's blowing a gale out there!' Clementine shut the kitchen door behind her eldest granddaughter. She took in the Barbour wellies and quilted jacket, the cold, windswept face. 'Have you been out walking? In this weather?'

'I needed to clear my head.' Caro took off her jacket and went to hang it in the utility room.

Clementine waited until she'd come back. 'Would you like a cup of tea? I was about to put the kettle on.'

'Yes, please.' Caro was frozen. She leant against the kitchen worktop, looked round at the familiar surroundings, the cork-board of family photographs on the wall. 'Something smells nice.'

'I'm making a fruitcake. For the old people's home. Somebody has to feed those poor people properly; the food they serve up there is all that ghastly processed stuff.' Clementine got the teapot out of the cupboard. 'Now then, what would you like? I've got Earl Grey, builder's or some of that herbal stuff I know you like.'

She didn't think she'd been heard, but when she

363

turned round she was aghast to see tears pouring down Caro's cheeks.

Caro covered her face with her hands. 'Oh, Granny Clem!'

*   *   *

Fifteen minutes later Clementine had heard the whole awful story. 'But why?' she asked for the umpteenth time. 'Why would he want to do such a thing?'

'Because he's trying to make out I'm an unfit mother.' Caro felt empty, as if there were no more tears to cry.

For only the second time ever, she heard her grandmother swear. 'I've a good mind to go round there right now.'

'Granny Clem, please don't,' Caro begged. 'I don't want all hell breaking loose and Sebastian using it against us. Don't tell Mummy or Daddy, either, will you? They're so far away, and they'll only worry. I just want to get this conciliation thing done, and hopefully we can sort it out . . .' She trailed off.

'Of course,' Clementine said reluctantly. She reached across and took Caro's hand. 'My dear, I hate to think of you going through this by yourself!'

'I didn't mean to be pathetic and start blubbing. It just all got to me.'

'Of course it did,' Clementine said passionately. She passed her granddaughter another tissue. 'Does Milo know anything's up?'

Caro wiped her nose. 'No, and I want to keep it that way. Benedict and I don't want to say anything unless we have to. Sebastian still wants to see Milo

364

while this is going on. We can't stop him.'

Clementine pursed her lips. 'For goodness' sake! The sheer front of the man is unbelievable.'

'I know, but I don't want Milo getting wind of anything, and being upset.'

'You're right, of course.' Clementine frowned. 'I just don't understand this abrupt turnaround.' She shuddered. 'Thank God we never made him one of Milo's trustees. Bertie would turn in his grave if that man had any say in our money.'

'That's one thing we don't have to worry about. Milo's inheritance is watertight.'

Clementine sighed. 'If this really is about Sebastian wanting a bigger role in Milo's life, why does he have to rock the boat? Milo can still stay with you and Sebastian can just see more of him.'

'Because Seb doesn't do sharing, Granny Clem. You know what he's like: he has to have control of everything. He's decided he wants Milo, and that's that.'

'You'd think he'd have more respect for you. Caro, he was married to you for five years, and you're the mother of his son!'

'That means nothing to Sebastian. I honestly believe this comes out of his sick desire to win all the time. Everything's a bloody competition, even access to his own son!'

Clementine was furious. 'All I can say is, Sebastian Belmont has picked the wrong family to mess with.'

CHAPTER FIFTY-SEVEN

Kizzy cleared her throat and pressed the button. It seemed to take an agonizingly long time before anyone answered.

'Hello?' It was a woman's voice, youngish.

'Um, hi.' Speaking into this stupid thing on the wall was never going to get any easier. 'It's Kizzy Milton?' she said, hoping whoever it was on the other end would recognize her name.

'Have you got an appointment to see someone?' the woman asked curtly.

'No, but Javier said to come any time,' Kizzy said, feeling foolish. She should have called first. 'He does know me.'

'I'm sorry, but no one sees Mr Hamilton-Scott without an appointment. You'll have to ring the office.' The intercom went dead.

Kizzy was left staring at the mouthpiece. *How embarrassing*. She shouldn't have just rocked up like this. Javier was a busy man.

Just then the little mouthpiece on the wall crackled into life again. 'Kizzy?'

'Yes?'

'It's Nigel. I'll buzz you in.' Moments later the gates started to swing open.

*   *   *

As Kizzy drove up to the house, Nigel came out of a little stone building to the right. He pointed to where Kizzy should park, and came over.

'Sorry about that, Elizabeth's my new assistant.

She can be a little overzealous, but that's why I hired her.' He looked at her enquiringly. 'Is Mr Hamilton-Scott expecting you?'

'No,' Kizzy said again. She blushed. 'He did say to come and see him whenever.' She knew this had been a bad idea. 'I'll go if it's not convenient.'

'No, stay here. Mr Hamilton-Scott is down at the centre.' Nigel raised his eyes to the heavens. 'Where else! I'll call his mobile, and let him know you're here.'

It didn't take long. 'Would you like to go down? He's trying out a new horse.'

She got a lift down with a groom called Jules on the back of a quad bike. The yard was busier today, with grooms pushing wheelbarrows and carrying feed-buckets round.

'Try the indoor arena,' Jules said. 'He should be in there.'

Kizzy thanked him and walked across the yard, conscious of eyes on her. A door to the side of the building stood slightly ajar.

Classical music filled the huge space. Javier stood in the middle, in leather riding boots and jodhpurs, watching as Oliver Foster put Love's Dream into an extended trot down the far side of the school. Neither seemed to notice as Kizzy crept up the steps to the viewing gallery and sat down.

She had a marvellous view from here. Love's Dream was such a *hunk*, she thought, gazing admiringly at the beautiful conformation of the horse's body. His proud head was held high, silky mane bouncing up and down on the awesome neck.

It soon became clear Javier was some taskmaster. He kept his eyes trained on horse and rider as they moved round, his deep voice cutting across the music.

'Head too high! Back hollowing! Watch out, you're losing engagement with the back legs!'

Kizzy wasn't sure if Javier was talking about Oliver or Love's Dream as he worked them round and round. Under the saddle the horse's back had started to foam with sweat.

As they went up into a canter, Dream's legs rearranged themselves mid-stride, so that the left one was leading instead of the right. To Kizzy it looked like the perfect flying change, but Javier had other ideas.

'OK, Oliver, hold it a minute.'

The boy slowed the horse down and walked into the centre of the ring, toward Javier. The frustration was clear to see on his face. Kizzy watched as they had a quick conversation, Javier making a point with his arms. Oliver nodded, taking it all in. He gave a quick grin at something Javier said, and then slid off and dismounted.

Next thing, Javier was up on the eighteen-hand horse, adjusting the stirrups. Kizzy sat up; now *this* was going to be something! She couldn't believe she was about to see an Olympic gold medallist this close up in action!

Javier pushed the stallion forward into a trot, and started to circle the arena. Kizzy had thought Oliver had been good, but now she could see what a world-class talent Javier was. The horse visibly collected itself under him, lifting its head forward and up.

They started to do an amazing collected trot diagonally across the school. Dream's knees were up high, reminding Kizzy of military marches. There was nothing stiff or jerky about this, though, and it was a sign of just how good Javier was that the horse looked as if he was doing the routine on his own. They were as one, with their elegant legs and powerful upper bodies, Javier's hands resting lightly in front as if he were doing nothing.

Kizzy watched spellbound as Dream went into an amazing movement, where he seemed to be going sideways and forwards at the same time. It was like Dream was *floating,* and there was a magical moment where all four hooves were suspended in the air. As the music slowed again, Javier brought the horse back down to a walk.

He glanced up and saw Kizzy, registering her presence with a little smile. Then he dismounted and patted Dream's neck. Saying something to Oliver he started to walk towards the viewing gallery.

Kizzy met him outside, where he gave her an affectionate kiss on the cheek. 'What a nice surprise.'

'You don't mind me turning up like this?' Javier looked even more gorgeous hard at work, with his hair ruffled and those oh-so-physical shoulders rippling under a long-sleeved black polo shirt.

'Not at all.' Javier pulled his gloves off and looked across to where one of the grooms was leading Love's Dream out of the arena, with Oliver Foster walking alongside. 'So what did you think?'

'I've never seen anything like it,' she admitted. 'It was spectacular.'

'Dream's a hell of a horse, and Oliver's a great kid.' He smiled at her. 'We'll get there.'

They walked back out to the yard again. Javier didn't seem to find it awkward that Kizzy was there. He exchanged pleasantries with another of the grooms, asking after his wife and new baby. Dusk was starting to fall as they made their way up to the house again.

'Do you always use classical music?' she asked.

Javier shook his head. 'No, not at all. The genre depends on what's suited to the horse. The Germans like their rap, and believe it or not, there's a big Spanish electro funk thing going on at the moment.'

'Really? I'd never have thought that.'

'What would you choose for Dream, then?'

'God, I don't know.' Kizzy thought. 'Something by Tinie Tempah, maybe. Dream's got that lovely power and energy, I reckon it would make for really explosive movements.' She didn't really know the technical terms for anything.

Javier raised an eyebrow. 'Tinie Tempah?'

'Er, yeah. He's this British rapper . . .'

He looked very amused. 'I do know who Tinie Tempah is, Kizzy. I'm not that old.'

She blushed. 'Sorry.'

He looked ahead, grinning. They walked in a comfortable, happy silence for a few moments before Javier spoke. 'I'm afraid I've got a meeting now, back at the house.'

'No worries.' She tried not to be too disappointed. Javier hadn't known she was coming, after all.

'It's with patrons from several of the coma charities. I try to help in any way I can. We meet every few months to talk about developments or new findings.' He turned to her. 'There's a man in America called Terry Sandling, who was in a coma for twenty years. Doctors had given up hope, but one day he woke up and started speaking. A few

370

days after that he could move his arms and legs, and five years on he's made a remarkable recovery.'

'That's amazing. What happened?'

'The doctors still aren't sure, but they think that for some reason his brain gradually started to rewire itself. Do you know what an axon is, Kizzy?' He had become very animated. 'They're the long nerve fibres that pass messages between neurons. For some reason Terry Sandling's axons decided to start working again, and no one knows why. Can you imagine if one day someone discovered *how*? What that could mean for coma patients, and how it could advance the treatment of brain injuries?'

Kizzy had decided to make a conscious effort not to shy away from the subject if it ever came up. 'Do you think, I mean, could it help Sarah?'

'Ah, well.' Javier's voice flattened again. 'Of course I live in hope, but whatever progress a patient makes in the first six to twelve months is generally about as good as it gets. Sarah's health is poor. She's picked up a lot of infections.'

'Does she know you're there?'

'It's hard to tell. Occasionally she'll have some movement in her fingers, but it could just be a muscle reflex. Some patients have a sense of what's going on around them, but are unable to respond in any way.'

Sarah was imprisoned in her body: in a living hell. Kizzy couldn't even start to imagine what it would be like. It would be especially bad for someone like her, who'd been so vibrant and physically talented.

They walked on, towards a silvery moon that had appeared over the horizon. Javier had gone quiet again. Kizzy wondered if he was thinking about his

371

wife.

His hand brushed tantalizingly against hers. Kizzy felt a thousand electric shocks go through her body.

'Kizzy.' Javier stopped and looked at her. 'I'm really glad you came.' He started kissing her, with all the exhilaration and passion of last time. Kizzy's legs went wobbly underneath her again.

Eventually he pulled away. 'I have to go,' he said reluctantly. 'There are people waiting.'

He took her hand as they walked; only releasing it as they got near the house. There were three more cars next to Kizzy's in the parking area. Nigel came out of the office looking slightly stressed.

'Ah, there you are, Javier! Our guests have arrived.'

'I'm sorry. I'll be in now.'

Nigel smiled a tad impatiently, so Kizzy took her cue.

'Bye, then.'

'Thanks again for coming over,' Javier said in a slightly more businesslike manner.

Kizzy walked off, leaving the two men standing there. *When will I see you again?* A familiar dejection took hold.

She was unlocking her car door, determined not to look back, when Javier called.

'Kizzy!'

He was standing by the office door. 'Tinie Tempah, hey? You could be on to something there.'

He gave her a wink that made her tummy roll over. Heart full again, Kizzy grinned back.

CHAPTER FIFTY-EIGHT

At the end of January the Fox-Titt contingent drove Nobby up to the Heythrop Hunt point-to-point. Buoyed up by his success at Chaddesley Corbett they had decided to try their chances and enter him up a level into something called a 'restricted'. The fifteen-strong field he was competing against was more experienced, but everyone else seemed to make mistakes, and he and Edward ended up yomping past the finishing post first.

The gang returned from Heythrop giddy with delight, and Angie and Freddie promptly threw a champagne celebration. Clementine and Brenda Briggs, who had gone to the race in Clementine's Volvo estate, phoned round the village to round people up. By the time Nobby had been put to bed with an extremely big pat on the back there was quite a party going on in the kitchen at the Maltings. A slightly tiddly Angie had her arm round Edward's waist, telling her audience how amazing he'd been.

'We were in third and screaming like crazy anyway, and then Edward spurred Nobby on, and he flew past the post by a nose!'

For once Edward didn't look like he was about to curl up and die at being the centre of attention. Like everyone else, he was riding high on exuberance and was full of giddy disbelief that everything had gone in his favour.

There was a knock at the door, and the Turner family piled in. The two women were all boobs and mascara, while Jack had a bottle of bubbly under each meaty arm.

'Hello, folks!' He pumped Edward's hand vigorously. 'Great result, mate. You must be over the moon.'

Stacey Turner, in a tight top and leather shorts, looked more like she was going out on the town than attending a Sunday soirée in the country. She cast an unimpressed eye over the surroundings. Then she caught sight of Archie, refilling Clementine's and Brenda's glasses on the far side of the kitchen. 'Oh my God, is that Archie Fox-Titt?'

'Yes, Stacey, he does live here.' Beryl Turner rolled her eyes at Angie.

'Oh my God. When did he get so fit? He used to be, like, a total drip.'

'*Sta*-cey,' Beryl said. 'Sorry, Angie.'

'It's fine,' Angie said, trying not to smile.

Stacey shot her mum a look through kohl-rimmed eyes. 'I was just saying how fit he was!'

Freddie came back with three full flutes. 'There you go, folks, get that down you.'

Stacey took a sip and pulled a face. 'That is rank! Urgh.'

'Oh.' Freddie looked rather crestfallen. 'It's actually a Krug Grande Cuvée, I thought we'd celebrate with some of the good stuff.'

Stacey handed him the glass back. 'Give it to Mum; she'll drink anything. You got any vodka?'

Clementine slipped away to phone Calypso again. 'There you are! I've been trying to get hold of you.'

'I'm just driving back.'

'On the hands-free, I hope?'

'*Yes.* Anyway, you called *me*!'

'I know. Marvellous news, darling, Nobby won

his race!'

'Cool. Where are you now? Sounds like a party.'

'At the Fox-Titts, having a drink. They've asked you along.'

'I'm heading home for a bath, actually. I'm knackered.'

'All I ask is that you come down for half an hour. Angie and Freddie will be so pleased.'

'OK.' Calypso sighed. 'I'll go past Camilla's and see if she wants to come, too.'

'Excellent! We'll see you soon.'

*　　　*　　　*

By the time Calypso drove up with her sister, the Pikes' Ferrari was parked across the entrance, blocking everyone's way in or out. In the kitchen Barry was handing out vodka jellies like sweeties. Stacey Turner was already on her fifth, and had trapped Archie with her chest over by the Aga.

'Hey, everyone! Hey, Kizzy!' Calypso planted a kiss on her cheek. 'Long time no see, how's it going?'

'Good, thanks.' Kizzy had a new radiance about her. Her eyes were clear and sparkling in her strawberries and cream complexion.

'You look fab! Have you been somewhere?'

'I wish!'

They stood back to let Cheryl past. 'Where's Caro, then?' Cheryl asked. 'Me and Baz knocked on them but there was no answer.'

'She and Benedict have gone to Babington House with the kids.'

'Aye aye, I smell a dirty weekend away. I could do with one of those.' Cheryl elbowed Calypso in the ribs. 'Mind you, every weekend's dirty at our gaff.'

Calypso tried not to wince at Cheryl's rat-a-tat-tat cackle.

Archie got her as she came back from making a work call. 'Do you fancy grabbing something to eat after this?'

No matter how big and strapping he'd got, Calypso couldn't get the image of him as a snot-nosed seven-year-old with a *Sesame Street* T-shirt out of her head.

'Are McDonald's doing a special deal on Happy Meals, then?' she asked.

He gave her a look.

'It was a joke,' she said lamely.

'I was thinking more of Giuseppe's. It's meant to be all right.'

The Bedlington Italian was an institution. Calypso hadn't been there for years. The thought of a hearty plate of pasta was suddenly very appealing.

'Aren't you going down the pub with the others?' she asked.

He grinned. 'That depends on you.'

*   *   *

Thirty minutes later they were sat across from each other in the lively Italian restaurant.

'I've only come out because I'm starving.' Calypso reached for the bread basket.

'What other reason would there be?'

He was definitely flirting with her. 'Archie,' she warned.

'What?'

'Stop looking at me like that!'

376

'Like what?' he asked innocently.

Calypso shot him a look. 'I'm surprised you didn't ask Stacey on your little date, she was very taken with you.'

'So this is a date?'

'Of course not,' Calypso said hotly. Why was she letting him wind her up like this?

Two huge bubbling lasagnes turned up. Archie proceeded to get through his, and then scoffed Calypso's leftovers.

'Fatty,' she said, watching him wipe the remnants up with a bit of garlic bread.

'Hey, I'm a growing boy.'

'Boy's about right.'

He gave her a winning grin and shoved the plate back. 'That was good.'

'So I see.' Calypso picked up her glass of red. 'So tell me, Archibald, any nice young ladies on the scene?'

'No, not really.' He wiped his mouth with a napkin. 'There was this girl Sue-Beth in New Zealand . . .'

'Sue-*Beth*?'

'She was American. Nice girl.'

'How come it didn't work out?'

He shrugged. 'I came home. It wasn't serious, anyway.'

'I'm sure Stacey would be up for something.'

'Why do you keep going on about Stacey? Are you jealous?'

'What?' She spluttered into her glass. 'As if.'

Chuckling, Archie crossed his big arms and sat back. 'What about you, Calypso? Any exes you want to talk about?'

'Exes, yes, but none that I want to talk about.'

'Not heard from old Jamesy boy?'

'No, thank God.'

'Is there any man out there who's managed to steal the great Calypso's heart?'

'What does that mean?' Calypso paused, wondering whether to say something. 'There was this one guy I was seeing. Rafe.'

She was never sure how many of the villagers had ended up finding out about their affair. Rafe had told her he wanted to keep it quiet to protect her from the media, and, stupidly, Calypso had believed him.

'Oh, right. Where did you meet him?'

'Uh, in Churchminster?' Usually Calypso didn't like going on about it, but Archie's lack of reaction was so irritating she couldn't keep quiet. 'Rafe Wolfe? That actor who came to the village to film *A Regency Playboy*.'

'Yeah, I remember now. Mum went to see it and said it was rubbish.' Archie shrugged. 'I was at uni at the time, it kinda passed me by.'

It had only been just over two years ago. Once again Calypso was reminded how young Archie was.

'So what happened?' he asked.

'There's nothing to tell, really. I got taken in by his bullshit, and he somehow conveniently forgot to tell me along the way he had a fiancée.'

Archie frowned. 'What an idiot.'

'I called him a bit more than that. In fact, I think the exact words were 'You fucking, lying, cheating, arsehole, scumbag.'

'Sounds like he deserved it.' He gave her a cheery smile. 'Is that why you're so defensive now?'

'Excuse me, I'm not defensive,' she said

defensively.

'Don't worry, I think it's quite cute.'

'Ha! *You* think *I'm* cute?' She fixed him with a look. 'The reason you think I'm defensive is probably because I'm tired from my job—one day you'll grow up and have one, too—and have better things to do with my evenings than spend it with an adolescent.'

'I've got a job as well.'

'Yeah, working for Daddy.'

'What's wrong with that?' Archie sat back and put his hands behind his head. 'And I don't know why you're so worried about going out with me; people will probably just think I'm your carer.'

It was like water off a duck's back with him. 'You are *so* annoying,' Calypso said, trying not to laugh.

His eyes twinkled. 'So you keep saying.'

*   *   *

On the way out Archie actually tried to hold her hand. 'What are you *doing*?' Calypso said, outraged.

'What does it look like?'

'Someone might see!' She pushed him away. 'Despite what you may think, this is not a date, so don't even think about going round telling people that.'

'You're the one who's mentioned the word "date" twice this evening.'

'I didn't mean it like . . . oh, forget it!' Tucking her bag under her arm, she started striding down the street away from him.

'The car's this way,' he called.

With as much dignity as Calypso could muster, she turned and stormed back past him.

CHAPTER FIFTY-NINE

It was the first of February. The day Caro had been dreading.

'Are you all right?' Benedict asked her again.

Caro gave the tiniest of nods. They were driving to the county court at Gloucester, and the upright figure of Granny Clem sat on the back seat. Clementine would never say it in so many words, but Caro knew her grandmother thought she should tell the family what was going on. But Caro just couldn't. Not at the moment, anyway. Rightly or wrongly, she just felt too embarrassed about the whole thing. Embarrassed that she was the one who had let Sebastian back into their lives—and that now he was causing all this hurt again.

Clementine was far too discreet and loyal to disregard her granddaughter's wishes, but the one thing she had insisted on was coming along today. In the end Caro had been glad of her grandmother's reassuring presence, and of the light, familiar smell of Je Reviens gracing the car.

The journey had been quiet and tense. Each of them had looked out of the windows, immersed in their own thoughts. Ironically it was a beautiful day, white clouds dotted across an open blue sky. Caro stared at the line of oncoming traffic, wondering where the drivers were going. Were any of them on their way to the most terrifying, nerve-racking ordeal of their life? Or, were they simply carrying out some mundane errand they'd been putting off, or going to do the weekly shop at Tesco? How she envied them if they were.

Gloucester Crown Court was an ugly seventies building that looked more like an office block than a place where the fate of countless families was decided. As they drove into the car park they saw a woman in a navy suit standing on the steps outside with an angry-looking man in a tracksuit. He was smoking furiously and waving his arms about, while the woman—who looked like his solicitor—had a large bundle of papers under one arm and was trying to placate him with the other.

Once inside the security arch, Caro's sense of foreboding didn't ease. She joined her husband and grandmother in the large waiting room for visitors. It was easy to spot the lawyers: the men and women in suits, holding bundles of paper, and having hushed conferences with their clients. There was a palpable air of tension, as warring parents sat glowering at each other from opposite sides of the room. There was little privacy, and several people were having to endure the indignity of discussing their case details with their brief while everyone else listened in.

Louise Rennison was already there waiting, her neat blonde hair freshly cut. 'How are you?'

Benedict squeezed his wife's hand. 'We're doing fine.'

They took the stairs up to the first floor, passing another harried lawyer-client conference on the landing. They came out in a long corridor, smelling of polystyrene and despair. Caro's stomach dropped as she saw Sebastian and Suzette at the other end. Sebastian was standing outside a door talking closely with a man in a loud pinstripe suit, while Suzette sat looking bored on a beaten-up chair. Her smart camel coat and gleaming bob were at odds with the desolate environment. She looked through Caro as if she wasn't there, and went back to fiddling on her BlackBerry.

Sebastian said something to his companion, and he turned around. The man's rat-like face lit up. 'Louise! How are you?' The man strode towards Louise as convivially as if he was meeting an old friend at a wedding reception.

'Patrick,' Louise said, with considerably less warmth.

The first thought Caro had was *unscrupulous*. With his slicked-back hair and white-collared blue shirt Patrick Carver clearly embraced the arrogant lawyer stereotype with glee. 'All ready?' he said. 'Not sure where the Cafcass officer is.'

'She should be along in a minute.'

Patrick smiled, displaying shark-like teeth. 'Good stuff! I'm sure we can have this all wrapped up in time for lunch.' He looked at the massive Rolex on his wrist. 'I've got a two o'clock back at Le Caprice with a very important client.'

Without even gracing the others with a glance, Patrick turned on his heel and walked off.

'Amazing,' Benedict muttered. 'Sebastian's managed to find someone who's a bigger, smugger prick than he is.'

Caro was as pale as a ghost. 'Do you want to go and sit down?' her grandmother asked. There was another row of chairs halfway down the corridor.

'Maybe you should, darling,' Benedict said. 'I'm worried about you.'

'I'm fine, really.' Caro didn't want to be any closer to Sebastian than she had to.

The door to the stairs opened and a woman came through, looking slightly stressed.

382

'Sorry I'm late,' she said, blinking through tired eyes. 'Mrs Towey, is it? I'm Belinda Winters, your Cafcass officer.'

Belinda Winters didn't look like the kind of person who would wield so much power over this case. Small and mouse-like, with long frizzy hair and a nose stud, she seemed more suited to manning a bean-burger stall at a festival.

'Hello,' Caro said, feeling quite sick.

Sebastian came striding down the corridor, the epitome of smiling charm.

'Belinda, isn't it?' He shook her hand like an old friend. 'I do like your shoes.'

She blinked again and looked down at her snot-green Crocs. 'Oh, thank you.'

Caro felt Benedict visibly tighten beside her. They watched as Sebastian treated the Cafcass officer to another dazzling smile.

'Can I carry anything for you? Poor thing, you look rather weighed down there.'

Caro hoped Belinda Winters would see through the charade, but she seemed flattered by the attention. 'Oh no, I'm fine, thank you.'

'If you're sure.' Sebastian stood aside. 'Shall we?'

He shot Caro the briefest of looks, before following Belinda down the corridor.

Caro felt even sicker. Sebastian thrived on confrontation. 'I can't go in there,' she said.

'You'll be brilliant,' Benedict told her. 'Just tell it how it is. That sorry excuse for a man hasn't got an ounce of credibility to his name.'

'He's right, darling,' Clementine told her.

'We'll be waiting right here,' Louise said.

Caro managed a weak smile. 'OK. Wish me luck.'

*   *   *

Caro was like a lamb to the slaughter. The face-to-face chat she'd been told to expect was actually a character-assassination; Sebastian even produced a dossier of lies to back his stories. A joke Caro had once made about having a minor breakdown had been turned into a serious concern about her fragile mental state. When she'd come to collect Milo after the point-to-point, Sebastian claimed she'd been unstable and stinking of alcohol, when Caro had specifically told him Calypso had spilt a drink over her.

It went on and on: the time Milo had run round to Sebastian's after Caro and Benedict had been so drunk they couldn't look after him, and when Sebastian had had to step in and stop her from driving drunkenly to pick up her son from school. He claimed he had only held back from going to the police because she'd promised him she'd get help . . .

There were even allegations that Benedict was so violent that Sebastian was worried about Milo being left in his care. Caro and Benedict's inappropriate sexual behaviour was also mentioned, and how Milo had told his father he wasn't happy living at home. And there was a witness, of course: Suzette. Blindsided, Caro had become more and more upset and angry. Belinda Winters's idea of mediation was sitting back and letting Sebastian do his work.

Benedict was so infuriated by the state Caro was in when she came out that Patrick Carver made a big show of standing protectively in front of Sebastian. He waited until Belinda Winters was in earshot before telling Benedict they already had

384

a transcript of his abusive behaviour against his client, and that he advised him to keep his temper under control. Benedict had to be pulled away by Clementine to calm down. All the while Belinda had watched, blinking, through dark little mole-like eyes.

As no agreement had been reached between the two parties, they then had to go in front of the judge. This wasn't in the main courthouse, but in another room, where District Justice Madhabi, a solemn-faced Indian man with half-moon spectacles, came out to listen to both parties' statements. The two versions were so at loggerheads with each other that a newcomer could have been forgiven for thinking they were talking about entirely different scenarios. At least Caro had Louise with her this time, engaging in a quick battle of wits with Patrick Carver across the table, and rubbishing the allegations.

At present the two lawyers were arguing over Sebastian's claim that the reason he'd hardly seen his son for five years was because Caro had deliberately prevented it. Caro's side had expected this, and Louise had asked Caro if she'd ever kept any of Sebastian's texts or recorded his phone calls as evidence, but of course she hadn't. How could she have known that a two-year-old phone call could be used as vital evidence in a custody battle over their child? Now it was just her word against his. It was frightening how vulnerable she was starting to feel.

Patrick Carver was on the attack again. 'My client has always had concerns that his ex-wife started up an extra-marital relationship with her current husband, and had designs from the start to get my client out of the picture so they could set up home together.'

The audacity of this took Caro's breath away. 'You bloody *liar*, Seb! You were the one who had all the affairs!'

District Justice Madhabi frowned at her language. Caro felt Louise put a reassuring hand on her arm. 'That claim is entirely untrue, and even if it was not, would have no relevance.'

'Just thought I'd mention it,' Patrick said breezily.

Sebastian's expression of someone unjustly accused of a crime was making Caro's blood boil. 'What about your counselling sessions with a therapist?' she shot back, desperately using all the ammunition she had. 'Are you sure you're in the right frame of mind to take full-time care of a child?'

Sebastian looked at her in astonishment. 'I have no idea what you're talking about! Why would you make up such a thing?'

Her mouth dropped open. 'Benedict was there! He heard you say it.'

'So was Suzette, and she will assure you I didn't.'

Caro slumped back in shock. My God, had he been planning this from the beginning?

The judge held his hand up with the weary air of a man who had seen this sort of thing too many times before.

'Miss Winters, you say you do have welfare concerns?'

The Cafcass officer scratched at a spot on her cheek. 'Based on what I've seen and heard so far, sir, I'd have to say yes.'

'This is madness!' Caro was trying so hard to

386

be calm, but she couldn't help it. How could this woman claim to have any say over her life after a thirty-minute meeting? She felt Louise touch her arm again.

The judge peered over his glasses round the table. 'As no agreement has been reached between mother and father, I am going to order the Cafcass officer to prepare a full report on the issues of residence and contact.'

Sebastian had been a model of calm and fake concern throughout, but as he looked across the table at Caro now, she saw the gleam of triumph in his eye. Round one to him. And it had been won so alarmingly easily.

*   *   *

They retreated to a greasy spoon afterwards for a much-needed cup of tea. Caro was completely numb, and furious with herself for losing her cool. Benedict's hand was closed round hers, gripping it hard. He hadn't let go of her for the last ten minutes.

'It isn't the outcome I'd hoped for, obviously,' Louise Rennison was saying. 'But think of it as a good thing, Caro. You've got nothing to hide, and the Cafcass report will prove that.'

'I had nothing to hide in there, and Belinda Winters still bought all Sebastian's lies,' Caro said bleakly. 'If I read Sebastian's statement and didn't know better, *I'd* think I was a bad mother.' Caro was starting to realize just what victims of a miscarriage of justice must go through, when no matter how desperately they pleaded, everyone just turned a blind eye to the truth.

'That bloody man!' Clementine exploded. 'I can't believe he could sit there and blatantly lie like that.'

'He obviously fed us the story about the counselling to get us onside.' Benedict shook his head. 'How could I have fallen for it?'

'Because I made you.' Caro stared down at the chipped tabletop. 'What if other people back up his claims? The fact that Belinda is involved is enough to make people suspicious.' It was horrible to think the Cafcass officer was going to be raking through their lives, as if Caro was a criminal.

'They can't and they won't.' Benedict's voice was vehement. 'You're a good person. Louise is right, this report will prove it.'

'We have to carry on,' Clementine said. 'Think of Milo.'

In a crystallizing moment Caro saw her son, the beautiful untainted little boy who was stuck in the middle of this dreadful thing. A love so fierce it almost hurt swelled in her heart. In that moment, Caro knew she would fight to the death for him.

CHAPTER SIXTY

Kizzy hadn't let her phone out of her sight, just in case Javier got in contact again. Her perseverance paid off. She was in the middle of the unglamorous task of pushing a wheelbarrow of muck across the yard when she received her first text from him.

It was short but oh-so-sweet. *'Dinner at mine?'*

Kizzy wanted to punch the air with glee. She'd almost sent Javier a text so many times in the past few days, but had held off. Just when she had

388

been losing hope again, he'd got in contact. It was becoming quite a game between them.

Fingers fumbling, she typed a reply. *'Sounds great. What time?'*

The text came back instantly. *'7.30 x'*

A kiss! He put a kiss! Deep breaths, she muttered. *Stop acting like a teenager.* She did a little skip of joy and picked up the wheelbarrow again.

Javier wasn't just invading her waking thoughts, but her dreams, too. Kizzy had lost count of the times she had woken to find her breath short and heavy, and a wetness between her legs. There'd be images of Javier in her head, too: of him taking her against the kitchen table, of his powerful body thrusting into hers, or a passionate, tearing-clothes-off embrace on the cold dewy grass. All she could think about was seeing his naked body, running her hands over every sinew and muscle . . .

Jesus. She'd never felt like this before. If things carried on like this, she'd have to take herself off to a bloody convent.

*   *   *

Her smelly work clothes were a thing of the past by the time she made the journey to Homelands that evening. Kizzy had to admit it: she was feeling good. Her new skinny jeans from Topshop showed off the length of her legs perfectly and the pale pink camisole matched her skin tone. Not wanting to go OTT, Kizzy had tamed the outfit with ballet pumps and a black Zara cardigan. Just enough, but not too much.

She was just about to knock on the front door when it opened. Nigel stood there, looking smart in

389

a bow tie and dinner jacket.

'Kizzy!' He looked surprised.

'Hi, Nigel. You look great, off anywhere nice?'

'The Woodborough Opera Festival are putting on a special performance of *Adriana Lecouvreur* at Berkeley Castle. It's one of my favourites.'

'Sounds very cultured!'

Nigel smiled back, an unexpected twinkle in his eye. 'It's wonderful to remember what a social life feels like.' He glanced back. 'Would you like me to show you through? Javier's in the east wing study.'

She thought she knew roughly where that was. 'Don't worry, if you tell me how to find it from the kitchen, I'll be fine. You have a great time.'

Nigel nodded. 'Goodnight, then.'

Kizzy found Javier in a small square room a few doors down from Mary's sitting room. He got up from behind his desk when he saw her.

'Did you ring? I didn't hear anything.'

'Nigel was just going out, so he let me in.' She stood in the doorway, awkward for a moment, and watched Javier come round the desk towards her. There was no kiss on the mouth, but she still thrilled as she felt his soft lips on her cheeks.

'It's about time he went out, that man works far too hard. Take a seat.' Javier indicated the chair in front of the desk, and went back round to his own. Kizzy went over and sat down, feeling a bit like she was going for an interview.

'He said he was off to the opera.'

'How he sits through three hours of death and despair is beyond me.'

'I thought you liked things like that,' Kizzy said, remembering the Wikipedia entry about Javier being a talented musician. She quickly blushed, in case she sounded like a mad stalker fan.

'Did you? I prefer my entertainment a little more light-hearted.'

'Has Nigel been with you long?' She was eager to get off the subject in case he found her out.

'Three years. The man's a godsend. He's so good at organizing things that I'm surprised he hasn't run for PM.'

Kizzy giggled. 'Where did he come from?'

'You've heard of Devon Cornwall?'

'My mum loves him!'

'Your mum and Mary both. Nigel was Devon's PA for years, but when Devon moved to the Cayman Islands Nigel got homesick and wanted to come back. Devon put up a fight by all accounts, but his loss is my gain.'

Their eyes locked, cancelling everything out. Kizzy's heart started to do a good impression of a bird fluttering in a cage again.

'It's good to see you, Kizzy.' Javier was wearing a black shirt that hugged his shoulders, the first two buttons undone to reveal a tantalizing glimpse of chest.

'You, too.' Why did she always blush like a schoolgirl in front of him? Not wanting to go any redder under his stare, she wrenched her eyes away and looked round the room. Javier's study wasn't as grand as she had imagined it would be. There were photographs of horses and dogs tacked up on the wall, including one of Love's Dream in training and another of Arthur the rescue horse, teeth bared in a funny grin. A pair of riding boots had been kicked off in the corner, and the sagging shelves revealed an assortment of equestrian books, medical textbooks, and a battered old French novel.

'I must think a lot of you,' he said. 'Bringing you into my shabby inner sanctum. Most visitors are treated to the delights of the study in the west wing.'

'I've never heard of anyone needing two studies before,' she said dryly. 'Then again, that was before I saw the chandelier in the stables.'

Javier threw back his head and laughed, exposing a smooth brown expanse of throat. 'You must think I'm a pretentious bastard.'

'I don't think you're a bastard.'

They grinned at each other, enjoying the moment. 'Would you like something to drink?' Javier said finally. 'It's my turn to cook, I'm afraid. I hope you won't be too disappointed.'

*   *   *

Javier turned out to be a natural, going on instinct rather than cookery books. They ate over candlelight at the kitchen table again: pheasant breasts from birds freshly shot on the estate that day, and vegetables from the garden. The game was moist, the apple sauce sweet and tangy. Compared to last time, when neither of them had been able to eat much, Javier fell hungrily on his plate and Kizzy followed. At the end she put her knife and fork together and sighed happily.

'That was so good, thank you.'

'I'm pleased you liked it.' He was an unselfconscious eater, devouring his portion with pleasure.

'Lasagne's about the best I can do, I'm afraid.'

'Lasagne's good.' Javier reached for the bottle of Merlot. 'Some more?'

'Just a little.' She sat back as he poured the liquid into her glass. There was a new stillness about Homelands tonight, with just the unearthly shriek of a nocturnal animal outside in the distance, the occasional moan of wind against the windows.

'Is it Mary's night off, as well?'

Javier nodded. 'She's gone to see her niece in Woodstock. Thomas is picking her up later.'

'We're all alone, then,' she said softly.

The flames in the solid silver candelabra quivered, as if a spirit had just walked through them.

'Yes, we are.'

The air felt as thick as velvet. The candlelight fell on Javier's face, carving out every angle and contour. Holding her breath, Kizzy slid off her stool and walked over to him.

'Javier.'

She reached up to feel the contours of his face, and the slight prickle there, from the start of his five o'clock shadow. Motionless, he let her run her hands through his hair and round his neck, and move out to test his powerful shoulders.

'Oh, Kizzy,' he said. The simmering emotion she could feel under her fingertips surged up, and he swept her clean off the ground. He carried her out of the kitchen, his deep brown eyes burning into her. Tiny gold flecks danced across the irises, hinting at the heat underneath. Kizzy was a prisoner in his gaze. She half-registered some back stairs twisting up, and then a long wide landing, before Javier kicked open the door to a bedroom.

It was colder in here than where they'd just been. Kizzy had enough time to appreciate the grandeur, the floor-to-ceiling curtains and four-poster bed, but the place was strangely sparse and unlived in, as flat and impersonal as a hotel room.

He laid her down on the chilled silk covers. 'Is your back all right?' he murmured.

Kizzy reached up and answered him with a kiss, her cardigan falling off one shoulder. Javier started covering her skin with butterfly-light kisses, and it was exquisite, but she wanted more. Pulling her jumper off Kizzy reached her arms above her head for Javier to take her camisole off. He paused to look at her, and she knew he was holding back, but Kizzy wanted him, *needed* him pressed on her, inside her, staking claim to every part of her body.

He couldn't resist her long. The silky camisole trailed through his manly hands and he stared at her perfect breasts, full and round behind a rose-pink bra. He groaned and started to nuzzle them, his hands crossing her narrow back to seek out the clasp.

His eyes took in the swell of her hips, the small, feminine waist. 'You are so beautiful, Kizzy.'

She arched her back as Javier's mouth moved on her, feeling the almost painful throb between her legs.

'Let me see you,' she gasped, scrabbling at his shirt. Taking his eyes off her, Javier sat back and ripped the last few buttons off as if they were of no consequence.

Oh, wow! Kizzy gazed at the beautiful man straddling her, at his wide expanse of chest and the textbook 'V' of his upper body. The amazing core stability that gave Javier such a flawless seat in the saddle was evident in the corrugated six-pack, a line of dark hair running down his olive-skinned stomach. His whole body was carved and sensuous, with the inherent power you only saw in a world-class athlete.

Kizzy was over-awed and almost terrified. She had to touch him, but she felt the way you do about a beautiful wild animal—she was scared of what might happen when she did. Javier's skin was taut and dense, layered by tightly packed muscle. Her hands were tentative at first, then bolder and hungrier. As she swept them down his back to the curve of his buttocks Javier groaned loudly. His rock-hard erection was pushing against her. Kizzy started rubbing the fabric, teasing the zip open.

'Christ, Kizzy.'

She thought he was telling her to stop, but then his jeans came down and she saw his enormous cock for the first time. For a moment Javier's eyes looked so black and wild that Kizzy felt a frisson of fear, but then he started kissing her breasts and stomach, moving down, down, until she could feel his soft tongue on the edge of her knicker line. Pulling the lacy triangle, he stroked her neat, light-gold bush. His eyes flashed up at her as she watched him pull her legs open and bend his head.

Kizzy lay back, blissful, as she felt Javier's mouth kiss and tease, bringing her up to the point of orgasm as if he'd done it a thousand times. It was delicious, stunning, yet still not enough. Lifting her hips, she pushed herself into him.

'Make love to me, please!' she gasped. Javier lifted his head, face heavy with lust. He moved himself up, kneeling on both elbows beside her. 'Kizzy, we shouldn't.'

Kizzy could smell herself on him, sweet and fresh. An almost angry longing took hold. 'I don't *care.*'

A curious expression entered his face. 'Are you sure? We can stop it right now, walk away . . .'

'I don't want to stop!'

His mouth was on hers. 'Nor do I.' He was almost smothering her with kisses. 'I don't think I can . . .'

She felt him position himself, and then suddenly he was inside her, filling her up. 'Oh God, oh God.' His cock felt glorious. Even this was almost enough to make her come.

'Hush, baby, my darling,' he crooned, moving back and forth with a sensuous rhythm. Kizzy wrapped her legs round his back, pulling him deeper inside. Her whole body was electrified, on the warm edge of orgasm, the very brink of exploding.

This is the most amazing thing I have ever experienced in my life . . . she thought.

They stayed like that, lost in each other, until Kizzy felt herself start to topple off the cliff. As her breathing intensified she felt Javier's hands grip her buttocks. Violently, he pushed into her, the sudden movement making her gasp. At once she felt the true might of his power and realized that even if she wanted to stop now, Javier had her completely. This feeling of surrender only turned her on more. Harder and faster he drove into her, making her cry out with exquisite agony. Kizzy tumbled into orgasm, wave after wave washing over her. She was soaked in sweat, oblivious of everything except her shivering body. It was as if there'd been no one before Javier.

Afterwards they lay entwined together, listening to the wind sighing through the trees. Kizzy propped herself up on one elbow and looked at him.

'What?' His face was full of contentment and warmth; the loveliest she'd ever seen him.

'Nothing.' Smiling, Kizzy started to trace her fingers over the rugged chin, the mouth that could have been conjured up by a Renaissance painter. His broken nose almost looked like it belonged on a different face.

'How did you break it? Your nose, I mean.'

'My father.'

Kizzy was really shocked. 'Your dad did that?'

Javier caressed her back with his fingers. 'He was rather concerned I was getting too wild and following in my mother's heathen footsteps. His words, not mine.'

'Javier, that's awful.'

'He was an awful man,' he said frankly.

'I'm sorry.'

'What have you got to be sorry about?' He kissed the top of her head. 'My mother would have liked you.'

Kizzy rested her face against the soft warm flesh of his chest. 'I would have liked to meet her, too.'

A gust of wind howled at the window. Despite Javier's embrace, Kizzy shivered. This house was filled with so much sadness.

CHAPTER SIXTY-ONE

Caro's belief that things couldn't get much worse was sharply revised when Milo managed to get a black eye the day before Belinda Winters's home visit. Benedict had broken up the fight in the living room between him and Rosie, but not before the little girl had scored a direct hit at her brother's head with the remote control. Milo had got a little cut under his eye, which had blown up even more by the next day.

Caro took him to the doctor's, just in case. Luckily the prognosis was that there'd be no lasting damage.

'I don't believe this!' She returned feeling completely fraught.

'Darling, these things happen.' Benedict was beating the sofa cushions to death, probably imagining they were Sebastian. 'Belinda Winters will understand.'

'What, that we're abusing Milo?' You couldn't make it up; Caro didn't know whether to laugh or cry.

'Hey, come on. Don't torture yourself like that, of course she won't think that.'

He was putting on such a brave face. Caro looked round at the pristine living room. Anything that might cause offence—including the beautiful black and white nude portrait hanging on the far wall—had gone. Next door in the kitchen there were homemade biscuits and fresh coffee was brewing. 'You have taken all the bottles out of the wine rack, haven't you?' she asked him. The *'I like to cook with wine, occasionally I put it in the food, too'* fridge magnet a friend had bought her as a funny little birthday present had long since been chucked away.

'Yes.' Benedict came over and put his arm round her. 'People can be responsible parents and still have alcohol in the house. We shouldn't have to act like we've got something to hide.'

'I know, but I don't want to give Belinda any cause for concern.'

He gave her a little squeeze. 'Even binning the lime cordial in case it gets mistaken for Chardonnay?'

Caro sighed. 'Do I sound like a complete madwoman?'

'Mildly, but I still love you.' He was trying to put her at ease.

'Oh, Benedict, I'm just so worried!'

He hugged her fiercely. 'Everything's going to be fine, Caro.'

*   *   *

Belinda Winters was perching sparrow-like on the opposite sofa. 'Poor Milo.'

'I know! He and his sister were having a little to-do, and I'm afraid she got him at close range. Takes after her father in the aim department, obviously.'

Benedict shot her a quizzical smile. Caro coloured, thinking that what she'd said had probably sounded dodgy. 'I'm not saying Benedict hits me or anything, ha ha!'

'*Dar*-ling.' His expression said, *calm down.*

Caro smiled apologetically at the Cafcass officer. She was so nervous of tripping up that everything coming out of her mouth sounded guilty. *Or is it just me who thinks that?* Benedict was right. She needed to calm down.

'As you say, these things happen.' Belinda's gaze travelled round the room, settling on something on the far wall. Even though she wasn't openly taking notes, there was something thoughtful about

Belinda that made Caro feel her whole home was on trial.

The Cafcass officer had turned up twenty minutes early—Caro wondered if it was deliberate—stinking the whole of the downstairs out with patchouli. Even though it was February Belinda was wearing Birkenstocks with no socks, long dark hairs sprouting from both big toes. Caro found herself transfixed by the sight. As an uneasy silence fell over the room, she realized she had been caught out, and blushed.

'Do you want to interview Benedict and myself together or separately?'

'I wouldn't like to call it an interview, Mrs Towey.' Belinda may have meant to reassure her, but her tone came across as faintly patronizing. 'Just go about your normal routine, and I'll grab you at some point for a little chat.' She smiled guilelessly. 'You won't even know I'm here.'

*   *   *

The smell of patchouli lingered long after the Cafcass officer had departed. 'That went all right, all things considering,' Benedict said. 'At least Cheryl didn't turn up in her latest risqué fancy-dress outfit.'

'I don't trust her.'

'Belinda? Why?'

Caro went to pour herself another coffee, and thought better of it. She was feeling jittery enough as it was.

'I don't know, it was just the way she *snooped* around.' When Caro had walked back into the kitchen, the drawer on the dresser had been

400

half-open as if Belinda had been having a rummage. 'I didn't like the way she questioned Milo, either. You know I walked past his bedroom door when she was in there, and heard her asking him to rate me from one to twenty?'

Benedict frowned. 'I'm sure she has her methods.'

'I'm sure she looks round our house and thinks I'm just some rich stay-at-home mum. She made that comment twice about kids needing love, not material wealth.'

'She's meant to be impartial.'

'She's human, and I know what Sebastian's like when he goes on the charm offensive.' Caro rubbed her face, trying to get rid of the tension. 'It's just so *unsettling*, this stranger coming into our lives and basing opinions on God knows what. How can the family courts place so much faith in such a one-sided thing?'

Before Benedict could answer, her mobile started ringing. Caro went over to her handbag, and her stomach twisted when she saw the name. 'Sebastian.'

'Hello, Caro.' The bastard couldn't have sounded more pompous if he'd tried. 'I'm ringing about our son. It is my day to see him, you know.'

'I know it is,' she said tightly. 'Are you coming over here?'

'I'd rather not, I don't know what sort of mood that husband of yours is in. Meet me in the pub car park, will you?'

*   *   *

Half an hour later Caro faced her nemesis. It was

too early for opening time, so the Jolly Boot's windows were dark and silent, with gusts of wind skittering across the tarmac. At least Milo didn't seem to have picked up on the bad vibes, and was happily playing 'vroom vroom' in the front seat of Sebastian's Aston Martin.

'Can I ask you something?' she said, fighting to keep her calm. 'Why would you make up such lies about me?'

'Lies?'

'I told you what happened with the non-alcoholic wine! How dare you imply I would drink and drive with my own son in the car?'

'Oh please, darling!' he said harshly. 'Stop this charade; you're embarrassing yourself. I should have aired my concerns at the time, but out of some misguided sense of loyalty I gave you a second chance.' He shuddered. 'When I think what could have happened to Milo if I hadn't happened to come over . . .'

'Don't—you—even—*dare*.'

Sebastian stuck his hands in his pockets. 'I hear Belinda came to see you today.'

'How do you know that?' she asked sharply.

'Unlike yours, my lawyer is good enough to keep me informed.' He smiled, mockingly it seemed. 'Belinda's a nice girl, isn't she? She was very sympathetic to my concerns: Milo growing up not knowing his real father, all the bonding experiences I don't want to miss out on.' Sebastian's eyes glazed over. 'Helping out with his homework every night, seeing the little chap's face light up when I take him to see the England boys play at Twickers for the first time . . .'

The gushing sentimentality repulsed her. 'Do

402

you take pleasure in fucking up people's lives, Sebastian?'

'Don't use such disgusting language in front of our son.' His eyes narrowed. 'Have you been drinking again?'

She contained herself. 'I'm not stooping to your level.'

'No, you don't stoop to anyone's level, do you? I think you'll find it's actually called not thinking about yourself the whole time. Have you ever thought about what Milo wants?'

'He's six!' Caro lowered her voice. 'For God's sake!'

'He's a human being. You've been obsessed with that poor child from day one, and for all the wrong reasons. What's good for you isn't necessarily so for him.'

'How *dare* you!' She forced a smile as Milo looked up from behind the steering wheel.

'I'm taking Milo home before you start a public slanging match.'

Caro fought the urge to smash him in the testicles. Sebastian suddenly grabbed her arm and leant in, his Hermès aftershave nauseating.

'Stop being a selfish bitch.' His lips were against her ear. 'You know you're not going to win.'

'Fuck you, Seb.'

'I'd watch what you say to me, I really would.' He stepped back, his smile horrible. 'Ciao for now, *Mrs Towey.*'

CHAPTER SIXTY-TWO

Out of the landing window Calypso watched her sister put her head down and walk off quickly in the opposite direction. What was Caro doing with Milo and the mushroom-haired twat in the pub car park? Surely Benedict hadn't banned him from the house? Her brother-in-law was far too self-controlled and charming for that.

'Big car, small dick,' she muttered as the Aston Martin started up. Sebastian probably wanted to make a big show of collecting Milo in the middle of the village so everyone could see what an amazing father he was. She had to grudgingly admit, he hadn't put a slip-on loafer wrong yet, but she lived in hope. How her sister could have let him oil his way back into her family was beyond her.

But then she wasn't Caro. Her older sister had always been amazingly forgiving. Maybe Calypso should take a leaf out of her book and try to get on with Sebastian. *I should bake him a cake and take it round,* she thought wickedly. If her cooking skills didn't polish him off, nothing would.

Long shadows were starting to creep down the corridor. As Calypso flicked the switch on the wall there was a loud 'pop' and the light bulb above the staircase blew. *Great.* She stood there in the darkness, thinking this was one more thing she didn't need right now. She didn't even know if she had any spare ones. Normally if a bulb went out in her cottage, Calypso would do what she always did, simply shut the door and stop using the room until Jed or Camilla gave in and came round to change it. It was going to be more hazardous negotiating the staircase in pitch darkness, however, especially when she'd had a glass of wine or three.

She turned and looked back out of the window, unwilling to go downstairs and face the arduous pile of paperwork awaiting her. The lights in the Jolly Boot had come on; the windows were warm orange rectangles against the dusky evening. Calypso stared into them longingly. What she'd give to be sat next to the fire drinking a nice shiny big glass of Merlot!

Unfortunately those invoices weren't going to write themselves, and send themselves off to get paid. The most fun she could hope for tonight was some pitta bread out of the freezer and a half-eaten pot of hummus. If she really wanted to go overboard, she could add a tot of Clementine's firewater sloe gin to her orange squash. *Woo hoo!* It was hard to contemplate just how exciting her life was.

She'd just got to the bottom step, and was pondering if she was talking to herself too much these days, when the front doorbell rang. Someone's shadow loomed through the glass panel.

'Hello?' She wasn't expecting anyone.

'It's me, Archie.'

Calypso groaned inwardly. She'd grabbed the first thing out of the wardrobe that morning: old jeggings with a hole in the crotch the size of Antarctica, and a bobbly black cardigan. A pair of her father's socks pulled up unattractively to mid-calf, and dark circles under her eyes completed the bag-lady look.

So what? she thought defiantly. *It's only Archie.* She went over to pull the door open, but not before she'd had a quick look at her face in the mirror on the wall.

'Hey.' Compared to her bedraggled state he looked annoyingly handsome, his eyes light and merry in a still-brown face.

'How come you're still tanned?' she demanded. By contrast, her holiday tan had faded, and she was feeling cavernously white. Well, for her, anyway.

'I don't know, sunbeds?'

'That is so gay,' she scoffed.

'I'm joking.' He grinned. 'Just lucky, I guess. Can I come in?'

'I'm actually a bit tied up.' She smiled sarcastically. 'You know, with that thing called work? You might have heard of it.'

'You'll be needing a break, then.'

'Oh, for God's sake,' she said, stepping back. His shoulders seemed to fill the entire hallway as he walked in.

She took him through to the living room, where he proceeded to take off his jacket and sit back on the sofa like he owned the place. Calypso perched on the arm of the leather armchair and hoped he'd get the hint.

'I'd offer you a drink, but I haven't got any milk.'

'That's all right,' he said cheerfully. 'I'll have my coffee black. One sugar.'

Calypso gritted her teeth. 'Fine.' It wasn't as if she had loads of important paperwork to do. As usual, there were no clean mugs in the kitchen, so she fished two out of the dirty dishwasher and rinsed them under the sink.

'Can I use your toilet?' he called.

He was totally invading her house. 'Sure, it's upstairs. First on the right.'

She stirred a sugar in his mug and two into hers. Might cover up the taste of the out-of-date coffee. Brenda Briggs in the village shop still hadn't quite grasped the concept of sell-by dates.

It sounded like the ceiling was about to come down. Calypso took the mugs out and stuck her head up the stairs. 'What are you doing up there?'

'Your landing bulb's gone. I almost broke my neck.'

If only.

His long legs appeared down the stairs. 'Have you got a spare bulb? I'll change it.'

Moments later he was rifling through her kitchen cupboards. 'Where do you keep them?'

'I don't know, try under the sink.' Calypso flushed as he opened it and a dozen empty wine bottles looked back at him. She really had to get down to the bottle bank.

'Let's see what we've got here.' He knelt down, making his jumper ride up a few inches at the back. Calypso ignored the smooth tanned skin and looked at his head instead. He did have nice thick hair, sort of light-brown with sun-kissed blond tips. From nowhere, she imagined running her hands through it.

As he stood up Calypso hastily diverted her gaze. 'You all right?' he asked. 'You've got a funny look on your face.'

'I'm fine,' she said, flushing again. 'It's probably from having your big arse shoved in it.'

'You've got a beautiful way with words.'

Feeling like Archie was the adult, and not the other way round, Calypso followed him back up the stairs. The light-shade was in a precariously high place on the sloping ceiling. The banisters creaked

407

as he climbed on them to get in a better position.

'Careful!' All this looking upwards was making her feel a bit dizzy. 'Shouldn't you have a stepladder?'

'Have you got one?'

'Why would I have a stepladder?'

His hands were rummaging around in the shade. 'I can't really see what I'm doing . . . Here we go.' He reached down and handed her the old bulb. 'Pass me the new one.'

'I'm not your bloody apprentice,' she grumbled, well aware he was doing her a favour. He was just so full of himself!

'Turn on the switch,' he told her. Moments later the landing and stairs were visible again.

'We have light!' she said. 'Hurrah.'

Archie had his feet wedged between two different rungs of the banister. 'Right. Now I just need to get down.'

'Be careful.'

'Don't worry, I'm always careful.' Twisting his body he went to jump off, but one of his boots got stuck between the banisters.

'Archie!' Calypso screamed as he lost his balance and lurched forward. As he put his hands out to stop himself the boot flew out, catapulting him back down the stairs. There was a sickening thud as he tumbled down the first few steps. Calypso looked over the banister. He wasn't moving.

'Oh my God, Archie!' Almost falling over herself in her haste to get to him, Calypso crouched down over the limp body.

'Can you hear me?' His eyes were shut. Bending down, Calypso put her face to his mouth. He was still breathing.

'Archie!' She had to get help. Just then he gave a little moan. She leant even closer. 'Archie? Can you hear me? It's going to be OK.'

She watched as his eyes fluttered open, and the next moment was astounded when he lifted his head up and kissed her full on the mouth.

'What the . . .' She wrenched herself away and fell back. 'I thought you'd bloody killed yourself!'

'Course not. I'm indestructible, me.' The little shit looked delighted with himself.

'This was a *trick*?'

'Well, no. But when I got to the bottom and knew I was all right I thought I'd come and wait for you to rescue me.' He put his arms behind his head, revealing big brown biceps. 'You give very good mouth-to-mouth.'

'Right, you.' Calypso sprang up. She was fuming! Marching over to the front door she pulled it open. 'Out, now! I've got better things to do with my time than play your juvenile games.'

'Don't be like that.'

'I mean it, *OUT*!'

He didn't move, so Calypso went to haul him up. Seconds later she found herself lying on his chest, inches from his face.

'Let go of me!' she said wriggling, but his arms held her firm.

'I'm feeling a bit funny again, nurse. I think I've had a relapse.'

'I'll give you a bloody relapse.' And then suddenly they were snogging frantically, all lips and tongues, hands raking through each other's hair.

'We are not doing this!' Calypso gasped, feeling Archie's strapping young body underneath her.

'Shut up and kiss me.' He deftly swapped

409

positions, so she was lying under him. Her leggings and cartoon socks were pulled off in record time. 'What are you doing?' she said for the umpteenth time.

'What does it look like?' He pushed her T-shirt up and ran his hands over her flat stomach and hipbones. Then his fingers trailed back down between her inner thighs.

'No!' she protested feebly as he found the soft curl of her bush.

'Why not?' he murmured. 'I know you like it.'

'No, I don't!' Calypso said, the wetness in her knickers giving her away. Archie started to gently rub her clitoris, his hand moving back and forth between her legs for lubrication. 'We . . . can't . . . do . . . Oh my God!' As he made a sublime circular moment, a delicious thrill rippled through her body.

'What's that? You want me to stop?' He took his hand away and looked up at her. He was as turned on as she was, his throat taking husky breaths.

It was unbearable. 'Don't stop now, you little shit!' Calypso grabbed his hand and shoved it down there again, arching her hips up. As he played with her she started to feel the heat building up . . .

'Oh my God, I'm going to come. Don't stop!'

BAM! The orgasm went through her with all the force of a high-speed train. Calypso moaned and rubbed herself furiously with his fingers, wanting to eke out every goddamn last sensation. Her breathing had barely returned to normal before the self-hatred set in.

'You need to leave.'

'Don't be like that.' He was lying on his side next to her, arm curled over her stomach.

'I mean it!' She suddenly felt vulnerable and

angry. What was she doing in the hallway with her muff out in front of Archie Fox-Titt? She jumped up, trying not to give him a bird's-eye view, and grabbed the nearest thing, which was her grandmother's old gardening jacket.

He was totally unruffled. 'You need to work on your post-coital chat.'

It only enraged her more. 'Archie!'

'All right, I'm going,' he said, unhurriedly getting up. Calypso tightened the hideous dog-patterned fleece around her. Brenda Briggs had brought it back for Clementine from a holiday in America. 'Nice coat.'

'Sod off.'

'Well, I'll see you soon, then.'

She ducked away as he went to kiss her. 'Don't hold your breath. And don't tell anyone about this!'

He grinned. 'Don't fight it, Calypso. You and I are meant to be together.'

'On the billion to one chance I start to take an unhealthy interest in schoolboys, I'll let you know.'

'Speak soon.'

There was a blast of cold air as the door opened and shut, and then he was gone.

'No, no, no, no, *no*.' Calypso leaned back against the wall and stared into space. She was in a weird parallel universe, and she couldn't even blame it on drink. Like it or not, she was reeling from the inescapable fact that Archie Fox-Titt had given her the best orgasm she could remember.

As far as she was concerned, it had never happened.

411

CHAPTER SIXTY-THREE

There was something up with Caro, Camilla was sure of it. Normally they were as close as anything, yet the past few weeks it had felt as if her older sister had dropped off the face of the earth. Which was no mean feat, considering they only lived on the other side of the green from each other.

When Camilla called the house, Caro would snatch up the phone almost immediately, but then there would be some reason she couldn't talk. Either the kids were playing up, or she was tired, or she had a million and one things to do. Camilla understood that her sister was a busy mum, but Caro seemed . . . distant. Secretive almost, and that had never been how Camilla would have described her in the past. When Camilla popped round, it almost felt like Caro was trying to get rid of her. It was strange, because her sister was such a lovely hostess, and usually always had time for people.

Camilla hoped Caro and Benedict weren't having marriage problems. They were such a perfect couple, so happy and beautiful and devoted to each other, but who knew what went on behind closed doors? Ominously, Caro had been the same when her marriage to Sebastian had been failing, retreating inside herself and not confiding in anyone. Sebastian. The thought suddenly struck Camilla: it couldn't be anything to do with him moving back again, could it? Surely not. Caro and Benedict were stronger than that. The situation, although less than ideal, seemed to be working out better than any of them had hoped.

It was meant to be Camilla's turn to cook that night, but as she let herself into the cottage a delicious smell of cooking filled the air.

'Jed?' she called, hanging her coat up on the hook. 'Is that you?'

He called back. 'Through here.'

'Something smells nice,' she said, walking through to the kitchen. 'Oh, Jed!'

The room had been turned into a scene from a romantic restaurant. The lights were dimmed, and candles were flickering in the middle of the table. The usual gingham cloth had been replaced by an antique white lace one Camilla only used for special occasions, while two place mats had been set opposite each other. Five stunning sunflowers—Camilla's favourites—had been positioned carefully at the head of the table. Camilla noticed the ice bucket and champagne glasses on the side; Jed wasn't normally much of a drinker.

'Oh my God, look at you!' Gone were the usual scruffy work clothes and faded blue overalls tied round his waist. Jed was looking utterly gorgeous in his black tuxedo, black hair brushed back over his temples. His green eyes had never looked so bright, nor his cheekbones so razor sharp. For the thousandth time, Camilla thought what a head-turner her boyfriend was.

'Mussels in Thai green sauce all right to start?'

'More than all right! Jed, what is this?' she said, as he came across and wrapped his arms round her. 'Our anniversary isn't for ages.'

He didn't answer her for a moment. 'I've got something to tell you.'

'Uh-oh, I knew there was something,' she joked.

He smiled, green eyes glowing in the gloom. 'I'm

413

ready, Cam.'

She didn't understand. 'Ready?'

'I've been selfish for too long, with my stupid male pride. I'm sorry.'

'Jed, what have you got to be sorry about? You've done nothing wrong.'

His eyes gleamed. 'I want to adopt with you, Cam. I want to start our own family.'

This was the last thing she had expected. 'I don't . . . what's brought this on? How long have you been thinking about this?'

'A while.' He held her tighter. 'I do owe you an apology, Cam. All this time I've been thinking about how *I* feel, not about what you want. The way you've dealt with all this . . . me. It's made me realize more than ever what an amazing person you are. What an amazing mother you'd be.'

She felt herself well up. 'Oh, Jed. You'd make a great dad, too, I know it.'

'Only one way to find out, isn't there?' Smiling, he stroked her face.

'It's a long process,' she warned. 'And even then . . .'

'I know all that. And I know I love you.' He started to undo the top of her trousers.

'I'm all hot from work. I should take a shower . . .'

'You're lovely as you are.' His eyes strayed. 'I want you on the table. We may as well make the most of the freedom while we can.'

'What, the sleepless nights, no time to ourselves, having no money?' She laughed as Jed picked her up. 'Are you really sure you want to do this?'

His green eyes burned into hers. 'I've never been more sure of anything.'

This time when he entered her, there was no

414

look of love or shame. Both knew the next stage of their lives had just started. As Camilla had said, it would be a long, arduous journey, but they'd found something again tonight: hope that they might still have that family after all.

*   *   *

Kizzy hadn't been able to stay away long. Tonight, however, Mary was buzzing about, so Javier had respectfully asked if Kizzy would like to see the music room. Once inside he'd closed the door and taken her from behind across the grand piano. It was urgent and animalistic, and afterwards they lay in a breathless heap on the floor.

'I hope Mary didn't hear us,' Kizzy whispered. 'I bet she was a good Catholic girl.'

'Don't you believe it, Mary was quite a catch in her day.' He shifted position slightly. 'If she does say something I'll tell her the piano needs tuning.'

'Cheek! I wasn't that noisy!'

Javier nuzzled her, laughing. Even in the wildness of his lovemaking he retained a sweet protectiveness. That side was out in force now: his strong arms were round her as if he'd never let go.

'I'm only joking, angel.'

Kizzy stuck her tongue out and rolled back to gaze up at the piano. From this distance she could see the swirls of mahogany in the polished wood, the yellow-gold pedals. 'What is it?' It looked expensive, nothing like the battered old one they'd had at school.

'It's a Steiner, commandeered from one of the great musical halls in Vienna during the Second World War. I picked it up at auction in Christie's

415

years ago.'

'Do you play much?'

'Not any more.'

'I'd love to have musical talent.'

His hand trailed up a satin-smooth thigh. 'Oh, you've definitely got a talent.'

'I'm talking about your piano playing,' she giggled. His fingers were creeping tantalizingly up her inner thigh. Javier had the stamina of a man half his age, she thought. She was still in a state of blissful exhaustion from the last time.

'Will you play something for me?' she asked.

'Now?'

'Yes.' She kissed his cheek. 'I'd love to hear you play.'

'All right then.' He got up, like a great leopard uncoiling, and went over to the seat. 'Normally I'd wear clothes of course, but this is rather liberating.'

'I can see that,' she grinned, gazing at his delicious buttocks. If someone had told her this time last year that she'd be treated to the sight of Javier Hamilton-Scott sitting butt-naked at a piano, she'd have laughed in their face. The rippling contours and posture reminded her of the men out of those eighties Athena posters her mum used to have in the kitchen.

The plink plonk of 'The Grand Old Duke of York' started up. Kizzy nudged him with her foot, smiling. 'Play something nice!'

'Like this?' He switched to the opening notes of 'The Entertainer'.

'Javier!'

'I can see you're not impressed with my repertoire so far.' His hands swept up and down the keys as if testing them. Sweet lilting notes rose up into the air as he started to play.

Kizzy propped herself up to hear. It was a classical piece, haunting and delicate. Where had she heard it before? She was transfixed, both by the quality of playing and by Javier. His eyes were closed; lost in the music, the smouldering tension he always carried with him had gone. Each note made the hairs on the back of Kizzy's neck stand on end. As she listened her eyes travelled across the sinewy back, to the scar snaking across Javier's left shoulder from a riding fall, and to his long muscular legs. Seeing him here, now, in all his glory, playing music of such beauty was the most erotic thing Kizzy had ever experienced in her life.

The last notes lingered in the air several seconds after he'd finished.

Kizzy got up and went to put her arms round him. 'That was incredible. I mean, exquisite, Javier.' She'd never heard music like it.

'*Clair de Lune*, by Debussy.' He sounded far away. 'One of my favourites.'

The name rang a bell. *That* was where she'd heard it. 'You know the *Twilight* films? That was in the first one, when Edward and Bella dance in his bedroom.'

'The vampire films? I'm not really into blood and gore.'

'Oh my God, they're so much more than that, Javier. It sounds really cheesy, but it's this most amazing tale of forbidden love.'

'Like us?'

Kizzy's smile dropped. 'Don't say that.'

'I'm sorry, I didn't mean to upset you.' Javier's great shoulders rose up in a sigh. 'Oh, Kizzy.'

Everything had been so perfect up till then. Kizzy

417

was desperate not to spoil the mood. 'I don't care about the age gap, I told you.'

He was silent for a long while. 'I have a wife. When I took my wedding vows, I meant them. I thought Sarah and I would be together for ever.'

'I understand. I respect that. Look . . .' Kizzy blinked back tears. 'If Sarah ever woke up, I'd be gone. Out of your life for ever. Can't we take it one day at a time? Please.' Her voice broke. 'I just want to *heal* you.'

'Oh, my darling. Come here.'

She got up and went to sit on his lap. 'It's not fair putting this on you,' he murmured into her golden hair. 'You can walk away at any time.'

Kizzy pulled back to look at him. 'Do you want me to?'

A look of anguish entered his face. 'No, of course I don't.'

'I *can't* stay away, Javier. Don't you understand? Not until you tell me to.'

He hugged her so fiercely it took her breath away.

CHAPTER SIXTY-FOUR

The last week of February saw Nobby back at Chaddesley Corbett claiming his second win in the Men's Open. By now Goldenballs, or 'Thunderpants' as he was affectionately known by the racing fraternity because of the earth-shattering sounds that came out of his rear end, was starting to be a force to be reckoned with. The day afterwards, Freddie and Angie invited Edward and Kizzy over for dinner, and a powwow round the kitchen table. Their unexpected success had given them serious food for thought.

Angie smiled at their lanky protégé over the duck curry. 'Edward, Freddie and I have been talking. You know, we're so delighted with the progress you've made this season, and if you wanted to carry on just doing the point-to-points we'd be more than happy, but . . .'

'Are you thinking about the hunter chase at Newbury?' he asked matter-of-factly.

Angie glanced between her husband and Kizzy. 'Well, yes, darling. But we'd never want to push you into something you didn't want to do.'

It had been Freddie who'd lightly remarked the previous evening that with Edward's flush run they might as well enter the upcoming hunter chase at Newbury Racecourse. It was a major step up. The horses were better quality, the fences and prize money a lot bigger. Unlike the farmers' fields they'd only ever been on, Newbury Racecourse was a 'Grade One' track, the highest level in British horse racing. It was the home of the renowned Hennessy Gold Cup, and countless legends had raced home past the post. When she thought about Edward and Nobby treading the turf there Angie suddenly felt rather sick.

'I mean, obviously it's the qualifier for the Cheltenham Festival, darling, but we're not even thinking like that,' she said hurriedly. 'All we thought was that it would be a fabulous experience for you to run on a proper track. We just want you to get round in one piece.'

Freddie's eyes twinkled. 'Still, Edward, not a bad race to get under your belt, eh?'

None of them could say the thought hadn't crossed their minds when Edward had won the last Men's Open. A first, second or third placing at Newbury was *the* golden ticket as far as the point-to-point world was concerned—and meant a place in the Foxhunter Steeplechase at the Cheltenham Festival. This four-day event was held at Cheltenham Racecourse and was one of the most prestigious events in the racing calendar. Traditionally held in the middle of March, a bout of equine flu had postponed the races for only the second time ever. Now the Festival was being held in the third week of April, after Aintree. The notion that they might, just *might*, have a chance to get there was the most unbelievable thing ever.

'Freddie, don't scare Edward off.'

'He's not.' Edward's long face was resolute.

'That's fine, Edward,' Angie told him. 'We really didn't expect you to want to do it. It's a huge leap up.'

'I mean no, you're not pushing me.' He gave a little smile. 'I want to do it. Me and Nobby, we're ready.'

They all looked at each other. A ripple of excitement went round the table. 'Wow!' Kizzy said. 'The Cheltenham qualifier!'

Freddie chortled. 'Who'd have thought it?'

Angie had been expecting a terrified reaction from Edward, but his eye had a positive glint. 'No harm in having a go, is there?'

*　　　*　　　*

Things weren't just looking up on the racing front for the Fox-Titts. Their business was starting to

420

make a profit for the first time in years, mainly down to Archie's energy and ideas. Angie walked into the study the next day to find father and son hard at work.

'I don't want to interrupt, I just thought you might like refreshments.' She put the tray of coffee and biscuits down.

'Thanks, Ma.' Archie was sat at Freddie's desk with his laptop open. The small sleek machine made Freddie's bulky old PC look like it was from another century. Angie glanced over her son's shoulder at the bullet-point paragraphs filling the screen.

'What are you up to?'

Freddie answered for him. 'Arch is doing me a business plan,' he said through a mouthful of chocolate digestive. 'We've already doubled our profits from this time last year. I don't know how I've been managing without him.'

'You just needed a gentle nudge, Pops.'

'Our website was terrible, apparently,' Freddie told his wife. 'Archie's redesigned it, so we're getting a lot more traffic.'

'You are clever, Arch,' Angie said. 'Maybe you could do me one for the shop.'

Archie looked up and grinned. 'Sure.'

Angie watched him type. Her son had grown up into such an easy-going, capable young man. She'd had her reservations about him going into business with his father, not wanting to pressure him into doing something he didn't want. She needn't have worried. Archie was showing a natural aptitude for running The Maltings Inc. He understood the land and had a brilliant business brain, too. Hard-working and popular, he was equally at home

421

creating a spreadsheet or mucking in with the rest of the workers on the estate. Only that morning he'd held a conference call with some prospective clients and then headed straight out on the quad bike to mend one of the jetties on the trout lake.

'Ma, stop looking at me,' he said, his eyes fixed on the screen.

'I'm just admiring my favourite boy.' Freddie was right; Archie was an absolute godsend.

Now all he needed was a nice girlfriend!

PART THREE

PART THREE

CHAPTER SIXTY-FIVE

March arrived. With it came the first signs of life after a long-drawn-out winter. The village green stopped resembling a muddy wasteland and started to take on the fresh new colours of spring, bare trees came out of hibernation, and there was even an early bloom of snowdrops across the Meadows.

Calypso noticed none of this. She'd had a particularly trying few days: first a corporate team-building course in Monmouthshire, at which she'd been 'encouraged' by the manic-eyed MD to take part in the activities—which had included a bungee jump and white-water rafting. She'd come back traumatized and exhausted, straight into a Harry-Potter-themed birthday party for a thuggish six-year-old. She'd found an amazing venue for this—the recently renovated Chowdry Castle—and had spent weeks sourcing top-notch magic paraphernalia.

Unfortunately, all hell had broken loose when one of the owls had escaped, taking a child's wizard hat off with it, and a rabble of snot-faced little shits had started pelting the grown-ups with the themed cupcakes. It had culminated in a 'Ron Weasley' being aimed with military precision at the snooty wife of an MP, and her expensive blouse getting stained with bright-red icing. Calypso had been dragged aside and told her party was totally unsuitable for young children, and her services would never be required again.

There had been a brief moment of hope when she'd got home and someone had emailed her about putting on a product launch. Calypso had clicked on the attachment, imagining some fashion store or perfume line, to find it was actually a local agriculture firm wanting press for their new fertilizer. Even though she'd always been loath to turn down work, Calypso had promptly emailed back to say she was taking a six-month sabbatical in the wilds of South America and would be uncontactable for the foreseeable future.

'To be honest, I don't give a shit. I'm up to here with whining, pampered kids and their stupid parties.' Calypso had gone straight round to Camilla's, and was now lying face down on the sofa, having recounted the whole Harry Potter debacle.

Camilla wiped away a tear of laughter. Her sister did have a way of telling stories.

'Hold on, you've got something in your hair.' She got up and came over to inspect the back of Calypso's head. 'It looks like bird poo.'

'I thought I felt something when that bloody owl took off! Great, so now I've got a bonce-full of bird shit to top it all off.'

'Shall I get a cloth?' Camilla was trying not to laugh.

'If you want, I'm beyond caring.' Calypso sighed and looked round the immaculate living room. There were fresh flowers in a vase on the windowsill and the floorboards had been newly polished.

'Can I move back in with you? It's so much nicer round here than at mine.'

'You don't really mean that, you're just having a bad day,' Camilla said hastily. The last time Calypso had lived here the normally pristine cottage had looked like a bomb had hit it.

'Bad day, bad week, bad life. God!' Calypso

426

turned over and stared up at the ceiling. 'How did it get to this, Cam?'

'Get to what? You've got a great business with lots of clients . . .'

'Clients I don't *want*. I'm seriously thinking of moving back to London.'

'Really?'

'Yeah.' Calypso struggled up. 'Oh, I don't know. It's just all so unglamorous and boring. Is that what real life is?'

''Fraid so, sweetie. Most of the time.'

'God. *Animal dung*. Wherever I look, there's poo. Poo in my hair, poo in my job. My social life is the biggest poo of all. It's poo-ma-fucking-geddon! You hear that, Bills? My life is literally *shit*.'

The pair of them started giggling for a good minute. 'Oh dear, poo-mageddon.' Camilla wiped a tear from her eye. 'My stomach hurts.'

It was amazing what a laugh could do. The doomy feeling that had hung over Calypso's day suddenly wasn't there any more. She threw her legs over the back of the sofa. 'So what's been happening with you guys? I feel like I haven't seen anyone for ages.'

'Well.' Camilla paused. 'Jed and I are going to see where we get with adoption.'

Calypso sat bolt upright. 'Seriously?'

Camilla grinned. 'Course, it might not happen, but we're going to try . . .'

She was flattened by her sister leaping across the room and giving her a big, perfumed hug. 'That is so great!'

'Thanks, sweet pea.' Camilla pulled a bit of Calypso's long hair out of her mouth. 'I'm pretty thrilled, too.'

427

Calypso went and sat back down. 'What's brought all this on? I thought Jed wasn't keen.'

'I think he just needed time to come around. You know, accept . . . our situation. We're both being realistic about it. These things can take a couple of years, and even then, you never know . . .

'But at least you're giving it a go.'

Camilla smiled again. 'Exactly.'

'Put it there, sister.' Calypso held her hand up in a high five gesture. 'You know, if the worst comes to the worst, you can always adopt me.'

Camilla started laughing. 'We're not that desperate!'

'Oi! I'm not that bad.' Calypso gave a throaty chuckle. 'Oh well, at least someone's sorting out their life round here. Talking of perfect lives, have you seen Caro recently?'

'No.' Camilla frowned. 'Do you think she's been a bit, well, weird lately?'

'What do you mean?'

'I don't know, she just seems on edge. I went over and called on her yesterday, and she slammed the study door shut in front of me, as if she didn't want me to see something.'

'Maybe Benedict's got some top-secret work project on that he doesn't want anyone to know about.'

'Maybe. But I hope Caro knows I wouldn't say anything.'

Calypso thought about what she'd said. 'Caro's always rundown coming out of the back of winter, with all the bugs the kids pick up. It's probably just that.'

'Maybe.'

Calypso felt a bit bad that she hadn't been round

428

to see Milo and Rosie for a while; she'd been so flat out with work. 'Maybe we should organize a girls' night, just the three of us.'

'Deffo! I've forgotten what one feels like.' Camilla got up from her armchair. 'It's nearly lunchtime. Are you hungry?'

'Does a bear shit . . . actually, let's not go there.'

*   *   *

Caro put the last of Rosie's socks away and closed the drawer. She heard the washing machine beep downstairs, indicating the cycle had finished, but instead she sat down on the bed and stared around at the pink room.

She knew she'd overreacted in front of Camilla. The custody paperwork had been laid out on Benedict's desk, and she'd been gripped by a sudden fear that her sister would see it. It was ridiculous, of course. How would Camilla be able to see from the doorway anyway? And even if she had, Caro knew she'd have been as supportive and sweet as ever.

New waves of emotion washed through her daily. She was exhausted and not sleeping properly, a tight ball permanently lodged in the pit of her stomach. She felt anxiety and fear, yes, but also such *shame*. Every aspect of their private life was being put under the spotlight, and Caro was terrified she would trip up. She and Benedict had even had to suffer the indignity of going to Louise Rennison's office and having strands of hair cut off by a representative from a drugs and alcohol screening company and sent off for analysis. Caro had barely touched a drop of booze in weeks, but she had still had a totally unfounded fear that perhaps there were traces left in her system from her life before, when she would enjoy a couple of glasses of wine and not feel as if she was committing a cardinal sin, or that it would be flagged up and used against her.

This paranoia was extending to every recess of her life. Had Belinda Winters been in yet to talk to Milo's teacher? Miss Ekins seemed normal when Caro went to pick Milo up, but she couldn't look her in the eye. Once or twice she was sure she'd caught Miss Ekins looking at her in a funny way. The worst thing was not *knowing*. A stealth assessment was being carried out on their lives, and Caro had no idea what the conclusions were likely to be.

Benedict was a true rock, as always, but Caro could see his anger about Sebastian starting to eat him up. Her husband was furious that they had been put in this position, that Sebastian had dared to treat the mother of his child so badly. The worst thing of all—and she would never admit it to anyone—was that Caro was starting to have nasty little doubts about herself. They were few and far between, and normally surfaced at four in the morning after hours of tossing and turning, but when they came it was like a sucker punch to the head.

What if she *wasn't* good enough to look after Milo? Motherhood didn't come with a handbook, but there were things she could have done differently, weren't there? These desolate moments of despair were normally vanquished by morning, but Caro felt more despondent each time. When she thought about all Sebastian's outlandish claims—and the fact that she'd given him any ammunition at all—she wanted to bloody slap herself.

Caro put her head in her hands. She wasn't going to lose the pride and joy of her life, was she? Her *raison d'être,* along with Benedict and Rosie. Caro squeezed her eyes shut, keeping the tears back. This wasn't doing her any good at all. She started sucking in long, noisy breaths of air. *Calm down. Focus.* By sheer mental strength she managed to will herself back to the present. The washing machine still needed emptying; Milo had to be picked up from school. There was nothing else to do but get up and carry on being a mother.

CHAPTER SIXTY-SIX

Dawn crept in through the sash windows. Kizzy stirred and blinked her eyes open. She turned over and saw the empty space beside her. Kizzy had always been an early riser herself, but Javier made her look like a positive layabout.

It was fascinating, and a real privilege, to be so close to someone in training for the Olympics. Every spare minute of Javier's time he was down at the yard with Oliver and Love's Dream. If they weren't in the indoor or outdoor arenas (it was better to train outside, so the horse got used to the sounds), Javier and his protégé were in the conference room, going over hours and hours of footage; of both the GB team and their competition. As always the Germans were a threat, and veteran Carl Hester, European, world and

Olympic champion, was the big one to beat. In the up-and-coming stakes, Great Britain's own Laura Bechtolsheimer was fast becoming a force to be reckoned with, too.

Before she'd met Javier, Kizzy had been vaguely aware of the rules of dressage, and a few of the big names, but now she was fast falling in love with the sport. Not to the extent that she'd ever do it herself—racing was still her true love—but Javier was so passionate and knowledgeable about it that she couldn't help being drawn in. She now knew the difference between a passage and a piaffe, and how many strides made the perfect flying lunge.

Kizzy had always thought of dressage as a nice, pretty sport, and that the real blood and sweat was in horse racing, but she'd come to appreciate the incredible endurance involved. The riders were marked both as a team and as individuals, and only the top 25 per cent would go through to the all-important Grand Prix freestyle round. The 'kur' music test, as it was known, was the chance to perform to your choice of music and ultimately win a medal. The highly anticipated event was the most prestigious part of the three-day competition.

The amount of time and money that went into choosing the music, which horse and rider might not even get the chance to perform to, was staggering. As marks were awarded for both technical and artistic ability, the music selection and choreography were crucial in showing off a horse's talents to their full potential. Kizzy's choice of Tinie Tempah aside (which Javier had told her was definite food for thought for another competition), Javier's team had decided that the Rolling Stones' 'Paint it Black' was the perfect choice to showcase

432

Love's Dream's powerful elegance.

This didn't mean just whacking on the CD player and hoping for the best. The London Philharmonic Orchestra were recording an instrumental version especially for Love's Dream to perform to. The team were even in the process of trying to get Mick Jagger to record a special introduction to the piece. The whole thing blew Kizzy's mind.

Like every event at the Olympics, dressage had received its fair share of Lottery funding. As well as paying for top-class coaches like Javier, it helped secure access to the best physios, nutritionists and sports psychologists. And that was just the horses; Oliver Foster had a strict diet and exercise routine, including his own private Pilates instructor to help perfect that crucial posture in the saddle.

Now only four months away, Olympic coverage was everywhere: television, radio, Twitter, newspapers. That month's *Horse and Hound* had a six-page feature on Great Britain's dressage team, with a fabulous photograph of Javier putting Oliver and his horse through their paces in the indoor arena. The article had made much of Javier's return to the equestrian world, and the great things expected from him.

Kizzy would've been sick with nerves if that had been her, but the pressure barely seemed to affect Javier. Nothing else mattered for him, expect those six minutes or so out in the arena. That was where Oliver Foster and Love's Dream—and Javier's prowess as a trainer—would be judged. In a funny way, Kizzy understood. Not that she'd ever compare her amateur racing career to that of a legend like Javier, but they were about the same things. All those months and years of hard work, all that frustration and sacrifice—all coming together for a precious few minutes. That's why Javier was at the top of his game; his focus was ferocious.

Kizzy saw the cup of tea he'd put by her side of the bed. She'd barely been awake when he'd come in earlier, murmured something in her ear and dropped a kiss on her head. Kizzy looked at the white swirl on the top of the liquid, where it had gone cold. It was amazing really, considering how busy Javier was, that he always had time for her. Even if they didn't really get to talk until Kizzy came over for a late supper, Javier was always full of questions about her day and how everything was going at the yard. As if she were the one with the big training job. The fact that he made Kizzy feel like the centre of his world every time only intensified the strength of her feelings for him.

Kizzy sat up, pulling the bed sheets over her naked breasts. She felt wide awake and clear-headed, even though they'd been up until the early hours making love. It had been wild and abandoned, just as it always was, and then there'd been a perfect moment of tenderness afterwards.

Just thinking about it made Kizzy ache with desire. She leant over and buried her face in Javier's pillow, inhaling the faint tang of his musky aftershave.

Her parents thought she was staying at Lauren's. Kizzy felt bad lying to them, but there was no way she could tell the truth. Her mum had been really pleased, saying it was nice Kizzy was spending more time with her friends again. It had made her even guiltier. All Kizzy could do was pray her mum didn't go and bump into Lauren in Bedlington or something. How the hell would she get out of that one?

She sat up, sighing at the customary stiffness in her back. It would take a few minutes to get going again. Kizzy rubbed her eyes and looked round the room. There was definitely a masculine feel in here, with the dark wood and navy curtains, but the room had a bareness, as if it had been set up for a purely functional purpose. There were few personal mementos here, and no perfume bottles or toiletries, or silk dressing gown hanging on the back of the door. Kizzy couldn't imagine Javier had ever shared it with Sarah, and she would never dare to ask. It was just another unknown, left undiscussed.

Javier rarely brought up Sarah's name, aside from the odd comment about something she'd liked, or a place they'd been together. Kizzy tried not to mind too much; she had no right to. It was so hard not to obsess about it, though. Javier obviously visited Sarah, but how often or for how long, Kizzy had no idea. Sometimes when she phoned and it went to voicemail, she imagined a beautiful old house that had been converted into a hospice, sitting in the middle of parkland, Sarah in her own private room, Javier sitting by her bed holding her hand . . .

The long shards of morning sun were moving up the wall. It was time to get a move on, not sit here brooding. Kizzy climbed out of bed and went to her overnight bag, trying to shake off her feelings of anguish.

She'd brought her work clothes, as she was going straight to the Maltings. Dressing quickly, she picked up her bag and the mug from the bedside table, having a sudden urge to get down to the yard and be surrounded by noise and people.

The great house was quiet as she padded out on to the landing. It was still before seven, and none of the staff were at work yet. Light was filtering in through the big front windows, warming up the dark panelled wood that dominated the interior of Homelands.

Normally Kizzy would use the back servants' stairs down the far left of the corridor, but her car was parked at the front. She started to descend the huge sweeping staircase leading to the entrance hall. It was funny to think of all Javier's glamorous and aristocratic ancestors who'd stepped down these stairs in the past. And here she was, in her socks and old joddies, and a sweatshirt that probably had Nobby's slobber across the front of it.

She'd just started down them when there was a faint 'thump' somewhere to her right. Kizzy looked up across the enormous landing. It sounded like it had come from behind one of the doors on the far side. She'd never been round there, because she and Javier normally went straight to their own room. He'd told her all there was in that direction was 'just another lot of bedrooms'. Not for the first time, Kizzy got the impression Javier was irritated by the size of the place.

It was all quiet now, but Kizzy started back up the stairs. She'd thought she'd better just make sure, and she was curious about the other rooms. Ignoring an inner voice that told her not to, she started to walk round the landing. There was a row of five doors at the very far end, all closed. Behind the first one was a cavernous, old-fashioned bedroom with another four-poster bed. A spooky portrait of an old man with a handlebar moustache hung over the fireplace. His eyes seemed to

436

be looking directly at her, reproaching her for snooping, and Kizzy beat a hasty retreat. The next door revealed a similar bedroom, sparsely decorated with grand bits of furniture. There was a pile of cardboard boxes in one corner. Both rooms had that musty, stuffy air of not being used very often.

It was in the second from last bedroom, on the windowsill outside, that Kizzy found the cause of the noise. A blackbird lay dead on the wide ledge, with a floppy body and staring eyes. The poor thing must have flown into the window and broken its neck. Kizzy would have opened the sash and moved it, but it was a steep drop below. She'd mention it to Mary later; there was a maintenance man around for that sort of thing.

Kizzy came out and closed the door behind her. There was still one more door, set slightly apart from the others, further down the corridor. Now she'd found out what the noise was there was no reason for her to go on exploring, but curiosity made her go and try the handle anyway. It was locked.

Kizzy raised an eyebrow. Maybe it was more of Javier's art collection; on her first tour round the house he'd pointed out a real-life Picasso. Apparently it was only an etching, and one of the cheaper ones, but still! He had a real *Picasso* hanging in his house. Even Kizzy, who was the first to admit she knew next to nothing about art, knew this was a big deal.

Maybe he had a whole load more of expensive art in there. Why would it be hidden away, though? More likely it was just a cupboard or junkroom, full of more cardboard boxes. Kizzy suddenly thought how it would look now if Mary or Nigel came along and found her nosing round. Turning back, she went to get her car.

CHAPTER SIXTY-SEVEN

Calypso was determined to start making time for herself before she had a complete mental breakdown. That morning she'd been out doing recces for new venues, but, after a quick sandwich for lunch, instead of tackling the omnipresent pile of paperwork on her desk she went upstairs for a long hot bath. Feeling more human, she was in her dressing gown doing a pedicure for the first time in weeks when the doorbell rang. She hobbled across the bedroom to look out of the window. Her stomach dropped. Archie's pick-up truck was parked on the verge. She was just about to duck away when he stepped back from under the porch and saw her.

Bollocks. She pushed open the window. 'Hi.'

'Hey, Calypso. What are you up to?'

'This and that.' *Bog off.* Just seeing him there, all spruced up in the wax Carhartt jacket she had a bit of a thing for in men, was bringing up all sorts of unwanted feelings.

'Do you fancy a walk? May as well make the most of the evenings getting lighter.'

'I'm busy,' she lied.

He cocked his head. 'Oh, doing what?'

'Really important work stuff.'

'Come on.' He grinned. 'You shouldn't be stuck indoors on a day like this. Come and take a walk

438

with me.'

*   *   *

Twenty minutes later they were ambling out along Bramble Lane. Archie breathed in deeply, and looked up at the pale blue sky. 'Nothing like a bit of fresh country air.'

'Nothing like an afternoon in front of the telly, either.'

He raised an eyebrow. 'For someone born and bred here, you're not really an outdoor girl.'

'Course I am, when it's hot and sunny. Summer's a long way off.'

There were a few merciful moments of silence. 'How's work?'

'Oh God, don't ask. I've just had it up to here, you know? *This* place. I'm seriously thinking of moving to London.'

'London?'

'Yeah.' She was secretly quite pleased at the look on his face.

'You don't need to go to London.' Archie went to grab her hand but she pulled away. He stopped and turned to look at her.

'Calypso.' He looked faintly amused. 'Why are you always so horrible to me?'

'I'm not horrible!' she said, though she knew he was right.

'Yes, you are. You bite my head off whenever I ask you something.'

'No, I don't,' she said defensively. 'Can we carry on walking, please?'

He wasn't going anywhere. 'Is this about what happened at yours?'

439

'*No.*' She covered her eyes. 'Archie, I really don't want to talk about this.'

'Why not?'

'Because it should never had happened. You're twenty-three, for God's sake, and I'm twenty-eight. We want different things, Archie.'

Archie shook his head. 'How do you know that if you don't give it a try?'

'I just do, trust me. I'm a different person now from when I was twenty-three.'

'I don't think you are.'

'Well, I am, and I'm not going to end up with someone who I've known all my life and who used to throw frogspawn in my hair. Anyway,' she added defiantly, 'you know what this place is like for gossip. I'm not becoming the sole topic of conversation for Brenda Briggs and her cronies.'

'Stop worrying about other people. Why can't we have fun and see what happens?'

Have fun and see what happens. Calypso had used a similar line many a time before. *When had she got so uptight?*

There was an opening in the hedge coming up, leading into a ploughed field. Calypso had a devil-may-care moment. 'All right, you.' She started to push Archie through backwards.

'Whoa, what's going on?'

'We're about to have sex.'

He looked round. 'What, here?'

'You wanted to have fun, didn't you?' She started unbuckling his belt. She'd show this boy she still knew how to have a good time!

His cock was satisfyingly hard. Calypso dropped to her knees and put it in her mouth. She felt like she was the one with all the power again.

'Oh my God.' He put his hands on the back of her head, grabbing chunks of blonde hair.

'Don't pull my hair.' She shook herself free and started licking round the rim of his bell-end again. He tasted of clean skin and the faint tang of washing powder.

'Let me touch you.' His hands were fumbling for her breasts under her jumper.

'I'm the one in charge.' She pushed him down on the ground and sat astride him.

'Have you got any condoms?'

'I'm on the pill. Unless you picked up some sheep-shagging disease on that farm of yours?'

'You bitch,' he said, snogging her. Calypso was wearing culottes and tights, which were going to be a bugger to get off, but before she could wriggle out of her right welly there was a tearing sound and Archie had ripped the crotch of her tights open with his bare hands.

'Those were expensive!' she exclaimed.

'I'll buy you a new pair.'

'Don't bother.' Calypso looked into his eyes. Pulling her knickers aside, she slid on to his cock. He moaned softly. *Control back to her again.*

She wrapped her legs tightly round him. 'Is this what you wanted?'

'You know it is. Jesus.'

It looked good in clothes, but naked, Archie's body was even more impressive. He had one of those modern-day rugby physiques, lean and muscular without an inch of spare fat. And those arms! Bloody hell, they were *massive*.

'Not bad.'

'Not bad yourself.'

'Let me go on top,' he told her. 'I want to make

441

love to you.'

'No, it's called having *sex*, and I'm perfectly happy here, thank you.'

'All right, then.' The next moment she was flat on her back.

'You like this manoeuvre, don't you?'

He grinned. 'It's called the surprise element. It's the only way I can get you to do something.'

'I thought you were doing *me*,' she gasped, as he slid back inside her.

He kissed her neck. 'I am now.'

Calypso couldn't help giving a little moan. It felt *good*.

Five minutes later they were walking back down the lane. 'Someone's going to see your muddy arse and wonder what you've been doing,' she told him.

'They'll probably say the same about yours.'

This time, when he took her hand, she let him. 'Only because there's no one about.'

'Yes, ma'am.'

CHAPTER SIXTY-EIGHT

In all her fifty-six years Angie had never, ever, imagined she would own a horse that would come second in a Cheltenham qualifier. When she looked back on that strange, crazy and wonderful day it was the silliest little things that stood out. Cheryl Pike's high-heeled wellies, the board on the other side of the track advertising Dubai Airport duty-free, the strangely frozen forehead of an old hunting chum she hadn't seen in donkey's years. The journey there, the stand packed with spectators, even the race itself, had passed in one giant blur.

All Angie could remember clearly was checking Nobby's girth for the umpteenth time and saying something to Edward, Lord knows what. When she watched the race back online on *Racing UK* she saw every little detail with crystal clarity, yet at the time it was all she could do to keep up with the field as they streaked past the endless miles of white running rail. Edward had stuck to his normal tactics: lurk midfield for the first fifteen fences until Nobby's motor was firing nicely, then let the horse have his head on the home straight. It wasn't perfect; playing it differently, Edward might even have been able to get the front runner, but Nobby had flown past the finishing post in second, beating a very good bay from Ireland by a whiskery nose.

They'd all gone mad, then. Angie vaguely recalled kissing the old chap next to her, and Edward had triumphantly punched the air. The crowd had hooted with laughter as Nobby had farted his way back to the paddock, tail high in the air. A man from the *Racing Post* had come up to Angie, and then someone from the *Bedlington Bugle*, who wanted to come round and interview them the next day . . .

Half the village had come down in a minibus driven by Brenda's husband, Ted, and by the time they'd eventually hauled everyone out of the bar the racing had finished. It had been a very raucous journey home along the M4, with even Edward joining in the laughing and joking.

Everyone piled into the Fox-Titts' for more celebrations. It wasn't until Angie had been handed her second glass of champagne that the enormity of what had happened actually hit home.

443

'Oh, Fred! We're going to bloody Cheltenham! I can't believe it!'

Her husband had been grinning like a loon all afternoon. 'I was wondering when it was going to sink in.'

'Well, it has now.' Angie put a hand over her mouth. 'Oh, Fred.' She felt quite overcome.

*   *   *

Jack Turner turned up with more champagne from the pub and it was gone eleven at night by the time a very tiddly Calypso, the last guest standing, was poured into the minibus by Ted Briggs and taken home.

It was only when Angie had put her eye cream on and climbed into bed, exhausted but exuberant, that she brought up the one thing that had been nagging at her all day.

'Don't you think it's strange how none of Edward's family came along?'

Freddie looked up from *The Field* magazine. 'Hmm?'

'That Edward's parents weren't there? I mean, it's not my place to say anything, but . . .'

'No, it's certainly not.' Freddie put his magazine down. 'I wouldn't make a big deal of it, darling. Maybe he didn't want the distraction.'

'Like you banning me from going clay pigeon shooting with you?'

'Something like that.' He grinned. 'It's those strange little sighs you make just as I'm about to pull the trigger.'

'I understand,' Angie said, snuggling under his arm. 'Edward's parents would be so proud of him,

444

though. Even if they don't like horse racing.'

'I'm sure they'll come to Cheltenham,' he told her. They cuddled together, each lost in their own thoughts.

'Darling?' Freddie said eventually.

'Yes, Freds?'

He hugged her so tightly she could hardly breathe. 'We've got a horse running at Cheltenham!'

It still seemed surreal. 'I feel sick.'

Freddie gave a sigh of wonder. 'If someone had said, when I saw that poor bugger up at Melton Mowbray, that eight months later he'd be running in the Foxhunter Steeplechase at the Cheltenham Festival, I'd have told them they were bloody barking.'

'I think we *are* bloody barking!' Newbury had been overwhelming enough. How were they going to cope when Nobby was led out in front of a fifty-thousand-strong crowd at Cheltenham?

'You know what you need.' Freddie started gently nibbling her ear. 'Celebration sex.'

'Do you think it will keep the nerves away?'

'Don't know. We'll just have to try it every time you get nervous.' Freddie's voice became muffled as he disappeared under the duvet. Angie felt her nightie being lifted. 'Hello, are these new?'

She'd forgotten what French knickers did to him. 'Marks are doing a new line. I thought I'd wear them for good luck.'

'They certainly worked.' His face resurfaced, a bit red and ruffled. 'I think it's my turn for a bit of riding, don't you?'

Maybe it was the high emotion, but she hadn't felt as randy for ages. Angie parted her legs and grinned. 'Come on then, stallion.'

CHAPTER SIXTY-NINE

Next morning
Archie trailed a finger across Calypso's flat warm stomach. 'Your skin is so soft.' His hand started to move up towards her armpit.

'Don't, that tickles.'

'What, this?' He went to work on her properly.

'Archie!' she screamed, laughing and retaliating. 'Stop it.'

'Ow,' he said lazily. 'OK, that really hurts. I'll stop now.'

Calypso shook her head. 'Dick.'

They were curled up in her bed together, after a rather nice doggy-style shag. Calypso had to admit Archie wasn't like other boys his age, who only cared about whether they came or not. He was an energetic, considerate lover who often made her crack up with some stupid joke mid pump. It was nice to have a laugh in bed. Overcome by a moment of affection, Calypso went to hook her leg over his and accidentally let out the most almighty fanny fart.

'Oh my God!' She jerked away and buried her face in the pillow. 'I'm so embarrassed.'

He was killing himself laughing. 'You got a trumpet up there?'

'Archie!' In spite of herself Calypso started smiling. James would have been completely mortified. Archie on the other hand, seemed impossible to offend.

446

Pity he was so *young*.

Archie misinterpreted her sigh. 'Hey, don't worry about it! I think it's nice you feel so comfortable in front of me.'

'Whatever,' Calypso grumbled, pushing herself up on her elbows.

He touched her cheek. 'I've got something for you.'

Calypso watched Archie walk across the room, completely unselfconscious in his nakedness. As he bent down to get something out of his jeans, the muscles in his upper back rippled. He pulled a white envelope out of the back pocket and came back over. 'Sorry it's a bit crumpled.'

'Is it a letter?' She sat up and pulled the duvet round her. 'About what? You're not coming out to me, are you?'

'You won't know unless you open it, will you?'

It was a voucher for a massage and facial at the spa in Bedlington, to be taken whenever she wanted. Calypso was completely taken aback. 'Archie, you shouldn't have. That's a really sweet thing to do.'

He pushed a strand of hair away from her face. 'I wanted to. You seem kind of stressed out at the moment, and I thought a bit of R & R would help.'

Calypso didn't know what to say. She reached up and put an awkward kiss on his cheek. 'Thank you.'

'Wait, was that you being nice?'

'Don't push your luck.' She flopped back on the pillow and looked at the voucher again. A facial and massage did sound *really* good right now.

Archie remained sitting on the side of the bed. 'Can't we start saying something?'

'About what?'

'Us.'

'Archie.' She tried exasperated patience. 'There is no "us". I thought we were clear about that.' Calypso waved the voucher. 'Is this a sort of bribe to win me over?'

'No.' He frowned. 'Of course it's not.'

Calypso immediately felt bad. 'Look, I didn't mean it like that.' She sighed. 'Archie, I've never made out we're going anywhere with this.'

'I know. You probably want some older bloke with his own house and plenty of "life experience", preferably suffering from a bit of erectile dysfunction.'

'Not the last bit, no.' She tried again. 'You know, Archie, just because we're virtually the only two single people in this village under forty doesn't mean we have to end up together.'

'Spoilsport,' he said, leaning across.

'Archie!' She tried to push him off. 'I'm being serious here.'

He stopped mid-kiss. 'I thought you didn't want serious?'

*　　　*　　　*

'You off to the stables, kid?' Kizzy's dad was standing at the front door in his pyjamas.

'I didn't want to wake you.' He'd been on the night shift.

'Say congratulations to the Fox-Titts from us, won't you?'

She looked at him over the car roof. 'Sure thing.'

'We're really proud of you, you know.' Her dad cocked his head to one side. 'The way you've handled it all. I know it hasn't been easy.'

'Thanks, Dad, that means a lot.'

'I'll try and keep your mother at bay a bit longer. About finding that proper job.'

Father and daughter shared a wry look. Kizzy was about to open the door when he stopped her. 'Just a minute, love.'

'Yes, Dad?'

Her dad came out on to the drive in his bare feet. 'Are you all right?'

Kizzy looked up. 'What do you mean?'

'I don't know.' He stopped by the boot. 'You just seem in a world of your own these days. I mean, I know you've got all the race stuff going on, but it feels like we hardly see you. Not that a twenty-four-year-old girl shouldn't have a social life, of course, but I just wanted to make sure you're OK.'

She swallowed. She and her dad never kept secrets from each other. Well, not big things like this. But how could she tell him? There was no way he'd understand; he'd freaked out enough when Javier had sent her the coat.

'It's not drugs, is it?'

'God, no!' He was so far off it provided a welcome laugh. 'Dad, you know I'd never do anything like that.'

'Good.' He looked relieved. 'You know us oldies, we like to worry.'

'You've got nothing to worry about.' She came over and kissed him on the cheek. 'See you later, Dad.'

'See you, kid.'

The heavy rains of yesterday had drained away, leaving behind a glossy green landscape. Normally it was a view Kizzy relished, but not today. Her dad was right; she had been in a world of her own.

Two things dominated her life these days: Nobby and the unimaginable excitement about getting to Cheltenham—and Javier. It felt so weird that she couldn't share the second with anyone, no matter how much she wanted to shout about it from the rooftops sometimes.

How *could* her dad understand? His daughter was head-over-heels in love with a man nearly two decades older than her. A man devoted to a comatose wife, who might—just might—wake up again one day. However she tried to dress it up, Kizzy was having an affair with a married man at the most traumatic time of his life. What if she'd been completely taken advantage of?

And yet, when she was with Javier Kizzy knew she hadn't rushed into anything recklessly. It was weird: Javier was such an icon of masculinity and prowess, yet it was his vulnerability that touched her the most. Kizzy didn't dare even try and explore his inner turmoil—which, at odd, unguarded moments, would show itself in his face and eyes— but it made her want to reach out and try and comfort him. She could see how beautiful his soul was. It was terrible to think he'd endured so much pain in his life.

What about how Javier felt for *her*? Kizzy was pretty sure her feelings were reciprocated, but, over two months in, there were no promises or declarations, no plans for next week, or even for a weekend away—or all the other things couples did in the early days of courting. The little voice she'd been trying to ignore suddenly piped up with savage clarity: *That's because you're not a couple.* Kizzy felt a deadening sensation in her stomach. How *could* they talk about the future, when they didn't

450

have one? She'd been floating round until now in a euphoric state of denial. The sudden realization they would never go out on dates, or move in together, or get married and have children, brought a despair so great that Kizzy wanted to stop the car and weep. *What are you doing?* the voice of reason said again. *You're chasing a dream that will never come true.*

There was a lay-by up ahead. She swerved in suddenly, earning an angry toot from the driver behind. She didn't hear them. She screeched to a halt and pressed her forehead hard against the steering wheel, as if that action would stop the questions screaming round in her head.

The old Kizzy would have been more sensible. Why invest in a relationship that could go nowhere? For a second she nearly turned back and went home again, but the thought—the awful, gut-wrenching, desolate thought—of never seeing Javier again, never having him touch her, make love to her, or hold her in his strong arms again, was so appalling that there was only one thing to do.

She turned on the ignition and started for Homelands.

CHAPTER SEVENTY

Javier was waiting for Kizzy on the swing in the sun-dappled garden, Salvador and Pablo dozing lazily at his feet.

'It's nice to see you sitting down for a change.' She smiled.

He grinned back and pulled her down into his

arms, smelling of fresh air and the musky aftershave he always used. Kizzy kissed him and pulled back to look up into his face. Warm, lively eyes met hers, no longer the impenetrable black masses she'd found so unnerving.

'Are you all right?' Javier touched her cheek with the back of his hand. 'You look a little pale.'

'I'm fine.' As soon as she laid eyes on him all her doubts about their relationship always melted away.

He ran his finger down her jawline and touched her chin. 'I thought we could have a little lunch and then head off down the yard.'

'Perfect.' Kizzy couldn't remember the last time she'd had a whole Saturday off. And here she was, spending it with *him*. Heaven.

They had homemade quiche and salad for lunch, outside in the garden with Mary. The housekeeper was as warm as ever to Kizzy; fussing over her and making sure she was eating enough, but Kizzy noticed a few unguarded moments when Mary seemed rather strained and preoccupied. Once or twice Kizzy caught a look between her and Javier she couldn't quite make out. She tentatively broached the subject as she walked down to the stables with Javier afterwards.

'Is Mary all right with me being here?'

He glanced at her. 'What do you mean?'

'You know, with Sarah . . .' Kizzy looked at the ground. 'I mean it must be pretty weird for Mary, especially as she's from an older generation. I'd hate for her to disapprove of me.'

Javier stopped. 'Kizzy, that's the last thing Mary thinks. She adores you. If anything, she's cross with me.'

'That's OK, then.' Kizzy was so relieved Mary

452

didn't hate her she only just picked up on what he'd said. 'She's cross with you? About what?'

Javier started walking again. 'Nothing.'

She glanced at his rugged profile, set resolutely. He clearly didn't want to talk about it. Instead Kizzy changed the subject to something benign about the weather, wondering what it might be Javier had done. They had nearly reached the centre when William, the head groom's nine-year-old son came running out towards them. He looked like he was bursting to tell them something.

'Mr Hamilton-Scott! I've just . . .'

Javier put his finger to his lips. 'Ssh now, if you're about to say what I think you are.' He ruffled the boy's hair. 'We don't want to give away any state secrets now, do we?'

William blushed, enjoying the intrigue.

'Secrets about what?' Kizzy was intrigued.

Javier shot her a sideways grin. 'You'll see.'

The yard was quiet, most of the horses having had their exercise already. Javier bent down and whispered something in William's ear. William shot Kizzy a delighted look, and skipped off.

'What *is* going on?' she asked.

'This way.' Javier started in the direction of the stables.

'Ah, I get it. Is it another new purchase?'

'You'll just have to wait and see.'

*   *   *

The chestnut thoroughbred wasn't what Kizzy would have expected Javier to go for, but still, she was a complete stunner. Around sixteen hands two inches, her leggy appearance was emphasized by

453

four flashy white stockings. The mare swung her pretty head round to look at the newcomers.

'Becca's Delight,' Javier said. 'Or Delly for short.'

'She's totally lush!' Kizzy admired the horse's strong hind legs. 'Where did you get her from?'

'A racing yard near here.'

It took a few seconds to register. 'A racing yard?'

Javier grinned. 'Yes, I bought her for you.'

Kizzy's jaw practically hit the floor. 'You did what?'

He grinned. 'I thought it was time to kick-start your racing career again.'

'But how . . . what . . .' Kizzy was speechless.

Javier looked anxious. 'It's not too much, is it? A friend mentioned he was looking to sell her, and I thought she'd be perfect.' He stopped. 'I can always take her back . . .'

'Oh my God!' Kizzy screamed. 'Of course I don't want you to take her back! I love her! Oh, thank you, thank you, thank you!' She wrapped her arms round Javier and started covering his face with kisses.

Javier gave a relieved laugh. 'I take it you're pleased.'

'Beyond pleased. *Ecstatic.*' Kizzy felt like crying. No one had ever done anything like this for her before.

'Kizzy?' he said into her ear.

'Yes?' She was still in shock.

'You're strangling me.'

'Oh! I'm so sorry.' She stepped back and looked over the stable door. Delly was looking at her with the softest brown eyes ever. *Her* Delly. Kizzy had to go in right now and hug her.

'I can't believe this is happening,' she murmured, burying her face in the horse's hay-smelling neck.

'Believe it,' Javier said. 'I don't know many people who would stand aside like you did and let someone else have their shot. I know I couldn't.'

A lump rose up in Kizzy's throat. She'd known for a long time now that Nobby was really Edward's. Javier had given her a one-in-a-million chance to start chasing her dream again.

'Can I get on?'

'I really got her for when your back was better . . .'

'Oh, please,' Kizzy cajoled. 'I've only got a month left. Really, it's nothing. I promise not to go any faster than a trot.'

'I kind of asked for this, didn't I?' He chuckled. 'OK, but we'll stay in the school. Better safe than sorry.'

*   *   *

Delly came with brand-new tack and a very smart red and yellow saddlecloth. Once Kizzy had tacked her up and borrowed a hat from Jules, they were up and away.

Javier leant on the fence round the riding school and watched as she rode round. 'How does she feel?'

'Fantastic!' Kizzy called back. Even at a gentle trot, she could feel how athletic Delly was.

'Your back doesn't hurt?'

'No,' she lied. To be fair, it was more stiff than painful. It had been months since she'd been in the saddle, and everything felt a bit rusty. Rusty, but still *amazing*. Kizzy bent down low against the

455

horse's neck.

'I'm back, Delly,' she whispered in delight. 'I'm back!'

It was all decided then. Kizzy would keep Delly at the yard, in one of the spare stables.

She tried to offer Javier livery money, but he wouldn't hear of it.

'It's enough to see you riding again,' he told her as they walked back to the house afterwards. Kizzy had literally had to be prised apart from her new mount. Javier had teased her about it, and told her she could come and see Delly whenever she wanted.

'Oh my God!' She did a little jig of excitement. 'I can't believe it.'

'But promise me, angel: no haring around or jumping five-bar gates until you get the all-clear from the doctors. OK?'

'I promise.' Javier had been about the only one who hadn't fussed over her back and treated her with kid gloves. Kizzy would honour her word to him; it was the least she could do.

'The Grand National isn't going anywhere,' he told her.

She smiled at him. 'Do you really think I could get there?'

'Oh yes,' he said softly. 'I think you're capable of anything.' He stopped and touched her face. 'Reach for the stars.'

Kizzy gazed up into his strong, handsome face. 'I love you.'

The words were out before she knew it. A look of shock passed through Javier's face before she saw his jaw tighten.

'Kizzy . . .'

'Don't,' she said desperately. 'I didn't mean to make you uncomfortable, you don't have to say it back.' *Why did you have to go and ruin things?* A dull flush of embarrassment crept up her neck. 'I'm sorry,' she added dully.

'You don't have to be sorry about anything. Kizzy, look at me.' Javier smiled, but there was still that tension round his mouth. 'I'm just happy that you're happy.'

She thought of Delly. 'I've never been happier, believe me.' *Or as unhappy.*

But that's what she'd signed up for, wasn't it?

CHAPTER SEVENTY-ONE

The last place Caro expected to see Suzette was at the fruit and veg section in Waitrose. 'Hello, Suzette.'

'Hello.' Suzette shot her an unfriendly look and started studying the organic oranges.

Caro hovered on the aisle, not sure what to do. Aside from tense handovers in the Jolly Boot car park—in which little was said—the only form of communication between the two camps was through their solicitors. In Caro's mind Suzette had become a Cruella De Vil type, sweeping in with her partner in crime and wreaking havoc. It was rather a shock to see her looking her normal groomed self, and doing something mundane like picking out courgettes.

Caro stared down at Suzette's basket. In it were two duck breasts, the new *Vogue*, and a pack of filter coffee. The Frenchwoman was ignoring

457

her, but Caro could see two little pink spots in the centre of Suzette's flawless cheeks. A human being did exist under that ice-cold exterior, after all.

Caro looked down at her own trolley. It was full to the brim: bread, four litres of milk, chicken, squash, Rosie's Cheerios and Milo's ice-lollies. Suzette's basket was positively spartan in comparison, and Caro tried to imagine her doing a weekly shop and remembering all Milo's favourite things. It wasn't easy.

She realized that Suzette had walked off, obviously anxious to extricate herself from the awkward situation. Caro bit her lip. What she should do was get the hell out of there. But the urge to talk to Suzette was too strong. She had to endure so much turmoil and stress on a daily basis, and felt she had no control over the situation. It was too much. Did Suzette really have any idea what she was going through? She needed her to *see*, to realize the effect Sebastian's actions were having. Caro had detected a vulnerability in the woman. At the very least, at a human level, she could try and ask for some answers.

For a moment she thought she'd lost Suzette and her chance, but then she spotted her at the end of the bread aisle. She manoeuvred her trolley round the other shoppers, approaching cautiously as if Suzette was a wild deer that might be startled and run off.

'Suzette.'

Dismay flashed across Suzette's face. 'Yes?'

Caro tried a smile. 'Look, I know this isn't the easiest of meetings, but I really need to talk to you.'

Suzette's eyes went up and down the aisle, desperately looking for escape. 'Caro, I cannot talk

458

to you. If you have any sort of complaint you need to go through Patrick Carver.'

A *complaint*? It was such an inappropriate word—as if Caro were moaning about a slight annoyance, like her meal being overcooked—that she wanted to laugh. And then she snapped.

'Having my son taken off me is hardly a complaint!' As a nearby shopper looked round, Caro lowered her voice and bent over the trolley. 'Suzette, this is destroying my family. Milo's family.' Had Suzette had to endure the indignity of Belinda Winters rifling through her life? Caro very much doubted it: she was the one on trial here.

'You know what Sebastian's like. He has to win at everything, and if he did, and he got hold of Milo, he'd get bored, Suzette. You'd be the one left looking after him.'

'Sebastian only wants to see his son grow up!' It was the first sign of emotion Suzette had really shown. 'I am the one with him, not you. I *know* him.' Her voice dropped to a low hiss. 'This jealousy and controlling behaviour has to stop, Caro. You need therapy.'

This time Caro did laugh, in outrage. 'My God, what crap has Sebastian told you?'

Suzette snatched up a packet of croissants. 'Let me pass.'

Caro tried again. 'Suzette.' She put a hand on the other woman's wrist, to try and appease her, but it was shaken off.

'Let go of me! How dare you!'

'Is everything all right?' The security guard who'd been standing by the entrance had wandered over.

Caro realized their hushed slanging-match had

attracted quite an audience.

'This woman is harassing me!' Suzette declared dramatically.

'No, I'm not!'

The security guard looked down at Caro's huge trolley, which was inadvertently blocking Suzette's path. 'If you'd like to follow me.'

'This is all a horrible mistake,' Caro protested, but the security guard held firm. 'You can either come quietly, madam, or make this a whole lot more difficult for yourself. Now, please follow me.'

*　　　*　　　*

Benedict stared at his wife across the kitchen table. 'You've just been thrown out of Waitrose?'

Caro nodded miserably. Her declaration of innocence had fallen on deaf ears, and she'd been ejected, leaving all her shopping behind. Even worse, one of the mums from Milo's school had been coming in as Caro was marched out of the entrance. The news would be all over the school by Monday.

'Oh, God.' She sank down in a chair. 'I don't believe this.'

'Don't worry.' Her husband came and put his arm round her. 'It's not a big deal. I should phone Louise, though, and tell her.'

There was something odd about his voice. Caro looked up at him. 'You do believe me, don't you? I wasn't harassing her!'

He hesitated a moment too long. 'Oh, great,' she said emotionally. 'Now my own bloody husband thinks I'm crackers.'

Benedict knelt down. 'Of course I don't.'

460

'Shit,' she said despairingly. 'I shouldn't have gone up to her. I just thought I could try and make her see sense.'

'I know, sweetheart. Christ, I can hardly talk, can I?'

'Do you think Suzette recorded it?' she said in a panic.

Benedict raised an eyebrow. 'I know what that pair are capable of, but even I don't think Suzette goes around with a Dictaphone on the off-chance she might bump into you.'

He was right, of course. Her ridiculous paranoia was rearing its ugly head again. Benedict tucked a strand of hair behind her ear.

'You acted how I guess any decent, loving mother would. But the harsh fact is that this is a custody battle, and, like it or not, we have to follow a certain code of conduct and not put ourselves in potentially incriminating situations. You've already seen what a dirty game Sebastian plays.'

'And I just added more fuel to the fire. I should have kept my cool, Benedict.' She sighed. 'When I saw Suzette in there, walking round like she hadn't a care in the world . . .'

Benedict studied his wife's tired face, the dark circles under her eyes. 'You're running on empty, darling. You need to start taking care of yourself.'

'I know.'

He kissed her and stood up. 'I'll call Louise first thing Monday, OK? There's nothing to worry about, but we need to keep her in the picture.'

'OK.'

'Shall I make you some lunch? There's a bit of leftover chicken from last night. I can put it with some salad.'

461

'Actually, I might go for a walk. Do you mind?'

'Are you sure you should be by yourself?'

'I'm not going to do anything silly, darling.' Caro got up and put her coat back on. 'See you in a while.'

*   *   *

She went down to the bottom of the garden and out into the fields. In the distance Clanfield Hall rose up out of the landscape. Caro unzipped her jacket—it was warmer than she'd expected—and set off down the gentle slope towards the stream at the bottom. If she turned right and carried on, she would eventually hit the far edge of the Maltings estate. *Maybe I'll go and see Angie.* Unable to face other people, she'd become a virtual recluse in the last few weeks.

Milo and Rosie were at her grandmother's for the afternoon. Clementine had been an absolute brick, offering to babysit, and popping over to No. 1 Mill House every day to check in. Caro knew Benedict agreed with her grandmother: that they ought to tell the immediate members of the family about the custody case, but Caro still couldn't. She didn't even want to tell Clementine what had just happened at Waitrose. God knows what Louise Rennison would think when Benedict called her.

Caro went over the encounter again, torturing herself with every detail. Why had she ever thought it would be a good idea to corner Suzette like a madwoman? Christ! Since when had she gone round having confrontations with people in supermarkets? She'd tried to think back to the normal, sane Caro she used to be, who had never

462

lost her temper, and always tried to work things out rationally.

The problem is, I have no idea how to solve this one, she thought. God only knew when the Cafcass report would be ready. Louise had said it could take up to three months. Three months! Three more days of living like this would send her mad. And she still didn't have a good feeling about Belinda.

Caro made her way down to the far end of the field, where a winding stream trickled past. She looked down into the water. Just in front of her was a rocky bit, where the stream started to trip and stumble, before negotiating its way round. It was a metaphor for her life. Caro's eyes followed the current, transfixed.

Please God, let me find calm waters again.

CHAPTER SEVENTY-TWO

The point-to-point meeting at Goatsford in April was the ideal 'pipe opener': a chance for Nobby to give his lungs one last good clear-out before Cheltenham. Six miles from Churchminster, it was a winding, often boggy, track across a farmer's field, with little in the way of amenities. After a taste of high-level racing at Newbury, Goatsford would seem even more basic, but Angie didn't care. It was the perfect place for Edward and Nobby to race without any pressure and have some fun. A bit of calm before the storm.

The response to their Newbury triumph had been quite phenomenal. So many people had been in touch to offer congratulations, one of the first being the Bedlington hunt master, who'd spotted Nobby's potential all those months ago. Everyone was thrilled that a local horse and jockey had made it through to the biggest race in the point-to-point calendar, and the *Bedlington Bugle* had run a story on Page Three. 'THE RED RUM OF CHURCHMINSTER!' the headline had screamed. Angie had cut it out and pinned it up in Nobby's stable.

Preparations were put in peril the day before Goatsford, though, when their star mount had escaped from his stable despite the new latch. Luckily the gate leading to the main road had been locked. Nobby had still managed to get into the orchard, where the underripe apples were a test for even his iron constitution. He'd spent the whole night lifting his tail and letting out smatterings of yellowy diarrhoea. The stable had stunk to high heaven when Angie had gone down the next morning.

'Do you think he'll be OK?' she asked Edward. He'd been up since the crack of dawn, and his ears and nose were glowing from the morning chill.

'He's taken plenty of fluids.' Edward massaged the base of Nobby's right ear. 'Just a bit of an upset stomach, isn't it, boy?'

'Just take it easy round there,' Angie said. 'We've got nothing to prove.'

She was met with a grin over Nobby's back. 'On the contrary, I think we've got quite a lot.'

Angie watched Edward walk off towards the feed shed. The difference in him, even since Newbury, was quite remarkable. He was never going to be the most outgoing of people, but inch by inch his guard was coming down. Conversations were no longer excruciating forms of torture for him, to be avoided

464

at all costs, and he was eating with the family more and more. Angie actually found Edward's quiet nature very restful. While her husband and son would be shouting at the rugby in the living room, she and Edward would hang out with the dogs over tea and biscuits in the kitchen.

Archie came to the back door in a T-shirt and pyjamas, his hair sticking up all over the place. 'Ma, phone for you.'

'Won't be a minute!' she said. 'Edward, come in for breakfast, won't you?'

A muffled shout signalled his reply. Giving Nobby a quick pat, she hurried back in.

'It's someone from *Cotswold Life* magazine,' Archie said.

'Blimey!' Angie replied, and went into the study to take the call.

Archie was making himself some toast when she came back in. 'What was that about?'

'They want to do an interview about Cheltenham.' She sat down at the table.

'That's good, isn't it?'

'I suppose, but I keep thinking it's tempting fate.'

'Hey, it's all good. You should start charging for interviews. At this rate I could be your agent.'

'On your current form, that's not a bad idea.' Only yesterday they'd signed a deal with a local company who ran stag and hen weekends, to start offering outdoor pursuits at the Maltings. Now, alongside the traditional pole-dancing lessons and beer crawl, people could go quad-biking through some of the most beautiful parts of the countryside, or learn to clay pigeon shoot. It was so simple, but something she and Freddie had never considered.

Archie stuffed a bit of toast in his mouth. 'Nobby

recovered from his great escape?'

She nodded. 'Christ only knows how he got out again. Your father's started calling him Houdini.'

'You should think about proper security. That's a prime piece of racehorse wandering round out there.'

'Do you really think it's necessary?'

'It might be a good idea, especially with all the tractor theft going on at the moment. I'll look into it.'

Angie watched him butter another piece of toast. Even in bare feet, Archie towered above her. 'We shouldn't be back too late, but there's plenty of food in the fridge.'

'It's all right. I might be meeting Calypso down the pub for lunch.'

Angie smiled. 'You're sweet on her, aren't you?'

He stopped mid-bite. 'What makes you say that?'

'Mother's intuition.' She'd seen the looks between the two of them at the party after Newbury, and noticed how Calypso's name kept cropping up in conversation.

'Yeah, I think she's cool.'

'Does she feel the same way?'

He shrugged. 'Don't think so. I'm too young, apparently, and Calypso reckons she wants to move to London. It's not hip and happening enough round here.'

'I wouldn't know anything about that.' Angie searched her son's face. 'Are you feeling down about it?'

'Ma, you don't need to start worrying about me.' He put his plate in the sink. 'I'm going for a shower.'

'Wish us luck, then.'

He stopped in the doorway and grinned. 'You don't really need it, do you?'

*   *   *

Goatsford was only the most basic of point-to-points but Angie was surprised to see white hoardings lining the entrance as they drove up later. She turned to her husband. 'They don't normally advertise here, do they?' You were usually lucky if there were two burger vans to choose from.

'They must have just started doing it.' Freddie looked down the road. 'Crikey, there's quite a lot.'

As they got nearer, it became apparent that the six-foot wooden erections were all advertising the same thing. 'Soapeez car wash! We get you in a lather!' screamed the bright-pink slogan. There was a phone number and a website address, accompanied by a picture of a scantily clad young woman bending over the bonnet of a Mercedes. Angie raised an eyebrow; they were certainly very different from the usual ads for local garages and garden centres. The organizers were obviously trying to be more adventurous.

On the course, there were Soapeez slogans everywhere, from the 'Soap's Up!' themed umbrellas in the eating area to the nubile young girl in a cropped slogan T-shirt handing out bumper stickers to people on their way in. They were making their way across to the horsebox park when Freddie suddenly hit the brakes.

'Careful, Freds!' Angie exclaimed as Edward lurched forward in the back. They were without Kizzy for once: she had a physio appointment her mum wouldn't let her cancel. Angie had heartily

467

agreed; today wasn't important in the scheme of things, anyway.

Freddie said, 'Is that *Barry*?'

Angie looked where he was pointing, to the edge of the car park. There were about a hundred vehicles there already, and a dozen of them were queuing up at a car wash entirely manned by what looked like Page Three models. A huge 'Soapeez' flag was flying high above, as more busty beauties delicately dabbed and swabbed with oversized pink sponges, doing very little dirt removal at all. In the middle of it all, in plus fours and a floor-length tweed coat, was Barry. He snapped his mobile shut when he saw the horsebox and came over.

'All right, peeps! What do you think to me new little get-up? I'm expanding the Bubblez franchise.'

'Are you really?' was all Angie could say. She noticed the occupants waiting to have their cars cleaned were all male.

'Yup, I had the idea at your first race. All those muddy cars, just waiting for a Soapeez lovely to come and wash 'em off.'

He slapped the side of the horsebox. 'No soapy tit wank jokes now, Freddie.'

Freddie went puce. 'I wasn't going to make any.'

Barry smoothed down the front of his too-tight plus fours. 'I think there's a real niche here.' He puffed out his chest. 'If we take off the way I'm expecting, we could have a "Pike National Derby" in a couple of years' time.'

They left Barry issuing instructions to his girls like he owned the place. 'You have to hand it to Barry, he's very entrepreneurial,' Angie said as they parked up. 'He'll probably make a complete success of it.'

Freddie gave her thigh a furtive squeeze. 'Maybe I'll get you one of those T-shirts.'

* * *

They were well-versed in what to do now, and fell into their roles. When Angie and Edward returned from getting weighed, Freddie was holding Nobby's head outside the horsebox and looking uncharacteristically cross.

'You all right, Freds?'

'That bugger just sounded his horn right next to the horsebox. Do people not know there are animals around? Poor Nobby nearly had a heart attack.'

A silver Bentley was bumping across the field. They all watched as it blasted another horse out of the way. The creature took such a fright the groom had a job to hold on to it.

'Who the hell do they think they are?' Freddie said. 'Any more of that and I'll report them to the steward.'

'Some people have no idea how to behave round horses.' Angie watched the car do a big sweeping U-turn and start back in their direction. A few seconds later her mouth dropped open. 'Is that Chip Mason? You know, Freds, the cricket chap who was on *Strictly*?'

Freddie frowned. 'I doubt someone like Mason would turn up at such a lowly event.'

'Apparently he's ghastly,' Angie remarked to Edward. 'Freds met him once.'

Freddie rolled his eyes at his wife's usual exaggeration. 'What I *said* was that he was a bit full of his own bluff. All these old sporting legends are.'

Angie stuck her tongue out at him, and looked at Edward to share the joke. Her smile faded. 'Edward, are you all right?' He was wearing an expression that could only be described as sheer panic.

Moments later the Bentley pulled up. A man got out of the driver's side. Angie raised an eyebrow. It was Chip Mason all right. Tall and sun-ravaged, the thick blond hair had mainly turned to grey. He'd put back on some of the weight he'd lost during *Strictly Come Dancing*, and was wearing a too-tight leather jacket over chinos that looked far too young for him.

Chip's sharp blue eyes travelled across the group and came to settle on Edward. 'There you are! I've been driving around all over the place.'

His voice was deep Yorkshire, and strident.

Angie and Freddie looked at Edward. He didn't say anything, just stared ahead in panic, like a rabbit caught in the headlights.

'I'm sorry, do you know each other?' Freddie asked politely.

Chip's beefy face flickered with confused annoyance. 'What the hell's this, Eddie?' He looked back at the Fox-Titts. 'Of course we bloody know each other. That's my son!'

CHAPTER SEVENTY-THREE

Freddie gaped at Chip Mason. 'I beg your pardon?'

Chip Mason looked at Freddie as if he was stupid. 'That's right, I'm Edward's father.'

'But you've got different surnames,' Freddie

470

protested weakly.

'Too right! I made Edward take his mother's name when he started riding.' Chip gave a snort of laughter. 'I don't want to be associated with this poofters' game!'

Angie couldn't believe someone would be so loudly obnoxious. They were at a point-to-point meet! Chip Mason folded his meaty arms and treated her to what he obviously thought was a winning smile.

'Unfortunately Eddie didn't take after me and my other lad when it came to the sports field.'

'Edward's a very decent rider,' Angie said coldly. She really didn't like the dismissive way Chip was speaking about Edward. Poor Edward had his eyes glued to the ground and was looking completely terrified.

Chip Mason let out a guffaw. 'Him? Good at anything? That'll be the day!' He gave Freddie a wink. 'The only thing that boy's ever excelled at is being tied to his mother's apron strings. If they gave out medals for being a complete nancy boy, Eddie would clean the board. Wouldn't you, Ed?'

He laughed loudly again, expecting the others to join in.

'Yes, well.' Freddie was disgusted. 'We should be getting going, Edward.'

Chip Mason's face fell. He was obviously a man used to adoring hangers-on. After giving Freddie a long stare, he focused his attention back on Edward. 'I'm expecting good things from you today, son! After that bloody great win of yours at Newbury.'

He turned and got back in the Bentley. He drove off with the windows down and the music just a little too loud, clearly wanting to be noticed.

'Edward, are you all right?' Angie asked. The poor boy's hands were actually shaking.

'Y-yes.' He nodded dumbly. 'Sorry about my d-dad. He doesn't really get what I do.'

That was an understatement. 'How about your mum?' Angie asked kindly. 'I bet she's proud of you.'

Edward gave a tiny nod. 'Y-yeah. But Dad doesn't really like it.' He hung his head. 'He says I should be playing a proper sport like him and my brother.'

Freddie put an arm round Edward's shoulder, trying to equate this skinny, lanky thing with sixteen-stone Ben Mason, Chip's other son, who played rugby for Gloucester. 'I'm sure he doesn't really mean it.'

'He bloody does!' It was the first time Edward had ever raised his voice. 'He's always said I'm not good enough!'

'Darling, don't get yourself upset before the race,' Angie said, shooting a surreptitious look at her husband. 'Just let your dad see what a marvellous job you're doing out there. That'll show him.'

Her words had the opposite effect. Even though Chip had driven off, Edward stayed a frozen wreck, incapable of doing anything. Somehow they got him down to the paddock, where Freddie gave him a leg up. As he led the pair round, Edward looked more like a nervous child at his first riding lesson than one half of the famous Cheltenham qualifier.

Angie's hopes that Chip Mason might disappear quickly faded. He stood purposefully by the start, arms folded. As the starter pulled his flag down

472

to go, Edward and Nobby were facing completely the wrong way. Even though the horse was raring to be off, Edward hung down on the reins as if he were scared to move. After what seemed like the most agonizing pause ever, Edward let go of the reins and they were finally off, a good ten furlongs behind the last runners.

Chip Mason was in full flow. 'Come on, Edward, this isn't a donkey derby!'

There were a few titters from the crowd, who'd recognized Chip's tall burly form, and he responded by playing the celebrity, all big smiles and laughs, and posing for camera-phone pictures with people.

'Arsehole,' Angie muttered. 'And to think I voted for him a few times on *Strictly*.'

Things were going from bad to worse. Edward was being more of a hindrance than a help to poor Nobby, every now and again pulling up sharply on the reins and making Nobby's head jerk backwards. And all the time that ghastly man's voice was cutting across the crowd, making jokes at Edward's expense.

Halfway round Nobby seemed to realize he was on his own. He put on a gallant effort, but as they approached the open ditch for the second time he misjudged his stride and stumbled. Edward had no chance. The crowd gasped as he was thrown forward, flying into the ground with the speed of a bullet.

'Edward!' Angie clapped her hand over her mouth. For a few terrible moments he didn't move, and Angie had terrible flashbacks of Kizzy. Even Chip Mason fell silent, and then there was a sigh of relief from the crowd as Edward rolled on to his side and sat up rather dazedly.

Of course, they were out of the race. After a quick check over by the St Johns Ambulance, who diagnosed nothing more than hurt pride, Angie and Freddie took Edward back to the box. Angie wasn't convinced he didn't have concussion; he was in a complete world of his own, not hearing what anyone was saying to him. He was mutely watching Angie bandage Nobby's legs for the journey back when Chip Mason walked round the side of the horsebox.

'You all right?' he asked Edward. He looked more cross than concerned. When Edward gave a nod, his father let him have it. 'Are you all having a joke at my expense, or what? What the hell was that out there, Eddie?'

Angie couldn't stand by and say nothing. 'How dare you! Edward could have been seriously hurt!'

'He wasn't though, was he? Might have knocked some bloody sense into him. What a waste of my time.'

Freddie stepped up, five foot eight of roundness to Chip's strapping six foot two. 'Right, that's enough. You're upsetting my wife, Edward, and the horse, and I want you to leave. Now.'

Luckily Chip Mason didn't take offence. He took one last disgusted look at Edward and sighed. 'Fine. Bloody embarrassment.' He stalked off, turning the charm on fifty metres away to a middle-aged lady who'd come up to ask for an autograph.

'Fool,' Freddie said angrily. He glanced at Edward. 'Sorry, son.'

Angie forced a smile. 'Never mind, darling, at least you got a good run out there. That's all we wanted.'

Edward was clutching Nobby's head collar so

474

tightly Angie thought his fingers might snap. 'I'm useless.'

'Of course you're not, Edward!' they both said in unison.

'I am, my dad's right.' He dropped his head and walked off.

*   *   *

Archie's pickup was gone when they got back, but Kizzy's car was in the yard. She'd been putting Nobby's bed down and getting everything ready, and watched in astonishment as Edward ignored her cheery greeting and walked straight into the granny annexe.

'Was it something I said?' she asked.

Angie shook her head. 'Let's get the horses to bed, and then you can come into the kitchen for a noggin.'

Over brandy for Angie and Freddie, and a squash for Kizzy, they told her about their day. Kizzy was as shocked as they were.

'I can't believe he turned up and acted like that! Poor Edward.'

'I know. Do you think I should try to talk to him again?' Angie asked Freddie. Her knock on the granny annexe door before they'd come in had gone unanswered. Edward hadn't said a word all the way home, despite Angie's attempts to persuade him to.

'Leave him for a while, darling.' Freddie rubbed his face tiredly. 'What a bad business.'

The office phone started going next door. 'I'd better get that,' Freddie said.

Angie looked back at Kizzy as her husband walked out. 'I always did wonder why Edward never mentioned his family. Now we know why. What a vile bully! How could Chip Mason not be proud of Edward? He's doing so well.'

'Not in his dad's eyes, obviously,' Kizzy said. 'It's probably made even worse by having a big rugby hero brother.'

'It's a wonder Edward has got this far at all.' Angie got up to slosh another two fingers in her glass. She needed a drink. 'Do you know anything about Edward's mother?'

'I think he's closer to her. He hasn't said much, but I get the impression she's as terrified of Chip Mason as Edward is.'

'I just wish he'd *said* something, instead of carrying this round all by himself.'

Kizzy looked a bit uncomfortable. 'I did see something, once.'

'See something?'

'In the annexe. I didn't think he was there, but I heard this voice coming from the bedroom.' Kizzy shook her head. 'It didn't sound like him. I thought maybe it was an intruder or something, but when I went upstairs Edward was standing in front of the mirror hitting himself with a whip.'

'He was doing what?' Angie was horrified.

'He was whacking a whip on his thigh. It was weird, Angie; it was like he was *punishing* himself or something.' Kizzy bit her lip. 'He didn't see me, and I got out really quickly.'

'Oh dear.' Angie came and sat down at the table.

'I should have said something sooner.' Kizzy realized how bad it sounded. Something like that wasn't *normal*.

'Do you think we should call a doctor or something?'

'Let's see how he gets on. It happened months ago, and he's been getting on so well since.' Kizzy raised an eyebrow. 'Do you think it's linked to his dad?'

'I wouldn't be surprised, the way he belittled Edward. What awful timing, Chip Mason popping up now.'

Freddie came back in the room, then, and both women changed the subject. It wasn't worth telling Fred anything unless they had to, and Angie sensed Kizzy's unease about speaking in the first place. She obviously felt great loyalty towards Edward.

Kizzy left as Angie was taking the dogs out. The pair walked to Kizzy's car, Avon and Barksdale scampering around them like a pair of loons.

The granny annexe looked dead to the world, the downstairs curtains still pulled shut from that morning. Angie bit her lip; Edward wouldn't do anything stupid, would he?

As Kizzy climbed in Angie noticed an overnight bag on the passenger seat. 'Are you off out somewhere later?'

'What?' Kizzy looked across and flushed. 'Oh that! That's just some old clothes.'

'Oh, right.' Angie smiled down at her. 'How are *you*, darling? Everything's been so mad I feel like we haven't had a proper catch-up for ages.'

'I'm good.'

Angie hesitated, wondering if Kizzy would say more. 'I'm afraid I've become a bit obsessed with things here, recently. The whole world could have turned on its axis and I probably wouldn't have noticed.'

'You and me both. I'll see you tomorrow.'

CHAPTER SEVENTY-FOUR

Calypso and Archie were sprawled on her sofa watching telly. The remnants of a takeaway curry lay on the coffee table in front of them.

'I'm so full,' she groaned, pushing the empty chicken korma out of the way with her foot so she could stretch her legs out.

Archie patted his belly. 'Good feed.' He put his head on Calypso's shoulder and for once she didn't move it.

'So I had an interesting phone call today,' she said.

'Oh, right, about what?'

'I spoke to my friend Olivia, who works in PR. The company she works for are looking to extend their events side, and Liv reckons it would be perfect for me. She's going to set up a meeting with her boss.'

'Cool. Where is it?'

'London.'

He kept his eyes on the telly. 'So you're serious about it?'

'Totally. It's something I'm going to have to do if I want to get anywhere in my career.'

'Do you want to go and work for someone else, though?' he pointed out. 'Your business seems to be doing really well. You've always got stuff on.'

Calypso screwed up her face. 'Now, let me see. Next week we've got the Rotary Club centenary dinner on Wednesday—*fascinating*—and someone's divorce party on Thursday, and Friday is the wildly exciting relaunch of Little Hampton Garden

Centre.'

'That's good isn't it? At least you're busy.'

'Doing things I don't want to do!' She sighed. 'You don't understand.' No one understood. 'I spent all yesterday on the phone begging some jumped-up knob from the local paper to come down and write about a new water feature. You'd think I was asking him to set fire to his pubes and run round Bedlington Square.'

'Maybe it'd be a good idea if he did do that. It'd be something different.'

'Ha ha. I'm just *bored*,' she added plaintively.

'Right,' he said neutrally.

'Oh God, I don't mean *you're* boring.' Calypso sighed again. Couldn't she say anything right? 'Have I upset you?'

'Of course not.' He picked up the remote and started flicking through channels.

'Archie!'

'What?' He stopped on the E! Channel.

'We need to talk about this.'

'Talk about what?' His big brown eyes glanced up. 'You said nothing was going on, right?'

Calypso opened her mouth and shut it again. Why did he always manage to turn the conversation upside down? 'So we're cool? You know, with keeping things casual?'

'Are you still going on about that?' he said, watching the screen.

'Oh, whatever.'

Calypso crossed her arms and pretended not to care, but it got the better of her. 'So we *are* cool?'

He dragged his gaze away, all amused eyes and shaggy hair. 'Yes, we're cool.'

'Good.' She flicked his knee. 'Twat.'

479

'That's really beautiful. Your charm is one of the few reasons I hang out with you.'

Calypso looked at the telly, smiling. The presenter was going on about some controversial photo shoot an actress had done. *'Next up is Rafe Wolfe, and his surprise role in a new art-house film . . .'*

Oh God. Before she knew it footage of her ex flashed up, from a recent red carpet premiere. Rafe's stylist had obviously persuaded him to work the Moroccan vibe that was going at the moment. His short blond hair was longer and slicked back, and he had an abundance of self-conscious necklaces under the unbuttoned white shirt. It didn't really work, not with Rafe's usual look being a preppy one.

Calypso waited for the sickening thud in her stomach. It didn't come.

'Isn't that your ex?' Archie asked.

'Yep.' Wanker. Calypso watched Rafe flash a cheesy smile for the photographers. God, he'd really overdone the teeth bleaching.

They watched Rafe lean over to kiss a screaming fan, and pose for a picture on her camera phone. He looked extremely pleased with himself. Calypso felt like a complete idiot: how could she not have seen through him?

Archie pressed rewind.

'What are you doing?' she asked.

He stopped on a frame. 'What's with the glow-in-the-dark teeth?'

Calypso giggled. Frozen on the screen with a rictus grin, Rafe did look ridiculous.

Archie sat up to look. 'You could see those bad boys from space. No wonder celebrities wear sunglasses at night-time.'

'Turn over,' she laughed. 'Archie, I'm being serious! I don't want to keep looking.'

'Nor do I, I might go blind.' He started flicking again. 'Ah, this is better. The History Channel.'

'We are *not* watching something called *Trench Detectives.*'

'It's interesting!'

'What are you, eighty?'

'I thought you were the old one.'

'Oh, funny!' Calypso sat back, enjoying the wonderful realization that she wasn't upset about seeing Rafe.

She must really be over him.

*   *   *

In the kitchen at No. 1 Mill House, Caro was leaning against the work surface watching her husband rustle up his special homemade crab cakes with hot pepper salsa. She took a sip of wine, savouring the rich apricot taste.

'You like it?' he asked. 'It's a new Viognier I picked up from the deli next to work.'

'It's really nice.' Caro smiled at her husband. Not many men could get away with wearing a pink apron over their smart navy trousers and white Gieves & Hawkes shirt, but Benedict pulled it off magnificently. She watched him expertly chop a tomato and add it to the bowl. The dear man was being a tower of strength at the moment. Despite travelling back and forth from London all week, he'd still managed to do a full shop at Waitrose, mend the dodgy latch on their en suite, and help Milo sort his out-of-control Top Trumps collection. That was without mentioning how he'd massaged Caro's stiff neck for hours on end without complaint on the sofa every night. Caro knew he was trying to make things as easy as possible for her at the moment, and she was eternally grateful.

'Have I told you lately I love you?'

Benedict wiped his hands on the tea towel and came over to kiss her. 'It's nice to see you smiling again.'

'It's nice to be able to smile again.' Caro looked up into her husband's handsome face. 'God, Benedict! I feel like the mists are finally clearing.'

These past few days had marked a massive turning point for her. They still had a long way to go, but Caro had learnt a lot about herself in a very short space of time. She'd been dealing in emotions, not facts, and it hadn't got them anywhere. Now the panic mode had relinquished its grip, Caro was able to have a much more rational approach to the situation.

Knowledge was power. Like Benedict, she'd been reading up on family law and custody battle case studies. Caro had come to realize what a volatile, emotionally-charged business it was, often based on one side's desire to inflict pain on the other, rather than any real concern about the child involved. There were often unscrupulous motives at work, and it was the job of everyone involved to sift through all the crap and see this.

Louise had told them from the start that the family court wouldn't rock the boat unless it was absolutely necessary. It wasn't the silly little things that Caro had initially been so worried about that concerned the court, but the biggies: drugs, domestic violence, mental disorders, criminal convictions. A child simply wasn't uprooted from their home on the basis of no evidence.

Benedict was still convinced Sebastian was doing this out of sheer spite, while Caro had her own explanation. Now Milo had got through the yukky, boring baby bit, he was a status symbol for Sebastian, a way to fit in and score marks with his fortysomething contemporaries. She still believed Sebastian had some feelings for his child—he had to—but there was a more sickening reason than that. Whatever he tried to pretend was the truth, Milo *validated* Sebastian.

If he thought he could just waltz in and take her child, Sebastian had another think coming. Caro had passed all the screening tests, so his little ploy to make out she was an alcoholic wasn't going to work.

Even more reassuringly, things had been going well with Belinda Winters. Her first visit had seemed like a disaster at the time, but, looking back, Caro could see she'd been overreacting. Belinda had been round three times since, and each time things had gone without a hitch. Caro felt she'd started to get past Belinda's evasive manner; they'd even sat chatting for half an hour over homemade cookies in the kitchen. Surely the Cafcass officer could see how things were? Caro was feeling a new wave of optimism. The next time she went back into that courtroom, she would be fully prepared. Sebastian wasn't going to run rings round her this time.

Their day-to-day life remained wonderfully, reassuringly normal. Caro still did the school run, made dinner, picked up toys from the living room floor. They went on nice long walks as a family, or over to see her grandmother for hot chocolate and homemade biscuits. Only yesterday Milo had had her and Benedict in hysterics as they walked back over the green, with his impression of Granny Clem.

'I was thinking we could invite everyone round for lunch next weekend,' she said, smoothing down Benedict's collar.

'The family?'

'Yes, and maybe Fred and Angie as well.' Caro felt bad that she hadn't seen much of her friends lately, but she hadn't been able to face talking to anyone.

'Great.' Benedict went back to his cooking. 'It'd be nice to catch up with them, especially with Cheltenham coming up.'

'I know, bloody hell. I still can't believe it!'

A trilling sound signalled the phone ringing. Caro looked for the handset by the microwave, but it wasn't there. Where was the bloody thing? She bet Milo had been playing cops and robbers again. Putting down her glass, she ran through to Benedict's study to use the one in there instead.

'Hello?' She grabbed the phone on the last ring.

'Caro, is that you?'

'Oh, hello, Louise! Sorry, I've been running round looking for the handset.'

'Sorry to call so late.'

'Of course not. How is everything?' They'd only spoken that morning.

'I've had some news.'

'Oh, right?' Caro sat on the edge of the desk. 'Nothing bad, I hope, my nerves can't take much more!'

Her jokey tone was met by silence. Something

was wrong. Caro sat up straight. 'Louise?'

'Don't let this set you back, OK? We're going to fight it.'

'What do you mean?' Caro suddenly felt scared.

Louise cut straight to the chase. 'Caro, the Cafcass report is in. Belinda Winters is recommending Milo should go and live with his father.'

CHAPTER SEVENTY-FIVE

They were back to square one.

Ever since the disaster at Goatsford, Angie and Freddie had hardly seen Edward. You'd think it would be impossible to avoid someone who only lived a few hundred yards from your front door, but Edward had done a pretty good job of it so far. Dinner times together in the main house were a distant memory. The only time he ventured out of the granny annexe was to see Nobby. But he was barely riding at all—at a time when training couldn't be more crucial.

Even worse, someone at the point-to-point had tipped off the local press about Chip Mason, and a reporter had turned up from the *Bedlington Bugle*, trying to speak to Edward. Freddie had shooed them off, but they'd still run a piece the next day about how Edward was carrying on a great sporting dynasty. It was a well-meant piece, but fearing it would send Edward into a complete tailspin if he saw it, Angie drove round buying up all the copies she could, and dumping them in the recycling bin.

Angie wondered what Edward's home life could

have been like, to make him so unhappy around his father. He was a sensitive boy who needed time and understanding, not hard-line brutish treatment. She wondered if his rugby player brother had treated him badly, too.

Chip's timing couldn't have been worse. His appearance had rocked Edward to the core, and Angie was seriously worried about Edward's state of mind now. How on earth could he deal with the pressure of Cheltenham? He hadn't been the most confident of people to start with. They were all feeling anxious in the build-up to the race, even Freddie, and *they* weren't the ones going out to risk life and limb.

When Edward did train Nobby, it was as if he wasn't *there* any more. He was so touchy and withdrawn, even with Kizzy, that Angie had resorted to watching him at her bedroom window through racing binoculars. It broke her heart to see Edward's stick figure crouched over Nobby like a broken toy soldier. One saving grace was that Nobby was his normal robust self, but it wasn't enough. They should all have been pulling together at such a crucial time, and instead Edward was out there by himself, thinking God knows what.

*   *   *

That morning Angie was in the kitchen, making carrot and coriander soup for lunch. She hadn't given up on Edward yet, and was going to leave a flask of it outside the granny annexe for him. Even if he didn't eat it, at least he would know they were still thinking about him.

She was in the middle of liquidizing the soup

when Avon and Barksdale jumped up and started making a terrific din.

'Dogs, shush!' she called over the whirring. It had to be a car. Angie switched the blender off and looked out of the window. She wasn't expecting anyone, and her first thought was that one of the fishing party they had booked in that day had got lost and driven down the private entrance by mistake.

A silver Bentley pulled up imperiously in the middle of the yard. Angie had gone to the door, ready to give directions, when Chip Mason climbed out, as big and brash as last time.

Her heart flew into her mouth. 'Hello,' she said guardedly.

Chip Mason stared at her rudely. 'Where's Edward?'

'He's not here, I'm afraid. He went out earlier.'

'Where?'

'I have no idea,' she said coldly. 'We don't keep tabs on him.'

Chip swaggered closer, only stopping when he saw the dogs' heads poking round her legs. 'No, but you are stringing Edward along with this little pipe dream.' He looked at her, half-curious. 'Come on, what's in it for you, then? I'm used to people trying to cash in on the Mason name.'

It was funny how he'd forgotten about having nothing to do with Edward up till then, or the fact that Edward hadn't been *using* the Mason name. 'There's nothing *in it* for us,' Angie retorted. 'And it's not a pipe dream. Edward's riding in the Foxhunter Steeplechase at Cheltenham! Hardly any point-to-point jockeys make it. We're very proud of him.'

'Proud of him?' Chip shook his big head. 'The day that boy makes me proud . . .' He stopped and looked down his nose. 'What's your name, again?'

'Angie,' she said, thinking how rude he was. 'Angie Fox-Titt. My husband and I—'

She was interrupted. 'You know, Angie.' He pronounced it *An-jey*. 'We've tried with Eddie. We got him in a good school, made sure he had tryouts with all the teams. Even when he came out with three GCSEs I bent over backwards for that boy and got work experience for him at a couple of mates' companies. We're talking big multinationals here, and all Edward did was embarrass me. He doesn't want to succeed at anything.'

'Maybe he doesn't *want* to do the things you want him to do,' she replied hotly. 'Have you ever thought about that?'

Chip Mason fixed her with a beady eye. 'I know it's hard to believe, but I was like Edward once, a scrawny little thing with no future. Sport was my passport to the outside world.'

Angie opened her mouth, but Chip was warming to his theme.

'I worked hard, An-jey, to make it. My family were piss-poor, you know, none of this private-school lark that Edward's been so lucky to have. If only that boy knew—'

If Chip had come here for a confessional, Angie wasn't in the mood. 'Actually, Edward does know. He's an extremely bright, capable young man. If you'd ever spared the time to actually *talk* to him, you'd know that.'

It was lucky Freddie was hidden away in his study because the physical change in Chip Mason was quite alarming. His ruddy face became even redder, anger swelling him so he towered above her. 'Don't you tell me how to bring up my own son! Where I come from women know their place. If my wife ever spoke to me in that way . . .'

'I feel bloody sorry for your wife! Don't you give me all your chauvinistic dinosaur crap.' Angie was seething. How *dare* this man come on to her property and try to intimidate her?

Chip's colour flared up again, but he obviously thought better of whatever he was going to do. 'Christ,' he said disdainfully. 'No wonder Edward's got all this rubbish in his head.'

'If you don't leave now I'll set the dogs on you,' Angie said. Avon and Barksdale were the most useless guard dogs ever but Chip didn't know that.

'Charming! I come all this way to make amends to my son, and you threaten me.' Barksdale gave a very convincing growl. Chip took a step back. 'All right, I'm going.' He stomped off back to the car, his bulky shoulders tight with anger.

'Tell him I called,' he shouted over one of them. 'Making me drive all this way for nothing!' The Bentley screeched out of the yard.

Angie realized her hands were shaking. It was nothing to do with her own feelings: the same thought kept circling in her head. *Thank God Edward wasn't here*. Chip had been kept at bay this time, but for how long?

CHAPTER SEVENTY-SIX

Calypso and Camilla were walking across the green on their way to Caro's. They'd been called over

489

there for a 'family gathering' as their grandmother had called it.

'I reckon she's duffers again,' Calypso declared.

'Duffers?'

'Pregnant. Up the duff.' Calypso dropped her sister a cheeky wink. 'Come on, grandma, get with the lingo.'

'Charming.'

'Are you telling them about you and Jed? Adopting?'

'I was going to,' Camilla admitted. 'But I don't want to steal their thunder.'

'You won't be! Oh, man, I love a happy occasion.' Calypso linked arms with her sister, making the stacked silver bangles on her wrist tinkle. 'I hope they've got some yummy canapés in, I'm starving.'

The two sisters carried on round the road, enjoying the sight of Churchminster's green on the cusp of spring. There was an early crop of buttercups over by the memorial bench looking like yellow dots on the flat green grass.

'Anyway,' Camilla said innocently. 'I was wondering how a certain Archie Fox-Titt was.'

'I really don't know what you're talking about,' Calypso said, very interested in a pair of magpies swooping past.

'Oh, right. It's just that Jed saw him streaking naked down your garden path the other night.' Camilla stifled a grin. They'd known about Archie for months.

For once Calypso was lost for words. 'Piss off! Did he really?'

'Yup, in all his crowning glory. I'd watch that he doesn't get a cold: we've had a frost this week.'

490

'OMG!' Calypso started laughing. 'I can't believe it! Archie had left his phone in his car, I told him someone would see . . .'

Camilla smiled. 'So it's all going well?'

'It's not going anywhere.'

'Why not? Sounds like you're having fun.'

'That's exactly it, fun.' Calypso stopped and looked at her sister. 'Bills, this is Archie Fox-Titt we're talking about! You know? Angie and Freds' annoying little brat of a son?'

Camilla laughed. 'He was a monkey. Do you remember when he set fire to the hedge outside the rectory? I think it's the only time I've ever seen Freddie get angry.'

'Yeah, and he was dragged off home howling like a baby.' How could Calypso ever move on from an image like that?

Camilla smiled. 'Still, he's turned out rather well.'

They reached No. 1 Mill House. 'May I remind you,' Calypso said, 'that he's only twenty-three and still lives at home with his mum and dad?'

'I think you'd make a nice couple.'

'And I think you need your head examined,' Calypso retorted, steering her sister up the front path.

*   *   *

Clementine answered the front door almost immediately. 'My dears.' She was doing her best Barbara Woodhouse impression today, in a checked skirt, wool jumper and sturdy lace-up shoes.

Camilla took her jacket off and hung it on the stand next to the door. 'It's very quiet. Where are

491

the children?'

'At a birthday party.'

'What's all this about, Clemballs?' Calypso dropped to a stage whisper. 'Is Caro up the duff again?'

She only did it to wind her grandmother up, but it seemed to wash over her. 'Caro and Benedict are in the living room.'

The sisters glanced at each other. 'Is everything all right?' Camilla asked.

Clementine's smile was strained. 'Come on through.'

They found Caro and Benedict having coffee. Caro's eyes were red, as if she'd been crying.

'Hello, darlings.' She came over and planted a kiss on their cheeks.

'Are you OK?' Calypso asked uncertainly. She'd sensed the strained atmosphere as soon as they'd walked in.

Her sister avoided eye contact. Benedict picked up the coffee-pot and turned to Clementine. 'Black, no sugar?'

'Yes please, Benedict.'

It seemed to take for ever, but at last everyone had a cup. Camilla and Calypso kept sneaking glances at each other.

Benedict looked at his wife. 'We've got something to tell you. We don't want you to panic—I'm sure it will be fine—but things have been happening that you need to know about.'

Calypso felt a bit sick. No one was ill, were they?

The room had gone quiet; all eyes were fixed on Benedict. He was very calm, but his hands were gripping his cup tightly. 'As you know, Sebastian moved back to the village saying he wanted to

492

spend more time with Milo.'

Calypso instantly relaxed. 'What's that idiot done now? Lost one of his hairbrushes?'

No one laughed. Benedict looked grave. 'At the start of this year we got a letter from a lawyer Sebastian had hired, telling us he was applying for a residence order for Milo.'

'A what?' Calypso said.

'It means going for custody,' Camilla said quietly.

Calypso snorted in disbelief. 'Custody? *Him?* Shut up.'

'Hush, darling,' Clementine said. 'Let Benedict finish.'

He gave Clementine a brief smile. 'Of course, we didn't agree. We hired our own lawyer to write back, and then had to attend a hearing at the family court in Gloucester. The outcome of that meeting was that a Cafcass officer—someone appointed by the court to monitor both sides of the family—had to do a report on Caro and Sebastian, and decide who Milo would be better off living with.' Benedict gave a tight smile. 'To the total amazement of everyone, our lawyer included, she is recommending Milo should go and live with his father back in London.'

Calypso and Camilla stared at him in shock. 'What?'

'This is insane!' Calypso spluttered. 'Sebastian's the worst father ever!'

'He's also very good at exploiting the system,' Caro said unhappily, 'and making people believe things.'

'But how often would we get to see Milo?'

'The Cafcass report is recommending half the school holidays and every other weekend . . .'

Caro's face suddenly crumpled.

Benedict put his arm round her. 'There, my darling.'

'I can't believe this.' Camilla looked on the verge of tears as well.

'Surely you don't have to hand Milo over just like that?'

Caro wiped her eyes. 'The Cafcass report is only a recommendation; it's not set in stone. Our lawyer Louise has already written back to the courts, challenging the report.'

'There's going to be a final hearing in front of the judge,' Benedict said. 'Caro and Sebastian will have to give evidence, along with the Cafcass officer, Belinda Winters.'

'When's the final hearing?' Camilla asked.

Clementine spoke. 'May the twenty-eighth, six weeks away. I've told Caro and Benedict we would like to go along to support them.'

Calypso and Camilla nodded vigorously. 'Of course.'

'Do Mummy and Daddy know?' Camilla asked Caro.

'I was going to call them, after this.' Caro saw her sisters' worried faces. 'Please don't worry. Nothing has been decided yet.'

'Our lawyer feels we have a very strong case against the report,' Benedict says. 'It's blatantly the wrong decision.' He clasped Caro's hand and gave her a reassuring smile. 'Milo's going nowhere.'

*   *   *

By the time she got home, Calypso's rage still hadn't subsided. She wanted to go round and rip

494

that cheating, lying piece of shit's bollocks off.

It couldn't be true. Caro was such a lovely person, and she didn't deserve this. Unlike Calypso, all she'd ever wanted was her own family to love and provide for. The one good thing that had come out of her marriage to that arsehole had been Milo, then she'd met Benedict and they'd had Rosie, and now No. 1 Mill House was this happy, warm, beautiful home that Caro had worked hard to make perfect. The thought that all that happiness might be taken away made Calypso feel sick to her stomach. *How could I not have noticed?* She'd been so bloody wrapped up in herself and her own supposed woes, she hadn't been aware of how down Caro had become. She'd always thought of Caro as invincible: the kind, older sister who looked out for others and never put herself first. Caro had looked so small and pale sitting there, so vulnerable next to Benedict, that it had made Calypso's heart clench. *I'm there for her*, she thought. From now on, any time of day or night, she'd drop everything to help Caro.

Half of her still didn't believe it. Surely the court would be able to see what a scumbag Sebastian was? It was as obvious as the fact that Caro was an amazing mother. If Calypso could have stood up in court and testified, she would have. When she thought about the vile lies Sebastian had invented about Caro, she couldn't bear the stain on her sister's character. She'd promised Caro she wouldn't go round to Sebastian's, but the temptation was so very great. As for that sly cow, Suzette, Calypso knew there'd been something 'off' there, the moment she'd laid eyes on her . . .

If she sat here and stewed there was a good

chance Sebastian's entrails were going to end up hanging from the trellis outside Bluebell Cottage. Without really thinking about it, she rang Archie.

He answered quickly. 'Hey, what's up?'

'Nothing much.'

'You OK?'

'Yeah.' She looked out of the living room window. 'Do you fancy a walk or something? I need to get out.'

'You must be bored.'

She wasn't in the mood for jokes. 'Do you want to go or not?'

'Whoa, I was only joking. I'll be round in ten minutes.'

He turned up all big and outdoorsy in a white surfer's T-shirt. Calypso let him kiss her on the cheek passively. Archie raised an eyebrow. 'Are you all right?'

'Fine.' Grabbing her cardigan from the banisters, she banged the door shut. They'd nearly got all the way across the green before either of them spoke. 'Can you keep a secret?' she asked.

'Course.' He looked at her. 'What is it?'

'I've just heard something really shocking. Sebastian is going for custody of Milo.'

'What?' Archie frowned. 'Why?'

'Why? Because he's an evil bastard who doesn't want my sister to have any happiness.'

'He's not going to get it, is he?'

'That's what I said, but they've had this welfare report from a woman who doesn't even *know* my sister, and she reckons Milo would be better off with his father. I mean, what? I reckon Sebastian's done a job on her. In fact, I wouldn't be surprised if he's paid her off.'

'I don't think that would happen, would it? I'm sure this woman is meant to be impartial.'

'She's got a funny way of showing it.'

'I'm sure it will be OK. You've always said what an arsehole Sebastian is. He won't be able just to turn up and claim ownership of Milo.'

'You don't know what a devious little bastard he is, Archie.'

'The courts will see through it, I'm sure.'

'That doesn't help Caro much, does it? I hate what he's put her through.'

'Caro will be fine.' Archie put his arm round her. 'Don't worry.'

His optimism was starting to grate. 'How do you know she'll be fine? If you heard some of the disgusting things Sebastian's been trying to pin on her you wouldn't be so sure.'

'Do you want to tell me about them?'

'No.' Calypso didn't want to repeat a single one. It would be like poisoning the air.

Archie squeezed her. 'Come on, it will be all right.'

'Archie, this isn't some stupid little family argument, you know. It's serious.'

'I know that. Of course I do. I just think it'd help if you tried to remain positive, Calypso. It will eat you up otherwise.'

Christ, he had no clue. Calypso pulled away from under his arm. 'This was a bad idea. I'm going back.'

'We've only just set off. Come on, it will do you good. Just being outside makes you feel better. '

Did he really think a *walk* was going to solve the problem?

'I need to go,' she told him.

'Where?'

'I don't know. Caro's. Granny Clem's. Be with my *family*. I shouldn't have dragged you out.' She turned round, not caring if he came or not.

'I want to help you,' he called.

Calypso whirled round again. 'What, by drinking in the beauties of nature?'

He looked just like a puppy dog: all happy, innocent eyes and wet shiny nose. Not a care in the world. Calypso half-expected a tail to sprout out of the back of his jeans and start wagging.

'Sorry, Archie, I can't do this.' She walked off, leaving him standing in the lane.

CHAPTER SEVENTY-SEVEN

Kizzy ran the brush through Delly's thick tail. 'Good girl, that looks better now, doesn't it?' She walked round to the mare's head, kissing Delly on her velvety nose. 'You're such a gorgeous girl, aren't you?'

She was rewarded with a flick of the head in return. Delly was one of those horses that really made you feel like they understood what you were saying. Or maybe it was just that Kizzy was completely dotty about her new present.

Kizzy looked at the freshly groomed coat, appreciating Delly's lines. She'd started riding her in the outdoor school; only slowly and carefully— what she'd do for a good gallop! But the physio had been very firm: 'Keep doing your exercises and take it easy.' Even Kizzy knew 'take it easy' didn't mean haring round the countryside on her new mount. She was seeing Mr Sherbourne in a couple of weeks, hopefully to get the all-clear. And then there'd be no stopping her!

Even when Javier was away, like he was today, Kizzy had a free run of the place. The yard and house had become a home from home; her dad had joked that he'd soon start forgetting what his daughter looked like. As far as her parents knew, she was spending every spare minute at the Maltings, preparing for Cheltenham.

Another lie, but that's what Kizzy's life was built on now. Lies and secrets. She'd told no one about Delly, because even Angie would find it weird. In some ways, Kizzy didn't want to tell anyone, ever, because they'd only question what was actually going on. *If I keep it sacred, and to myself, things might not have to change*, she told herself. When the gates opened to Homelands and she drove in, it felt like she was entering her own little dream world where everything was perfect and had a happy ending. Kizzy existed one day at a time; she didn't want to think about the future—or reality. It was amazing how you could convince yourself everything was all right when you really wanted to.

Today Javier was up in London having a meeting with the Olympic committee. Aside from the rigorous training schedule, an increasing amount of his time was spent attending Lottery fund-raisers and sponsorship dinners, increasing the profile of the dressage. He'd also been approached to be a consultant for LOCOG—the London Organizing Committee of the Olympic and Paralympic Games—and had been up and down to the capital, making sure the dressage arena at Greenwich Park was going to be up to scratch. Javier had

499

initially been hesitant about taking on any more commitments, but he'd confessed to Kizzy that he was actually really enjoying himself. No longer the blank-eyed recluse Kizzy had first met, Javier was now charged with a new passion and zest. He was such an asset to the country and his sport.

She'd been at the centre all afternoon with her darling Delly. It was a relief to have somewhere to go to at the moment. The atmosphere at the Fox-Titts' yard was strained, to say the least. They only had two weeks until Cheltenham, and Edward showed no sign of breaking out of his odd, withdrawn state. Kizzy was seriously beginning to doubt if he would be able to take part. She felt for him, she really did, but also she wanted to take him by the shoulders and *shake* him. He'd achieved the most amazing things, and was poised to ride in the most important race of his life. Was he going to let his dad ruin that, as well?

Even so, it was hard to keep thinking such dark thoughts. It was a stunning day, hot enough to wear only a little vest top over her jodhpurs. As Kizzy walked back up to the house, riding hat in hand, Homelands was a sea of green and yellow around her, the rugged parkland colliding slap-bang with the neat, groomed lawns. Everywhere she looked there was new colour and life. The gloomy sadness that had pervaded the place when she'd first visited seemed a thing of the past.

Wherever she went now Salvador and Pablo followed, their black eyes darting back and forth, their sharp ears pricked. Kizzy walked across the gravel at the front, waving to Nigel through the office window as she passed. Pushing open the door in the wall to the back of the house, she said

500

hello to one of the gardeners—who was pruning an already pristine rosebush—and headed for the kitchen.

Mary was at the flour-smeared table, energetically kneading dough. She looked up when Kizzy came in.

'There you are, Kizzy. How's that horsey of yours?'

'As beautiful as ever.' Kizzy checked the door, to make sure the dogs couldn't get in. 'Something smells good.'

'It's a little chicken and tarragon pie. I thought you might like it for lunch.'

'You do spoil me.' Kizzy smiled. 'I'll end up the size of a house.'

'Nonsense, there's nothing to you. You jockeys don't eat enough.'

The housekeeper put the dough back into its mixing bowl and covered it with a damp tea towel. 'There, I'll leave that to rise. Shall I make us a cup of tea, Kizzy?'

'It's all right, I'll do it. You go through to your sitting room and put your feet up.'

Mary was perched in her armchair as Kizzy came in with the tray. The window was open, the smell of the wisteria climbing outside gently scenting the room.

'You be mother, Kizzy.' She sat back and took a sip out of her cup. 'Aah, that's better. What time is Javier back?'

'About five, I think he said. Depending on the traffic.'

Mary nodded. 'Grand.'

They lapsed into silence, with only the occasional clink of china as Mary lifted and set down her cup.

'What was the meeting about today?' she said at last. 'I lose track of Javier's movements at the moment.'

'With the Olympic committee? It's another one of those assessments again, where they get an update on your performance and fitness levels. Just to make sure everyone's winning medals and hitting targets.' Kizzy smiled wryly. 'So no pressure or anything.'

Mary didn't return the smile. There it was again, that moment of awkwardness. She met Kizzy's eyes over her cup and looked away.

The wedding photograph of Sarah and Javier was omnipresent above the mantelpiece, the bride radiant and dewy-skinned. Kizzy decided to come straight out with it.

'Mary, can I ask you a question?'

'Of course.'

'What will happen to Sarah? Do you think she'll ever wake up again?'

Mary put her cup down. It was a moment before she slowly answered.

'Sarah's condition is difficult. When she first came off the life support we could have lost her, but her heart kept going. Sometimes when you imagine you see the smallest eye flicker or murmur, your heart starts going like the clappers . . .'

She stopped abruptly. 'The doctors have always been straight with us. Sarah could go on like this for a long, long time but is that what she would really want?'

Kizzy imagined Mary in the hospice, sitting by Sarah's bed for hours. 'I'm sorry, I shouldn't have asked.'

'Of course you should have.' Mary shifted her

stout body in the chair. 'To be honest, it's nice to talk about her. Javier doesn't say much; it makes him angry he can't do anything about the situation.'

'What was Sarah like?' Kizzy was gripped by an urge to know, whatever the consequences.

Mary folded her arms and looked out of the window at the greenness beyond. 'Sarah was a lady, through and through. She had a kind word for everybody. In all the time I knew her, I never once heard her raise her voice.'

'I can see why Javier loved her so much.'

The housekeeper nodded. 'She brought a tranquillity to Javier's life that he'd never had before. You know Javier and his father never got on? Lord Douglas Hamilton-Scott was a hard man who ruled by discipline, not love. I think he actively disliked his own son and felt threatened by him. He was dreadfully harsh on Javier.'

Kizzy thought of how loving her own dad was. Lord Hamilton-Scott sounded like a seriously warped individual.

'It had a terrible effect on Javier. He was always fighting, Kizzy: fighting about what happened with his mother and father; fighting against his brother dying; fighting about feeling such an outsider in the world he was born into. When he met Sarah, she calmed him. She saw past the looks, the money, Javier's career, to see something there no one else was aware of. With Sarah, Javier found peace in himself for the first time.'

Mary stopped as she saw Kizzy's face. 'Now I've upset you.'

'You haven't, really.' Kizzy's throat filled up; she could never, ever dream of being able to share what Javier and Sarah had. 'It's just really sad,' she said

503

instead.

The old lady suddenly looked troubled. 'Kizzy, there's things you don't understand. Things you should understand.'

'It's OK,' Kizzy said awkwardly. 'I know there's no future for me and Javier.'

Mary set her mouth. 'It's not right. Javier needs to be straight with you.'

'About us?' Kizzy registered Mary's disapproval and wanted to die. 'Mary, I really don't want to cause any problems. I'm sorry if you think . . .'

'Think? What does it matter what *I* think?' Kizzy was startled at the anger in her voice, but it was gone in an instant. 'I'm sorry Kizzy, it's just been a long day.'

'It's a difficult situation for you, Mary. I do appreciate that.'

Mary looked at her for a long time. 'You're a grand lass Kizzy, so you are. You deserve better than this.'

'Please don't worry.' Kizzy gave a tentative smile; 'So are we friends? You don't mind me being here?'

'Mind? I love it, there's too much boy's talk in this place!' She was back to her normal robust self. 'Now Kizzy, would you mind fetching me my handbag from the kitchen? I think I've got one of my heads coming on.'

CHAPTER SEVENTY-EIGHT

Mary's eyes were closed when Kizzy came back in. She didn't stir when Kizzy put the tissue on the table beside her, her chest rising and falling gently under the green cardigan. Kizzy quietly closed the door behind her and left.

She wandered down the corridor, feeling drained. Mary had voiced what Kizzy had been trying to block out, all the way along. Until now Sarah had been almost a mystical figure, existing mostly in the dark recesses of Javier's mind. Of course she'd been there in other ways too, no matter how wonderful the time Kizzy spent with Javier was. There was her horse, Aphrodite, at the stables, bearing the physical scars of that terrible day; there were the photos, there was even her presence whispering through the house. Kizzy had lived with these since the very beginning of her relationship with Javier.

By joining Javier she'd agreed to be haunted by the past—trapped there, even—unable to go forwards. He hadn't forced this on her; Kizzy had *chosen* it. Her life was very different from before, in countless mundane, domestic ways. Even Nobby, her racing . . . it all diminished when she was with Javier. And she knew that Javier would never really be hers. She'd learned to live with it no matter what Mary thought.

Ahead of Kizzy was the great entrance hall, then the doors stretching into the west wing. It was very much the 'business' end of the house: hired out for corporate events and functions, the place where Javier oversaw the day-to-day running of the estate and equestrian centre from his study-cum-office. Kizzy had hardly ever stepped foot in there. She had no need to.

Kizzy looked at her watch. Javier would be back soon. Maybe she'd take the dogs down and meet him at the gates. Kizzy was about to turn back when something caught her eye. The locked door at the end of the landing. Why did it stand out today of all days?

To an outsider it might seem weird that there were parts of Homelands Kizzy had never been in, but that was just how it was. The place was so vast that Javier and his small staff only used the areas they needed to. Kizzy supposed it was like that in a lot of stately homes. If Javier had wanted to show her something, she would surely have seen it by now.

And yet . . . Kizzy's curiosity was piqued again. Why *would* you lock a door unless it was to keep people out? Without even really thinking about it, she started to climb the sweeping staircase.

There was the door: glossy and panelled, with an ornate doorknob. It was identical to the others. And yet there was something *different* about it, too: secretive. Expecting it to be locked again, Kizzy tried the handle. To her surprise it moved easily, and the door clicked open.

The sound seemed really loud. Kizzy looked round guiltily, but there was no one listening. Holding her breath, she put her hand on the door and pushed it open.

What a shock! Instead of a store cupboard or stuffy bedroom, Kizzy found herself looking down a long, wide, sun-filled corridor. It felt different from the rest of Homelands, with its light wooden floors and pastel walls. Kizzy took a step over the threshold, saw the duck-egg blue curtains pooling on the floor, a tall cut-glass vase filled with white lilies. Even the atmosphere was lighter and more rarefied. She noticed a trio of beautifully executed charcoal sketches hanging on the wall.

Despite the pleasant surroundings, it was too quiet. There was no sound of the house's internal workings or of human life in here. Sunlight streamed in through a large window, tiny dust particles swirling in the air like stardust. Their bewitching patterns made Kizzy feel slightly unnerved.

A magpie swooped past outside, making her jump. Kizzy went over to the window to get her bearings. The orangery was directly below, so she knew she was on the east wing of the house. *Get out,* whispered the voice of reason in her head.

Kizzy's feet moved forward again, as if she was being controlled by someone else. She passed more doors on the way down the corridor. Several were open, and she stopped at one that looked like a living room, elegant in its minimalism, a transparent Phillipe Starck 'ghost' chair artfully displayed in the corner. Over the fireplace was a vast painting of a ballerina, crouched over herself exquisitely like a dying swan. In another was a library, but not like the one she'd seen downstairs. This was all shiny-spined books on photography and dance. One door opened on to a stylish dressing room, with one of those mirrors with bulbs round them that Kizzy had seen in the movies, pristine, with a simple silver hairbrush and art deco perfume bottle standing in front of it. A beautifully painted rocking horse, with what Kizzy guessed was real hair for the mane and tail, stood sadly in one corner.

On the landing at the far end there was a staircase. It led down to a wide hallway with a black and white chequered floor.

A sound floated up from somewhere. A voice. Kizzy nearly jumped out of her skin.

'Hello?' she called back.

She was met by more silence. *Am I imagining things?* She was sure she'd heard it. She leant over the stairs further, straining her ears. There it was again! She realized it wasn't a human voice but music, the delicate undertones too indistinct to make out. Kizzy started down quietly, trying to blend in with the house.

A different smell hit her in the middle of the stairs. Antiseptic; something sharp and pervasive that went straight to the back of her throat. At the bottom of the staircase she was confronted by yet more corridors, running off from the hallway like a six-pointed star.

'Hello?' The music was coming from the corridor to the left, so Kizzy turned and walked down it. The walls here were flawlessly white, punctuated only by one striking piece of modern art.

The music was louder now. Kizzy's stomach turned over as she recognized *Clair de Lune*, the piece Javier had played to her on the piano. The door to the room it was coming from was open. Kizzy approached hesitantly.

Inside, the room was large and dimly-lit. Kizzy's gaze was immediately drawn to the near wall, which was dominated by a stunning, blown up, black and white photograph. Her stomach jolted again. It was Sarah, on stage, arms held aloft, one long leg poised elegantly behind the other. She was wearing a feathered tutu as she smiled into the camera at an unseen crowd.

Kizzy swallowed. The sheer size of the thing was overwhelming, as if Sarah was a saint looking down from a stained glass window. As Kizzy stared at it, the hairs on her arms prickled in warning. There was someone else with her in the room.

Kizzy turned round slowly. There was a bed on the far side of the room, high and mechanical like the ones you saw in hospitals. She went cold as she saw a person lying in it.

'I'm so sorry! I had no idea anyone was in here . . .' Kizzy trailed off. Something wasn't right. Digging her nails into her palms, she took a step towards the bed. Just then a breeze rippled the blinds on the windows, letting a shard of sunlight into the room. It highlighted the figure under the sheet, and Kizzy's knees nearly went. She saw the spun-gold hair fanned out across the pillow, the delicate chin tipping up.

Sarah. Kizzy put a hand over her mouth, averting her eyes as if she shouldn't look. When it became perfectly clear the figure hadn't reacted, Kizzy forced her gaze back and took another step forward.

There was a stand by the bed with a pump and a bottle filled with a milky brown fluid. A clear plastic tube ran from it to somewhere under the covers. Kizzy stared at the pristine white sheets for a moment before dragging her gaze upwards.

Sarah was beautiful, even now. From the prominent collarbones and hollowed cheeks Kizzy could see Sarah was very emaciated, but she still radiated a kind of ghostly perfection. Her complexion was translucent and tight, showcasing the exquisite bone structure. She was dressed in an exquisite white nightgown, the silk pooling against the flattened chest. The way Sarah's hands were serenely clasped together reminded Kizzy of an angel statue she'd once seen in a graveyard. She registered the gold wedding band and spectacular diamond ring on Sarah's left hand. They looked loose, as if they could fall off at any minute.

The last part really got to Kizzy. It felt wrong staring at someone who shouldn't be like this, who couldn't talk or speak back. She dropped her eyes and saw the camp bed set up close by. It was narrow and rudimentary, a single pillow and blanket neatly folded up on it. There was something familiar lying at the other end. Kizzy's stomach thudded as she recognized Javier's jumper. She needed to leave, fast. She knew instantly this was something not meant for her eyes, or those of anyone else from the outside world. Javier could never find out she'd been here.

'Can I help you?'

Kizzy nearly had a heart attack. She whirled round to see a dark-haired woman in a white tunic and trousers. She didn't look much older than Kizzy.

'I'm sorry,' Kizzy said. 'I didn't mean to barge in.'

'How *did* you get in?' A quizzical smile.

'I, er. Javier . . .'

The woman's face brightened up. 'You're Kizzy, aren't you? Javier mentioned you.' She went over to Sarah and looked at her face.

Kizzy wasn't quite sure what was going on. 'Sorry, I didn't catch your name.'

'Tracey, I'm Sarah's nurse.' She crossed over to the window and pulled the blind up a few inches. 'Let's get some more light in here.'

Kizzy didn't want to look at the tragic figure in the bed. 'I'm so sorry, I didn't know Sarah was here.'

Tracey turned round. 'Javier doesn't know you here?'

'I was kind of exploring,' Kizzy said guiltily.

A door banged outside in the corridor, follow by a familiar voice. 'Tracey! Are you about?'

Javier. Kizzy felt sick to the stomach.

'In here!' Tracey called back. She looked Kizzy, face suddenly serious. 'You'd better go.'

Javier's voice was nearing down the corrid 'I stopped at Jo Malone and got a few treats f Sarah.' Upbeat, cheery.

Kizzy started for the door. *I'll just say it w a big mistake*, she thought frantically. *Javier w understand . . .*

He was nearly outside. 'One of those wild fig an cassis candles, and the gardenia scent she likes. thought we could . . .'

Javier stopped dead in the doorway, hunkily dar in a crisp white shirt. He looked shocked.

'What are you doing here?'

'Javier, I'm so sorry.' The words fell over each other. 'I didn't mean to come. I found this place by accident. I'm so sorry.'

She watched him put the Jo Malone bag down on the floor.

'Tracey, can you give us a moment?'

Tracey shot Kizzy a look and hurried out. Kizzy had an insane urge to run after her, beg for sanctuary. Anything but be left to face Javier . . .

Kizzy made herself look at him. The colour had drained from his face, his eyes were black and terrible. He was glaring at her as if she was his worst enemy.

'I said, what are you doing here?'

'I'm sorry,' she said again, sheer fright making

her stutter. 'I was exploring, and I didn't realize . . .
I would never have come down here if I'd known.'

'Wouldn't you?' He'd moved in front of the bed,
as if to shield Sarah.

'No!' Kizzy was horrified. 'Of course not.'

'I gave you as much of me as I could.' His look
was destroying her. 'I thought you *understood*. Why
could you not respect my wishes!'

This wasn't happening. 'That's not how it was!
I'd never go behind your back.' Kizzy couldn't bear
him thinking badly of her.

'How many times have you been here?'

'Just this once. Javier, I swear, you have to
believe me.'

Something rippled through his face, giving Kizzy
a moment of hope. Instead Javier looked as if he'd
aged a thousand years in an instant.

'Please, leave.'

'Javier . . .'

His voice rose to a shout. 'I said, get OUT!'

Blinded by tears, she fled the room.

CHAPTER SEVENTY-NINE

Angie was in her antiques shop, unpacking some
boxes from an auction she'd been to. She was just
admiring a rather nice carriage clock—French,
nineteenth century—when the doorbell tinkled. She
looked up to see Caro.

'My darling!' She came round the counter to give
her a hug. 'How are you? It feels like an age.'

'Hello, Ange.' Caro looked tired. There were
dark circles under her eyes.

'Have you lost weight?' Angie was quite shocked at how wan Caro looked.

'A bit, I think. For once I haven't been trying to lose it.' Caro smiled, but it didn't reach her eyes.

There was something wrong. 'Darling, are you all right?' Angie watched in horror as Caro sat down on the nearest chair and burst into tears.

*   *   *

'I can't believe it!' Angie said, half an hour later. 'That bloody man, who does he think he is?'

They were sitting in the little boxroom at the back, which Angie used as an office. A packet of biscuits lay untouched between them.

Caro took a sip of coffee from an old mug with a horse's head on it. She felt exhausted.

'Belinda Winters has certainly been taken in by him, otherwise she wouldn't have written what she did.'

The twelve-page report made for galling reading. In neat paragraphs Belinda Winters had documented Sebastian as being 'open and friendly' while Suzette was praised for being 'helpful'. Her views of Caro were less favourable. The Cafcass officer felt Caro 'hadn't been entirely honest and candid', while Benedict had come across as 'detached' and 'guarded'.

'I was just so nervous, I wasn't myself,' Caro said. 'It's all horribly uncomfortable. And Benedict's been so angry about everything, that he's been fighting to keep his emotions in check.'

'Of course you'd be nervous,' Angie said soothingly. 'I'd be a wreck, any decent mother would. It doesn't mean you're trying to hide

513

something!'

'You'd think so, but nothing surprises me any more,' Caro said wearily. She'd been right to worry about Milo getting a black eye from the remote control, after all. It had been flagged up as an example of a 'chaotic home-life' and 'an inattentive mother struggling to cope with two children'. She didn't know whether to laugh or cry. Didn't every family have a chaotic home-life? Sebastian on the other hand, had been praised for his 'stable' environment and 'meticulous planning when it came to arrangements for Milo'. Of course he had time to organize everything: he didn't have two children to look after!

'It's ridiculous that the court puts so much store by what this woman thinks,' Angie said. 'She's clearly a terrible judge of character.'

'She's got to come down on one side, and unfortunately it's not ours.' Caro had always thought those Fathers 4 Justice were publicity-seeking vigilantes, but she was starting to have some sympathy for them.

'So now you've got this final hearing,' Angie said.

Caro nodded. 'As we're never going to agree, Louise says we may as well go straight to it, rather than apply for any more interim hearings.' She sighed. 'I'm dreading the whole thing. I'll probably go to pieces and blow it again.'

'You won't. But most of us would struggle in such a high-pressure situation.'

'Sebastian doesn't! You'd want to give him an Oscar if you'd seen some of the performances he's given, Angie.'

Angie reached out for her hand. 'Oh, Caro. What a dreadful thing to have to go through!'

Caro smiled bravely. 'We'll live to fight another day. It's amazing what you can do when you have to.'

'It'll be fine,' Angie said firmly. 'I know it will.'

'I know.' Caro tried to smile. 'Let's talk about something cheerier. You must be so excited about Cheltenham.'

Angie took her cue. 'Excited, shocked, terrified; all those things!'

'I heard about Chip Mason turning up. I can't believe he's Edward's father.'

'I don't think Edward can, either. He's been in a world of his own ever since. Fred and I are so worried about him.'

'What will you do?'

'At the moment, I'm seriously thinking of pulling him from the race.'

*   *   *

Calypso was feeling pretty bad about how she'd spoken to Archie. She decided to pop round to the Maltings and see if she could buy him lunch at the pub. A peace offering, and maybe even a shag back at hers afterwards. She'd got quite used to having Archie in her bed.

There was an easyCar rental vehicle parked next to his pickup when she drove in and parked. Calypso got out and looked at it. It was a bit odd. Who needed a rental car in these parts? She knocked on the front door and stepped back.

Archie took so long to answer Calypso was about to give up, but then she heard footsteps and the door was pulled open.

'Hey.'

515

'Hey.' He looked really cute: his faded baggy jeans were hanging just low enough to show off the waistband of his pants. Calypso had an urge to push him inside and do it right there in the hall.

'I was wondering if you fancied lunch.' She shot him a cheeky look. 'I owe you after leaving you stranded in the lane.'

'Don't worry. They didn't have to get search and rescue out.' Archie smiled. 'That's really nice of you, but I've actually got a guest.'

'Archie?' It was a girl's voice, American. Then a dark-haired waif of a thing materialized beside him, doll-pretty in a floral tea dress. She eyed Calypso curiously.

There was an uncomfortable pause. 'Calypso, this is Sue-Beth,' Archie told her.

'Hi!' Sue-Beth chirruped.

'Yeah, hi,' Calypso said cursorily. She looked back at Archie. 'Well, *sorry* to interrupt your cosy little set-up. I'll see you later.'

Fuming, she turned her back on them and walked off. She couldn't believe the bloody nerve of him!

He came after her just as she was about to start the engine. 'Calypso.'

'Don't "Calypso" me.' She shot a look at him through the open window. 'No wonder you've been so quiet the last few days. You've obviously been shacked up with Miss American Pie in there. Didn't take you long, did it?'

'It's not like that. Sue-Beth is over in the UK for a few days, visiting. She drove out to see me today.'

'How nice for you.'

'Sue-Beth is my *friend*.'

'Oh? Like I'm a friend? Do you fuck all of us?'

516

For the first time she saw a flash of irritation. 'What do you want from me, Calypso?'

'Want?' she said defensively. 'I just wanted to know if you fancied going out for lunch. It's what friends do, isn't it?'

Archie shook his head. 'You're impossible. And you were really rude to Sue-Beth then. Don't take out your bad mood on her.'

She was surprised how much his words stung. Calypso turned the key in the ignition. 'You know what, Archie. Go back to your little playmate in there—or whatever she is—and carry on with your childish fun.'

'Calypso, if anyone needs to grow up round here it's you.'

'I beg your pardon?'

'You. You're so down on everything. This place, your job. If your life is so rubbish, why don't you do something about it instead of moaning all the time?'

She was stunned. Archie had never spoken to her like that before. 'I am, thank you! I'm going to London, remember?'

'Fine, go to London.' He turned on his heel and walked back towards the house.

'Fine!' she yelled. Shaking, she put the car into gear, doing an embarrassing accidental wheelspin. At the top of the drive she pulled up abruptly and stared out of the windscreen.

What the fuck? *She'd* just been told to grow up by *him*!

'Screw you, Titt-Head,' she muttered. Whatever they'd had, it was over.

517

CHAPTER EIGHTY

Kizzy emptied the bucket into the water trough. As it settled she saw a ladybird floating on the top, being tossed around like a tiny figure lost at sea. Putting her hand in the water, she carefully closed her hand round it and scooped the insect up. It was too late. The tiny speck lay lifeless in the palm of her hand, its red shell crushed and flattened. Kizzy stared at it for a moment, then laid it down gently in the grass.

It was just another thing she'd destroyed.

Suddenly the tears came back, just when Kizzy had thought she had no more to cry. Covering her face, she dropped to the ground next to the trough. It was only here, out in the middle of one of the Fox-Titts' paddocks, that she could let herself sob for the first time. Anyone happening to pass nearby would have been forgiven for thinking an animal was wounded and in pain.

She cried and cried, great heaving sobs that racked her body and made it hard to breathe. *I've lost him.*

It had been twenty-four hours since she'd fled Homelands, pulling out of the drive so erratically that she'd narrowly missed an oncoming van. The screech of brakes and drawn-out horn had made her stop, hands shaking so hard she could hardly hold the steering wheel. How she had got home and managed to have any sort of conversation with her parents she would never know.

Twenty-four hours of agony. Once she'd calmed down enough to speak, Kizzy had kept calling

Javier to explain. His phone had rung out; her texts had gone unanswered. It was so sudden and unreal. There were moments when she felt like she was in a nightmare.

The fact that Sarah had been in the house all along was too much to take in. Javier had said she was in a private hospital, but never in a million years had Kizzy imagined it was under his roof! How could she not have realized? But then again, Homelands was so vast, with so many different wings and entrances, that it was entirely conceivable Sarah could have been nursed there. There were cars coming in and out all the time; Kizzy had just assumed they'd been to do with the business, or belonged to the support team visiting Love's Dream.

All the time Kizzy had been floating round in her own world, Sarah had been lying a few corridors away. This was what Mary had been trying to warn her about! Kizzy kept replaying their conversation: 'There are things you should understand, Kizzy.' Why *hadn't* she been told? Who else knew? Did they *all* know? Kizzy felt sick thinking about it.

When Kizzy looked back now, she could see other little signs. The way Javier had sometimes seemed to fall off the face of the earth—unreachable and his phone switched off—until morning. The time he'd received a text and jumped out of bed, saying one of the horses was ill down at the centre. Yet the next day, none of the grooms had mentioned anything. It must have been some health scare to do with Sarah. It was clear how ill she was.

Javier had obviously created a cocoon, a sanctuary for Sarah, and Kizzy had committed the cardinal sin by barging in there. She felt like she'd *violated* Sarah. No wonder Javier was so angry.

The thought of how much Javier must hate her made Kizzy cry even harder. It was only when someone coughed that Kizzy realized her private show of grief wasn't so private after all.

Looming over her was Edward, with a dripping mug of tea in each hand. Kizzy silently took the one being offered and had a sip. He sat down on the side of the water trough, his long legs curled up messily under him. 'I saw you were upset.'

'Oh, right.' She wiped a hand quickly across her face.

'I don't mean to embarrass you.'

'You haven't.' She looked out over the paddock. 'Thank you for the tea, Edward.'

They sat and drank in silence, undulating hills surrounding them. In the far corner of the paddocks two wild rabbits were nibbling on the grass. Kizzy watched as they raised their ears and took off, sprinting into the undergrowth.

Edward didn't press her, and she was grateful. It felt comforting just to have him there.

Half an hour must have passed before he got up. 'I'd better get back,' he said.

'OK.' She managed the tiniest of smiles. 'Thank you, Edward.'

To her surprise he leant down and put a huge hand on her shoulder. It was unexpectedly warm. Kizzy could feel the heat going into her chilled body.

'I'll see you in a bit.'

*   *   *

Angie was putting away the groceries when there was a soft tap at the back door. The dogs jumped up and started their usual din.

'Avon! Barksdale!' She really was going to have to take them to training classes; they had to be the noisiest dogs in the Cotswolds. Pushing a large paw off her foot, she went and opened the door.

'Edward! Hello.' She was taken aback to see him there. He was in his usual jodhpurs and polo shirt, his hair flattened round the front from his riding hat.

'C-can I come in?'

'Of course. Perfect timing, I was about to put the kettle on.'

He came in and hovered while she shooed the dogs into their baskets.

'Sit down, darling. I've got some of those Mr Kiplings from the shop that Fred has a thing for . . .' Angie got the packet out of the treats cupboard. 'Oh. Expiry date June 2008.' She'd only bought them yesterday.

'I'm fine with squash, thank you.'

'Coming right up.'

Angie came back and sat down, handing the tumbler to Edward. 'So, darling, how are you?' She decided to play things naturally, in case Edward got scared off.

'I'm good, actually.'

Edward looked different, she thought. *Calmer.* The haunted, stretched mask he'd been wearing the last few weeks had relaxed, giving him back the sweet, kind expression Angie had always found so endearing.

For only the second or third time since she'd known him, Edward looked her straight in the eye.

'I've come to say thank you.'

'Thank you?' She didn't understand.

'You know, for everything you and Freddie have done for me. I know I'm a bit quiet about stuff, but I really do appreciate it.' He scratched his arm, more of a twitch.

'We love having you here. You're part of the family now.'

White-blond eyelashes framed Edward's lilac eyes. 'I'm sorry I've been a bit weird lately. You know, with my dad . . .'

'It's perfectly understandable, darling,' she said gently.

Avon came over and put his big head on Edward's lap. He stroked the dog, twisting his hands round Avon's ear. 'Me and Dad have never really got on. We're different people. He's really confident and outgoing like my brother. I'm not like that. I guess I find it difficult to let others in, make friends.'

It doesn't help having a domineering dad that knocks the self-confidence out of you, Angie thought, smiling encouragingly at Edward.

'I did really try, you know,' he told her. 'To get into the stuff he liked, so he'd be proud of me, but I was never good at sports. He just used to get angry, and say I wasn't fulfilling my potential.'

'You can't go through life trying to live up to other people's expectations, Edward, you just have to be yourself.' Angie wasn't going to bad-mouth his father, no matter what she thought of Chip. 'Some people—men especially—find it hard to express themselves. I'm sure your father doesn't mean to be the way he is. Of course he loves you.'

'Maybe.' He looked thoughtful. 'My dad is an

amazing man in a lot of ways, you know. So many people look up to him.' A wry smile. 'He's just not a very good dad, at least to me, anyway.'

'Oh, Edward.'

'It's fine, really it is. I've spent a lot of time thinking about stuff. I haven't been in the right head space, and it's not fair on you all. Especially with Cheltenham coming up.'

Angie kept quiet. She was starting to get a bad feeling.

'So anyway, I've made a decision.'

'OK.'

'It's time to move on. I need to do something different with my life.'

He was leaving. Angie was shocked at how upset she was. She didn't care about Cheltenham, only about him. Edward had achieved so much, and now he was giving it all up.

Edward glanced at her nervously. 'I thought you'd be happy.'

'*Happy?* That you're leaving us?' Did he really have that low an opinion of himself? Angie made herself smile. 'Of course Freds and I will support any decision you make, but Edward, I'm so sad!'

'Leaving?' His forehead wrinkled. 'I'm not leaving. What makes you think that?'

'But you just said you were moving on.'

'Oh.' He blinked. 'I meant from all the stuff with my dad. I'm not going to let him rule my life any more.' He had a look of defiance. 'He can take me as I am or not at all.'

'Christ!' Angie gave a nervous giggle. 'You nearly gave me a heart attack.'

Edward looked doleful. 'Sorry, I didn't explain myself very well. I'm not really good at this stuff.'

He blinked. 'God, I'd *never* want to leave here, or Nobby.'

'So you still want to go to Cheltenham?'

'Go?' His eyebrows shot up, his long face looking comical in surprise. 'Of course I want to go! It's the best thing that's ever happened to me!' Edward suddenly stopped, looking anxious. 'Unless you don't want me to any more . . .'

'Of course we want you to!' Angie looked at the huge, skinny young man sat at her kitchen table. 'Oh, Edward, I'm so happy!'

She went round to give him a hug. Even sitting down, Edward's head nearly came up to hers. He reached up and put his arms round her awkwardly. Angie's heart melted even more.

'I think we should celebrate by breaking open that box of Belgian truffles, don't you?'

CHAPTER EIGHTY-ONE

Cheryl Pike was filling Caro's kitchen up with her Boudoir perfume and bawdy cackles. She'd come round to show Caro her outfit for Cheltenham—a specially designed purple and black catsuit to match Edward's racing colours—and showed no sign of going an hour later. Barry was in the Costa del Sol on a business trip.

It was a nice spring day, warm enough to have the back door open. Caro was actually quite pleased to have the company. There was something about Cheryl that was relentlessly chirpy. Even if the rest of civilization was wiped out by a massive asteroid Cheryl would be there at the end, tottering round in her stilettos and false nails. She was telling Caro about a couple she knew who'd just got matching boob jobs.

'I didn't know there was such a thing for men,' Caro said. She was at the ironing board, pressing name-tags on to Milo's new sports kit.

'Ooh, God, yeah.' Cheryl shifted in her chair and pulled at the crotch of her catsuit. 'Men worry about their pecs just as much as us girls and our boobies. They're not all as lucky as your Benedict, you know!'

Caro smiled. 'Benedict is one of the blessed ones, it has to be said. He doesn't suffer ugly days like the rest of us. Well, me, anyway.'

'Don't put yourself down, Carol, you've got a great pair on you.'

'Thanks, but they're feeling gravity a bit these days.'

'Nah, you just need to winch 'em up a bit. Like this.' Cheryl stood up and advanced on Caro. She put a hand on each boob and jammed them together. 'See! They look better already.'

Caro looked down. Her cleavage was suddenly somewhere under her chin. 'I'm just not sure it's practical for every day . . .'

'Nonsense.' Cheryl started tugging her bra straps up. The material dug into Caro's shoulders.

'Ouch, that's actually a bit painful . . .'

'That's better!' Cheryl stood back and surveyed her handiwork. 'Old Benedict's not going to be able to keep his hands off those tonight.'

Caro blushed slightly and sat back down again. Moments later there was a light tap at the back door. Caro nearly jumped out of her skin.

'Terribly sorry to intrude,' drawled a familiar

voice. Sebastian was standing at the open back door looking at them.

*   *   *

It was the first time she'd seen him since the Cafcass report had come back. 'Why are you here?' she asked.

Sebastian ignored her and flashed a smile at Cheryl. 'Hello, Cheryl, how *are* you?'

'Can't complain, you?'

'I'm wonderful, thank you for asking.'

He turned back to Caro, slightly cooler. 'I've come to pick up my son.'

'But you're having him tomorrow.'

Sebastian shook his head. 'Nope, sorry. We agreed on today. Both Suzette and I have it written down on our online calendars.' He treated Cheryl to another megawatt smile. 'I'm afraid I'm a bit of a stickler about keeping to arrangements.'

Caro knew exactly what he was getting at. If he brought it up again . . . Crossing over to the dresser, she got the diary out of her handbag. *Damn, damn, damn!* It was there, bold as anything.

'Sorry,' she said stiffly. 'For some reason it was in my head as tomorrow.'

'No problem,' he said smoothly. 'You've been under a lot of pressure.'

Pressure brought on by you. Caro was alarmed by the hatred she felt welling up inside her. 'He's not ready yet, I'll bring him up to you.'

'Fine. If you could get yourself together, and make it sooner rather than later.' Sebastian directed another smile at Cheryl. 'Bye, then.'

'Excuse me,' Caro said to her neighbour. She

caught up with Sebastian as he was going back round the front. 'I want a word with you.'

He swivelled round. 'What?'

Caro faced up to him. 'You may have won Belinda Winters over, but this is a long way from being the end. The Cafcass report is just one person's recommendation.'

'One person whose opinion the judge takes extremely seriously.'

'You're not going to drag my family's name through the mud. You'll have to try harder than that.'

He looked at her as if she had just crawled out from under a stone. 'Oh, darling, I think you're doing a good enough job of that by yourself, don't you?'

Caro's hands were shaking when she went back in. 'You all right, love?' Cheryl asked. 'Is old Sebastian giving you gyp?'

'No, it's fine. I'm just feeling a bit off.' Caro tried to recollect her thoughts. 'I'd better get Milo ready . . .'

'I'll get off.' Under the layers of eye make-up Cheryl was watching her curiously. 'You're trembling like anything! You sure you're OK?'

Caro managed a weak smile. 'Completely.' The biggest trauma in Cheryl's world was being unable to find a nail varnish to match her latest car, or the postman not delivering her copy of *OK!*. There was no way she could understand something like this.

CHAPTER EIGHTY-TWO

Kizzy stared up at her bedroom ceiling. Muted sounds from the television were coming up through the floor from the living room below. There was a sudden explosion of canned laughter, followed by a barely discernible snort from her father.

Laughter. She couldn't ever imagine laughing again. Or smiling, or waking up and looking forward to the day ahead, or going to sleep at night and sleeping right through, dreamless and happy. It had been six days since her world had come crashing down and Javier had ordered her out of his life.

Her desperate attempts to reach him had stopped. If he wanted to speak to her, if there had been any chance of a reconciliation, he would have made contact by now. As the days had gone by Kizzy had fallen into a hopeless despair, punctuated by moments of anger as well. How could he cut her out like this? Did she mean nothing to him? She hadn't meant to hurt anyone, or defy his wishes. Surely she'd have to have found out about Sarah at some point? Had Javier really thought he could keep on lying and hiding it all from her for ever?

These thoughts made her feel even worse. Kizzy realized how little she knew about Javier; maybe they'd never really had anything together. Their relationship—if you could even call it that—had been built on shifting sands. Sarah would always be there; Javier had made that clear from the very beginning. Kizzy was a fool. No matter how much she'd told him that she accepted the situation, she'd been kidding herself. Fatally, she'd hoped for a future with him.

Stupid, stupid girl. What must they all think of her? Sarah *was* Homelands for Javier, Mary, and the staff employed there to look after her. It was the one place Sarah could be kept safe, for the rest of them to try and find some kind of peace. And she, Kizzy, had gone barging in there, into a place where she'd had no right or privilege to be. They must all hate her, even Mary.

When Kizzy thought about never being in that kitchen again, never having a cosy cup of tea with the housekeeper, or walking with Salvador and Pablo in the grounds again, or at the very worst, being able to see her beloved Delly, she felt as if her heart would break. And at the centre of it all was Javier.

I've thrown it all away. I've got nothing.

Her phone started ringing and Kizzy had a fleeting moment of hope. *Javier.* She reached to her bedside table and looked at the screen. It was Lauren instead. Kizzy's spirits sank. She didn't want to talk to anyone at the moment, but Lauren was always upbeat and bubbly. At the last moment she answered.

'Hey.'

'Hey, girl! How you doing?'

'Oh, you know.'

Lauren sounded like she was in a bar. 'So listen, I'm just out shopping at the moment, but my cousin has given me two tickets for the opening night of that new club, Base, and whose name pops up in my head? The Kizmeister! We haven't been out in like, *for ever.*'

'I'm not sure, babe, I'm not in a great mood at

the moment.'

'All the more reason to come out! What are you doing otherwise? Hanging out with those smelly horses of yours?'

'I think I'm just going to stay in, actually.'

'Kizzy Milton, don't you dare give me that! Or the "I'm skint" line either; we'll get all our drinks bought for us.'

Despite everything, Kizzy had to laugh. 'You don't give up, do you?'

'*Somebody*'s got to save you from turning into an old granny! So what do you say, babe? You, me, cocktails, a boogie and little flirt with all the boys. Just like old times.'

Kizzy hadn't heard from Lauren in months, and she'd chosen now of all weeks to get in touch. Maybe it was a sign.

'All right, I'm in.'

*   *   *

Three hours later Kizzy was regretting the decision. The club, a converted town house just off Bedlington High Street, was packed to the rafters with punters screaming to be heard above the pounding house music. To be fair, most of them looked like they were enjoying themselves, and a couple next to Kizzy had been chewing each other's faces off for the last five minutes, but Kizzy really wasn't into it. Her feet hurt, she'd had her drink spilt down her top, and she'd lost Lauren ages ago. Looking around the rammed, wall-to-wall crowd of people, Kizzy didn't even know where to start looking for her.

A hand grabbed her bare shoulder and she

turned to see a sweaty-faced guy, leering. 'Can I buy you a drink?' His eyes travelled blatantly up and down her body.

'I'm fine, thanks.' He stank of booze. Kizzy turned away, hoping he'd get the message.

A few seconds later the hand was back, this time gripping her arm more persistently. 'Why can't I buy you a drink?' He went to touch her thigh. 'Nice legs, sexy.'

'Get lost!' She pushed him away. Where was Lauren?

The drunk guy's eyes narrowed. 'Who do you think you are? Stuck-up cow.'

Normally she would have let it go, but Kizzy's temper was frayed enough. 'Who do I think I am?' She fronted up. 'Who do you think *you* are? You're the one who came up and started ogling me like I'm a piece of meat.'

He swayed, eyes glinting over his lager bottle. 'Slag!'

'You all right, Kiz?' Freshly-shaved, and smelling of aftershave, Brett was standing there.

'Brett!' She'd never been so pleased to see anyone.

He gave the drunk bloke a challenging look. 'What's going on?'

'He's just really drunk.' It wasn't worth getting stressed about.

Brett frowned. 'I'd make myself scarce if I were you, buddy. The owner's a friend, so don't start hassling any more girls unless you want to get chucked out on your arse.'

Brett was a big guy and he wasn't looking friendly. The drunk went to say something and thought better of it. Muttering under his breath, he slunk off into the crowd.

'Thanks, Brett, you saved me.'

He grinned at her. 'No problem. What are you doing here by yourself, Kiz?'

'I'm not, I've lost Lauren.'

'All the same, babe,' he said reproachfully. 'Hot girls on their own are going to get the wrong type of attention.'

'You are funny. Still as protective as ever?'

'Hey, just looking out for the lady.'

Brett was looking good: his dark hair was cropped close to his head and carefully gelled, and he had a nice tan. The smart black blazer he was wearing had probably cost more than Kizzy's entire outfit put together.

'Can I buy you a drink?' he asked.

'Thanks, but I've kind of had enough. I think I'm going to call it a night.'

'Let me drive you home, then.'

She tried to protest, but he wouldn't hear of it. 'I'm only parked outside. I'm not having you walking home by yourself.'

They left, Brett guiding her by the elbow. Kizzy noticed quite a few girls giving her dirty looks when they clocked who she was with. Brett was obviously still quite a catch.

His car was parked a few spaces down the street: a sleek silver machine with curves in all the right places.

'Nice wheels,' she said, climbing in.

'BMW M3 Coupé, had it delivered last week.'

'You're obviously doing all right for yourself.' The BMW pulled out, past a queue of shivering people waiting to get in the club.

'Can't complain. I'm MD with my dad now, in

charge of a team of forty.'

'Well done.'

The leather seat was soft against her bare legs. Kizzy crossed one leg over the other and wished her shorts didn't ride up quite so high. A flicker of eye movement from Brett indicated he'd noticed the unintentional show of thigh.

'So what's new with you, Kiz? Got yourself a proper job yet?'

'Ha ha. Actually, the horse I'm looking after has made it to the Foxhunter at Cheltenham.'

'Cheltenham? That's a pretty big deal isn't it?'

'Just a bit,' she smiled. Brett had never understood her obsession with horses.

They carried on down the High Street, past a police car pulled up on the side of the road, and out of the town centre. 'I haven't seen you out for months,' Brett commented. 'What have you been up to?'

'This and that.'

'You OK?' Brett asked after a few minutes. 'You don't seem yourself.'

'Don't I? Sorry, I'm just a bit tired.' Her estate was coming up. 'It's the next left . . .'

He shot her a grin. 'I know where you live, Kizzy. It hasn't been that long.'

The BMW pulled up on the drive behind hers. 'How are your parents?' he asked.

'They're good.'

'And Dan?'

'Safe and well, touch wood.' She tapped the side of her head.

Brett nodded. 'That's good. Tell your dad I've got a couple of spare tickets for the Gloucester/Wasps match if he wants to come. One of my mates has got a box.'

'That's really nice of you.' Her dad had always approved of Brett: a man's man who'd looked after his daughter well. Kizzy reached for the handle. 'I'll let him know.'

'Get him to call me. Kiz.' Brett put his hand out. 'Hold on a minute.'

She turned. 'Yeah?'

'Why don't you give me a call as well?' His hand was still on her arm. 'I miss you, Kiz.'

She looked into the dark eyes. They'd always been his best feature: dark and fringed with long lashes. All the girls loved Brett's eyes. They still didn't have a tenth of the depth or emotion of Javier's.

'Oh, B.'

The leather creaked as he sat back in his seat. 'You got a fella?'

Kizzy sighed. 'No. Well . . .' She looked down at her lap. 'It's complicated.'

Brett didn't push it. 'He'd better be treating you well, I can tell when something's up with you.'

Kizzy turned her head to him. 'You're such a lovely guy. You know that?'

'How about I'm your guy again?' It was said with a confident twinkle, but she could tell he was nervous.

'You deserve more, believe me.'

'How do you know, if you won't give us a chance?'

'It's not that.' She put her hand on his knee. 'You've got so much to offer, but I can't give that *back*. Do you understand?'

'I never had you,' he said. 'I always knew it, really.'

She touched his face. 'Some girl is going to be so lucky to have you.'

When he leant forward to kiss her, Kizzy didn't stop him. It was a soft, aftershave-filled peck that made her feel nothing. She pulled away sensitively. ''Bye, babe.'

''Bye, Kiz.' She saw the flash of disappointment, before his handsome face resumed its untroubled look.

*   *   *

At the entrance to Shakespeare Drive, Javier watched Kizzy trip up the path. As she reached the front door, she turned back and smiled at the man, her lovely face happy. The BMW reversed back down the drive before flashing past, giving Javier a glimpse of the driver. He sat there in the dark for a few moments, before putting the car into first. As quietly as it had arrived, his black Land Cruiser disappeared back into the night.

CHAPTER EIGHTY-THREE

Calypso had been having a super-productive day. She'd spent three hours that morning driving all over the Cotswolds hand-delivering the funky new postcard flyers she'd had made up to advertise the all-new and improved Scene Events. Every bar, restaurant, deli, café and clothes shop had been on her hit list. The expedition had cost her two hundred pounds in flyers, eighty pounds in petrol and a sore bum from sitting down so long, but it was all part of her grand new master plan. If this didn't get new business, nothing would.

Not that Calypso would *ever* admit Archie had had anything to do with it, but she'd had a massive wake-up call. It was either the Cotswolds or London. She'd sat down with Camilla and Jed one night and worked out a business plan if she were to take up Olivia's offer and move Scene Events to the bright lights of the capital. It had proved just too expensive. As Camilla had pointed out for the millionth time, surely it was easier to stay and build up what she had here?

Calypso realized her sister was right. If Scene Events was going to become the company she wanted, it was down to her and no one else. She had a gold mine in her well-connected friends, which she hadn't made the most of. So Calypso had begged, borrowed and stolen all of their contacts, and put out a massive group email, bigging up Scene Events and offering a 25 per cent discount to anyone who made a booking in the next fourteen days. It was a bit cheeky, in a kind of SPAM-invading-people's-in-boxes kind of way, but Calypso didn't care. If she wanted to get somewhere, she had to be inventive.

It was exciting and nerve-racking, and by lunchtime that day her tactics had started to pay off. First she had an email from a millionaire who was opening a Cheltenham branch of his cool London bar, enquiring about Calypso's prices for putting on a red-carpet-style opening night. Next was a phone call from a Tatler-friendly socialite who lived in a mansion outside Bourton-on-the-Water, who wanted Calypso to put on an after-show soirée for her rock star friend.

After assuring the socialite she would indeed be able to provide something different, with lots of high drama, Calypso put the phone down and sighed happily. This was the kind of party she could get a year's worth of work from just because of the kind of people going. Amazing, cool work that would make Scene Events one of the best out there. Finally things were happening!

Up yours, Archie, she thought defiantly. *I'll bloody show you.*

*   *   *

Caro was flicking through Nigel Slater, wondering what to cook that evening. She had the whole family coming round. Camilla had offered to cook at hers, but Caro had insisted that she wanted to do it. As much normality as possible was essential at the moment and, besides, it kept her busy.

She was staring at the contents page, trying to make the words register, when her mobile rang. It was a private number.

'Hello?'

'Caro?' A heavy accent.

Caro's stomach dropped. 'Suzette?'

'Yes. I hope I have not inconvenienced you by calling.'

She sounded positively ingratiating. Caro stared across the kitchen. Why was she calling? 'No, you haven't.'

'Good.' There was an awkward pause. 'Caro, I was wondering if we would be able to meet up and talk.'

'I tried to talk to you before, and you weren't interested.'

537

'I know, forgive me.' Suzette gave an embarrassed laugh. 'I was a little, how do you say it, *thrown*. I was not expecting to see you there.'

'I was surprised to see you, too.' Caro sighed. 'Suzette, I think it's a little too late for talking, don't you? What is it you want to say?'

'Will you come over here? I'd prefer to talk in person.'

'Is Sebastian there?'

'No, he is at work.'

'Does he know you're calling me?'

Suzette hesitated for a split second. 'No.'

Despite everything, Caro's interest was piqued. 'I've got to pick Rosie up from nursery in an hour.'

'It won't take long, I promise. I'd be so grateful. Please, Caro.'

*   *   *

Suzette was dressed in her usual black, and, if such a thing was possible, she looked like she'd lost weight. Her watchful, feline eyes seemed almost too big for her thin face. She double-kissed Caro in a mist of Thierry Mugler's Angel on the doorstep. 'Please, come in.'

The living room table had already been set out with dainty little biscuits and a cafetière of freshly brewed coffee. Suzette ushered Caro over to the French Louis XV armchair, and sat down on a hard-backed chair opposite. She busied herself pouring out the coffee. She was wearing the antique diamond ring Caro had admired before, the only flash of opulence in her otherwise minimal surroundings.

The coffee was strong and bitter. 'What was it

538

you wanted to talk to me about?'

'Ah yes.' Suzette placed her mug down. 'Caro, perhaps I haven't been as open with you as I should have.'

'What do you mean?'

'Sebastian. He is my world. I was in a very unhappy relationship before we met, with a man incapable of showing any love back. Too many years wasted.' Suzette twisted the diamond on her bony finger. 'I am lucky to have a second chance. When you get to my age and find the man you are meant to be with, it makes you feel very . . . blessed.'

Caro never expected such a baring of emotion. Where was Suzette going with this?

'I would do anything to make him as happy as he has made me,' Suzette said. 'Despite how he might seem, he is a very different man underneath. Vulnerable.'

'Are you talking about him having counselling? He told me it never happened.'

Suzette flushed. 'His issues, they are all true, you know. He told me, and I believe him. I did tell him it wasn't wise to lie about the counselling, but he said you would use it against him otherwise.'

Caro wasn't about to concede the point. 'Suzette, do you want me to have sympathy for Sebastian?'

'No. I understand that is . . . difficult for you.' The dark eyes fixed on her. 'Despite what you think of Sebastian, he is not a monster. He truly believes Milo should be with him. I know he perhaps hasn't gone about things in the best way, but that is Sebastian. He has changed, Caro. He just wants the best for us, a better life. Surely you can't begrudge him that?'

'And Milo?' Caro said sharply. 'Do you both want a better life for him?'

Suzette flushed again. 'Of course that is what I meant,' she murmured.

Caro rubbed her hands over her knees. 'Suzette, I appreciate you asking me over here, but this is difficult.'

'I agree. I just wanted you to know, from one woman to another, that I wouldn't seek to find myself in this position. I know I can't understand how, as a mother, you must be feeling . . .'

'No, you can't.'

Suzette leant forward, giving Caro a flash of bony chest. 'But I still have feelings, Caro! It has taken its toll on me as well.'

Her chin trembled, as if she was about to cry. Caro couldn't help but feel a bit sorry for her. No one thought about the partner in these situations. 'I know it's hard for you as well.'

'I just want to support the man I love. Whatever happens, I hope that one day we can be cordial, Caro. So you know I am not some evil person, but a human being with real thoughts and feelings.'

Caro studied the tight, pale face. Suzette did seem genuine. It would be good to have an ally in Sebastian's camp, even in the unlikely form of his girlfriend.

'Thanks, Suzette, I appreciate us having this chat.' She stood up and reached for her bag. 'I really must get Rosie.'

'Before you go . . .' Suzette smiled hesitantly. 'Could I ask your advice on something I have just bought? I'd appreciate a woman's opinion.'

'I'm not sure my taste is quite up to yours,' Caro said wryly.

'*Au contraire.* Please, come upstairs.'

She took Caro into the spare room, where a painting stood against the wall. 'What do you think?'

'It's stunning.' The silvery rooftops of a city landscape shimmered off the canvas at her.

'You like?' Suzette sounded pleased. 'It is by Aubrey, an up-and-coming artist from Paris. Sebastian, he likes more abstract art, but I saw this and fell in love. And so good to support new talent, *non*?'

'*Non.* I mean *oui.* It's really lovely, Suzette.'

'Thank you.' She was standing close enough for Caro to smell her perfume again. 'And now you must go, little Rose will be waiting.'

At the bottom of the steps Suzette picked up Caro's handbag. 'Don't forget this.'

'I don't think I'd get very far if I did.' She turned to face Suzette, so close she could see the little blue veins under Suzette's eyes. 'What do you think, Suzette? About Milo? Do you think it's the right decision for him to come and live with you?'

'What do you mean?' She didn't seem to understand the question.

'Do *you* want Milo to come and live with you?'

'Of course!' She nodded her dark head assuredly. 'I adore Milo. He is Sebastian's flesh and blood, is he not?'

Caro didn't say anything. If Sebastian ever did tire of Milo, would Suzette do the same? Caro suddenly felt very afraid for her son.

She was halfway down the path when Suzette called out again. 'Caro!'

'Yes?' Suzette was still standing in the doorway, wearing an expression Caro couldn't quite

541

decipher. 'Suzette?'

The curtain of composure was drawn across again. 'It was nothing, I forget. Goodbye, Caro.' She smiled briefly and shut the door.

CHAPTER EIGHTY-FOUR

Caro took her chance while they were alone in the kitchen. 'I went to see Suzette today.'

Benedict looked up from uncorking another bottle of Prosecco. 'Right . . .'

'She rang me this morning.'

Her husband put the bottle on the side. 'What on earth for?'

The rest of the family were sitting in the garden, enjoying an aperitif. It was warm enough to sit outside, providing you had a jacket or jumper on. Jed was just firing up the giant heater that sat on the patio.

'It was some kind of peace offering; quite bizarre.' Caro glanced out of the window. Calypso had her hand in the bowl of Kettle Chips, devouring them. 'I actually think Suzette feels quite guilty.'

'So she should,' he said shortly.

'I know, darling, but it's made me think a bit. I've never once considered things from Suzette's perspective. It must be really difficult, being dragged into a situation that has nothing to do with you. She was saying earlier that all she wanted to do was support Sebastian.'

'Is that why she invited you over? To show she's not all bad? I bet Sebastian bloody put her up to it, to try and get things out of you. '

'Sebastian didn't know.'

Benedict raised an eyebrow. 'Really?'

'That's what she said. I don't know, darling. Why else would Suzette have me round?' Caro frowned. 'It know it sounds silly, but it felt like she was trying to *reach* out to me.'

*   *   *

Benedict had excelled himself. After a dinner of spring Cotswolds lamb served with cucumber raita and perfectly roasted new potatoes, picked only that morning from Clementine's vegetable patch, the six adults sat round the table, watching the night sky darken into purple. Somewhere at the end of the garden two birds were calling to each other.

'Benedict, I swear you should go on *Masterchef*,' Calypso said. She was looking very elfin in a big camouflage parka, her blonde hair spilling out over the hood.

'It really was excellent,' Clementine agreed. 'I will have to give the recipe to the WI. I'd never think of putting cucumber with lamb, but it worked wonderfully.'

It had been a lovely evening. For once they'd all studiously avoided the subject of the court case and concentrated on good food and company instead of on the family.

'Hey, Camilla's got some news,' Calypso announced. They all looked at her, sitting next to Jed. He had his arm round her.

'Good news?' Caro said enquiringly. 'We could do with some of that!'

The pair looked at each other and grinned.

'Go on!' Calypso urged. 'If you don't bloody tell

543

them, I will.'

'Well.' Camilla took Jed's hand. 'Jed and I have decided to try and adopt.'

There was a stunned happy pause. 'Oh, dear boy, dear girl!' Clementine exclaimed. 'What wonderful news!'

There were handshakes and embraces all round. 'This is so great, guys!' Caro said, giving Jed a big hug. 'Why didn't you say anything before?'

'Oh, I don't know,' Camilla said. 'I just felt a bit bad with all that's been going on . . .'

Suddenly there was a loud hammering on the front door. They all jumped. 'Who the hell is that?' Benedict frowned.

The pounding started again, along with a muffled shout.

'What on earth is going on?' Clementine exclaimed.

'I don't know, but I'm going to find out.' Benedict threw down his napkin and got up. 'Stay here, darling,' he told Caro.

'No, I'm coming.' As they walked into the hallway, a sleepy eyed Milo was standing at the top of the stairs holding his teddy bear. 'What's going on?'

'Nothing, champ,' Benedict told him. 'Go back to bed now.'

'*Police, open up!*'

The police? Caro and Benedict stared at each other. What were they doing here?

'What if it's about Mummy or Daddy?' Caro said fearfully.

'This is your final warning!' The male voice brokered no discussion. 'Open up or we're going to have to force our way in.'

'For God's sake!' Benedict rushed over to the front door. 'This has to be a mistake, you've got the wrong address or something . . .'

Three uniformed police officers—two men and a woman—filled the front porch. The biggest male officer stepped forward. 'Does a Caroline Towey live here?'

Benedict glanced back at his wife. 'Yes, but why do you want to know that?'

'I'm Caro Towey.' She stepped forward. 'What's this about?'

The officer had what looked like a piece of A4 paper in his hand. He held it up so Caro could see the address of the local magistrates' court across the top.

'What's going on?' Benedict was as confused as she was.

The police officer shook the piece of paper. 'We have a search warrant for these premises. We have information that stolen property and Class A drugs are being kept here.'

'What?' Benedict said, aghast. 'This is some kind of joke!'

'I can assure you we're serious.' The policeman gave the warrant to Benedict and stepped in.

Caro had a fleeting glimpse of her children's scared faces at the top of the stairs. 'You heard my husband. There's been some kind of horrible mistake!'

Without waiting for an invite, the female police officer went straight into the living room. Caro chased after her. 'There are no drugs or stolen goods here!'

The rest of her family came through, their faces dropping with shock as they saw the three police officers in the house.

'What's going on here?' Jed asked.

'There's been a mistake!' Caro repeated. Benedict followed her in, his face ashen. 'Caro, they're saying you went on to private property and stole an item of significant value.'

'What?' She laughed out loud. 'That's ridiculous!'

She watched as the female officer picked up her handbag and put it on the coffee table. 'Excuse me, what are you doing?' she cried, as the woman started to pull things out. 'You can't just come in here and start rifling through my stuff!'

Benedict put a hand on her arm. 'Just let them do it.'

'Fine!' Caro crossed her arms and watched. One by one her personal belongings were brought out: purse, diary, hairbrush, lipstick, wet wipes, an empty flapjack wrapper.

'See?' she said defiantly. 'I can't imagine what you thought you were going to find.'

The female officer opened the side pocket inside and put her hand in.

'There's nothing in there but some of my daughter's hair grips,' Caro started to tell her, but suddenly something else was brought out. Something small and shiny that Caro knew she'd seen before . . .

'Hang on a minute, that's Suzette's ring!' she said, totally baffled.

'So you do claim to know it?' asked the first officer.

'Yes I *know* it, but I have no idea what it's doing in there.' She turned to Benedict. 'I don't understand how that got in my bag . . .'

546

'Sir, there's something else.' The female officer brought out a small white packet. Flat, it was rectangular in shape and looked like it had been wrapped in cling film. Caro frowned; was it an old bit of chewing gum? She watched as it was handed over and the package held up to the light in a male police officer's hand.

'Oh my God,' she heard Calypso say faintly, and then the man in charge turned to her, his face as stern as anything she'd ever seen.

'Caroline Towey, I'm arresting you on suspicion of handling stolen goods and being in possession of Class A drugs. You do not have to say anything, but it may harm your defence . . .'

CHAPTER EIGHTY-FIVE

It was a horrible nightmare. In front of her own children, Caro had the indignity of being handcuffed and marched out to the patrol car outside. Benedict wasn't allowed to go with her, and the last thing Caro saw was Granny Clem at the front door, trying to usher a confused Milo and Rosie upstairs. Rosie had wanted to go with her, and Caro had left the house to the sound of her little girl's screams and cries. It was the most distressing thing she'd ever heard.

Down at the police station she was booked in in front of the custody sergeant and put in a tiny cell, no bigger than her double bed at home. Her one phone call went straight to Benedict, who had already spoken to Louise Rennison, who in turn had recommended someone from her sister firm, who practised criminal law.

Caro had to wait three hours in a bare little room that smelt of stale sweat and urine, with nothing more than a plastic mattress and an open toilet. She still wasn't allowed to see anyone bar her new lawyer, who turned up in less than an hour.

Guy Glanville was tall, thin, and as sharp as a tack. He listened to Caro's side of the story, provided tissues, and advised her to speak openly and freely, telling the truth.

It wasn't going to be as easy as that. By the time she was hauled into the interview room, in front of DS Partridge and DC McBeth, Caro was tired, emotional and shell-shocked. The situation was quickly put to her. Caro had been invited to Bluebell Cottage, Bedlington Road, Churchminster, by the occupant, one Suzette Strasbourg. Ms Strasbourg had said she wanted to talk in a conciliatory manner about the ongoing residence order over the son Caro had with Ms Strasbourg's new partner, Sebastian Belmont. During the conversation, Caro had made several references to using cocaine, and asked Suzette at one point if she had ever used it. When Ms Strasbourg had said no, Caro had then brought a small white packet of an unknown substance out of her handbag and suggested that she and Ms Strasbourg 'do a line' together. Ms Strasbourg had become uncomfortable, and asked Caro to leave, but had discovered some time later that a valuable diamond ring of hers, which Caro had admired on previous occasions, had gone missing. Ms Strasbourg had waited until her partner, Mr Sebastian Belmont, had returned from work, and then the two of them had made the decision to call the police.

Caro was beside herself. 'Do a line?' She'd never said anything remotely like it in her life. Her pleas fell on deaf ears. At 2 a.m. she was released on bail, pending further inquiries, to reappear at the police station in four to six weeks. Benedict, who had been waiting outside in reception all the time, was incandescent as he drove them home.

'Just when I thought that piece of scum couldn't stoop any lower.' He slammed his hand down on the steering wheel. 'The damn bastard set you up!'

'Benedict, don't.' Caro couldn't believe it. She felt like a common criminal.

He glanced at her face and controlled himself. 'It will all be disproved.' He put his hand on her thigh. 'They absolutely have no case against you.'

'They have, though! Benedict, you weren't there.' Caro was convinced the police officers didn't believe her. Only last month there'd been an article in the *Daily Telegraph* about the rise of cocaine addiction amongst middle-class housewives. What if the police thought she was one of those people?

'I could go to prison.' Panic was starting to win over reason.

'You are not going to prison,' Benedict said firmly. 'You heard what Guy Glanville said. At the very worst, you'll end up with a fine and a community service order.'

'And a criminal record.' She felt sick. 'How are the family courts going to view that?'

'You're going to be fine,' Benedict repeated quietly. His shoulders were rigid.

They drove the rest of the way home in silence. Benedict pulled the Porsche up outside the house and cut the engine. 'Here we are.'

Caro sat in her seat for a moment before bursting into tears. 'I can't bear it! What have we done to deserve this?'

Benedict was clearly distraught and furious himself. He reached across and cradled her in his arms. 'Oh, my darling.' He kissed her hair. 'I can't bear what that bastard is putting you through.'

Caro clung to him as if she were hanging on to a rock for dear life in a ferocious storm.

*   *   *

Louise Rennison rang at half past seven that morning. 'I haven't woken you?'

'No.' She hadn't slept a wink. Caro sat down on the top step of the stairs clutching the phone, and stared at her slippered feet.

Louise was as calm and professional as ever. 'Are you happy with the instruction you are receiving from Guy Glanville?'

'Yes, he seems very competent.'

'Good. I'm pleased.'

'Louise, I didn't do any of these things!' Caro burst out. 'The nearest I've come to drugs is a puff of a joint at university. I would never bring that stuff into our home.'

There was a pause. 'I know, Caro,' Louise said quietly.

Caro looked down the stairs. The postman had been already; a few white envelopes were scattered on the mat. 'The court will have to know about this, won't they?'

'I'm afraid so, yes.'

'My next appearance at court is right about the same time as the final hearing. Great timing, eh?'

'It's not ideal.'

Louise had never been one to sugar-coat things, and Caro was grateful for that. 'This could drag on for months. Even if I do get found not guilty, it could be too late, couldn't it?'

She heard the lawyer sigh. 'It's hard to measure these things, Caro. It could depend on how strongly District Justice Madhabi feels about drugs.'

'You always told me that as long as the four biggies weren't involved—drugs, domestic violence, mental disorders or criminal convictions—we had a pretty strong case. Well, I've got two out of those four. It's not looking good, is it?'

Louise took a long time to answer. 'No, I'm afraid it isn't.'

*   *   *

When Caro put the phone down afterwards, she just sat there. Tears filled her eyes, dissolving the envelopes by the front door into fuzzy shapes. Putting her head between her knees, she started to cry. She'd lost him. Her darling, precious, irreplaceable son.

'Oh, darling,' she wept to herself. 'Mummy's let you down. I'm so sorry.'

Someone touched her gently on the shoulder. Milo was standing there in his dinosaur-patterned pyjamas, cowlick ruffled.

'Mummy? Why are you crying?'

Caro hastily wiped her eyes. 'Mummy just got something in her eye, sweet pea, don't worry.'

Her son crouched down and put his arm round her. He smelt of sleep and sweetness, the kind of innocent, untouched smell only little children had.

551

'Don't be sad, Mummy. I love you.'

Caro put her arms round him and it took all she had to stop herself howling. 'Oh, my darling. I love you, so very much too.'

CHAPTER EIGHTY-SIX

Next day

Cheryl Pike tottered down her front path on to the green. Normally she'd drive round to the shop, but the Range Rover had been making a funny noise and was in the garage, so Cheryl was stuck without wheels until later. Which meant she'd have to suffer the indignity of using her own two feet if she wanted some more milk for her afternoon cup of tea. Cheryl didn't do walking, unless it was the three kilometres she did on the treadmill in the conservatory every morning to *Kylie's Greatest Hits* on the iPod.

Still, it was a lovely day. Maybe she and Barry could go for a Pimm's in the pub garden later when he got back from work. They wouldn't eat there: Pierre was a little heavy on the butter and cream side for Cheryl's liking, and Barry preferred her home-cooked grub anyway. Eggs, chips and peas, and he was as happy as a pig in muck. Cheryl preferred a nice salad herself. *A second on the lips, a lifetime on the hips* was a mantra she heavily subscribed to.

As she walked in to the village shop, Brenda Briggs was behind the counter deep in the latest edition of *FHM*. ''Ere, Cheryl, you'll never guess what I'm reading about: this dwarf and his deep-frozen poo poo.'

552

'I don't think I want to know.' Cheryl pushed her Versace sunglasses up on her head and went over to the chiller. 'The bloody Ocado man forgot my skimmed milk again. What are we paying them for?' She came back to the counter with a carton. 'I tell you; I've had a day of it, Brenda. First I broke one of my nails and had to get my technician out on an emergency call, then the Sky Plus didn't record *Neighbours*, and now I've had to walk all the way round here in my Jimmy Choos and ruined the heels. I mean, what's going on?'

Brenda made a sympathetic noise. 'I've saved you a copy of the new *25 Beautiful Kitchens*, if that makes you any happier.'

'Thanks, babes.' Cheryl snapped open her massive Dior clutch bag. 'What are you wearing to Cheltenham?'

'Ooh, I dunno. I hadn't really thought about it.' Brenda leant on her elbows on the counter and looked enviously at Cheryl's stick-thin figure. 'What about you? Bet you've got something lovely and glam.'

'Yeah, I've had this amazing jumpsuit made. In Nobby's colours. With a *stunning* pair of heels from Roberto Cavalli.'

Brenda looked knowledgeable. 'Arabic, is he?'

'Something like that.' Cheryl handed over a fifty-pound note for the milk. ''Ere.'

Cheryl had important things to mull over as she trotted back round the green. Brenda had got her thinking about her outfit again. What nail polish was she going to wear? Bright purple to match her outfit, of course, but was it going to be the Dark Angel by MAC or the Christian Dior? MAC did do a lovely deep colour, but Dior never chipped . . .

There was a car parked ahead on the side of the green. Cheryl recognized it straight away: that little Aston Martin owned by Caro's ex-fella and his snooty French bird. The girlfriend—Susan, she thought her name was—was standing against the driver's door gabbling away into her mobile.

Cheryl stopped dead in front of the car. It was right in her way! You couldn't just pull up and park where you liked. Bloody foreigners, they hadn't got a clue.

'Excuse me? You're blocking the *road*,' Cheryl said exaggeratedly. The woman probably couldn't understand her, anyway.

Suzette shot her a cursory look and turned her back on Cheryl. She gesticulated wildly with her free hand. *'Oui! Oui!'*

Cheryl started to walk deliberately slowly round the car, making her point. What a rude cow!

*   *   *

Caro was staring out of the living room window when a turquoise-clad figure walked up the front path. It was Cheryl in matching pedal pushers and a tight Juicy Couture T-shirt. Caro went to duck behind the curtain, but it was too late. Cheryl lifted a gold-encrusted wrist and waved.

Moments later the doorbell rung. Caro blinked tiredly. Running her hands over her face, she willed herself to look relatively normal and went to get the door.

'Hi, Cheryl.'

'Hello, Carol. You'll never guess who I just bumped into? Sebastian's bit of fluff, Susan. She was parked on the green like she owned the place.

554

I could have got killed walking in the road. She was lucky there was no cars around.'

Cheryl was like a parakeet: all noise and squawks and garish colours. It was making Caro's head hurt.

'. . . I mean, the only reason I walked over there in the first place is because the Range Rover's in the garage. She wouldn't have been so hoity flipping toity if I'd driven up in the Ferrari . . .'

Caro hadn't eaten, hadn't slept. She also hadn't cried for five minutes, which was a record. As Cheryl started on about how Suzette had nearly made her step in a pile of horse poo and break her neck, Caro finally snapped.

'For God's sake, you ridiculous woman! And my bloody name is *Caro*!' As Cheryl's lipsticked mouth fell into a shocked 'O', Caro slammed the door in her face. She stormed off down the hallway, ignoring the muffled squawk outside.

'B-but wait! I've got something really important to tell you!'

CHAPTER EIGHTY-SEVEN

That evening
People could say what they liked about Brenda Briggs, but they couldn't accuse her of having a dirty house. Every inch of Hollyoaks Cottage was always scrubbed, swept and dusted to within an inch of its life. 'You could eat your dinner off my kitchen floor,' Brenda was fond of saying. In fact, her husband Ted once had, when he'd come back late and drunk from the Rotary Club dinner, and Brenda had thrown his egg and chips at him.

Brenda was happily beating the living daylights out of the hallway rug in the back garden. It was one of those glorious Cotswold evenings when the air smelt good and everything was green and ripe and lush amongst Brenda's collection of gnomes. In the oak trees at the bottom of the garden, the blackbirds' chatter would give Brenda a run for her money.

Brenda gave the rug another wallop with Ted's old tennis racket, feeling it work her bingo wings. After talking to Cheryl, she'd been busily thinking about her own Cheltenham outfit. It sounded like pink was the colour to wear, and Brenda had a lovely cat jumper with sequins for eyes, which would go well with her sparkly trainers. Or should she go really smart with the plastic mac she'd just bought from the stall on Bedlington market? It was a dead ringer for the one Brenda had seen Jenny Eclair wearing on *Loose Women*, and probably a tenth of the price.

Suddenly the sound of shouting erupted from next door. Brenda stopped mid-*thwack*, ears quivering like a terrier's. They never heard much from Sebastian and Suzette, unless Suzette was playing her opera music full blast out of the bathroom window. Brenda had had a mind to go round there about it, but her Ted, knowing about opera because he had a lovely baritone himself, had told his wife to keep her beak out. 'Raises the tone of the neighbourhood,' he'd said. 'It could be bloody Meatloaf.' The cheek of it! He was only saying that because he knew Brenda wanted 'Bat Out Of Hell' played at her funeral.

There was more shouting. Suzette was babbling away in French now, so Brenda didn't have a clue what she was talking about. She sounded pretty upset, though. Brenda put the tennis racket down and crept up to the fence. Suzette might seem a bit up herself, but that—as Beryl Turner had explained—was only because she was French. She was actually all right. She kept her garden nice and tidy, which Brenda approved of, and had even given Brenda some lovely bubble bath and body lotion she hadn't wanted. It had had some posh label Brenda couldn't pronounce, but it had been a nice thought. It was a pity Brenda couldn't say the same for old Smarmy Pants Sebastian. He might have come round with a bottle of bubbly when they'd moved in, but as far as Brenda was concerned a leopard didn't change its spots. The champagne was still in the cupboard under the kitchen sink, as Ted was a real ale man and Brenda didn't drink. Who did Sebastian think he was, coming in here with his fancy ways?

The back door flew open and Suzette came storming out. Her normally composed face was agitated and tear-streaked. 'I can't do it any more, Sebastian!' She stood on the patio, breathing heavily and hugging her body with her thin arms.

He followed moments later, shirtsleeves rolled up from the office. 'For God's sake, darling! Can we stop with the histrionics?'

'It is not histrionics!' Suzette shrugged Sebastian's hand off her. 'Caro is a nice woman.'

Brenda was agog. This was better than being in the front row at *The Jeremy Kyle Show*! They were so caught up in their argument that neither of them realized she was there. Brenda didn't think to move inside; besides, she'd been out there first.

'Caro is a manipulative bitch, Suzette.' For once

Mr Smarmy Pants didn't look so pleased with himself. 'Haven't I told you that enough?'

'She is the mother of your child! How can you say such a thing?'

Sebastian stared at her with his ice-blue eyes for a moment, then sighed heavily. 'She's got to you as well, hasn't she? My own girlfriend, the love of my life, taking the side of my ex-wife . . .'

Brenda rolled her eyes; anyone could see the silly sod was playing with Suzette's heartstrings, but the poor cow looked like she was falling for it. Her pale face faltered, expression unsure. 'I just . . . isn't there another way?'

'No. We've talked about this,' Sebastian said smoothly. 'All I want is for us to be happy.' He put his arms round her. 'That's what you want, isn't it, my darling? For us to be one happy family?'

The French woman's scrawny shoulders sagged. '*Oui*. I am sorry, Sebastian. All this, it has just got to me.'

'Of *course* it has,' Sebastian said, as if talking to a child. 'Have you taken your spirulina today? You know how overwrought you get without it.' As he kissed the top of Suzette's head, his eyes came to rest on Brenda. They widened with surprise, before being replaced by their usual smugness. 'Well, well, Brenda. Spying on us, were you?'

'Bloody cheek!' Brenda lied. 'I was doing no such thing.'

Suzette touched Sebastian's arm. 'Don't, darling. Brenda is our neighbour.'

He gave an irritated tut. 'Oh, who gives a shit, darling? The sooner I can stop pretending to actually *like* this backwater and its inbreds, the better.'

Brenda was outraged. 'Now you just hang on a minute . . .'

Sebastian's doorbell rang from inside the house.

* * *

Caro took her finger off the buzzer and stepped back.

'You all right?' Cheryl was standing beside her, silver handbag under her arm like a weapon.

Caro nodded. She was calm, powerfully so. The rage of half an hour ago had sharpened her mind, bringing everything into clear focus. For the first time in months, she had no fear or worry. *I know what to do.*

She pressed the buzzer again. If no one answered, Caro would start knocking instead, until someone did. Even if the skin on her knuckles started to tear and bleed.

Loud footsteps approached and the front door was pulled open. Sebastian stood there, nauseatingly oily in his expensive pink shirt and red braces.

'Yes?' He looked down his nose at her. 'I'm afraid we can't allow *convicted criminals* on the premises.'

'I haven't been convicted of anything.' Caro heard her voice, as calm as a flat sea in summer.

'Yet.' Sebastian looked at Cheryl, no pretence of being nice this time. 'What's she doing here?'

'She's with me.'

'*She's with me,*' Sebastian mimicked in a horrible baby voice. 'What's this, Caro, brought your friend along to fight your battles?'

'Sebastian.' Suzette appeared at his elbow, a

559

slight puffiness round her eyes the only indication that anything was amiss.

She gave Caro a cautious look. 'What is it, Caro?'

Caro stared her out, until Suzette eventually dropped her eyes. 'I know what you've been up to,' Caro said, turning back to Sebastian.

He raised an eyebrow. 'And what might that be? Apart from rescuing my son from the clutches of his degenerate mother?'

'I *know*,' Caro said, this time louder. 'About your plans for Milo's inheritance. The only reason you went for sole custody was to make it really difficult for me to see him, wasn't it? And the only way I would have had any relationship with Milo again was if I made Milo's inheritance over to you, and made you the only executor. A desperate mother, who would do anything to get her son back . . .'

Sebastian's expression didn't change, but the shock on Suzette's gave the game away.

Caro's calm started to slip away. She wanted to fly at Sebastian and gouge his eyes out, mark his flesh with her fury. How dare he! With a superhuman effort, she controlled herself. 'You were going to squander Milo's money, that *my father* gave him for your own means!'

'Oh, Caro, you really have lost it now,' he sneered. Caro ignored him and turned to Suzette.

'It's true, isn't it?' she said steadily.

Suzette's chin quivered defiantly for a moment, then her face crumpled. She put her manicured hands up to it, and started weeping.

'I am sorry, Caro, but we need the money. It is the only way.'

'Shut up, you stupid bitch,' Sebastian hissed. His

features rearranged themselves into a mask of calm malevolence. 'So what if I am? You're not the only one entitled to a dream life you know.'

Cheryl gave a little gasp. 'Why, you . . .'

Caro's hands bunched into white fists by her sides. 'So you admit it?'

'I told you it would come to this!' Suzette fled weeping into the depths of the house. Sebastian gave a cursory glance after his girlfriend and leant on the door frame, hands in pockets.

'Admit what, darling? That for the first time in twenty years I'm getting a little tired of the five a.m. starts and twelve-hour days at my desk to keep *your* leeching self in the manner you've become accustomed to?'

Caro actually laughed out loud. 'I don't leech anything off you. The only money I've ever taken is maintenance payments for *our* son, after you cheated throughout *our* marriage.'

'Yes, well.' Sebastian studied a well-groomed fingernail. 'Any real man would play away from home if they were married to the likes of you.'

He glanced up to see her reaction, but Caro kept calm. She planted her legs firmly, matching his pose. 'What about your savings? The bonus you told Benedict and me about?'

His nasty smile faltered for a second. 'Yes, well, maybe I didn't escape as lightly from the banking crisis as I made out. It happened to the best of us, you know.'

Caro let his words hang in the air. 'So basically you've done this whole thing—framed me for drugs and stealing, and made out I'm a bad mother—for financial gain? Just so you can get out of the city and start again?'

'Something like that.' Sebastian sounded utterly bored, as if he was having a conversation about the weather, not admitting to trying to destroy her life. 'Sorry, darling, but I'm not going to be one of those stupid bastards who drops dead at his desk aged fifty, while his wife is busy fucking the gardener at their six-bed pile in the Home Counties.' He smiled easily. 'Suz and I have found this super little chateau in the Loire. Vineyards, three hundred acres, the lot. Main house is spectacular, needs a couple of hundred thou spent doing it up. Of course, money's not what it was, and my London place has taken a hit, so . . .'

'And Milo? Where does he fit in while you lounge round in the sun drinking wine?'

Sebastian watched a car drive past. 'Prep school, and then Wellington College of course, like his pater. Once you do the honourable thing and sign on the dotted line, adding in a few new clauses of course, you can have the little bundle of joy back as much as you want. Hell, have him *all* the time. Holidays, Christmas, bar mitzvahs. He'll only be bored out of his brains at boarding school otherwise.'

Sebastian wasn't just a smug bastard; he was rotten to the core.

'You had it all planned out, didn't you?' she asked.

'Pretty much.' He checked his watch and yawned. 'Well, as much as I've enjoyed this, I've got things to be getting on with.'

Suzette appeared back on the doorstep, eyes red-rimmed. 'There, there.' Sebastian put his arm round her. 'Let's get you inside, away from these lunatics. Because that's what people will think if you ever try to put this story about, Caro.'

'Before we go,' he hovered on the door, looking intrigued. 'How *did* you find out? About our plans. Not that it matters now, of course, but I am rather surprised. I thought you were too stupid to work it out.'

Cheryl stepped forward in a jangle of gold. 'So you did, sunshine. I overheard *her*,'—she jerked her head at Suzette—'talking to someone about what you two were up to.'

Sebastian shot his girlfriend a murderous look.

'My sister,' Suzette murmured, not meeting his eye. 'I had to talk to someone, Sebastian! This whole thing has been very upsetting for me.' She turned to Cheryl, looking at her properly for the first time. 'You speak French?'

'Course I do, you silly cow.' Cheryl's tone was pure acid. 'Me and Baz had a villa in St Tropez for five years, how else did you think I got my acrylics done?'

The other two looked stunned for a moment, then Sebastian laughed out loud. 'Well now, Cheryl, we obviously underestimated you.'

Caro put her foot in the door. 'Cheryl's not the only one you've underestimated,' she said quietly.

Sebastian sighed. 'What's this? Some pathetic last-ditch attempt to get me to change my mind? Sorry, darling, but you should know me better by now.'

'I could say the same to you.'

He frowned as Caro produced the small silver device from her pocket. 'What the hell's that?'

'I'm surprised you don't know.' Caro looked at the machine. 'You used something very similar when you recorded Benedict and me that time.'

She watched confusion, realization, and then rage ripple across his face. 'You fucking bitch.'

Her moment of triumph was clouded by the rank disappointment Milo had such an award-winning shit for a father. Caro tucked the recorder back in her pocket. 'I think that just about wraps things up.'

It was like watching a great statue fall apart. Sebastian's face caved in, his body crumpling like a broken deckchair. He advanced over the threshold, angry spittle flecking colourless lips. 'Give me the recorder, you devious bitch!'

Caro found herself staring into the eyes of a madman. She started backing away.

'It's all right, Carol, I've got my rape alarm!' Cheryl shouted, but just then there was a squeal of brakes. Like something out of an action film Granny Clem's Volvo Estate skidded up on the front lawn, Benedict behind the wheel. He jumped out in his work suit, tie flapping over his shoulder. Three steps and he'd hooked his fist firmly under Sebastian's chin, sending him flying back into the flowerbeds.

'Come near my wife again and I'll knock you into the next century.'

Sebastian lay groaning on his back. 'Jesus! I think you've broken my jaw.'

'Oh my God, Benedict!' Cheryl squawked. 'That was so sexy! Just like Jean-Claude Van Damme.'

With a final contemptuous look at Sebastian to make sure he wasn't seriously injured, Benedict put his arm round his wife and they walked off. Suzette gave a whimper. Cheryl picked up her Louis Vuitton handbag and shook her head.

'Get shot of him, love. Otherwise you're going to end up in that dirt as well.'

564

Behind next door's net curtains Brenda was already reaching for the phone. *Hell's bells!* They'd seen some things in this village, but nothing like this. Churchminster's grapevine was about to go into meltdown.

CHAPTER EIGHTY-EIGHT

'The sad thing is, I think she really loves him.' Caro lifted her glass so Benedict could refill it with ice-cold Moët. The whole family had gathered in the living room at No. 1 Mill House to celebrate the fabulous turn of events. A jubilant Louise Rennison had called earlier. Sebastian had dropped the custody battle, and both he and Suzette had withdrawn their charges against Caro.

Calypso shook out her mane of hair. 'Then Suzette's more of a stupid cow than I thought . . .'

'I know, but she's under Sebastian's spell. It's what he does to people.' Caro sighed. 'I wouldn't like to be in Suzette's shoes right now. You know how Sebastian will take all this out on her.'

'You're really not going to go any further with it?' Granny Clem was upright in the armchair by the fire, two fingers of champagne in the bottom of her glass.

Caro felt her whole family's eyes on her. 'We've won, anyway. Milo is staying, and that's all that ever mattered. Sebastian has his own repercussions to deal with: he's missing out on a relationship with the most wonderful little boy in the world.' Caro shook her head. 'I don't want to waste any more time or energy on some hellish revenge.'

'Some might call it justice,' Granny Clem said shrewdly.

'As far as I'm concerned, justice has been done.' Caro had agonized long and hard, but she'd made her decision. Sebastian had wreaked enough havoc. All she wanted was to get back to the one thing that made her life worth living: being a wife and mother.

'Besides,' she added with a wry smile, 'Sebastian didn't get off scot-free. There was the small matter of Benedict laying him out on the flowerbed.'

'That sounded amazeballs,' Calypso said. 'I so wish I'd been there!'

Benedict actually blushed. 'Ah yes, when I got home from work and the house was empty, I went straight over to Clementine's and found the kids there. I'm afraid I saw red when she told me what was going on, and went straight to Bluebell Cottage.'

'I would have done exactly the same,' Clementine told him. 'I mean, given him a jolly good punch.'

'Go, Clemmie!' Calypso said. 'What I love the most about all this is the fact that Cheryl is fluent in bloody French! Next up she'll be telling us she's got a PhD in neuroscience.'

Everyone laughed. Cheryl was the heroine of the day. After overhearing Suzette's conversation with her sister about how terrible she felt at using Milo's inheritance to fund their new life in France, Cheryl had hotfooted it round to Caro's.

'The tape recorder idea was Cheryl's, too,' Caro explained. 'Apparently one of her friends caught her husband out the same way.' Caro exhaled in admiration. 'She scripted all the questions, you know. I wasn't sure if Sebastian would confess, but he's such a show-off I guess he couldn't resist the

566

chance to gloat.' Cheryl might still be calling Caro by the wrong name, but Caro would be eternally grateful for her support. It had turned out that their Barbie doll neighbour ate the likes of Sebastian for low-fat, high-protein breakfast.

'Where is Cheryl now?' Camilla asked. 'I thought she'd be round here dissecting every detail.'

'We did ask them over, but she's gone to take Barry to get his teeth whitened before Cheltenham.' Caro looked up at her husband. 'We're going to get her something nice to show our gratitude, aren't we?'

'A new set of boobs?' Jed said mischievously.

Milo wandered in from the playroom, clutching his Ben 10 plastic figure.

'Are you all right, darling?' Caro sat up and ruffled his hair.

'Yeah.' Milo's intelligent brown eyes settled on her like a laser beam. 'Were you talking about Daddy, then?'

Everyone went quiet. Milo hadn't asked for his father yet, but that didn't mean he wasn't missing him. 'Yes, darling,' Caro said awkwardly. 'I was going to have a talk with you about it. You see, some urgent business has come up, and Daddy has had to go away again ...'

The lies told to cover up a grown man's despicable behaviour ... Milo didn't respond at first. Caro was ready for him to be upset, but he just nodded.

'OK, cool. I'm staying here, though, aren't I?'

'Of course you are, my darling.' She put her arms round him, savouring his sweet, soapy smell.

'Urgh, Mum!' He squirmed as she kissed his ear. 'Can I go back and play now?'

Caro released him. 'Of course you can.'

'Let's go and play, Benny-dict.' Milo held out his hand. 'Us men need to stick together.'

Everyone cracked up again. 'What about me?' Jed asked.

Benedict got up and grinned at the rest of the room. 'Come on, champ, let's go and see what your sister's up to.'

*   *   *

Calypso left with her grandmother an hour later. Clementine seemed in a reflective mood as they came out of the gate and started round the green.

'That all turned out pretty well, then.' Calypso tried to gauge what her grandmother was thinking.

'Indeed.' Clementine suddenly stopped dead and put her face in her hands. For a horrible moment Calypso thought she was going to see her cry for the first time, but the old lady's face was alive and happy.

'It's over, Calypso! It's really over! I can't tell you how relieved I am.'

Calypso hugged her grandmother, aware of how sparse her figure was. 'Me too. Tell you what, though, if I ever see that big-haired tw—'

'Hopefully you won't,' Clementine finished firmly.

Bluebell Cottage had already been vacated. Brenda Briggs had reported Sebastian screeching off in the Aston Martin, hours after the showdown, a weeping Suzette by his side.

Clementine smoothed down her bun, something she always did when her nerves were fraught. 'I just feel for Milo in all this. God knows what will happen further down the line, when he's older.'

'We'll deal with it as a family, just like we always do.' Calypso squeezed her grandmother's liver-spotted hand. 'Don't worry, Granny Clem.'

Clementine smiled gratefully. 'You are a good girl.'

They went round to Calypso's front gate. 'You want me to walk you home?' she asked.

'Thank you, darling, but I'll be fine.' There was a glint behind Clementine's glasses. 'I might pop in the shop on my way past, see what Nobby's odds are in the *Racing Post*.'

With Cheltenham only days away, the whole county was gearing up for the hundreds of thousands of racing fans who were about to descend.

'A horse we know, running at Cheltenham! It's the most exciting thing to happen to the village for years!' Clementine walked off at a rare old pace towards the shop, making Calypso smile. She could already see the change in her grandmother. Thank God! It wasn't bloody fair to put her through something like that at her age. Now it was all over they could move on with their lives.

Calypso started up the path, counting her blessings. Milo was safe, that bastard Sebastian was out of the village. Business was going amazingly well: if she carried on taking bookings at this rate she'd have to get someone else in to help. The weather was getting warmer and the days longer, and as a summer person her mood always picked up around this time of year. And yet she still felt strangely flat . . .

Archie still wasn't speaking to her. She'd tried texting and Facebooking him, tagging him in a funny pic she'd found from New Year's Eve—her attempt at initiating a reconciliation and saying sorry—but Archie hadn't responded. It was a nasty shock that she hadn't won him over, and Calypso hated to admit it, but she *missed* him. Missed his funny, easy-going nature, his warm, twinkly eyes that did that cute turning-down thing at the corners. Missed his redoubtable self-confidence, a trait even people twice his age rarely possessed. Missed his long kisses and ripped body, the things he did in bed, and the way he held her afterwards . . .

Another person, with not quite so many barriers round them, might have gone round to the Maltings by now to apologize. Calypso wrestled with herself every time she drove past, wildly deliberating whether to turn into the drive—until the last second, when she'd always carry on. She just couldn't do it. She might have been out of order, but her natural stubbornness and pig-headedness had kicked in. If he thought she was going to go round on her hands and knees begging for forgiveness, he had another think coming.

Calypso glumly slid her key in the lock. She'd even thought of avoiding him by not going to Cheltenham, but people would only ask her why she hadn't been there. Sod it; she'd have a great day out with her family, wear something amazing to show that pipsqueak Archie what he was missing. Like she cared anyway . . .

I tried, and he wasn't interested. It was as simple as that.

CHAPTER EIGHTY-NINE

With just a few days to go until Cheltenham, the inhabitants at the Maltings were careering between huge excitement and sheer terror. Every time Angie thought about the race her stomach turned over, and even Freddie was on edge. Twice that week already he'd put his cheese and biscuits down and completely forgotten where he'd left them. It was most unlike of him to be distracted, especially when it came to his beloved Bath Olivers and Stinking Bishop.

They'd gone as far as they could with the training, and it was now just a case of keeping Nobby rested and happy, so he was nice and fresh for the big day. Angie kept herself busy washing and ironing Edward's silks and packing and repacking the race bag. The holdall held all the gear Edward would need, and things like a first-aid kit and Nobby's racing bridle and paddock sheet. It reminded Angie of when she'd been about to go into hospital to have Archie: all that waiting around for the big event, with the bag packed and ready by the front door.

The response from the village and beyond had been amazing. Based on his previous form, the online gambling site Betfair had Nobby down at initial odds of thirty-three to one, which was a great price to start with. Everywhere Angie went people wanted to know about Nobby, and said they'd be placing a bet, and the kitchen was starting to look like a Clinton Cards shop with all the good-luck messages.

But Angie was seriously concerned about one person, and it wasn't Edward. Kizzy had been a complete wreck for the last two weeks. Angie suspected it was something to do with Javier, but Kizzy had closed up every time Angie had tried to talk about him. It was as if she and Edward had swapped personalities: Kizzy had become withdrawn and distant, while Edward seemed to grow in confidence every day, even with Cheltenham approaching.

*   *   *

Angie tried again, when she took a cup of hot sugary tea out to Kizzy that morning. She found her round the back of the stables, forking up the muck-heap. Kizzy was looking dreadfully thin, Angie thought, her little face sharp and drawn, the famous chest flattened under the big baggy hoodie she was wearing. From the back she looked like a pre-teen.

'Thought you might need warming up.' Angie balanced the cup of tea on the top of the gatepost so one of the dogs wouldn't knock it over.

Kizzy looked up. Aside from the two spots of colour in her face from the physical exertion, she was deadly pale.

'Thanks, Angie.'

'Will you come in for some breakfast soon?' Kizzy had been avoiding the house like the plague.

'I'm not really hungry.'

'You're wasting away on us, Kizzo!'

Kizzy managed a wan smile. 'I'm all right.'

Angie hesitated, choosing her words carefully. 'Are you really OK, darling? It's just that you don't

572

seem yourself at the moment.'

All the light had gone out of Kizzy. She looked at Angie with dull blue eyes.

'Do you want to talk about it?' Angie asked.

Kizzy didn't respond.

'Is it Javier?'

At the mention of his name, Angie saw a ripple of anguish pass across Kizzy's face. 'I can't talk about it. I'm sorry . . . I just . . .' She shook her head helplessly.

'OK,' Angie said gently. 'You know where I am if you need me.'

She left the little figure mindlessly sweeping the concrete and walked back to the house. First Edward, and now poor Kizzy; and this at a time when they should be out celebrating the simple joy of being young. Angie shut the back door with a troubled mind. What on earth had happened?

Kizzy looked like the heart had been ripped right out of her.

CHAPTER NINETY

The Christie's Foxhunter Steeplechase was on the Friday of the Cheltenham Festival, right after the famous Gold Cup. The evening before, the whole of Gloucestershire had lit up like a fireworks display after the most terrific thunderstorm, but thankfully it blew out as quickly as it had come. The next day rolled in under sedate grey skies, with a discernible fizz of excitement in the air.

As the eight-seater minibus driven by Ted Briggs had quickly filled up, Calypso got a lift in the back of Caro and Benedict's 4×4 with her grandmother. The raceground was on the outskirts of the town, and the winding streets of Cheltenham were chock-a-block with people heading out there. But finally they reached the daffodil-adorned roundabout at the entrance and were directed in.

If Calypso had thought the first point-to-point at Chaddesley Corbett had been good for people-watching, Cheltenham was on another level. There were thousands of racegoers converging on the hill to get in, and every walk of human life was there. It seemed the predominantly green-and-brown-coloured crowd were split into two groups: the serious racing fans and those who were just there for a day on the lash.

There were smart couples in matching deerstalker hats and felt jackets; groups of lads suited and booted with one eye on the ladies; the odd Guinness hat; and bleary eyed characters looking shell-shocked—probably at how much cash they'd blown on horses and booze in the past few days. Calypso, who'd gone all Alexa Chung in a trilby and Topshop waxed jacket with her trusted dark skinny jeans, couldn't believe how many women looked more like they were going off to dance on a nightclub podium than tramp round one of Britain's most famous racecourses. One woman tottering past had fishnet tights on and a coat barely covering her bum, and was holding on for dear life to her shaven-headed boyfriend.

Then there were the Eton schoolboys, fresh out of sixth form, in their smart blazers and jeans, self-consciously drawing on cigarettes; people on office days out; ruddy-faced outdoor types with the red noses of people who liked their good port and whisky. In amongst it all were the touts, weaving their way through the crowd with a practised swagger, and shouting for custom.

The air was full of the smell of greasy fat from burger vans and the sound of race officials with loudspeakers telling everyone which gate to go to. As the women waited for Benedict to park the car there was another loud buzzing overhead.

'I wonder if that's Cheryl and Barry?' Caro said.

In typical style, the Pikes had eschewed Brenda's offer to come in the minibus, and were flying in on Barry's powder-blue helicopter. For those who preferred to travel by air or had the money to do so, the helicopter park was situated in a field behind the racetrack. The skies were almost as busy as the roads below, as millionaires and pop stars were ferried in to start their day of gambling and drinking.

A Bentley glided through, chauffeur at the wheel and a pair of Charles and Camilla lookalikes in the back, no doubt being whisked away to the VIP entrance rather than suffer the indignity of having to queue with the hoi polloi.

'This is a-mazing,' Calypso declared, transfixed by another fake-tanned dolly bird with goose-pimpled legs and a bright pink parasol. She couldn't believe she'd always turned down the chance to go before.

They'd all splashed out on club tickets, which meant they'd be able to see the horses parade before and after the races, and get a real flavour of all the action. It was also the enclosure where all the owners and trainers mingled, and they wanted to see the Fox-Titts and wish them luck. Not that Calypso was particularly looking forward to seeing

Archie. Part of her wanted to avoid him completely, and the other wanted to get the inevitable awkward hellos over and done with.

Once Benedict joined them, the group made their way down the hill past the main entrance and the racing Hall of Fame to the club turnstiles a little further down. Camilla and Jed were already there under the huge scoreboard, where they'd arranged to meet.

'What ho, chaps!' Camilla said. She looked well, her freshly coloured brown hair as thick and glossy as any of the horses' tails there that day. She and Jed were standing close together, with the sweet intimacy of a couple happy in love.

Clementine went straight off to the Totes betting stall to check Nobby's odds, while Benedict and Jed went to join the long queue at the cashpoint. The three sisters were left standing together. Calypso thought how radiant Caro looked today in her camel coat with the fake fur collar, which brought out the warm tones of her skin and hair. The stress had literally melted away, and she looked like her old self: vivacious and full of life.

Caro caught her sister looking and smiled. 'Exciting, isn't it? I do love Gold Cup day.'

The club enclosure was definitely the place to be. In the shadow of the huge stands overlooking the racecourse, it was a large area housing multiple bars, restaurants and the ubiquitous Totes betting stalls, their green flags flapping in the breeze. The place was a seething mass of activity as people shopped, socialized and wandered round putting money down. Camilla had already bought everyone a race card, with the programme for the day and information on each runner. There was Nobby,

No. 22, along with a little sketch of Edward's black and purple colours, and the names of the owners and rider.

'Has been making hay between the flags this season,' the blurb said about Goldenballs, 'but will have to take a step forward today to meet the challenge.'

Brenda Briggs had wasted no time hitting the shops, and had dragged the long-suffering Ted down to an expensive hat stall to watch her try on a selection of furry ones twice the size of her head. Calypso and her sisters were giggling at the pained expression on Ted's face as he was forced to try on a Stetson, when the Reverend Bellows materialized in front of them.

'H-hello, girls.'

'Hello, Reverend!' Caro said brightly. 'Having fun?'

His beard had something of dubious origin stuck in it. 'Y-yes thank you.' He looked round nervously, as if the prospect of being left alone with three attractive women was a terrifying prospect. 'J-Joyce has popped to the Ladies, I can't think why she's taking so long.'

There was suddenly a huge kerfuffle in front of them. As people jostled and flashbulbs went off, Calypso saw a skinny, heavily tanned woman who looked vaguely familiar.

'Is that Katie Price?' Camilla asked. 'She's tiny!'

'Yeah,' Calypso said. 'She's well into her horses.'

The celebrity was sporting new hair extensions and, even though it was cloudy, huge sunglasses that covered half her face. Clad in the tiniest dress and fur jacket, her long bare legs were set off by the highest pair of bright-pink heels.

577

'Who's Katie Price?' Reverend Bellows enquired. Luckily the girls were saved from having to explain to a man of the cloth how someone could be famous simply for having fake boobs and a colourful love-life, by the arrival of two more Churchminster residents.

'Did you see that?' Cheryl squawked, eye-popping in head-to-toe Ronseal tan and a low-cut zebra-print dress. 'Katie Price has got the same shoes as me! I don't believe it!'

'You're the original and the best, babes, don't you worry,' Barry said, equally startling in a striped suit and pointy white shoes. He grinned at everyone. 'Ready to make some lovely jubbly spondoolies?'

Cheryl, the outfit drama already forgotten, was rifling through her handbag. 'Bollocks, I left my chewing gum in the helicopter. Baz, you got some?'

Clementine came back, clutching a race card in her gloved hand. 'Nobby's odds have gone up to a hundred to one.'

'Is that good or bad?' Calypso asked. She hadn't got a clue about betting.

'Bad, I suppose, but Nobby hasn't run here before.' Clementine gave a nervous shudder. 'I can't imagine how Freds and Angie must be feeling!'

It was only one o'clock and the race wasn't until four, so they decided to go and have a wander. The parade ring was filled with the media filing pre-race reports for their respective news channels. One poor sod, with a *Racing UK* microphone, kept fluffing his lines, much to the amusement of a wisecracking crowd clutching plastic pints of Guinness.

'Ooh, look, there's Clare Balding,' Camilla whispered. Resplendent in a lilac coat, the presenter was standing in the middle of the ring talking to a camera crew.

Calypso was just trying to work out if the tiny, dishevelled thing in a long tatty cardigan was Lily Allen when Angie turned up, wearing her 'Owners and Trainers' badge, and looking every inch the part in a brown felt hat and smart new chocolate-coloured suit that matched her huge eyes. Everybody fell on her, wanting to know how Nobby was, and how it was all going.

'We're all fine. Nobby travelled up well, and we've got him settled in the stable now.' Angie looked round the racecourse. 'Christ! I still can't believe we're here!'

'Believe it.' Caro smiled. 'You've done so bloody well! We're so proud of you.'

'Afternoon, all.'

Calypso's stomach dropped. Archie was sauntering towards them, looking like he didn't have a care in the world. He'd swapped his usual jeans and T-shirt for a checked shirt and smart blazer, the cut of which only emphasized his broad shoulders. Calypso crossed her arms and tried to ignore the fact that Archie did preppy *really* well.

'How are we all?' His brown eyes rested on Calypso for a fraction of a second. She gave a lightning smile, blushing when it wasn't immediately reciprocated. She turned away and pretended to study the scoreboard.

'We're all gunning for you a million per cent!' Clementine said.

'Thank you, darling,' Angie said gratefully. The theme tune to *Only Fools and Horses* went off somewhere. 'Oh, hold on a minute.' She pulled her phone out and looked at it. 'It's Freds, probably wondering where we are. I'd better shoot. I just wanted to pop down and say hello.'

'Go!' urged Caro. 'We'll all be cheering you on madly.'

'See you all later,' Archie said easily. He didn't look at Calypso. Mother and son walked off, Archie head and shoulders above Angie. As Angie said something on the phone, Archie draped his arm round her shoulder and leaned down to listen.

'If that boy was any more laid-back, he'd be horizontal!' laughed Caro.

'He's good for Angie's nerves, at any rate,' Clementine said. 'Archie is clearly not a young man who's fazed by much.'

Clearly, Calypso thought. While her hands were suddenly all clammy, he'd acted as if she didn't exist. The little bit of hope she'd been pretending not to hang on to had just been extinguished. *He's so full of it.* From that moment on, she decided to erase Archie from her day.

CHAPTER NINETY-ONE

Instead of going in the main stand, they'd all clubbed together and hired one of the chalet rooms next to the club restaurant on the side of the track. It afforded them an excellent view, and they had their own waiter service so they could avoid the scrum at next-door's bar. The wine and champagne were swiftly brought out, and people enjoyed their first glass, poring over the racecard and arguing about what to put bets on. Barry Pike proved extremely knowledgeable, and gave out lots of tips, even generously insisting on buying Ted and Brenda's tickets for them when he went off to the William Hill shop, where all the big players put their money down. The atmosphere was brimming with anticipation as people watched and waited for the day's fun to start.

Calypso got stuck into the Moët with Brenda, and had to keep nipping off for loo breaks. On her way back from one she got waylaid by a group of Irish lads outside a bar, and it was there that Camilla found her at three o'clock, as she went to place a last-minute bet on one of the favourites running in the biggie, the Gold Cup.

'I've been looking for you, the Gold Cup's about to start!'

'Soz, I got a bit waylaid.' Calypso's dirty blonde hair was wild and free; her eyes a little glittery by now under the black kohl.

'Have you put any bets on yet?'

'Shit, I'd forgotten about that!' Calypso looked for somewhere to put down her half-drunk pint of Guinness. 'Better be off. See you, Seamus,' she said, trying to remember all their names. 'And Barney, Ronan, and . . .'

She caused a right old palaver at the Totes betting stall because she couldn't decide who to back in the Gold Cup, eventually deciding on a horse called Gay Boy because she thought the name was funny. Most people had put five quid each way on Nobby; with his odds still firmly at a hundred to one there was no point putting any more down. Ignoring Calypso's plea that she wanted a quick hog-roast burger, Camilla pulled her away.

The Gold Cup flew past in a hail of glory, and then it was time for them all to make their way down to the parade ring again, to watch the horses being brought out for the Foxhunter. The main event might be over for a lot of people, but the Churchminster contingent were a jangle of nerves as they walked down to the pre-parade ring. Calypso heard someone shout her name, and turned to see Seamus, the tallest and cutest of the Irish boys, waving at her from under the stand. It was so busy there, with onlookers streaming out to go and collect their winnings or commiserate with each other at the bar that Calypso quickly lost sight of him in the throng.

'I feel sick with nerves,' Caro whispered to her. Calypso felt a bit queasy as well as she caught sight of Archie, standing in the middle of the parade ring with his parents and all the other owners and trainers. Calypso watched as he started talking to a middle-aged blonde woman wearing a bright red fitted coat, and tried to block out a pang of jealously.

Get a grip, loser, she muttered. *You don't even like him.*

The grooms started to bring the horses out, then the jockeys following on foot in all their different-coloured silks. They were all absolutely minute, with the exception of Edward, who towered above them like an anorexic stick-insect. At least the other jockeys seemed to be talking to him, though, as they joined the owners and trainers in the middle of the ring. Kizzy gave the Churchminster lot a quick grin as she led Nobby past, Edward's number-patch on her arm. She'd lost a bit of weight, Calypso thought, and was almost lost in the sky-blue jacket she was wearing, her bottom half tiny in a pair of figure-hugging jeans.

Under the glare of the big outdoor lights and the noise of the crowd, some of the horses were playing up, but Nobby was ambling along as normal, more interested in what was going on around him than anything else. There were some beautiful horses there, and Nobby's head looked more donkey-like than ever, but even Calypso could see he was in great shape: his body was strong and firmly muscled, with not an ounce of fat anywhere.

A bell rang for the jockeys to mount and the grooms started to lead the horses out of the gate down to the course. People started to move in the middle of the ring, but Archie still had his back to Calypso. For some reason it felt like a giant 'fuck you', and Calypso tried to stop her blood from boiling. Was he trying to be deliberately rude?

'Right then, chaps,' Clementine announced. 'We'd better get back to the chalet.'

*   *   *

The crowds weren't as big as they had been for the Gold Cup, but the stands were still pretty full. Hundreds more people were milling round the railings at the side of the track, waiting for it all to start. In the Churchminster chalet their waitress had put more Moët in the ice bucket but no one even noticed. All eyes were trained on the big screen by the start.

'*Twenty-four runners going down to the start for the Christie's Foxhunter, and they'll be underway shortly,*' announced the commentator.

583

An air of expectation rippled through the tiny room. Calypso briefly wondered where Angie and Freddie were, and how they'd be feeling. She was shitting herself, and it wasn't even her horse.

A loud cheer went up from outside, and they saw the horses start cantering down to the start.

'Oh, my life, there's Nobby and Edward!' squawked Brenda Briggs as the two of them flashed up on the big screen.

'One of two new runners to the race today is Goldenballs at a hundred to one, trained and ridden by Edward Cleverley and owned by Mr and Mrs Frederick Fox-Titt.'

'Go, Edward!' shouted Calypso. She tried to shove all thought of Archie out of her mind. Her grandmother was standing next to her, gripping her arm.

The field assembled at the start line and the ten thousand-strong crowd held its breath. There were a few horses playing up, but then the starter pulled his flag down and the pack surged forward. The roof of the Guinness stand next door was nearly lifted off by the cheers of the crowd.

'And they're off for the Christie's Foxhunter two thousand and twelve!' shouted the commentator. The mainly brown pack surged off down the first straight. Calypso hadn't paid much attention to the other horses, and had no idea who was who aside from Edward, but Clementine had told her the favourite was Super Injunction, ridden by eighteen-year-old feted rider Billy Forster. It quickly became clear that this was still a race up for grabs.

'Reigning champion Super Injunction is bounced out by Space Cowboy who takes an early lead ...'

The pack streamed over the first fence, one after

584

the other. Calypso's eyes were swivelling between the big screen and the track, trying to keep up.

'Which one's Nobby?' The colours were a blur from here.

'Midfield, look.' Her grandmother handed her the binoculars.

'*Goldenballs jumps the second in tenth place. With two circuits ahead of them, it's Space Cowboy leading, Super Injunction in second, Puzzle Man in third, Deb's Delight in fourth . . .*'

The pack raced round the far straight, followed by a jeep with cameras on its roof. They all looked so small and faraway from here, Calypso thought, as if they weren't real horses and humans at all, but little toy figures that had been wound up and let off. She watched as they all made it over the next fence.

The field started to stretch out, but Nobby was doing a solid job remaining somewhere in the middle.

'He's going well,' Clementine said excitedly, but moments later they all screamed as Nobby hit the next fence and stumbled forwards.

'*Bad mistake by Goldenballs then. The horse did well to recover!*'

'Dear God,' Clementine murmured. 'Angie and Fred must be having heart attacks!'

As they came to the end of the first circuit, the field had strung out into the four front runners, the middle pack quite a long way behind, and a few stragglers at the rear. Two horses had already been pulled up by their jockeys.

The commentary was fast and flowing. '*And Super Injunction has moved back up into first over the fourteen, after a bad landing by Space Cowboy.*'

Calypso was staring at the big screen. Nobby had started to overtake several horses in front of him.

'It's Gone Bananas in fourth, Zeinko and Planter's Boy in fifth and sixth, and Goldenballs has moved up to seventh . . .'

'Go on, Edward!' they all shouted. The middle pack was still a fair way from the leading four, but it was a good place. If Edward could keep this up, he'd finish very respectably in the first ten.

By the time they'd all jumped the open ditch for the second time, two more horses had been pulled up and someone had fallen off, the loose horse galloping ahead with the front four. It was a messy, nail-biting race, far more so than the Gold Cup.

Nobby had dropped back down to eighth. There was no way his pack would catch up now.

'If they can just keep going,' Clementine said anxiously.

'Down to the last four from home, and it's Super Injunction ridden by Billy Forster, followed by Space Cowboy and Gone Bananas moving up to third.'

Three more fences to go. Stretching up on tiptoes, Calypso could see the first three horses approaching the final straight.

The commentator's voice was rising in excitement. *'And it's the reigning champion Super Injunction, who's clear by two and a half lengths!'*

The roar of the crowd rose to deafening proportions.

'It's Super Injunction and Billy Forster to Space Cowboy and Brian Cox in second, Go Bananas and Clare Williams in third. Zeinko and Planter's Boy are tucking in nicely behind them in fifth and sixth, and Goldenballs is now in seventh. Surely the rest don't count now? These seven are a long way clear

586

as they have three fences left to take in the Christie's Foxhunter.'

Everyone in the chalet was on tenterhooks. They couldn't believe Nobby and Edward had got this far.

'They're now twenty lengths clear of the eighth horse. Super Injunction is streaking out in front. And on the second to last fence, terrible mistake by Super Injunction! He's unseated his rider!'

There were cries of 'Oh no!' from outside. The boyish little figure of Billy Forster scrambled up from the Cheltenham turf and ran to the side of the track.

The crowd went bonkers. Super Injunction's unexpected departure seemed to have thrown everyone behind him into disarray. All except Nobby. As the pack closed towards the final fence, he started to creep forward.

'It's Space Cowboy left out in front. Gone Bananas has run out of gas on the last stretch.'

'Go on, Edward! Go on, Nobby!' they all screamed. Even Benedict and Jed were jumping up and down on the spot. Nobby had overtaken fourth place and was now passing third . . . As they thundered up towards the posts Nobby started to edge past Gone Bananas . . .

'And Goldenballs has moved up into second place.'

Nobby was stretching out, back end going like no one's business. On top, Edward's long skinny legs were urging him on.

'Oh my God! Fucking hell!' Calypso screamed, but it was lost in the other shouts reverberating round the room.

'The Christie's Foxhunter is going back to Ireland

587

this year for Brian Cox and Space Cowboy . . .'
Nobody heard as Goldenballs flew past the finishing post to take a magnificent second.

CHAPTER NINETY-TWO

Everyone started screaming and hugging each other. Clementine shrieked like a schoolgirl as Jed picked her up and swung her around, while the Reverend Bellows repeatedly crossed himself in the corner. Ted Briggs, normally the most taciturn of men, ended up kissing Caro full on the mouth in his excitement, and then started apologizing profusely to Benedict. Joyce Bellows was so overcome with the emotion of it that she burst into hysterical tears, and had to be taken off to the loo by Cheryl to get her make-up redone.

Then it was back up to the winners' enclosure to see Edward and Nobby come in. On the way it started to dawn on people just how much they'd won. Nobby had come in second at a hundred to one, an unbelievable result. Barry did the maths quickly in his head as they hurried up; from the big smile on his face he'd clearly done very well himself, but even two pound fifty bets each way, like Brenda's, would net her nigh on ninety quid. It would be champagne bottles at the ready after all this was done.

They got to the winner's enclosure just as Space Cowboy and his Irish jockey were being brought in, but the biggest cheer came when Edward and Nobby walked in behind them. It wasn't just the Churchminster lot; as Edward was a local jockey,

Goldenballs's amazing performance had touched a lot of people. Edward's mud-splattered face, already euphoric, reached a beatific state of consciousness as strangers called out his name and clapped their congratulations.

Angie practically had to be carried up from the track by her husband and son. Voice croaky from screaming, she was also in the stunned stupor of someone who'd just won the lottery. As she walked in arm in arm with Kizzy, and saw all her friends there cheering Edward and Nobby, it took all Angie had to stop herself blubbing in front of them.

Kizzy was grinning from ear to ear. Far from Angie having to worry about her, she'd been an absolute star all day, from the moment she'd turned up at five o'clock in the morning to plait Nobby. She'd been there every step of the way for Edward, Angie remembered, a source of cheer and reassuring comfort. And what a result! Second in the Foxhunter, with a horse she'd helped to train! Angie watched Kizzy wave at the others, and fervently hoped she'd started to get over whatever had happened between her and Javier.

There was the prize ceremony, then, and the winning jockey Brian Cox was presented with the humungous silver Christie's Foxhunter Steeplechase cup. A still-beaming Edward stood and watched, along with the third and fourth placed jockeys, and then it was nearly time for the jockeys to get weighed back in and their horses untacked.

There were still people four-deep round the sides watching, and a sports reporter with a BBC microphone was moving round and picking individuals out to interview. As Angie walked up with Kizzy towards Edward and Nobby, she suddenly heard a name that made her stop dead.

'Chip Mason! It's a surprise to see you here. Aren't we more used to seeing you on the dance floor these days?'

There was a chuckle from the crowd, and Angie swung round to see the florid face of Edward's dad to her left. Instinctively she looked over at Edward, but he didn't seem to have heard.

'*Shit*,' Kizzy said under her breath. 'What's he doing here?'

'I have no idea,' Angie replied through gritted teeth. She looked back at Edward, who was bending down to talk to a race official who'd come up to him. Angie saw Edward grin in response to something the woman said. If Chip Mason butted in now, and ruined Edward's moment . . .

The reporter, who'd been scouting for celebrity racegoers to interview all day, wasn't about to give up his prize find. He pushed the microphone into Chip's face. 'Who did you back today? Had any luck with a win?'

For once Chip looked rather discombobulated. 'Er, Goldenballs.'

Angie and Kizzy exchanged a look. This was a turn-up for the books.

'Wow, you did all right there, then! Did you have an inside tip?'

A woman beside Chip, as small and dark as Chip was big and blond, spoke up. 'Edward Cleverley is our son.'

Edward's mother! Angie did a double take and saw his sweet nature in her face.

The reporter was bristling with excitement: this would be a great little piece on the proud famous sportsman, there to cheer on his son. 'This is great!'

He turned and beckoned to his cameraman who was standing on the other side of the ring. 'You don't mind if we do a quick piece live for BBC South West, do you?'

Chip looked distinctly uncomfortable. Freddie came up and whispered in his wife's ear. 'What the hell's going on?'

'I can't bear it, Freds. They're about to get Edward and his dad together on camera!'

As Edward turned round to see what all the activity was about, he clocked his dad. Angie sagged as she saw the look on his face.

'Right, if I can just get you in here, Chip! You too, Mum.' The reporter practically hauled Nobby and the Masons in front of the camera.

'This is awful, I have to do something!'

Freddie grabbed her arm. 'Darling, you'll only make it worse. They've started filming, anyway.'

The BBC South West reporter had the four of them in a stiff semi-circle, Nobby looking bemusedly at the cameraman and the strange machine on his shoulder. At least Edward's mum looked like a nice woman, Angie thought, as she snuck Edward a delighted little smile. For a second his face relaxed, as the reporter jumped back in.

'Well, Chip! I expect you're very proud of Edward. Second in the Foxhunter with odds of a hundred to one is pretty special.'

Chip Mason went even redder, as if he felt he'd been put on the spot.

'We're extremely proud of him,' Edward's mum said. She had such a soft voice Angie only just made out what she said.

Edward shot his mum a grateful look. Angie was fully expecting him to go to pieces, especially in front of the cameras, but he was surprisingly together, sitting quietly atop Nobby with a watchful expression.

The reporter was getting frustrated by the lack of response from Chip Mason. He was never normally a man short on words.

'So Chip, anything you want to say to your son?'

Angie's heart sank. She watched as Chip turned stiffly to Edward. For a moment father and son looked at each other, saying nothing.

'Well, er . . . Eddie, me and your mother are very proud of what you achieved today.'

There was an 'aaah' from the crowd.

Edward's eyes were fixed on him. 'Are you really, Dad?' he asked softly.

'Of course I am!' he said crossly. There was a pause. The reporter looked rather anxious. Chip Mason shuffled on the spot and cleared his throat. 'You did an excellent job out there, and I was very impressed.' He looked up, and, for the first time, Angie saw softness in his eyes. 'I really was. Well done, son.'

The cameraman filmed as Chip Mason offered his hand up to Edward. For an agonizing moment Angie thought Edward wasn't going to take it, but then he leant down and grasped it firmly with a grin.

'Thanks, Dad.'

'Thanks, guys, and congratulations again, Edward.' The reporter turned to the camera with a cheesy grin. 'Well, I guess you could say Edward's a chip off the old block! Now, back to the studio.'

*   *   *

It was time for some serious celebrating. As the day's racing started to wind down, Angie and Freddie managed to sweet-talk everyone into the owners' and trainers' marquee. It was rather like a raucous wedding reception: crowds of smartly dressed people were sitting round the white-clothed tables knocking back champagne.

A magnum of Moët was brought out to the Churchminster table, a very generous present from Barry Pike. Even Clementine, who only ever had more than one glass at Christmas and New Year, was persuaded by Barry to let him give her a top-up. The Pikes were so funny and brash, and such good company, that pretty soon everyone was stuck in and getting rip-roaringly drunk.

Archie hadn't given Calypso a second glance the whole time. She'd been ignoring him, anyway, as he sat on the other side of the table, between his mum and Kizzy, one arm draped across the back of Kizzy's chair. Calypso tried to keep him out of her line of vision, and proceeded to get as drunk as possible.

An hour later the heat and noise had intensified and Calypso's eyesight was starting to get a little hazy. Leaving Brenda trying to coerce Jed into downing a shot of vodka, Calypso got up and wove her way across the packed room towards the Ladies. Several of the older, more distinguished-looking men in the room gave her ravishing blonde hair and long legs a second glance, but Calypso was oblivious as she concentrated on getting to the toilet in a straight line. Once inside she headed straight for a cubicle and sat down, her head in her hands.

The speed-drinking had weakened her resolve,

and Calypso was starting to fume again. Archie didn't even have the balls to acknowledge her with a smile or quick hello. OK, so he might still be in a huff for some reason, but Jesus, it wasn't as if she'd murdered anyone! *You're drunk*, she told herself. *If you were sober you wouldn't care.* Pulling up her skimpy knickers, she flushed the toilet.

Back outside, the crowd seemed to have doubled in minutes. Calypso was just trying to squeeze past a group of braying men blocking her way, when her heel caught on the carpeted floor. She stumbled, and would have fallen into the table next to her, if a pair of strong arms hadn't been there to catch her.

Calypso looked up, ready to thank her rescuer, and found herself looking into Archie's big brown eyes.

'You all right?'

'Fine, thank you,' she said tetchily, shaking his hands off her.

'Had a bit too much to drink?'

'What are you, my mother?'

He held his hands up. 'Whoa, I was only joking.'

'Well, it wasn't very funny.' Calypso was completely unnerved by his sudden close proximity. Archie had removed his blazer, and his shirtsleeves were rolled up, showing off his muscular forearms. *He's probably done it on purpose*, she thought savagely.

By contrast, he was annoyingly calm. 'Someone's in a good mood,' he said mildly. 'I've been wanting to speak to you.'

'Oh, wow!' she said sarcastically. 'The great Archie Fox-Titt has deigned to honour me with his company!'

He looked at her as if she was mad. 'What is

594

wrong with you?'

'Hey, Calypso!' Someone put their arm round her; it was Seamus, the cute Irish lad from earlier.

'Hey, babe!' She made a big show of cuddling a man she didn't really know from Adam. Not that Archie knew that.

'I got to see you after all.' Seamus looked at Archie. 'All right, mate? Not intruding am I?'

Calypso flashed a sugary-sweet smile and slipped her hand round Seamus's waist. 'Not at all, babe!'

Archie shrugged as if he couldn't care less. 'I'll leave you to it, guys, have fun.'

He walked off, back towards the table. Calypso tried to ignore the sinking feeling. He'd won again.

*   *   *

Kizzy was trying to get in the mood. It had been the most incredible day, and she was so unbelievably chuffed for Edward. He'd only come in for one drink, and told Angie his parents had invited him out for dinner. God knows how that was going, Kizzy thought, as she looked across the packed marquee, but today had done wonders. Chip had practically delivered a public apology out there to Edward, in front of the cameras.

Kizzy still wished Edward were here, though. At least she didn't have to pretend to be happy when she was with him, and they could sit together in a comfortable silence. Now she was flagging desperately, and the champagne had stopped going down so well. The Reverend's wife had been drunkenly shouting in her ear for the last ten minutes, but it was so loud in there that Kizzy hadn't got a clue what she was going on about.

The euphoria and adrenaline that had carried her through the day was draining away, and in its place, the crushing emptiness and devastation she'd felt since Javier had ordered her out of his life was returning. Kizzy watched the happy raucous crowd, wondering if she'd ever be capable of similar emotions again.

The weeks felt like years. Kizzy had only sent one more text message, saying for the last time how sorry she was, and how she'd never meant to upset him. Like her earlier ones, it had gone unanswered. She'd even driven up to Homelands, to do what, she didn't know—but just being near the place somehow calmed her. But as the entrance had approached she'd thought of Javier and Sarah behind those gates together, locked away from everyone. *I'll never belong in there*, she'd thought. She'd driven around for the rest of the night in an empty daze.

She wasn't eating or sleeping, she couldn't think straight. She had thought everything would gradually get better with time, but if anything she was feeling worse. It was as if the world she'd come back to, the world she'd been so happy and content in before, was now not enough. Kizzy hated this feeling of misery, but what could she do? Her life had stopped.

As she looked back across the room, she caught sight of a familiar dark profile near one of the far tables. Her heart instantly started to pound. *Oh my God, it can't be* . . . She sat up, trying to get a better look. A large fat man in a red waistcoat moved in front, frustratingly blocking her view, and Kizzy practically jumped up and ran round the table to get a better look. She caught a glimpse of broad shoulders and almost collapsed, but seconds later the man turned round, and Kizzy saw the too-close-together eyes and weak chin of a complete stranger.

Embarrassed, she glanced round to see if anyone had noticed, but everyone at her table was still immersed in their laughing and drinking. Kizzy stood still for a moment, cursing her stupidity. Of course Javier wasn't there. He was at Homelands with Oliver and Love's Dream, not in a hot, crowded tent full of drunken people banging into each other and talking complete nonsense. Kizzy knew where she'd rather be, and the realization was so bad that she had to get out, past the tables of rowdy people without a care in the world.

The raceground had practically emptied out, and most punters were back on the special buses and coaches laid on to take them home. It was starting to get dark across the Mendip Hills, giving the place a rather empty, deflated feel. It was as if the real party had moved on from this place—the way it had from her life. Kizzy wrapped her arms round herself, and looked up at the sky. It seemed unbelievable that Javier was somewhere under it, not far from here.

Two women were walking towards the marquee, the reddening sunset behind them. With smart matching blazers and leather boots, they were definitely part of the upmarket racing set. They were deep in conversation as they walked past.

'I heard some news earlier, from one of my dressage chums: Sarah Hamilton-Scott's died.'

Kizzy went cold.

The other woman said, 'Who, darling?'

'You know, Javier Hamilton-Scott's wife. She had that nasty fall from her horse.'

'I remember now! Christ, I thought she'd died years ago.'

'I know, sad though, isn't it?'

'Very. I do hope it won't affect Javier's focus for the Olympics . . .'

They walked through the open door of the marquee and disappeared into a wall of sound. Kizzy was left alone outside again, staring across the empty racecourse.

CHAPTER NINETY-THREE

One week later

The kitchen at the Maltings was overflowing with food.

'Do you think we've got enough?' Angie said, looking round at the piles of smoked salmon, breads and organic cheeses—and the miniature pork pies she'd been up half the night making with Gloucester Old Spot sausagemeat.

Freddie was lugging another box of Billecart-Salmon champagne into the utility room. They always got the decent, mid-range stuff in for a big party. 'More than enough,' he puffed. 'We could feed the five thousand here.'

'We didn't invite quite that many.'

In honour of Edward and Nobby's amazing performance, the Fox-Titts were throwing a big party. The whole village had been invited, as well as Fred and Angie's fantastically glamorous and fun friends. It promised to be quite a day.

'I hope the weather holds out.' Angie peered out of the windows at the thunderous skies. Their

Cheltenham wonder was grazing in the paddock opposite, happily snuffling round for tasty morsels.

'They're forecasting storms later,' Freddie said, coming back through.

'Oh well, we'll just have to stay indoors. Now, then.' Angie put her hands on her hips and tried to think. 'We've got the bubbles, beer, four cases of Oyster Bay, spirits, mixers . . . did you get the WKD for Stacey Turner?'

Freddie clapped his hand to his forehead. 'Damn, I knew there was something. I'll have to go back to the cash and carry.'

'There isn't time now, people are arriving in a few hours!'

'I'll go if you like.'

Edward was standing at the open back door. He was wearing a smart new T-shirt and jeans, and Angie thought how nice it was to see him dressed like other young people, and not in the tatty jumpers and jodhpurs he usually wore.

'Would you mind?' she asked. 'You're insured to drive the Range Rover.'

'Not at all.'

'There's the chap,' Freddie said gratefully, reaching into his pocket. He threw the car keys across the kitchen and Edward caught them in one hand.

Angie went for her handbag. 'I'll just get you some money.'

'No, Angie, this is on me.' Edward grinned. 'It's the least I can do.'

'It's meant to be your party! But thank you, Edward, that's very sweet.'

He was about to turn round, but stopped in the door. 'Is it OK if my brother comes to the party too?'

'Dear boy, of course!' Angie said. 'You hear that, Freds, we'll have one of your rugby heroes in the house!'

Edward laughed. 'I'll make sure he doesn't start chucking balls around and breaking things. See you in a bit.'

'See you soon,' Angie said. Alone again, she and Freddie stared at each other.

They'd invited the Masons, not sure what their response would be, but Edward had come straight back, saying his parents would love to come. He hadn't said much about the dinner he'd had with his family, but it seemed to have gone well. He'd told Angie that he and his father were working on things. She'd been rather touched when Edward had admitted that Chip might not be the best dad in the world, but, 'He's the only one I've got.'

'Let's hope Chip Mason behaves himself,' Freddie said. 'There's a new sporting legend in the family now!'

Angie smiled. 'I'm sure it will be fine. From the sound of it, Chip is starting to realize what a wonderful son he's got.' She glanced round again. 'Are you *sure* we've got enough food?'

'Darling!' Freddie went over to pour himself a glass of water from the filter jug. 'Where's Kizzo? I thought she'd be down here by now.'

'I'm not sure if she's coming. Don't look at me like that.'

'I'm not looking like anything. I'm just surprised.'

'Don't ask me why, I promised not to say anything.'

'Then I won't ask.' Freddie gave his wife a frown. 'She is all right, though, isn't she?'

Angie sighed. 'Oh, Freds, I just don't know.'

The guests were due to start arriving at one. At twelve thirty-six Angie hared up the stairs and bumped into her son coming out of the shower.

'All sorted, Ma?'

'Just about! Thanks for all your help this morning, darling.'

'No probs.'

Angie looked at her son. He was looking very tanned and strapping. He had one towel wrapped round his waist and another round his shoulders, so all you could see was wet chest and muscled calves.

'Are any of your friends coming?'

'I didn't ask, actually. I thought it was a village thing.' He started drying his hair with the towel.

'You can invite who you want, Arch! In fact,' she said, trying to sound innocent, 'I thought it might be a good idea for you to invite some girls.'

He raised an amused eyebrow. 'Girls?'

'You know. I *worry* about you. You should have a nice girlfriend, not be stuck out here with just your father and me.'

'Mum, you don't have to start fretting about me.'

'What about Calypso?' Things seemed to have gone quiet on that front.

He stopped rubbing. 'What about Calypso?'

'I don't know.' Angie hesitated. 'There seemed to be a bit of an atmosphere between you two at Cheltenham.'

Archie cut her off firmly. 'Ma, you don't know what you're talking about, OK?'

'But . . .'

'But nothing.' He looked at the bathroom. 'Are you going to get in the shower, or what?'

Angie watched him pad back down the corridor

601

to his bedroom, his broad back filling the corridor. Young people! Who knew what went on in their heads these days?

*   *   *

An hour later the house was starting to fill up. There was Clementine and her family, Milo on Benedict's shoulders as they came in. Calypso was working and coming down later, but Brenda and Ted Briggs were there with the Reverend and Joyce Bellows and the entire Turner family, on a rare day off from the pub. As they hadn't been able to make Cheltenham, Jack and Beryl were up for a celebration, while Stacey's denim hot pants, fishnets and neon-pink vest top looked more suited to a summer day in Vegas than a windy April afternoon in the countryside.

The Pikes caused a stir when they walked in: Cheryl had had so much Botox she could barely move her face, and she soon had Angie's posh viscount friend in fits of laughter as she regaled him with tales of all the cosmetic surgery she'd had. Edward was showered with congratulations and back-pats, and since everyone wanted to go and see the famous Goldenballs they traipsed across the yard to Nobby's stable, which Angie had decorated with balloons and streamers that morning.

She was so busy greeting people and rushing round getting them drinks that she didn't get a drop herself until Caro came and found her in the hall and presented her with a flute of champagne.

'You are a dear girl.' Angie took a long, luxurious sip. 'Lovely!'

'You've had a great turnout,' Caro said. 'I

haven't seen Kizzy yet. Isn't she here?'

'She's coming later,' Angie lied, although there was still a chance Kizzy would make it. 'How are you, darling? I must say, you look wonderful!'

'I feel it.' Caro did look so happy and rested.

'I don't suppose you've heard from that bastard? If you don't mind me saying.'

'I've called him worse myself.' It was the only time Angie had seen her friend's sunny mood falter. 'We're communicating through our lawyers now. Sebastian's claiming poverty, and wants to decrease Milo's maintenance payments.'

'What an utter shit!'

'Our solicitor, Louise, doesn't think he'll get away with it. She's unearthed an interesting piece of news, actually. Belinda Winters, the Cafcass officer who was put on Milo's case, has just been suspended for unprofessional conduct. Apparently she was caught taking a bribe in return for recommending that a child went to live with a particular parent.'

Angie's eyes widened. 'You don't think . . .'

'We don't know.' Caro shrugged. 'I wouldn't put anything past Sebastian any more.'

'That's disgusting. These people are meant to be in positions of trust, and . . .' Angie stopped. Chip Mason had just walked in.

Angie made her excuses to Caro, and went over to say hello. The Masons were standing with Edward by the front door. To her complete shock, Chip planted an awkward kiss on her cheek. 'An-jey. How are you?'

'Good, thanks! How lovely to see you all.' She smiled at Edward's mum, who looked very neat and pretty in a smart red dress—and at the tall, dark hunk of a young man standing beside her.

'Angie, this is my mum, Daphne,' Edward said.

'Hello,' Daphne said. 'You have a beautiful home.'

'How sweet of you to say so.'

Daphne had Edward's lovely smile. 'Thank you so much for looking after Edward,' she said. 'You've been such wonderful friends to him.'

'Your son is a huge star round these parts, let me tell you,' Angie said, embarrassed.

'I don't know about that.' Edward grinned. 'And this is my brother, Ben.'

'Delighted,' the rugby star said, shaking Angie's hand. He had a killer combination of height, width and puppy-dog eyes. Stacey Turner clocked him as she came out of the downstairs loo, and went straight back in again to apply another layer of bronzer.

Seconds later they were accosted by Brenda Briggs. 'Chip!' she said breathlessly, as she shoved a bit of paper into his face. 'Can I have your autograph?'

Chip was charm personified. 'It's Edward's day, not mine,' he explained with a winning smile. 'I hope you don't mind.'

Angie and Edward's mum exchanged a glance. *What do you know?* Angie thought wryly. This was all going rather well.

*   *   *

The level of voices and laughter in the kitchen was becoming deafening. Freddie tried clinking the side of his glass, but it went unheard, so he ended up pounding together the coffee and tea tins instead.

604

'Ladies and gentlemen!'

'There's none of those here!' someone shouted, and everyone hooted with laughter. Freddie grinned, basking in the sight of so many of his friends and loved ones.

'If I could drag you away from your conversations for just a moment, I'd like to take a few minutes to talk about why we're here today.'

'To clear out your wine cellar!'

'And the Fox-Titt Cuban cigar collection!'

'That's if the moths haven't got there first!'

Freddie let the banter carry on for a few more moments before he put his hand up.

'While you know my gorgeous wife and I never need an excuse to put on a knees-up, there is a very special reason we're all gathered here today.'

Everyone nodded their heads and made noises.

Freddie carried on. 'I think most of you know the story now, and it goes without saying that Angie and I still can't believe that the sorry wreck we picked up at Melton Mowbray last year has turned out to be our very own Desert Orchid.'

More cheers. Someone banged on the kitchen table.

'While Angie and I have gone on a somewhat nerve-racking journey by becoming accidental racehorse owners,' Freddie said, 'none of this would have been possible without the Herculean efforts of Kizzy and Edward at turning Nobby into a first-class racehorse.' He turned to Edward, who was standing between his brother and mum.

'Edward, you've become part of the family. We're all so proud of what you've achieved, and I know I speak for all of us when I say there's a stellar career ahead of you. When we see you lift that gold cup one day in the big one at Cheltenham, we'll be thrilled to know it all started here.'

Angie glanced over at Chip. She half-expected him to look cross at what Freddie was saying, but the big Yorkshireman was distinctly overcome. Daphne met her eye again, and gave a little smile.

Back in the centre of the room, Freddie was finishing his speech. 'And now a toast to Edward and Nobby. Our pride of the Cotswolds!'

A shower of flutes flew up in the air. 'To Edward! And Nobby! Long may their success continue!'

Chip Mason blew his nose so loudly it made everyone jump.

CHAPTER NINETY-FOUR

The skies were sombre, as if in mourning, over the tiny hamlet of Badger's Mount. Kizzy stood in her old riding clothes at the top of the hill, looking down into the graveyard of All Saint's Church. Sleek cars were parked on the narrow road outside, some with chauffeurs, as they waited patiently for their passengers.

The thicket of trees was a good place to stay unseen. The last thing Kizzy wanted was anyone knowing she was there, but she had instinctively wanted to come. She *had* to be there, to show her silent support for Javier. Out of respect for Sarah, too; this was a woman who'd given up her home and her husband—oh, for those wonderful, passionate, heart-stopping few months!—to Kizzy. In a funny way, she *owed* Sarah.

606

To anyone else her logic would probably have sounded completely crazy, but Angie had told Kizzy she had to do what felt right. The older woman had been a tower of strength ever since she'd found Kizzy frozen and distressed outside the marquee at Cheltenham. There hadn't been much Angie could say to make things better, but it had been such a relief for Kizzy to share the turmoil she had been carrying round with her.

There had been a half-page obituary about Sarah in the back of the *Daily Telegraph*, praising her as one of the stars of modern-day ballet and her photo had adorned the front page of several newspapers. There had been little known about the actual funeral, it was Angie who'd heard on the grapevine where it was taking place, followed by a private cremation.

The congregation had been in there for about half an hour, and every so often Kizzy could hear snatches of beautiful piano music and sonorous singing. She tried to imagine Javier in the front row, his rugged dark head bowed. Who would be sitting next to him? Sarah's sister, Pan? Her husband, Arkie? Kizzy desperately hoped one of them could reach out to him.

As she stood and waited, Kizzy looked over the blossoming countryside. Still waiting to be dried out by the summer sun, the land had never looked richer or more alive. And in the distance was Homelands, standing stoically, a mass of golden stone against the green. Kizzy could see the emerald squares of the paddocks from here, although it was too far away for her to make out Delly. Her heart literally ached at the thought of the horse that she'd only possessed for a short while.

Like Javier, really.

Kizzy jumped as the bell in the tower began to ring. A minute later the studded wooden door of the church opened and the pallbearers came out, carrying Sarah's coffin. Kizzy's heart caught in her throat as she saw Javier at the front left, looking achingly handsome in a tailored black suit.

Trying to get a clearer glimpse of him, she stepped out from her cover. She wanted to drop to her knees and weep when she saw the utter devastation on Javier's rugged face. It was carved out by grief. The blackness of his eyes and hair, the bleak expression; they all merged into a terrible mask of sadness and loss.

Other people started to file out behind him. There was Mary O'Gara, tiny in a black shawl and dress. A tall, slim woman with a veiled black hat had her arm round her, and Kizzy recognized the refined figure of Pandora. She saw Nigel, sombre, standing with a distinguished older couple; Kizzy wondered if they were Sarah's parents. Some of the older grooms from the yard had also come, looking stiff and uncomfortable in their black funeral suits.

The hearse was waiting outside the church gates, and the cortège started its slow procession down the front path. Kizzy moved forward without really thinking, and her movement must have caught Javier's eye, because he suddenly turned and looked right up at her.

Kizzy's heart nearly stopped. She went to duck, but it was too late. Javier's face was blank, making it impossible to know what he was thinking. Kizzy tried a tentative smile. It froze on her face as Javier turned his head and fixed his gaze back on the

608

ground in front of him.

Oh no. With a dreadful sinking feeling, Kizzy stepped back into the safety of the thicket. This had been a huge mistake. She desperately hoped Javier would realize she'd come to support him. *Admit it*, piped up the horrible little voice in her head. *You came for yourself. You just wanted to see him.*

In furious disgust at herself, Kizzy pressed her back against the tree, not looking down again until they'd all driven off.

*   *   *

Even by Calypso's high standards the event had been a success. Thirty of the music industry's most influential people had been enticed out of London to attend the showcase of a talented up-and-coming local singer. The singer's manager, anxious his protégé's first gig should be in suitably dramatic surroundings, had thrown the gauntlet down, but Calypso had still managed to come up with the goods: a ruined castle in the middle of nowhere.

The isolation of the place had been a massive gamble, especially as rain had threatened all day, but the weather had managed to hold off. The wild, spectacular surroundings had proved perfect for the Byronic singer's haunting voice, and as he'd roused the jaded audience with songs of lost love and broken hearts, even Calypso had been stunned by how wildly romantic it all was. It was the kind of experience you wanted to share with someone; a pity her choices were thin on the ground in that department at the moment.

The manager came up to her afterwards, as the distinguished guests were being moved towards a

609

moat bridge for champagne cocktails, and a string quartet began—rather aptly—playing the most exquisite version of *The Storm at Sea* by Antonio Vivaldi. No one could accuse her of not ramping up the atmosphere.

'Calypso, great job.' The manager was short and skinny, with a dodgy transatlantic twang and thinning hair gelled back to hide the bald patches.

'Thanks, Tony.'

His beady eyes flickered over her figure. 'Won't you stay for a drink?'

'Thanks, but I've got a party to be getting to.'

'That's a shame.' He put his hand on her arm, making Calypso shudder inwardly. 'Well, you know how to get hold of me. We should hook up.'

'Cool,' she said, thinking exactly the opposite.

Tony bared ageing nicotiney teeth at her. 'So call me, yeah? I'll see you soon, Cally.'

'See you, Tony.' She watched him walk off. WTF, *Cally*? She couldn't wait to get out of there: bony Tony had been giving her the eye all day.

On the way back to her car, her iPhone pinged. She scrabbled round in her oversized bag to find it.

'*Hey, Calypso! How you doing? I've got a couple more days over here if you want to meet up tomorrow? S xx*'

Calypso groaned inwardly. Seamus, the Irish guy from the races, had been plaguing her by text message all week. There had been some hardcore flirting between them in the marquee, before she'd collapsed and been carried out by Camilla and Jed. In the sweaty, hazy furore she must have given him her number, and he'd been bugging her ever since.

Go away. He'd been OK, but it had just been a boozy laugh, hadn't it? The final part of that night

610

was distinctly fuzzy. Calypso could barely remember seeing Archie again, except for catching a distinctly unimpressed look from him on the other side of the room, as Seamus had put his arm round her and whispered something in her ear.

And now she had to go and face Archie, at a party in his own house. God! Her phone beeped. Seamus again.

'*Or I could even do tonight, let me know* :) *Xx*'

'Get *off* me!' she groaned, humping her handbag on to the roof of the car. All these blokes she didn't fancy, when the one person she really wanted clearly thought she was a complete knob. Resting her head on the roof, Calypso succumbed to a moment of bleakness.

CHAPTER NINETY-FIVE

Angie had heard on the grapevine that the wake was being held at Sarah's parents' house so at least Kizzy knew she was safe for a few hours. Javier had given her an electronic key for the gates to Homelands, which she still had. It was with some trepidation that she watched them slide apart, the familiar winding road opening out in front of her.

There was only one place Kizzy wanted to be at the moment. It wasn't at home with her unsuspecting parents, or out with her friends, or even at the Fox-Titts' party celebrating their success. She knew that just a few minutes with her Delly, inhaling the sweet, grassy smell as she put her arms round the horse's neck, was the only thing that could give her comfort. Even if it was the last time she'd ever see her.

Kizzy tried not to look at the house as the road forked into two, and turned right down the road towards the equestrian centre. She parked in her normal spot and got out, noting the lack of activity. Most people must have gone to the wake. She'd just spotted Delly grazing in the far paddock with Deirdre and Javier's old horse, Gypsy King, when Jules, one of the newer grooms, came out of the staff cottage.

'Kizzy, hi.' He looked a bit uncertain.

'Hi, Jules,' she called, sounding more confident than she felt. 'I've just come to see Delly, if that's OK?'

'Er, yeah. You know they're all . . .'

Kizzy nodded quickly. 'That's why I came up now, I didn't want to get in the way.'

'Oh, I get you. Did you know her?'

'Who?' she said stupidly.

'Sarah. She was a bit before my time. Sounded really nice, though.'

'No, no,' Kizzy said awkwardly. 'No, I didn't.'

Jules seemed to realize he'd said the wrong thing, and changed the subject. 'You thinking of taking Delly out? There's meant to be a big storm on the way.'

'No, I only wanted to give her a quick groom. And these.' She grinned and brought a packet of Polos out of her pocket.

'OK. Well, I'll leave you to it. Give me a shout if you need anything.'

Delly had come walking up without Kizzy even having to call her, and now she was tied up outside her stable getting a thorough brush. The familiar, physical activity made Kizzy feel slightly less hopeless, even if she knew it wouldn't last.

'I've missed you, Del.' She started wiping the animal's eyes carefully with a dampened piece of cotton wool. 'You missed me, too?'

She was treated to a gentle snort and Delly's hot breath on the back of her hand. Kizzy stood back and admired the mare's glossy coat.

'They've certainly been looking after you.'

Who would have her now? she wondered, a sudden new wave of depression rushing over her. Delly was a racing horse, not a dressage one, so really, there was no need for Javier to keep her. Kizzy couldn't bear the thought of someone coming and taking her away in their horsebox.

Delly pawed the ground and snorted again, stopping Kizzy's tears. 'What's that, girl? You getting bored?'

The thought had been at the back of Kizzy's mind all along. *Just one more ride.* A proper ride, not in the riding school but out in the countryside, where there was space and fresh air. Should she? Dare she? Sod the bloody doctors and the consequences; she'd deal with them if she had to.

It was like a shard of sunlight shining into a dark room. 'Come on, Del. Let's get you tacked up.'

*   *   *

Jules was sweeping the yard when Kizzy led Delly out ten minutes later. 'Having a quick ride after all?'

'Yeah.' She did the chinstrap of her hat up.

'I'll open the gates for you.' Jules started to walk towards the riding school, but Kizzy stopped him.

'Don't worry, Jules, I'm taking Delly out.'

'Out?'

'Yeah, for a hack. That's OK, isn't it?' she said defensively.

The young groom scratched his head. 'It's about to piss down.'

They both looked up at the violet storm clouds that had rolled in from the east.

'It's only a bit of rain!' Kizzy looked at her watch. 'Look, it's only four o'clock. It won't be dark for at least a couple of hours. I won't even be that long, anyway.'

'It's just that Mr Hamilton-Scott said . . .'

'What did Mr Hamilton-Scott say?' Kizzy's cheeks grew hot with humiliation. 'I do know what I'm doing with Delly, Jules.'

'Course you do.' He was blushing now. 'OK, see you later.'

There was the faintest grumble of thunder in the distance. Kizzy felt another thrill. 'We'd better get going, then.'

*   *   *

The skies over Churchminster were so dark the Maltings was lit up like a Christmas tree as Calypso drove in. It looked like the party was in full swing: the driveway was packed with Range Rovers, 4×4s, and a plethora of nice sports cars. Calypso found a space on the far side, behind a maroon Jaguar with a 'Keep Hunting' Countryside Alliance sticker in the back window.

She was just struggling out in the pencil skirt that had seemed a good idea back in the cottage, when an astonishing sight caught her eye. There, doing a fearsome foxtrot across the yard in front of her, was

614

her grandmother in the arms of none other than Chip Mason.

Calypso watched in disbelief for a moment. Grabbing her handbag, she strode across to the yard and heard her grandmother give a distinctly girlish giggle as Chip Mason swung her round.

They didn't seem to have noticed her, so Calypso cupped her hands round her mouth. 'Oi, Ginger Rogers!'

Clementine looked round, her bun slightly askew.

'Oh, there you are, dear!'

The bun wasn't the only thing amiss. Clementine's eyes had a distinct gleam to them.

'Granny Clem, are you *drunk*?'

'Of course not! Maybe just a little squiffy. Oh, I am sorry, Chip, I think I just stood on your foot then . . .'

'Excuse me,' Chip Mason said in his strong Yorkshire accent, and swept Clementine away across the yard.

Convulsing with laughter, Calypso left them to it. If her grandmother was tiddled, Christ knew what the rest of the party would be like. A group of smokers were huddled on the front porch, fag in one hand, champagne glass in the other. They were screeching with laughter at something, and Calypso got another shock as she saw one of the nicotine gang was the Reverend Bellows, drawing heavily on a Marlboro Red. His face dropped when he saw her.

'Don't tell Joyce, will you? I told her I gave up when I started my theology training.'

Inside things were definitely getting raucous. With four hours of solid drinking under their belts, there were more than a few people in their cups. Rod Stewart's 'Maggie May' was blasting through the house, and every downstairs room was full of flushed-faced people laughing and joking and having shouted conversations with each other.

At the top of the stairs Calypso noticed a white-haired man and woman appear furtively, the man adjusting his shirt collar as he went down before the woman. Reaching the bottom, he grinned broadly at someone past Calypso. 'Ah, Tam, old chap! Don't suppose you've seen my wife anywhere, have you?'

The old ones were always the worst, Calypso decided, as she made her way down the corridor. Quite a few of the male guests had clocked her gorgeous, wild blonde hair, sexy heels and cropped-leather biker jacket, but Calypso didn't notice. She still hadn't seen any of the Fox-Titts yet, meaning Archie.

Bracing herself, Calypso carried on towards the back of the house. She passed the dining room, noticing as she did so that there was a man inside, slumped on one of the chairs, while the Fox-Titts' border collies stood on top of the table, eating their way through a huge green cake in the shape of Cheltenham racecourse. As she walked into the kitchen a buff, dark-haired guy who looked a bit like Mark Wahlberg gave her an interested look. Just then someone called her name.

'Calypso!' Caro came rushing over and gave her a huge hug. Camilla followed with the happy sway of someone just on the right side of pissed.

'You're here! Yay! Ooh, Archie's here somewhere . . .' Camilla said loudly.

'Ssh!' Calypso hissed. 'For God's sake, Bills.' Her

sister was never normally indiscreet; was the whole village hammered?

'It's Churchminster's most delectable woman!' Freddie was on them, brandishing a magnum of Billecart-Salmon.

'Top party, Freds!' Calypso kissed him on both cheeks and handed over the bottle of wine she'd brought.

'Coming from such a pro, I'll take that as a compliment.' Compared to his inebriated guests, Freddie seemed positively sober. 'Glass of poo?' he asked, proffering the huge bottle.

'Would I!' Calypso had never been more in need of a drink, but when he went to pour it only a few drops came out.

'Bloody hell, this is the third one this hour! Hold fire, I'll be back in a minute.'

'No worries.' Calypso turned back to talk to her sisters, but they'd disappeared into the throng. On the other side of the room Mark Wahlberg was definitely giving her the eye. Calypso flashed a quick smile back, idly wondering why Stacey Turner was giving her the evils. Mark Wahlberg picked up his drink and started moving confidently through the crowd. He was coming over . . .

Someone tapped her on the shoulder. Calypso didn't really have to turn round to know who. She steeled herself before she did. Compared to everyone else in the room, Archie's eyes were clear and alert: rude health and virility were oozing from every pore. He seemed to have got even taller and more strapping than the last time she'd seen him.

'Hey,' he said.

'Hey.' Just out to the left of her vision Calypso could see Mark Wahlberg hovering nearby.

'I didn't think you were coming.'

'I had to work.' Calypso fervently wished Freddie would come back with that glass of champagne; her mouth was suddenly feeling as dry as a sandpit.

'I hear it's all going great guns. Your work, I mean.'

'How would you know?' she said belligerently.

He looked at her. 'I still care about you, Calypso.'

She felt a funny little flutter in her heart. 'Funny way of showing it.'

'What's that supposed to mean?'

'Oh, I don't know.' She made a point of looking over at her admirer.

Archie turned his head to see what she was looking at, and clocked Mark Wahlberg.

Bingo! That would show him. Calypso allowed herself a smug little grin.

He turned back. 'Have you got a moment?'

'Sure,' she said airily. 'What do you want to talk about?'

'Let's go somewhere more private.'

*   *   *

Archie shut his bedroom door and turned round. 'You look pretty,' he said, giving her outfit the once-over. 'Is that new?'

'Did you bring me up here to say that?'

'Of course not.' He frowned. 'I just thought we needed to be alone.'

The 'thump thump' of music from downstairs was coming up through the wooden floorboards. Calypso looked round the room, noticing the ubiquitous gap-year photo-board showing Archie

618

and his equally young, fat-free friends on a powder-white beach wearing garlands. On the far wall there was a framed England rugby shirt with Biro signatures scribbled all over it, while a didgeridoo sat on top of the wardrobe.

'It looks like a teenage boy's bedroom in here,' she said cattily.

Archie glanced round as if he hadn't really noticed. 'I only use it to sleep in.'

Once again, he had somehow managed to make Calypso feel like a complete bitch.

'Take a seat.' He gestured to the double bed.

'I'd rather stand,' she said, folding her arms.

Archie shrugged. 'Suit yourself.' He went and leant against the desk opposite the bed. 'How have you been?'

If he wanted to play funny buggers Calypso wasn't joining in. 'Why have you been ignoring me?'

His right eyebrow shot up. 'I haven't.'

'I sent you a message on Facebook! And I texted you.'

She watched him get his iPhone out of his pocket and scroll down. *'Hey, Archi-baldy, you all right?'* he read out. *'I'm about to go into another meeting, BORING.'*

Calypso flushed, maybe her jokey-pokey approach hadn't worked. 'I was only trying to offer the olive branch,' she offered defensively. 'Sorry if it upset you.'

'It didn't.' Archie put his phone back. 'Calypso, we need to talk properly.'

'I tried to talk to you at Cheltenham.'

He gave a frustrated laugh. 'Yeah, it wasn't the best day for a heart-to-heart. I was a bit busy.'

'I didn't mean it like that.' She added, 'You didn't have to turn your back on me,' suddenly aware of how childish it sounded.

'What are you talking about? *You* were giving *me* the cold shoulder all day. You saw how mad it was: everyone wanted to congratulate Mum and Dad. When I finally got away, the first thing I did was come and find you. You blew me off, and then snogged that bloke all night.'

'Nothing happened,' she mumbled.

'I know that. You were just trying to make me jealous.'

It was said in such a cheeky way that Archie didn't come across as arrogant. Calypso looked at him, all big arms and ruffled hair, with that cute eye-crinkly thing he did when he smiled. It was impossible. She went across and punched him on the arm.

'You're *so* annoying.'

'Ah, that's better. Back on firm ground.'

Calypso stayed standing where she was. Through the window tumultuous skies cast a seductive pallor over the bedroom.

'So you're not cross with me any more?' Archie asked.

'I'm not cross with you.' Calypso sighed. 'Oh, Arch, I'm cross with myself. I've treated you like a child, when I'm the one who's been behaving like a complete brat the whole time.'

'I wouldn't say the whole time . . .' He was still smiling.

'I have. I owe you an apology, Arch. For the way I was in front of Sue-Beth, and my behaviour in general. I've been so down on everything, when my life is actually pretty darn cool. I'm sorry you've had to put up with me whingeing all the time.'

'It's all right, I like putting up with you.'

He casually pushed her jacket lapel open with his hand, and looked at the skull and crossbones T-shirt, her breasts full and high underneath. Calypso felt herself grow hot again.

'Archie, don't do this.'

'Why not?' He pulled her into him. Calypso tried to resist, but it was impossible. Archie gazed into her eyes.

'You're funny and infuriating and cute and sexy, and I love the way you always do a little shriek when you sneeze . . .'

'It wouldn't work,' she said half-heartedly.

'Why?'

'Because of the age gap.'

'Don't start that again.' He held her tighter, his big warm body pressed into hers. 'Since when have you cared about rules and convention? I care about you, and I think . . .' He smoothed Calypso's hair off her face and put it behind her shoulder. '. . . you like me, too. That's all that matters, isn't it?'

She mumbled something.

'What's that?'

'I said, it's just *easier* if we don't. You'll probably only want to go out pulling girls or something, and I don't need any more of that shit.'

'God, Calypso, is that what this is really about?'

'If I stay single, I won't get hurt again,' she whispered. 'At least I'm in control then.'

'I'd *never* want to hurt . . .' Archie stopped. 'Look, life's about taking a chance, isn't it? Meeting people, having new experiences, that's what shapes us. As long as the good outweighs the bad it's worth it, isn't it?'

621

'You make it sound so bloody simple.'

'That's because it *is*! Yes, you can stay single all your life, and know where you're going to be in fifty years' time, but that's pretty boring. When you get to eighty, what would you rather say? "I've loved, I've laughed and yes, I've fought quite a bit, but I've got the most incredible family out of it. I've been on this amazing journey with this person, through all the ups and downs, and I'm really proud of what we've achieved." Or, "I've stayed single because it's safer that way. The end?"'

Archie lifted Calypso's chin, making her look at him. 'I don't know what's going to happen in the future, but I do know we're great together. That's what it's about, isn't it?'

She studied his gorgeous, honest face. 'How do you put up with me?'

'Is that a yes then? Hey, don't cry.' He wiped her face and leant in close. 'I always knew I wanted you, but you had to come to *me*.'

'Oh, Archie,' she said, and then they were snogging passionately, hands and mouths all over each other. Calypso felt him grow hard instantly and was desperate to see that fabulously ripped body again. As she started to tug his T-shirt up, the door suddenly flew open and a male guest stood there, swaying in the doorway.

'Sorry, I was looking for the loo.'

They looked at each other and grinned. 'If you don't mind,' Calypso said, 'I was about to have sex with my boyfriend.' She shut the door in the man's face with a smile and turned back.

'Right, you.'

CHAPTER NINETY-SIX

The air was heavy, charged with the kind of electricity you only get before a colossal storm, as Javier walked under the arch into his equestrian yard. He'd already changed out of his black suit, and was back in jodhpurs, riding boots, and the faded blue denim shirt he'd had for years.

The wake had been beautifully catered, and brief. Pandora and Arkie had travelled back with him and Mary to the house. They'd understood when Javier said he'd needed some time alone. He'd made sure Mary was all right before he'd left, but Javier could tell she was still angry with him. She had aged impossibly these last few weeks, as if her indefatigable defence had finally started to crumble. Javier felt guilty every time he looked at her, knowing it was his actions that were partly to blame.

If only he'd listened. He'd been so bloody proud, no, who was he kidding? He'd been a fool. A selfish, pig-headed fool who thought he had known best. Javier had gone against the doctors' wishes and brought Sarah home. It had been his belief that, surrounded by her own things in a place she loved, Sarah might wake up again one day. The official story was that Sarah was in a private hospice and only a handful of people knew the truth; Sarah's family of course, his discreet PA Nigel, and Mary. Homelands was a business with people coming and going and Javier hadn't wanted Sarah turned into some kind of martyr. He'd been wrong. Keeping her a secret had placed unimaginable strain on the house, especially Mary. As for Kizzy . . .

Javier's stomach clenched as he thought about her beautiful, precious face. He couldn't believe it when he'd seen her standing at the top of the hill. But of course, that was typical Kizzy. Putting other people first and worrying about them, even when they'd treated her in the most unforgivable way . . .

'Hello sir.'

The voice made him jump. William, Rory's son, was standing uncertainly in front of him. Javier looked round; he'd wandered down to the stables without even realizing. Being round his horses always soothed him.

William's impish face was grave. 'I'm sorry to hear about Mrs Hamilton-Scott. I don't remember loads about her, but she smelt of flowers and was really nice to me.'

Javier smiled and touched the top of William's mop. 'Thanks, son, that means a lot to me.'

Everyone who'd attended the funeral was back at the yard by now. They kept a respectful distance, acknowledging their boss with stoic smiles and nods. It was nearly time to get the horses in now anyway, and everyone automatically fell into the evening routine. For Javier it provided a merciful retreat into normality.

The thunder was getting closer and more frequent; you could taste the rain in the air. Javier called to his staff to start bringing the horses in; eyes scanning the paddocks. He knew every inch of the place, and where each horse should be at every time of day. So Delly's absence was noticed almost instantly.

It quickly became clear no one knew where

the horse was. Concern started to mount; even a well-protected establishment like Homelands was not immune to theft. After an urgent search for Jules, the groom who'd been in charge earlier, Javier found him round the back of the staffroom having a sneaky smoke.

Jules dropped his cigarette like a hot potato, and quickly ground it out under his boot. Javier had bigger things to care about.

'Jules, where's Delly?'

'Delly?' The young man's face relaxed a little. 'Kizzy took her out.'

Javier stood stock still. 'Kizzy was here? You let her take Delly out?'

'Y-yes,' Jules said, with the dawning look of someone who is realizing they've massively fucked up.

'You know Delly's bad in thunderstorms! Why didn't you tell Kizzy?'

'She said she knew! I think she did, anyway.' The young lad gulped. 'I'm really sorry, Mr Hamilton-Scott.'

Javier was thinking quickly. They'd only found out about Delly's phobia when she'd reared up in her stable during a terrific storm the previous week. It had taken five people to calm the terrified creature down, and stop her from kicking her way out of the stable.

Kizzy wouldn't have any idea of the risk she was taking.

'Where did she go?' he said. 'Jules, this is important.'

'She said she was going up to Hangman's Hill.' Jules looked crestfallen. 'Sir, I'm really sorry.'

Javier put a quick hand on the boy's shoulder.

'You weren't to know.'

He strode back into the yard, issuing instructions.

'Rory, please go and tack up Gypsy for me.'

Looking at his boss's face, the head groom knew not to argue. In record time the huge grey stallion was brought out. Already restless from the impending weather, Gypsy King pawed the ground impatiently, sensing something was up. Javier put a restraining hand on his neck.

'All right, old friend, you're going to have to trust me on this one.'

The first splatters of rain had already started as they clattered out of the yard.

*   *   *

God, she'd missed this! It was the sense of *freedom*, of being out here with Delly, away from everything and everyone and the massive mess her life had become. As she drank in the sights and smells of spring, every little new bud and leaf bursting into life, something stirred inside Kizzy and gave her first glimpse of the colour she'd been missing. Until now, her life had been so grey and empty.

Above the greenery was the evening sky, and the biggest storm clouds that the Cotswolds had seen this year. Kizzy knew she should turn back—the belly-deep grumbles of thunder were almost upon them—but she couldn't face it yet. The static in the air was having a weird effect on her, as if it was tapping into her grief and misery. It made her feel high, on edge, and she wasn't sure whether that was good or bad.

Delly's mood was charged, as well. The mare's ears kept flicking back and forth, and her head was restless.

'Easy girl. We'll be OK.' In retrospect, it hadn't been the best idea bringing Delly out. Aside from Nobby, who wouldn't even bat an eyelid if you clashed a pair of cymbals in front of his face, most horses were antsy round thunder. Kizzy was sure it would pass, though. There was an old farm shed round here that she knew they could always go and shelter in.

The rain was coming down now: big fat globules that soaked her white T-shirt and jodhpurs, making them cling to her skin. The expanse of Hangman's Hill opened up in front of them. It swept up to a crest at the top, where a lone tree, bent over like a black crow and known locally as 'the dead man's oak', was silhouetted against the night sky. Javier had told Kizzy the local legend was that they used to hang highwaymen from that tree, and leave them up there until their bodies had rotted away.

Javier. The agony was like a knife going through her. For a moment Kizzy felt like one of those lifeless, hanging corpses, stripped down to nothing but cloth and bone. She had accepted that Javier would never love her, that they could never have a real future together. All that was left was a farewell ride on the horse he'd bought for her.

She dug her heels into Delly's sides. 'Come on, girl.'

They started off in a canter, which quickly gave way to a flat-out gallop. Kizzy's misery lifted as her wonderful, gorgeous Delly opened up and flew. It only confirmed what she knew already, that Delly was the horse for her. She hadn't even had this connection with Nobby. The mare streaked out in front, responding beautifully to her hands.

627

As they pelted up the undulating slope Kizzy was gripped by a dangerous abandon. She completely gave Delly her head, the reins loose and flapping as the horse ran out properly for the first time in its young life. The fact that the half-tonne of beast underneath her was now in control gave Kizzy the biggest head-rush. *I'll just sit here until Delly runs out of steam*, she thought blissfully. *I don't care where she takes me.*

*   *   *

On the track below, Javier pulled Gypsy up. The light was failing now, but he could still make out the tiny figure in white, bent low over Delly. He watched for a moment, heart soaring as he recognized the carefree girl he'd seen all those months ago at Clanfield Hall, going hammer and tongs across Frances Fraser's lawn.

'Kizzy!' It was no use; she'd never hear him from here. Javier glanced up at the sky again, bristling with fearsome intent. If he could just reach her in time . . .

CRACK! The heavens suddenly exploded. A lightning bolt flashed down, lighting up the clouds like an order from God. Javier's heart stopped as he saw Delly rear up on her hind legs, jerking Kizzy back like a rag doll.

Stay on, angel, he willed, as Kizzy managed to grab hold of the reins, falling forward again. It wasn't over yet. As another clap of thunder sounded maliciously right above them, Delly took off with the unstoppable terror of someone who had the Devil running at their heels.

The sharp pain in her back had been unbelievable, and Kizzy was still reeling as Delly dropped back down and took off. It was raining so hard now that Kizzy could barely see ahead as she desperately fought for control of the reins.

'Delly, stop!'

But months off riding had weakened her muscles, and her efforts barely registered with the terrified animal. The careless elation of moments earlier had given way to very real fear. Delly was completely out of control, and Kizzy was powerless to stop her.

The horse raced up the crest of the hill, towards the dead man's oak. By this time Kizzy was standing up in her stirrups, trying to haul the horse back, but every time another flash of pain down her spine made her flop back in the saddle, gasping for breath. Delly shot over the top and down the other side and Kizzy's innards curdled as she remembered what was waiting for them at the bottom. A long, twisting fence of barbed wire, put up by an over-zealous farmer to keep ramblers out. She had to pull Delly up . . .

'Stop!' she screamed again, but her cry was whipped away on the wind. The barbed wire was getting closer. All Kizzy could think about was Delly running into it, her flesh being ripped apart as she thrashed and struggled.

'Kizzy!'

Somebody else was *up* here? Kizzy turned in the saddle, and had one thought: *I'm seeing things.* Javier was galloping after her on the magnificent Gypsy King. He was hatless, his dark hair slicked back by the rain.

'Pull her up!'

Kizzy tried again, felt another agonizing spasm. 'I can't!' A note of hysteria had entered her voice. The barbed wire was metres away. In her mind's eye Kizzy saw the spiteful little knots of metal like sharpened teeth, ready to tear into Delly's legs and chest.

All of a sudden Javier was galloping beside her so close their knees were banging against each other. Kizzy could only watch as he reached a strong arm out and grabbed Delly's reins. It was too late; they were inches from the barbed wire. Kizzy shut her eyes, but a second later she felt Delly swing round violently, nearly unseating her.

As she opened her eyes, she realized they'd come to a grinding stop. Kizzy saw the deep skid marks from Delly's hooves, the barbed wire inches away from her leg. Oh God, it had been so close . . .

Javier was off Gypsy in an instant, his hand on Kizzy's knee. 'Are you all right?'

'Is Delly OK?' Her hands were trembling so much she could hardly hold on.

Javier quickly ran his legs down the horse's front legs and checked her head. Then he tied her and Gypsy to the fence. 'She's got a bit of a sore mouth, but she'll live.' His face was sheet white. 'Christ, Kizzy! I thought I'd lost you both then.' Suddenly he was pulling her down, holding her so tight she could hardly breathe. 'Are you all right? Are you hurt?'

Being flung against his muscular body, the broad chest she'd missed so much, was overwhelming. Kizzy stiffened and pulled away. Javier's face fell.

'Kizzy . . .'

'Why didn't you tell me!' The force of her voice surprised her, carrying across the wind. 'About Sarah!'

He looked pained. 'I know, I got it wrong. I'm so, so sorry.'

Everything that she'd been through, the stress and strain of not just the past few weeks but the internal conflict she'd had since meeting Javier, suddenly exploded inside Kizzy. She started hitting him with balled fists, wanting to hurt him as much as he'd hurt her . . .

'I hate you I hate you, I wish I'd never met you . . .' As she felt his arms close tightly round her, Kizzy fought for a second and collapsed. 'Oh Javier.'

There was a dilapidated old barn in the corner of the field. It was old and sagging, but at least there was a roof to shelter under.

'Come on, we'll be safe in there.' Javier picked up the horses' reins and waited for her to start walking. She tried not to notice his shirt was completely soaked through, showing off the taut brown skin.

Don't.

The inside of the building was dim and fusty, grass and weeds springing up through the concrete floor. Javier looked for somewhere to tie the horses, finding a rusting metal ring in the wall. He came back and went straight up to Kizzy, but she stepped away. Javier registered her awkward body language.

'Kizzy, I . . .'

He looked so sad and depleted, his shoulders sagging under the weight of his sorrow, that Kizzy forgot all about herself. The man had just attended his wife's funeral. She couldn't even imagine what he was going through.

'How are you?' she said softly.

'I've been better.'

Kizzy put her hand on his arm. The heat coming off his body was incredible. 'Javier, I'm so sorry.'

He put his hand over hers, keeping it there. For a moment there was only the sound of the rain on the corrugated iron roof, a gentle headshake from one of the horses. Eventually Javier fixed his gaze on her.

'If you want the God's honest truth, I'm relieved, Kizzy.'

Kizzy thought she'd misheard. 'Relieved?'

Javier gave a melancholy smile. 'I probably sound like a callous bastard, saying this on the day of Sarah's funeral.' He stared down at his big hands. 'The truth is, I said goodbye to her a long time ago. I knew she was never coming back when I saw her lying in the hospital bed after the accident. It sounds completely crazy, but standing in the church with the coffin, people crying all around me . . .' His remarkable eyes settled back on Kizzy. 'I just felt such relief. Sarah was finally being set *free*. She was too special a person to waste the rest of her life away in a hospital bed.'

It was a strangely uplifting moment. They smiled at each other. 'Sarah would have been proud of you,' she told him.

'I'm not proud of myself.' Javier took her hands. 'I've treated you appallingly. It was just such a shock seeing you in Sarah's room. I think I overreacted because I was so angry and scared at what I'd done.' He sighed. 'I should have been honest about Sarah from the start, instead of some misguided notion I was protecting her honour.

632

The truth is when Sarah had her accident my life ended as well. I thought that was the way it was going to be, that I'd had my shot at happiness and from now on it was going to be me, taking care of Sarah in the house we'd been so happy in. I never, ever expected to meet anyone again, I didn't even want to.' He was gripping her. 'It's not an excuse for my behaviour, Kizzy, but I didn't know what to do. Mary's been on at me since the start to say something, but then everything was moving so quickly with us and then I was afraid I'd lose you if you knew the truth. It was a coward's way out. I'm sorry, Kizzy.'

'I would have coped with the truth,' Kizzy said quietly. 'But I understand why you did what you did.'

Outside the storm was starting to ease, heralding new beginnings. Kizzy thought of her life without Javier and it was unbearable. 'I missed you so much.' She dropped her head so he couldn't see her tears. 'I know this is the world's worst timing.'

She wanted him to hold her so badly again, but Javier kept standing there. 'I did come to your house to see you, I was going out of my mind and wasn't really thinking straight.' He sighed heavily. 'Christ, what was I going to do? Throw stones at your bloody window?'

Kizzy couldn't believe it. 'Why didn't you let me know?'

'You were with someone else, in a black BMW.' Javier forced a smile out. 'He looked like a decent person.'

It took a second for Kizzy to catch on. 'You mean Brett? He's not my boyfriend! I mean he was, but it was over a long time ago . . .'

'You don't have to say that for my benefit. You deserve a good man, Kizzy, and he'd better treat you well.'

'I don't want Brett, or anyone else!' she cried. 'I just want *you*.'

A strange expression crossed his face and Kizzy was terrified that it was all too late. The next thing he'd pulled her in so fiercely it took her breath away again.

'Oh my gorgeous, perfect darling.' Then a second later: 'This bloody hat! I can't see you properly.'

Kizzy let him unbuckle her chinstrap. Almost throwing the hat down, Javier stood back up and cupped her face in his hands.

'I've wanted you from the first moment I saw you. It's no use, I can't hold back any longer.'

'I don't want you to!'

His mouth pressed down on hers. They kissed, half-crying, half-laughing, as the rain bucketed down round them.

'I'm not saying it's going to be easy,' he murmured.

'I don't care.'

'I'll be away a lot, with the Olympics.'

'I'll be away a lot with my racing. It's not all about you, mate.'

He gave a soft laugh. 'Your parents won't be happy about the age gap.'

'Sod my parents, sod everyone, Javier! As long as I've got you . . .'

They kissed even more passionately, arms wrapped round each other. Kizzy loved the wonderful familiarity of it: the way Javier kissed and held her, his muscled, protective body making her feel so safe and complete. Kizzy clung on to him, scared that if she released her grip Javier would disappear again.

'You're shivering,' he said anxiously. 'Are you cold?'

'I'm never cold round you.' It was true. 'Thank you for saving me earlier.'

Javier's eyes had never looked more alive, the tawny flecks dancing across his irises.

'No,' he said softly. 'You've saved *me*.'

For a moment there was silence round them, the wind and rain put on hold.

'Kizzy.'

'Yes?'

His face was full of the most beautiful warmth.

'I love you.'

ACKNOWLEDGEMENTS

Lots of people kindly gave up their time to help with *Horse Play*. Firstly, the lawyers; the brilliant Rebecca Mansell, Toby Atkinson, Carrie Rudge, Kate Edwards from Wendy Hopkins and Hannah Magee from Howells Solicitors. As with everything in this book, all mistakes are my own.

A huge thank you to my old Pony Club mucker Beckie Williams and her jockey husband, Tony. Also to supreme racing correspondent Aly Rowell, who also provided her expertise on the dressage side of things, as did the hugely knowledgeable Gay Bartle. I'd also like to thank Geoffrey and Sheila Libson for providing insight into being a racehorse owner.

Michelle Beynon, Mr Chirag Patel and Mr Asgar Baig from Cardiff Heath hospital on back and head injuries. To Simon Wright and Tim Barrett-Jolly for the culinary side of things and Niall Douglas on the world of travel agents. As always, my eternal gratitude to Emma Messenger and also DS Helen Rance for crime related matters. My family, friends and readers; all your continuing support and lovely Facebook/Twitter messages mean so much.

Lastly, my wise and wonderful editor Sarah Adams, literary agent Amanda Preston, Polly Osborn, Emma Buckley, Suzanne Riley, Lucy Pinney, Larry Finlay and all the team at Transworld, which must be the nicest place in the world to have your book deal.